s.H.

Station Wagon in Spain

Station Wagon in Spain

A NOVEL

FRANCES PARKINSON KEYES

FARRAR, STRAUS AND CUDAHY
NEW YORK

TO THE MEMORY OF
KATHARINE MCKIEVER
WHO SHARED WITH ME MY FIRST JOYS
OF
A STATION WAGON IN SPAIN
AND WHO THROUGHOUT THE LONG YEARS
OF OUR FRIENDSHIP
WAS A SOURCE OF ENCOURAGEMENT
AND INSPIRATION
A GUIDING STAR TOWARD
GREATER ACHIEVEMENTS AND HIGHER IDEALS

CONTENTS

FOREWORD

A STATION WAGON IN SPAIN

I.

THE FIRST IMPETUS to the book which I have called *Station Wagon in Spain* was given me by my dear friend Katharine—or, as we always called her, Kitty—McKiever, a staff writer and feature editor of the N.C.W.C. News Service, during the spring, summer and autumn of 1946, which we spent together in Europe.

I had determined to take the first feasible ship to France, partly because I wanted to help rehabilitate the Benedictine nuns, in whose *hotellerie* I had lived while writing the biography of Ste. Thérèse of Lisieux, and who had sustained much loss of life and complete loss of property during the invasion of Normandy; and partly because a novel, with its scene laid in France—Nantes, Saumur and Lisieux all in the picture—was pushing hard toward the forefront of my consciousness. Kitty had been with the American Red Cross and Graves Registration Service during World War I, and had kept a diary, which I knew would be of great help in creating the proper background for the earlier part of the novel, as I visualized this. Moreover, she could drive a car, which my lameness has always prevented me from doing; and we had been in France together when World War II began, and had managed not only to persevere with what we had been sent to do, but eventually to get ourselves, our car and our stories all safely home via a French freighter, over a sea infested with submarines. Therefore, I did not think she would find postwar France too hard to take and I urged her to ask for leave of absence from her office, beyond her normal vacation period. Permission for this was granted—on condition that she would spend part of the extra time in Spain.

I had made no allowance for such a journey in my calculations for the summer; the frontiers between France and Spain were closed to regular travel because of temporary tension between the two countries; and visas from the latter were hard to obtain no matter how it was approached. The situation was still further complicated because the only vehicle I had available was a decrepit wooden station wagon, secondhand when I had bought it several years earlier, an all-wise government having decreed that I could not have the necessary gas to get from my town house in Alexandria, Virginia, to my farm in North Haverhill, New Hampshire. This had left me with the necessity of buying a cheap secondhand car to keep in New England to ply back and forth between the Haverhill farm and my ancestral home in Newbury, Vermont—a distance of only five miles by highway, but fifteen by rail, with no train connections which permitted a traveler to go back and forth the same day. The whole situation was, and still is, a mystery to me: I had to use up space, then at a premium, on trains, to cover the long-range travel; I had to spend a lot of extra money on the second car, which could otherwise have gone into war bonds; and my efforts to raise foodstuffs on the two country places, as I had been urged to do by the government, became unnecessarily complicated. However, the second car—namely the decrepit station wagon—was just the thing in which to carry supplies to the stricken Benedictines, and the distance between Le Havre and Lisieux is short; the station wagon could be expected to hold out long enough to cover that; whether or not it would hold out for a more extended and hazardous journey was something else again. But Kitty and I decided to meet that problem later, and blithely set sail on a small, shaky, antiquated French vessel, resurrected to provide sketchy transatlantic accommodations for persons who insisted they must get to Europe for professional reasons—no passports to American citizens being then granted for anything else. With us went our station wagon and our supplies for the Benedictines, 21 huge pieces of baggage in all.

We had an amusing, if not a particularly comfortable voyage; reached our destination with no more serious mishap than tire trouble near Le Havre; and no great problems except those produced by a rather crowded crossing on the ferry at Quillebeuf, when a traveling circus, including all its animals, had pre-empted most of the limited space designed for passengers. Then we settled down at the Montellerie, the *manoir* at Norolles, a village near Lisieux, where the nuns had established temporary headquarters. As usual, I had worked hard on shipboard, though my makeshift for a desk was merely a board stretched across a washbasin; I already had a good head start on my novel when I was installed in the one room which was to serve me for sleeping, eating and writing at the Montellerie; and the book was progressing fast, since there were few distractions, when an invitation dropped into our hands which represented an irresistible temptation: if we would come to Rome, wrote a certain high dignitary of the Church, he could promise us seats in one of the diplomatic galleries at the canonization of

Mother Cabrini. Neither train nor plane reservations were available. There was only one thing to do: jump into the station wagon and trust that it would last long enough to get us to Rome.

"And, once we are there," Kitty, always the optimist, said cheerfully, "it will be much easier to get to Spain than it would have been from France. The Constellations are already making regular flights between Italy and the United States and there is a stopover for fueling in Madrid."

We were greatly buoyed up by this prospect. After all, the highways of France, yawning with craterlike gaps though they were, presented no more of a problem to us than when they had been blocked by newly mobilized troops, seven years earlier. And we were better off for gasoline: a special allowance had been given us for that by the French; how we were going to manage after we got to Italy, where nothing of the sort was in sight, we did not stop to ask ourselves.

As I look back on it, the trip seems compounded half of recklessness and half of miraculous protection. We left Menton with a tank and a can full of French gas and it enabled us to reach Genoa. There, through the good offices of a diminutive bellboy, we acquired a little bootleg fuel, into the exact ingredients of which we did not dare inquire. We were down to our last liter of this when we saw the Stars and Stripes floating over an encampment of the American Army of Occupation near Leghorn, and drew up at its entrance just as the engine gave its last gasp. The welcome—and the gasoline!—we received quickly raised our spirits, which had been at very low ebb; the craterlike roads in France had been nothing to contend with compared to the missing bridges and the complete nonexistence of any undamaged thoroughfare in Italy; while the mountain road between Rapallo and La Spezia, always breathtaking in character, brought us to the brink of one precipice after another, at the same time that we faced a head-on collision with some local bus, even more decrepit than our station wagon. (I should like to say in passing, however, that Kitty pronounced the Italian truck and bus drivers "the true gentlemen of the road," for not once did they fail to yield us the right of way and show us every other possible consideration; and I should like to add that when I returned to Italy, and went over the same roads and streams four years later, both highways and bridges represented a marvel of reconstruction, based on the indomitable courage of the Italian to survive and conquer, even more than on skill and equipment.) Still and all, we reached Rome on schedule, the evening before the canonization; I was able to guide Kitty, who had never been to the Eternal City before, straight to the hospitable doorway of the Grand Hotel, without making a single false turn; and there we found our rooms decked with flowers, an excellent cold supper and the coveted invitations duly awaiting us.

I have described the canonization elsewhere and so have many other writers. Suffice it to say now that, for the next few days, we gave ourselves over entirely to the pleasures and privileges provided for us. Then we asked Lorenzo, the incomparable concierge at the Grand Hotel, to get us the first available reservations for Madrid on a Constellation. He accepted the order with his usual efficient nonchalance, and told us he would give us an answer the next day. But when we returned hopefully to his desk, he confronted us with a downcast countenance.

"Two of the Constellations have had engine trouble this past week," he told us apologetically. "There are suspicions of sabotage, or of some imperfection in the mechanism. There have been no serious mishaps, but the company is determined that there shall be none. All flights have been canceled until further notice and there is no intimation of when such notice will be given."

For a moment, Kitty and I stood silent, looking at each other: how could we face a second time those teetering boards over rushing rivers, those hairpin curves with a sheer drop on one side and an onrushing bus at the other, those kilometers when we watched the gasoline gauge and wondered how we were going to reach the next source of supply? Yet we both knew that we must, just as we had known, in 1939, that we must stay in France, war or no war, until we had the stories we had gone to get. This time, we had promised to go to Spain. The next morning we were on our way—in the station wagon.

We entered Spain, after leaving Perpignan, through the frontier at La Junquera, where we went through a good many long-drawn-out formalities, but were treated with complete courtesy. Then we were on our way, via Gerona to Barcelona, which we reached late at night, and again found flower-decked rooms, a delicious cold supper and even newspapers spread out for us. We were pretty tired, and we gave ourselves a few days' leeway before starting on again. It was just as well. True, Spain had had more time to recover from the Civil War than France and Italy from World War II; the roads were in fair condition, the supply of gasoline, though rationed, adequate for our needs; and though we were frequently stopped by the *Guardia Civil* and asked to show our credentials—for, as I have said before, Spain was then a country of closed frontiers and all Europe still forbidden to tourist travel—this was always done with great politeness and we were never detained more than a few minutes. But much of our route led through desert country and this was early August; the heat was almost unbearable, even for anyone who rejoices in warm weather as wholeheartedly as I do; and there could be no midday siestas for us, since Kitty must get her Spanish stories as rapidly as possible, so that I could get back to mine in Lisieux— it had never occurred to us, when we left there, that I would be gone so long from my base of operations. The station wagon rattled on from Lerida to Saragossa, where again we paused just long enough to draw breath, see the main sights and enjoy another kindly welcome. Then we were on to Madrid, with a stop for lunch at the *Albergue de Carretera* at Medinaceli—the first of many restful and happy experiences at those wayside inns, first visualized more than 20 years earlier by the Marqués de la Vega Inclán, who had told me of his hope to provide comfortable, if simple lodging, and abundant, properly prepared food, at small out-of-the-way places, where hitherto decent accommodations for transients were nonexistent.

In Madrid, as in Rome, all problems and discomforts came temporarily to an end. No impediments were put in Kitty's way, as she went about searching for the material she had been asked to find; on the contrary, she met with kindness and co-operation everywhere. This experience, and many I myself have had, both before and since, has made me extremely skeptical about reports of tales allegedly "smuggled" out of Spain, because, otherwise, they would not have been allowed to leave there, and about dispatches "censored" past recognition. Even in those unsettled times, no one asked to see what we were writing and everything that was dispatched reached its destination unchanged.

After the fruitful interlude in Madrid, Kitty and I went out of Spain by a different and shorter route than the one by which we had entered it—Burgos, Vitoria, San Sebastian, the International Bridge; then, in France, Dax, Angoulême, Poitiers, Saumur—and finally Lisieux. Again there was a slight delay, but no difficulty at the border; again the poor old station wagon rattled bravely on. Not until our mission was safely accomplished did it give unmistakable signs that its days of rash adventure were over. When Kitty and I left the Montellerie, it stayed behind with the nuns. For a little while longer it served them for their infrequent and cautious errands. Then, like a good war horse that has gone unafraid and unscathed through a series of battles, it quietly went to pieces.

I had been to Spain twice before I went there with Kitty; since then, I have been back there four times—each of these four times in a station wagon. To be sure, these vehicles have been more reliable as to condition, more elegant as to appearance, than the one in which Kitty and I made our mad dash from Normandy to Rome, from Rome to Madrid and back to Normandy again. But, as I said before, it was this venture which gave the impetus to all the others; it is to this, in a very large measure, that I owe the wonderful sights I have seen through the length and breadth of the land; the many Spanish friends I have made of both high and low degree; the delightfully repeated experience of keeping house, with a Spanish staff, in the *palacete* of a provincial city; and the enriching expansion of learning that comes with increasing knowledge of the Spanish language and Spanish literature.

II.

Though Kitty's observations quickly took the finished form of articles which were immediately published, my random notes, made in both Italy and Spain that summer, did not get beyond the stage of penciled draft; my heart was in my Norman novel, and this also absorbed most of my writing time. I had a vague idea that eventually I might write a travel book based on these notes and call it *Station Wagon in Spain*. I finally mentioned this casually to my friend, Eleanor Carroll Brunner, who had been my "boss" when she was Associate Editor of the old *Delineator*, and later, when she had become Assistant Dean of the Columbia School of Journalism, one of my two best editorial advisors. "That title," she said, "does not belong on a travel book; it belongs on a suspense story. You have said you could never write one. Well, what about *Dinner at Antoine's?*"

Feebly, I defended myself. The key to the plot of *Dinner at Antoine's* had been provided by something which had actually happened; the account of this happening was already in the public domain; and I had had able help, amounting almost to collaboration, from a friend who had one or more suspense stories, written anonymously, to his credit. I still did not feel capable of tackling one alone. But Eleanor, who had been responsible for my first excursions into hagiography, when she insisted that I should write the life history of the Little Ste. Thérèse, now became equally vehement on the subject of suspense stories. "What about that 'Spanish Prisoner' theme that Muna Lee has been urging you to develop?" My erstwhile boss went on. "It's in the public domain, too, as far as that goes—several articles, and for all I know, some fiction has dealt with it already. But Muna's right —you'd approach it from an entirely different angle; and you know your way around Spain, literally and figuratively, as well as you know your way around Louisiana and almost as well as you know it around New England and Virginia. You don't need a collaborator. Do talk with Muna about that suspense story again!"

I said I would, but I already knew that I was lost. Muna Lee, who has a very formidable official title in the State Department—Director, North and West Coast Section, Public Affairs Staff, Bureau of Inter-American Affairs —is just as capable of giving advice as Eleanor Carroll Brunner, and just as hard to stave off, once she has made up her mind about something. Although the next time I went to Spain, it was with the sincere and declared purpose of writing about Avila, in terms of the human lives which have glorified it, I found I could not work on this as I wanted to until I was actually settled in that wonderful old walled city; meanwhile, ten glorious, empty days at sea were stretching out ahead of me. In the course of these, I wrote the first four chapters of *Station Wagon in Spain*. During a bout of illness the following winter, when I was back in Louisiana and could not do research because books of reference were too unwieldy to handle in bed, I wrote two more chapters. A second series of empty days at sea and a visit from Muna, during which she did not cease to prod me, when I went back to Avila, brought me through Chapter 17; and finally, during a blessed period of quiet at my ancestral home in Newbury, Vermont—the first of any length that I have had there in many years—the story took on new impetus, and I spent practically every waking hour working on it until it was finished.

My fictional Abbess resembles a real one in loveliness and wisdom, though not in name and background; but the descriptions of Santa Ana's Convent are factual, as to both architecture and history. Readers of George Santayana's *People and Places*—one of the most delightful biographies I have ever read—will recognize its location as directly opposite the charming house where he spent much of his boyhood. The Santayana residence has, alas! deteriorated from its erstwhile prominent position and is now a bakery. To an outsider, it seems unfortunate that some public recognition has not been accorded it as the family home of one of the world's greatest philosophers; but, both because he was a lapsed Catholic and an author who preferred to write in his adopted rather than his native tongue, Santayana's other great qualities and achievements have been either overlooked or misprized in Avila. Not so the Convent of Santa Ana, which still maintains its proud tradition. Rather amusingly, the two names sound so much alike that there is still confusion between the two in the spoken word. The first time I said I wanted to go to Santa Ana's, the sad reply was, "But, *señora*, nothing now remains of the Santayanas but their graves!"

The Spanish titles which I have given my fictional characters are all authentic, but obsolete for lack of heirs in the last hundred years or so. I have chosen them for both reasons: I did not wish them to be untypical of Spain, but neither did I wish to cause any possible embarrassment to living persons, or any misunderstanding on the part of readers who might attribute wholly imaginary characteristics to real individuals. All selections have been made from the *Guia de la Nobleza* by Felipe de Salvador, a Member of the Royal Academy of History.

Lest anyone think I have exaggerated the degree and faithfulness of care given by the employees of absentee Spanish landlords to the property of the latter, I may mention not only my own personal observations of these, but those so ably described in H. V. Morton's delightful book, *A Stranger in Spain*, published by Dodd, Mead & Company; Mr. Morton actually found flowers adorning the family photographs of owners who had not visited certain of their estates for as long a period as fifteen years! It was also Mr. Morton who first called my attention, in his book, to the excellence of chocolate in Astorga, which, thanks to him, I knew enough to recognize myself, on my way between La Coruña and León. On the other hand, no "overgrown Swiss chalet" disfigures the slope of the Guadarrama, where several excellent sanitaria are located, and no pseudo-Spanish doctors operate there. My inclusion of these is wholly poetic license.

Muna Lee's acquaintance with the "Spanish Prisoner Letter" began when she was working in censorship at New York during World War I. All foreign mail was, of course, opened then, and these particular letters, which came in by the thousands, were stacked in piles and labeled "Thought to be fraudulent"—exactly as I have had Harvey Wendell describe them in my story. So they never reached their intended victims at that time; but it is a matter of record that, almost ever since the discovery of America, many have got through. (It was in 1542 that the Seville courts recorded the first Spanish Prisoner swindle.) Among the various authoritative articles written on the subject are "The Perennial Prisoner" by Stanton Delaplane, which appeared in *Scribner's Commentator* for April, 1941; and "Spanish Prisoner," a section from *Crime is a Business* by John C. R. MacDonald, published by the Stanford University Press. Both of these articles were made accessible to me through the courtesy of the Library of Congress.

I am indebted to the Minister of Justice, under whose jurisdiction the Director of Prisons operates in Spain, for a cordial reception to Muna Lee and me, helpful information and an abundant supply of literature regarding penal rules and regulations, to supplement that already given me by the Spanish Consul in New Orleans. The Minister of Justice even went so far as to urge us to visit the prison in Avila—which, as he pointed out, was conveniently near the *palacete!*—and see for ourselves the existing conditions. I am also indebted to staff members of the French Consulate General and the Spanish Consulate in Boston, and to a highly placed official in the French Police in Paris for detailed information about police procedure and extradition, under the circumstances I have described; and to my eldest son, Henry W. Keyes, a Boston lawyer, and Sven Nielsen, my French publisher, for co-operation in securing this. Mr. Norman F. Page of the New York branch of the American Express Company has authenticated all references to the spurious use of checks and the steps taken when such frauds occur; and Dr. Nicholas J. Chetta, Coroner of the Parish of Orleans and ex-officio City Physician of New Orleans, has supplied me with the necessary information regarding the type of poison which would fit into my plot, as he did in the case of my novel, *The Royal Box*.

My thanks are also due to the members of both my secretarial and domestic staffs, English and Spanish as well as American, for the interest they have taken in my work. The secretarial branch has shown it not only by many hours of patient typing, but by several valuable suggestions as to plot structure; the domestic branch by the efficiency which has permitted me to spend long hours at my desk, unharassed by minor household problems. As all the latter part of the book has been drafted when I was badly crippled with arthritis, I could never have worked with the speed I have achieved and the comfort I have enjoyed if the burden of creative writing—always a heavy one, whatever the nonwriter may believe to the contrary—had not been lightened for me by these faithful helpers.

The Oxbow
Newbury, Vermont

F.P.K.

Part One A STATE OF
DEMENTIA

1.

ALLAN LAMBERT WAS profoundly bored. He had been comparatively poor and had worked hard all his life, that is to say, for nearly thirty years. Now he was rich, because his late father's brother Nathan—a bachelor, a recluse and a miser—had died, leaving all his money to his nephew, and Allan did not know what to do, either with the money or with himself.

His Uncle Nathan had owned a huge historic house, but had occupied only one wing of it, to save light, fuel and service. Since the house was part of the legacy, and was located on the outskirts of the New England town where Allan taught Spanish in a small select college, it was taken for granted that he would move into it at once, instead of trespassing further on the good will of the cousin with whom he had been living for some years. This cousin, Arthur Morse, was related to Allan on his mother's side and, therefore, had not come in for a share in Nathan Lambert's will, though he could have used the money much more handily than Allan. Like the latter, he taught, for inadequate compensation, at the small select college; but unlike Allan, he was married and had a rapidly increasing family of his own. Though Allan had always been scrupulously fair about paying his share of the expenses in the Morses' modest cottage, they needed extra space badly, especially now that Marian, Arthur's wife, was pregnant again, and her physician had informed her that twins should be included in her state of expectancy, as she always preferred to call it. So Allan had moved into the huge historic house as soon as his uncle's estate was settled, and that was very soon after the old miser's death, since there was no one to contest the will and very few formalities to meet in connection with it; and he was now living in the same wing which his uncle had occupied, and was served by Casper Brice, the same old houseman who had continued to minister to Nathan after all the other servants had been discharged as an economy measure, or had left of their own free will, because their wages were annually reduced instead of being annually increased. Casper, who, according to his late employer, was now so decrepit that he could not expect anyone else to hire him, had stayed on, partly because he himself feared this was true and partly because he had nowhere else to go. He had expected and dreaded dismissal immediately after Allan took over; surely, Casper reasoned, a personable young man, with no false ideas about the value of money, would want to keep open house for congenial company and, in order to do this, he would need a competent, up-to-date staff. But Allan, who was accustomed to living in a servantless cottage, was actually much impressed by Casper Brice and, in any case, would not have dreamed of dismissing so faithful an old retainer. As for opening up the entire house, such an idea did not occur to him, either, until it was presented to him, first by the president of the local historical society, next by the Dean of the college, and then by Charlotte Wendell, the girl who, a couple of years earlier, had decided she would like to become engaged to Allan. The historical society felt it was Allan's duty to permit the public to view his monument to Early American culture and elegance, if not every day and all day, at least two or three times a week at stated hours. The Dean saw in it an answer to his prayer for an adequate recreational center. Charlotte, who had not been blind to Allan's personal attractions when he was poor, found these so greatly enhanced since he had become rich, that, while she did not actually propose to him, she certainly gave him to understand how much she would enjoy being the chatelaine in such an establishment as he now possessed; and, since she was the soul of propriety, there was no question that she considered a church wedding the suitable prelude to such a role.

Allan told the president of the historical society that of course it would be necessary to have the long-closed house thoroughly cleaned and restored to its erstwhile splendor before it could be thrown open; otherwise the public would be not only disappointed but deluded. He reminded the Dean that he was due for a sabbatical year, and that he could not run the risk of having the house more or less demolished by carefree students during his absence. And he told Charlotte, solicitously, that he could not dream of asking a delicate girl to undertake a task which he was sure would be a tax on her strength—why, the house had thirty rooms in it! most of them enormous, some in a state of complete disrepair. To all he made vague half promises: when the house was renovated, when he returned from his travels, when he found a vigorous, middle-aged, experienced housekeeper, he would be glad to consider their various suggestions. But meantime . . .

Meantime he did nothing, either about renovating the house, or consulting a travel bureau, or engaging a vigorous, middle-aged, experienced woman. Nathan's death had occurred in late May and Allan was always genuinely tired at the end of the third semester, for he was a conscientious teacher, and Spanish, formerly included in the curriculum only of those who were looking for a snap course and were under the false impression that this was one, had increased in popularity along with the Good Neighbor Policy. He now had more pupils than he could handle easily by himself, and his only assistant was a more or less stranded Mexican of advancing years, whose scholastic qualifications were open to doubt and whose health was so uncertain as to require long periods of rest, but who was undemanding as to salary. Allan was sorry for him, so he saw to it that the college was satisfied with the course; but the burden of keeping it satisfied rested with him.

In a way, this burden had now been lifted, perhaps forever. But the thought that poor Perdido—as the students had aptly nicknamed the miserable Mexican—could not possibly carry on alone, and that it was doubtful whether anyone selected as a substitute for Allan would put up with such an assistant, troubled the young professor. The thought that the poor old man might be turned adrift obsessed him so greatly that he did not shake off his normal fatigue as quickly as he would have done if he had not been worried as well as weary. It was while he was still trying to find a solution for Perdido that he unexpectedly inherited the large fortune and realized that in some way he could provide for his assistant; but it took him a little time to recover from the shock of the legacy and adapt himself to an entirely new mode of life. It was when he eventually succeeded in doing so that he realized he was no longer tired or troubled, but bored.

He was sitting at a well-spread table placed under the shade of a beautiful copper beech, in a secluded part of the velvety lawn which surrounded his house, when this realization struck him in full force. Casper had suggested that he might like to breakfast outdoors, these beautiful summer mornings, and he had fallen in readily enough with the suggestion. It certainly was very restful to loll there at his ease, protected from the direct rays of the sun, but, at the same time, basking in its radiance. It certainly was very pleasant to consume, in such a setting, fruit juice thoroughly chilled, coffee perfectly brewed, eggs cooked to a turn and muffins that melted in his mouth, especially after years of breakfasting surrounded by Arthur's clamorous brood, on food which was of inferior quality, improperly prepared and presented in a most unappetizing manner amidst unattractive surroundings. He reflected with gratitude that he need never again see cereal shaken from a carton to a bowl, milk poured direct from bottles into tumblers and grubby children smearing butter on their faces, all to a chorus of parental pleading and infantile protest. But after he had finished his breakfast, he could not possibly eat anything again for several hours, especially as he had done more than justice to Casper's excellent cooking now; and, agreeable as it was to begin a day in such a leisurely manner, he could not spend the whole of it sitting under a copper beech. He was young, he was strong, he was used to activity, both physical and mental. Idleness was all very well for a while, but presently it began to pall. He had better start doing something. The question was, what? The college had closed for the season and he would not be going back in the fall, because this was his sabbatical year, the year to which he had looked forward so eagerly and for which he had saved so carefully. Now he did not need those savings; he might just as well have had a little fun along the way. When you came right down to it, perhaps it was fun he needed and not work. But how did you suddenly go to work to have fun, when that was one of the things you had never learned to do, and when there was no one at hand to teach you?

Of course some members of the faculty had been reasonably congenial; but they had now all gone their separate ways, to make the most of their summer vacations, except the Dean, who was not much of an athlete and did not indulge in games of chance, and who had never been one of Allan's favorite people anyhow. There was no one left on the campus with whom he might have a set of tennis or play a rubber of bridge. He was genuinely fond of his cousins, but the new baby—or babies—would be coming along any day now, and though Arthur and Marian would be glad to see him if he went around, the cottage would be in the usual turmoil, only worse. And of course, there was Charlotte. She had not gone away for the summer. She had told Allan she would not think of leaving him, in these first days of his bereavement. He had not asked her to stay near him and he did not feel in the least bereaved—it would have been hypocritical to pretend that he did. There had been no ties of affection between him and his uncle who, while living, had never made his nephew's lot in life any easier, and who would not have paved the way for it to be easier now if there had been anyone else to whom he could bequeath his money. However, since Charlotte seemed determined to comfort Allan, he had submitted, somewhat warily, to her ministrations; he could go to see her any time and be warmly welcomed. The reason he did not feel impelled to go was just that: the welcome would be a little too warm. Not that Charlotte was forward about any form of physical demonstration. True, she sometimes reached for Allan's hand and pressed it, but she did this in such a way that it only suggested sympathy. True, she sometimes sidled slightly toward him on the sofa, but she did that in such a way as to suggest that she did not want to seem stand-offish. She never invited, much less precipitated, an embrace. Nevertheless, something warned Allan that if he so much as put his arm around her waist or kissed her cheek, she would immediately leap to the conclusion that they were as good as engaged. And he was not ready to be engaged to Charlotte.

He could not have told exactly why. Though she was nearly always described, both by her more flighty contemporaries and by her parents' friends, as the "sensible type," she was also quite pretty; and though she had a mind of her own, and did not object to speaking it on occasion, she also knew how to make herself extremely pleasant. She was well brought up and well educated. Her father was a prosperous automobile dealer and she was his only daughter; he had wanted her to have a good home and go to good schools and he had seen to it that she did. Both he and his wife were fine upstanding citizens and they would have approved of Allan Lambert as their son-in-law. They had known him for some years now, ever since he had come to the college to teach, and had bought a battered second-hand car, which he was still driving, when he drove anything. The Wendells regarded him highly and even though he could not, until very recently, have supported their daughter in the manner to which she was accustomed, that did not trouble them. They had plenty and to spare. Besides, socially as well as scholastically, the match would have been a step upward for them. Town and gown did not customarily mingle very much, and the Wendells had been flattered when Allan had accepted an invitation to their house, shortly after the purchase of the secondhand car, and because he had intermittently continued his visits, even though he made no more purchases. The Lamberts, whether rich or poor, were aristocrats. The old miser had cut a dashing figure in his day—no one knew what had soured and suppressed him, but no one denied the charm and distinction of his earlier years. His brother, Allan's father, had been American Consul in Málaga, which was where Allan had learned his Spanish as a boy, and he had good connections everywhere, even though he had not been able to take advantage of them. Now that he was no longer hampered by the necessity of squeezing every nickel until it screamed, of course he would. The prospect of these connections was very pleasing to Mr. and Mrs. Wendell. No less than Charlotte, they would have welcomed Allan very warmly. . . .

"Beg pardon, sir. The mail, sir."

Allan had been thinking so hard about Charlotte, and pondering so deeply the question as to whether, after all, it might not be a good thing for him to get married, that he had not heard Casper coming toward him across the soft grass. Now the old man began to clear the table, quickly and noiselessly, while Allan opened one envelope after another and then threw them and their contents on the grass. Nearly all the communications which reached him nowadays were begging letters. The news of his good fortune had apparently reached almost every charitable and philanthropic institution in the country and they had hastened to put him on their mailing lists; innumerable needy individuals had also hastened to take pen in hand. At first, Allan had responded generously to all such appeals; then he had come to the conclusion that, rich as he was, he would soon be in the poorhouse unless he curbed his instinct toward prodigality and he had begun to weed them out. When the pleas started coming not only from every part of the United States, but from much more distant points, he decided it was time to call a halt, at least temporarily; and, among those which fell promptly to the grass this particular morning was one from the Philippines, two from India, and three from Darkest Africa. When he came upon an envelope bearing a Spanish stamp, he had a moment of hope that its contents would not belong to the same category as those of the communications he had so swiftly discarded. After all, it might well be from some boyhood friend, of whom he had had no news in a long time and it would be good to do so. He opened the letter with pleasant expectations.

"My dear sir,"—he read with rapidly mounting astonishment—"A person who knows you has made me trust to you a delicate matter on which depends not only the future of my dear daughter, but my very existence. I am writing you from prison. But let me explain . . ."

Allan turned the sheets rapidly, seeking the signature. At the end of the letter were initials and the number of a post office box in Madrid. Neither meant anything to him. But he was sufficiently intrigued to go on.

"I was formerly a respected banker in Avila, but after some unfortunate speculations, fled from there with my beautiful eighteen-year-old daughter in the hope of avoiding arrest for myself and disgrace for her. This hope, alas! was not fulfilled. I was seized, sentenced to pay a ruinous fine for pleading bankruptcy under false pretenses and incarcerated. My beloved daughter was forced to take temporary refuge in a convent, as her sainted mother is already with God, and all near relatives closed their hearts to us in our misfortune. However, before my arrest I was able to hide in a secret compartment of my suitcase a cashier's draft for $15,000 and a claim check for a trunk which I sent over the border into France. In the trunk are negotiable funds to the value of no less than $285,000. The prison authorities who, according to custom, separated me from all my belongings, are now preparing to sell this suitcase for some paltry sum, being, of course, unaware of the potential treasure it contains. Unless my fine can be paid and the suitcase retrieved, all will be lost!"

At this point, Allan tossed the letter on the pile surmounted by those from the Philippines, India and Darkest Africa. Then he lighted a cigarette and reached for another envelope. Almost immediately, however, he laid this aside and retrieved the letter he had just thrown away.

"In this desperate situation, I am throwing myself on your mercy. I am emboldened to do this, even though I myself have not the honor of knowing you, because the person to whom I referred, another North American, has told me how to reach you and advised me to seek your help. I cannot disclose his identity, for he is using an assumed name here in prison, not wishing to bring shame on his family. While he, like myself, is a victim of misfortune, he is nevertheless a compassionate and upright man.

"I am able to write you thus freely on confidential matters because I have made a friend of the prison guard, upon whose discretion you may rely completely, and who will receive your reply to this letter, if you are good enough to send one. He cannot himself open the suitcase seized by the prison authorities because it has been sealed and the broken seals would be discovered before the guard could cash the check. There is only one way out of the difficulty: you must come here, pay the fine and redeem the suitcase; the way will then be clear not only to repossess the wealth represented by the cashier's draft, but by the claim check to the trunk! For, as soon as you have satisfied the guard that you have the necessary funds to pay my fine, he will indeed break the seals, search for the secret compartment, and—thanks to my instructions—readily find it. You will next telegraph the cashier of the bank and the customs officials at the border. In a few hours you will receive replies from them, proving that I have told you the truth. Then and only then will you actually hand over the money for my fine!

"If you are willing to help me recover the sum represented by the cashier's draft—$15,000—and the negotiable funds to the sum of $285,000, I will gladly pay you a third of this, namely $100,000 as a reward for your time and trouble and a token of my appreciation for your act of mercy. I implore you, dear sir, heed my plea, not only for my sake, poor unfortunate creature that I am, but for the sake of my innocent, my precious child, who will be forced into a novitiate against her will, if she trespasses too long upon the charity of the convent where she has taken refuge. . . ."

"Beg pardon, sir, Miss Wendell is calling."

For the second time Casper had approached so noiselessly that Allan had not been aware of the old servant's footsteps and, this time, he looked up with a start.

"You mean she's on the telephone?"

"No, sir. She's here."

Allan rose slowly, still holding the letter with the Spanish postmark. Charlotte was already coming across the lawn. She had on a white suit, smartly but rather severely tailored, and a small, smart white hat. She looked both cool and striking. She did not go in for either soft dresses or exaggerated sportswear, both of which she realized were not exactly her style. She smiled and waved her hand.

"It's such a lovely day," she said, "that I thought a picnic would do you good. It might cheer you up."

"Thanks a lot. But I'm not in the least depressed."

"You say that because you're determined to hide your true feelings. You show a great deal of self-control. But, of course, after your terrible bereavement . . ."

Without answering, Allan looked around him—at the beautiful trees, at the blooming flower beds, at the great expanse of lawn and finally at the white-columned mansion of mellowed brick which dominated all these. Try as he might, he could not succeed in feeling bereaved, only somewhat overpowered.

"Anyway," Charlotte went on, disregarding his comprehensive glance and pretending not to understand it, "I've packed a lunch and brought it along, just on the chance you would go on a picnic. Dad's loaned me a new convertible to try out and I'd like your opinion on that, too. It's very good looking—olive and gray finish, not horribly flashy like most of the new models. And it's got plenty of power, though it's small enough to be cozy. What do you say?"

"Well, it doesn't seem like a bad idea," Allan answered, tardily returning her smile. "Sit down for a moment first though, will you? I'd like to show you a letter I've just received."

"Perhaps Miss Wendell would take a cup of coffee while she's reading, sir?" Casper, who had been hovering close at hand, inquired solicitously.

"A very good idea. Thank you, Casper."

"If you don't mind, Allan, I'd rather have orangeade. I've had coffee already."

"Well, so have I. I can always drink more coffee though."

"It's very bad for you, Allan, to drink so much coffee. I'm sure it's retarding your recovery."

"I can't seem to convince you that I haven't been ill—just tired. However, an orangeade is also a good idea. Bring us two orangeades and two cups of coffee, will you, Casper? Then we can take our choice."

Allan lighted another cigarette and watched Charlotte as she read. She did not seem to find the letter as intriguing as he had; she was going through it much more rapidly, but he knew this did not mean that she was doing so superficially; she was very quick about everything she did, whereas he was apt to be deliberate. However, when she thrust the letter back into its envelope and tossed it to him, he did not doubt that she had thoroughly grasped its contents.

"Whoever wrote that ought to have realized that no one in his senses would fall in with such a crazy scheme," she said. "Why didn't you throw it away with the others?" And she gestured toward the pile on the grass.

"I opened it because I thought it might have come from some long-lost Spanish friend. I don't know just why I went on reading it after I found it didn't. But now that I have read it, I think it might be rather fun to answer it."

2.

THE PICNIC WAS NOT an unqualified success. The weather was perfect, the lunch excellent and the convertible speedy and smooth riding. But Allan was preoccupied and Charlotte was annoyed. He did not refer to the Spanish letter a second time, but she was aware that far from dismissing it from his mind, like a sensible man, he was still dwelling on it. At last, when they had finished eating, she broached the subject herself.

"If you did answer that crazy letter, what would you say?"

"I don't know yet. I'm thinking that over."

"I shouldn't suppose it would take much thought."

"I don't come to decisions as fast as you do, Charlotte."

"So I've noticed. You haven't even decided yet, have you, where you're going on your sabbatical?"

"No, what's the hurry?"

"I should think you'd want to make the most of it. College has been over three weeks now. Before you know it, the summer will be gone."

"Well, I've still got another free summer ahead of me, not to mention a winter in between."

"Yes, you could do something really worth while in that length of time, if you'd only get started."

"But I'm not sure I want to do anything worth while. Teaching is considered worth while and I've been doing that for years now. Studying is supposed to be worth while and I've been studying all my life—both before and since I began to teach. I studied hard enough to get scholarships that would help me pay my way through a good preparatory school and a good college. Then I started teaching so I could go on and get post graduate degrees. I'm fed up with both studying and teaching."

"Allan, you say you're not depressed and you say you're not ill, but you must be both. If you weren't, you wouldn't talk like this. Studying and teaching are your life."

"You mean they have been. I believe there must be something more to life than studying and teaching. Anyway, I'm going to try to find out."

"How?"

"That's just what I'm thinking over."

"I thought you said you were thinking about how you'd answer that crazy letter."

"Yes, I did. The way I answer that letter may lead to just the discovery I'm seeking."

Charlotte gave up. They had found a delightful spot in which to eat their lunch, with a view of the river and the mountains beyond and no other picnickers around. She had been very hopeful that, under the benign influence of privacy, scenery and good food, Allan would cease to stand aloof. To be sure, he was apparently enjoying himself; he seemed contented and relaxed. But, as far as she was concerned, he was as withdrawn as ever—more so and in a worse way. Previously, he had been scholastically absorbed which, after all, was highly respectable and, indeed, highly commendable; now he was wasting his time—and hers—in shallow thoughts. The drive home was rather silent and, when they reached Allan's huge historic house, he did not suggest that she might like a cup of tea under the copper beech or ask when he could see her again. He simply thanked her for having thought of the picnic, without even saying he had had a good time, and then he disappeared between the white columns of the portico.

She was still nursing her disappointment and displeasure the next day when her father came home to lunch with an extraordinary piece of news. "Allan Lambert came down to the shop this morning and asked to see me personally," he informed his wife and daughter, as he did justice to an excellent steak. "I thought at first it must be about a rather private matter. I ought to have known better. Young men don't call on the fathers of the girls they're going with any more, to ask for the green light. Even if they did, they wouldn't make office visits—they'd beard the lion in his den. Well, I seem to be getting a little mixed in my metaphors, but I haven't come out of my daze yet."

"What dazed you?" Mrs. Wendell inquired practically, disregarding the first part of her husband's speech and helping herself to more mashed potatoes.

"He said he wanted to buy a station wagon. And he did. Right off the floor, without even trying it out. He said it was just the type he had in mind, so he didn't see any use looking further—he'd take my word for it that, mechanically, it was all right. Well, of course he knew he could do that. But you could have knocked me over with a feather, just the same. It was the new model with the scarlet body and the cream-colored upholstery he wanted. He paid cash for it and drove off, just like that."

"Allan has bought a red station wagon!" Charlotte exclaimed, pushing away her plate. "What on earth will he do with a gaudy thing like that? That style isn't suitable for a college professor, anyway. I should think he'd have better taste than to drive it around here."

"I don't believe he intends to drive it around here. He said something about taking it abroad."

"Taking it abroad!" Charlotte cried, echoing her father for the second time. "Why, it was only yesterday he told me he didn't know what he was going to do. He said he was thinking it over."

"Well, looks like he had thought it over. . . . Didn't say anything about a honeymoon trip to Europe, did he, sugar cookie?"

"I've told you a thousand times that I wish you wouldn't call me anything so silly. No, he didn't say anything about a honeymoon trip to Europe or anywhere else. If you want to know, all he talked about was a crazy letter he'd got in the morning mail from some foreign crook who wants to have a huge fine paid, so he can get out of jail—a lot of drivel about a cashier's check and a sealed suitcase and a friendly guard and a beautiful daughter and heaven knows what else."

"You're not talking about one of those Spanish Prisoner letters, are you, sug— Charlotte?"

"What do you mean 'one of those Spanish Prisoner letters'? Did you ever hear of anything like this before?"

Mr. Wendell laughed. In his turn, he pushed back his plate. Then he lighted a cigar. "Sure I have," he said comfortably. "I never got one myself, but I knew a bunch of other men that did, when we were living in Lakeville, before we moved here—druggists, grocers, plumbers, men with good businesses, but not so well off but what a nice fat sum of money would look pretty good to them. One of them, Hal Preston—you remember, Mother, he kept the hardware store on the corner of Main and Vine—smelled a rat right away and told his brother-in-law, Pell Nichols, up in Fairview, all about it. And come to find out, Pell had got the same identical letter! Presently, the whole crowd was comparing notes and had a good laugh over it—that was the last of the poor Spanish Prisoner as far as they were concerned. But in World War I the mails were full of letters like that. My pal Jim Hooker, who got a job in censorship in New York, told me they came in by the thousand—of course, all foreign mail got opened then. Those letters used to be stacked up in piles and labeled 'thought to be fraudulent.' So they never reached their intended victims at that time. But other times, plenty have got through."

"As far back as World War I, did you say, Harvey?" Mrs. Wendell asked incredulously. She was still eating mashed potatoes, but she paused, her fork poised in mid-air, and looked in bewilderment from her daughter to her husband.

Mr. Wendell laughed again. "Near as far back as Columbus, according to Jim Hooker. He said there were records in Seville, Spain, to show that the Spanish Prisoner swindle began along about 1542. The racket'll die down for a while, and then it'll start up again, livelier than ever. Some letters still come from Spain, like this one you're talking about, sug—

Charlotte. They keep on coming and they keep getting answered. Well, you know the old saying, there's another sucker born every minute. But I wouldn't have put our friend Allan in that class, not if you hadn't told me about this particular letter yourself."

"But who *sends* the letters?"

"According to what I've heard, there's regular 'Spanish Prisoner' gangs that make 'em up. In Mexico and I suppose in European countries, too."

"But how do they get hold of names?" Charlotte persisted.

"I don't know. You'd think maybe from the yellow pages of small-town telephone books, if the racket weren't some older than the telephone."

Mr. Wendell chuckled at his own understatement. However, it was soon evident to him that his satisfaction was to be short-lived.

"Dad, I think you ought to go right down to Allan's house and tell him what you've told us," Charlotte said with spirit. "I think it's your duty."

"Well now, I don't know about that." For the first time, Mr. Wendell spoke uneasily and, as he glanced from his daughter to his wife, his uneasiness increased and he regretted his expansiveness. He had been rather proud of his fund of information on a subject of which his wife and daughter—and obviously that learned highbrow, Allan Lambert—knew nothing. He had already noticed Charlotte's flush, but he had set it down to her annoyance at his incurable habit of calling her by an infantile pet name which she detested, and which he was obliged to admit did not suit her at all. Now he realized that she was not merely annoyed, she was angry and she was deeply troubled as well. There was no doubt about it, she liked the Lambert fellow a lot, and she did not want him to make a laughingstock of himself; what was more, she did not want to be separated from him by the width of the Atlantic Ocean for whatever reason, even a very sound one.

Mrs. Wendell's expression was no more reassuring than Charlotte's; she was not flushed, but her lips were set in a grim line. Her husband had not been married to her for twenty-five years without learning what such grimness meant. In a moment, she, too, would be urging him to do his duty and he would have to heed her words.

"After all," he said, conscious while he did so that it would do no good, "Allan's free, white and well over twenty-one and he's no fool. Far from it. I don't know's he'd thank another man for telling him what he ought to do with his time and money, especially a man that wasn't related to him in any way. I don't know as he'd even listen. Be that as it may, I wouldn't relish the job of trying to make him."

"But, Dad, if he *was* related—sort of. If he was going to be your son-in-law, for instance, wouldn't you think that then—"

Mr. Wendell regarded his daughter searchingly. "If I were sure he was going to be my son-in-law, I suppose I might feel some different," he said slowly. "But I haven't heard anything, so far, that would be liable to make me take a bet on it."

"Well, one thing's certain. He never will be your son-in-law if you don't take proper steps to keep him from falling for this swindle, hook, line and sinker. Once this gang you've told us about gets him in its clutches, there's no telling what will happen to him. I'd expect the worst."

Mrs. Wendell brought out the words with a snap; afterward, her lips closed again in a line even grimmer than before. Then she rose and began to clear the table. As she reached the swinging door that led into the kitchen, she paused, her hands piled high with dishes.

"Of course, if you don't care anything about your only child's happiness," she said acidly and disappeared.

Mr. Wendell continued to sit at the table, facing the child in question. At the moment, she did look very much like a little girl, a little girl who was rebellious and hurt and frightened, and not at all like a self-controlled, determined young woman. As he gazed at her, he saw two large tears overflow from her eyes and trickle down her flushed cheeks. It was more than he could bear. He laid aside his cigar and, rising, crossed over to her side of the table and put his arm around her.

"I'll see what I can do to bring this man of yours to his senses, sugar cookie," he said.

3.

Mr. Wendell spent a miserable afternoon. Not that there was anything the matter with business; on the contrary, his clerks kept invading his private office to tell him of more orders and more sales. The news that Allan Lambert had bought a station wagon was promptly noised abroad and hopeful inquiries about the possibility of obtaining the same model were coming in thick and fast. It was soon evident that the day's profits were to be the largest ever reaped in the course of many prosperous years. But Mr. Wendell was not able to dismiss from his mind either the picture of Charlotte as she had sat facing him with the tears rolling down her cheeks, or the prospect of confronting the richest and most influential man in town with the statement that he was a sucker. It would have been hard for Mr. Wendell to tell which of the two thoughts added more to his discomfiture. Nevertheless, he had promised Charlotte and he had always been a man of his word.

To his immense relief, he was granted a reprieve. Conscious that the longer he postponed his call, the harder it would be for him to make it, he went directly from his office to the Lambert estate.

His ring at the imposing front door remained unanswered and, in a moment of weakness, he told himself that he would be justified in going away and telling Charlotte afterward that he had indeed tried to see Allan Lambert, but that he had not been able to get into the house. However, he remembered that only one wing was inhabited, and knew that he should try the side. Here he was promptly welcomed by Casper, who was in a visible state of excitement.

"Mr. Lambert's stepped around to see Mr. and Mrs. Morse," the old servant reported, "and he told me that, afterward, he might go to see the Dean."

"Then you don't expect him back for some time? You don't think I'd better wait for him?"

"No, sir, I wouldn't think so. But if you'd care to leave a message—"

"Just tell him Mr. Wendell called. He bought a car from me this morning and I forgot to tell him something rather important about its operation. You see he's been driving a less up-to-date model."

"Well, sir, it's very kind of you to come in person to explain the difference. I'll let him know as soon as he comes in that you'd like to get in touch with him."

"Thank you. That'll be the best way to handle it, I expect."

Supper at the Wendells' was a gloomy meal. Neither Mrs. Wendell nor Charlotte renewed their admonitions and reproaches, but, on the other hand, they made it evident by their silence that they thought Mr. Wendell had been remiss in failing to await Allan's return, no matter how prolonged his absence might have been. Immediately after the evening meal, Charlotte, who generally stayed up to all hours, went to her bedroom, and Mrs. Wendell, who was a deft and expeditious housewife, remained in the kitchen much longer than could possibly have been necessary to tidy it up for the night. Mr. Wendell was not much of a reader, but he enjoyed television, so he took refuge in his favorite program and had succeeded in partially forgetting his worries when the telephone rang. As Charlotte had an extension in her room, and habitually leaped to use it, Mr. Wendell permitted the ringing to go on for some moments. Then, reluctantly, he tore himself from the screen and picked up the receiver.

"Hello," he said tonelessly. The response which came to him over the wire was cheerful and friendly.

"Oh, hello there, Mr. Wendell! Allan Lambert speaking. Casper tells me you came to see me—something about the car. Very thoughtful of you. Really, I'm delighted with it—I've driven all over town in it already. I can't imagine that I'll have the least trouble with it. But if you think there's something I ought to know before I take it out again, why not run over and have a drink with me? I've been thinking myself I might like to have it air conditioned and we could talk about that anyway."

"Why, thanks, Allan, I'd be glad to come over."

Mr. Wendell went upstairs to put on a clean shirt and a coat and, before going down again, he knocked at his daughter's door. "Allan's asked me to come over and have a drink," he said. "Maybe things will work out even better that way than if I'd seen him this afternoon. So long, sugar cookie."

She did not answer and he realized that though doubtless she was still wide awake, and had very probably listened in on the conversation, she did not intend to speak to him again until he had good news to report. Mrs. Wendell was equally unresponsive. She was taking the next day's roast from the freezer, and a blast of glacial air struck him as he strode through the kitchen. Allan, on the other hand, greeted him genially, receiving him on the rear veranda and indicating a chintz-upholstered wicker chair with an expression of hope that his visitor would find it comfortable, at the same time turning toward a laden butler's tray and inquiring hospitably as to Mr. Wendell's preferences in liquid refreshment. When they were both seated with tall tinkling glasses in their hands, Allan, on his own initiative, launched into an expansive account of the day's activities.

"I've been rushing around so that it's doubly pleasant to sit down for a quiet chat," he said. "I believe I told you this morning I was thinking of going abroad. In fact, I'd called up a travel agency in Boston before I came around to your place and they'd promised to call me back around noon and let me know what they could do for me. When they got in touch with me, they told me they'd been able to get me a single outside cabin, with private bath and veranda, on a Spanish ship sailing a week from next Thursday."

"A *Spanish* ship?" Mr. Wendell inquired, taking a quick swallow of his Scotch.

"Yes—perhaps I didn't mention Spain, specifically, when I said I was going abroad, but that's where I'm headed. Of course, American and Italian ships go there, too, but I thought I'd like to get into the Spanish atmosphere right away. I haven't been to Spain in years—hadn't thought of going back, as a matter of fact. My mother died while we were in Málaga, so I had some rather sad memories connected with the country, and it's taken me some time to dismiss them from my mind. I'd been rather vaguely considering a long trip to South America—down the east coast, through the Straits, then through the Chilean canals and lakes and up the west coast. Marvelous scenery, so I'm told. Besides, I've been rather curious to get acquainted with the various usages of Spanish that have sprung up in the different countries, and I've never been further south than Panama, which was my father's last post. Now, in Argentina, for instance, where the Italian influence is so strong, they go in for all kinds of expressions that aren't ever heard in Peru —the pronunciation's quite different, too, so I'm told. Well, I can look into all that another time. I had some good friends in Málaga when I was a boy and I'll enjoy looking them up, and finding out whether they still remember me. It'll be my own fault if they don't, I realize that. I ought to have made more of an effort to keep in touch with them. But if they've forgotten me, or aren't interested in renewing the acquaintance, I'll make others. I'm not worried about that."

Allan also took a swallow of Scotch, but less hastily and with more enjoyment than Mr. Wendell had gulped down his.

"Of course, I haven't much time to get ready, leaving a week from Thursday," Allan went on. "But I've still got some contacts in the State Department—my father's very favorably remembered—and I was assured there wouldn't be any difficulty about rushing through a passport, though I may have to fly down to Washington to see about it instead of getting it in Boston. The AAA's most co-operative, too. I have to arrange for a *carnet*, foreign insurance, all that sort of thing. So I'll need to keep on rushing. Not that I mind. I'm looking forward to it. But when I heard you wanted to talk to me about the car, I thought maybe it would be better if you did it right away. Then we'd be sure to get it in. Incidentally, I've definitely decided on the air conditioning. Now, what was on your mind?"

Mr. Wendell took another quick swallow. Then he set down his glass.

"I may as well come clean first as last," he said. "There isn't a thing I need to tell you about the operation of that station wagon. You'll handle her all right and she'll go like a breeze, anywhere you take her. But when I went home to dinner today, I mentioned to my wife and daughter that you'd been in and bought a car and that you were thinking of taking it abroad. I don't know how I came to do it. Most usually, at home, I don't discuss what goes on at the shop. But seeing that you're a friend of the family, not just a business acquaintance—"

"Why, Mr. Wendell, you don't need to apologize! I think it was perfectly natural for you to tell Charlotte and Mrs. Wendell that I'd bought a car and that I was thinking of taking it abroad. As you say, I'm a friend of the family. I'm very glad to be, too."

"Well, you've relieved my mind and that's a fact," Mr. Wendell said gratefully. "But I haven't told you the half of it yet, so you'd better wait until I tell you some more before you say I don't need to apologize. It seems Charlotte and you went on a picnic yesterday and you showed her a letter that you'd got in the morning mail."

"That's right. I did. I thought it might interest her. It interested me."

"So when I mentioned the sale of the car and said you were taking it abroad," Mr. Wendell went on doggedly, "Charlotte added two and two and got five, the way a girl will sometimes, you know. She took it into her head that the reason you were going abroad was on account of how you'd had this Spanish Prisoner letter."

"That's right, too. At least, it's partly right. Now that I've got it, I don't see why I didn't think of going to Spain in the first place. If I hadn't got it, I might have been trying to engage passage to Tierra del Fuego instead of La Coruña."

Mr. Wendell breathed hard. "Well, of course if you mean by that, getting this letter just put you in mind of seeing your old friends, and going back to the place where you lived as a boy and where your father did a fine job, that's grand," he said. "But if you mean it likewise gave you the idea that you might look up the 'Prisoner' who wrote that letter, it's something else again."

"Yes, it is. And I don't in the least mind telling you that after I've looked up the man who wrote that letter, I mean to look up my old friends."

Mr. Wendell breathed harder still. "Well, it so happens this isn't the first time I've heard about letters like that. And when I told Mother and Charlotte what I knew, they wouldn't give me any peace until I'd promised to come and tell you, too. I didn't want to. I said it wasn't any of my business what you did with your time and money. But they kept after me just the same. So I came. That's what I think I ought to apologize for. But when you get to be as old as I am, maybe you'll find it isn't so easy to say no to your wife and daughter—especially if your wife's got what's called a mind of her own and you see tears rolling down your daughter's face."

It was over. To his unspeakable embarrassment and with indelicate frankness, he had kept his promise. And now this cultured and wealthy young man, this highly desirable suitor, who could not have received him with more courtesy if he had been president of the college, would find a gentlemanly way of telling him to get out, and that would be the end of a beautiful friendship. What was worse, it might well be the end of all Charlotte's hopes and her parents' hopes for her. It would have been better, much better, if he had shown his wife and daughter who was the head of the house; in the end, the one would have had less cause for grimness, the other less cause for tears. . . .

"You say you've heard of more letters like the one I received yesterday," Allan Lambert was saying pleasantly. "I'd be very pleased if you'd tell me what you told Mrs. Wendell and Charlotte. Here, let me freshen that drink for you. And what about a cigar? I don't smoke them myself, so I very negligently forgot to have any put out. But my uncle did—it was his only extravagance! And there are some left, pretty good ones, I believe. Excuse me just a minute, I'll get one for you."

Mr. Wendell sat very still, hardly daring to believe his ears. Allan refilled his glass, not forgetting to add plenty of ice to replace that which had melted, and the grateful guest sipped the fresh drink with keen appreciation while his host sought out the cigars. When Allan returned with them and sat down again, he renewed his request, with every evidence of cordiality.

"Well, it was like this," Mr. Wendell began. "When we were living in Lakeville, before we moved over here, a bunch of men I knew . . ." And he went on to relate what Hal Preston, who kept the hardware store on the corner of Main and Vine, had told his brother-in-law, Pell Nichols, up in Fairview, only to find that Pell had received the same identical letter; and how finally the whole crowd got together and had a good laugh. At this point he paused, but sensing his listener's absorbed attention, he continued with the tale of what had happened in the Censor's Bureau during World War I, according to his pal Jim Hooker. And he ended up with the Archives of Seville.

"That's what I heard," he said. "And that's what I told my wife and daughter. It's all I heard—all I told them."

"Well, I'm very much obliged to you for telling me, too. I hadn't heard any of it before and it's very interesting. Not that I hadn't figured out that there was something phony about the whole thing, of course."

"You *had!*"

"Why, yes. If there had been a cashier's check and it had been any good, wouldn't this prisoner have immediately disclosed the fact that he had it and that he could draw on it, that he didn't need to pay a fine for bankruptcy—in fact, that he wasn't a bankrupt at all? As for the $285,000 in the trunk, if it existed at all, isn't it certain that it must have been embezzled? Otherwise, why write a total stranger about it? 'Prominent bankers' are bound to be men with wide acquaintances and quite a few friends. And there aren't many families so completely wiped out that an eighteen-year-old girl has to take refuge in a convent, in this day and age. Think of me, for instance. My father and mother are both dead and I was an only child. But I've got cousins who would do anything in the world for me—and just remember Uncle Nathan!"

Mr. Wendell set down his drink and rose. He might have known. According to reliable report, more than one seemingly intelligent man had been taken in by the Spanish Prisoner letter. Why they had not all followed Allan Lambert's clear line of reasoning, without supplementary information from anyone, he could not imagine—or why he had not instinctively known that no matter what anyone else had done or failed to do, Allan Lambert was quite capable of taking care of himself. His previous embarrassment was as nothing to the humiliation which now flooded his being. But almost instantly a startled query speared its way through his shame.

"Then if you know it's a swindle, why are you going to look up the scoundrel who wrote the letter and who's no more a prisoner than you are?"

"Because," Allan Lambert replied with a smile, "I think it might be fun. Don't go, Mr. Wendell. Sit down and have another drink."

4.

ALTHOUGH ALLAN ENJOYED HIS trip to Washington, which he had not visited in a long while, and was gratified by the courtesies shown him there, the impression that it had been necessary to speed up the normal procedure of procuring a passport proved to be entirely baseless. His ship, the *Tarragona*, had been scheduled to sail on the fourteenth of the month; when he failed to receive his ticket promptly after having sent a check for it, he telephoned and was told that the agent had been waiting for further information about the ship's movements before communicating with him; it appeared that there might be a slight delay. Yes, certainly, the *Tarragona* was a passenger ship, as up-to-date and luxurious as any on the Atlantic. But on the westbound voyage it stopped at Vera Cruz, at San Juan and at Havana; Mr. Lambert would, of course, understand that, if there were cargo to take on, as well as clients to accommodate, the cargo must be given consideration. The agent did not say *prior* consideration, but Allan had no difficulty in deciding that this was the case when the agent went on to inform him, rather hesitantly, that the *Tarragona* was now scheduled to sail on the twentieth. As this was the date typed on the ticket, now rather tardily sent in, Allan took it for granted that he had imagined the hesitation; and as he had been told that the car must be on the dock two days before the departure of the ship, he drove to New York on the seventeenth. As he still lacked information as to the hours for receiving automobiles, however, he telephoned again the following morning, to learn that there had been another unavoidable postponement and that the twenty-fifth was now the appointed date.

He derived a rueful amusement from the idea that a passenger who had embarked in Vera Cruz on schedule, and who had important engagements in Spain, might by now be feeling somewhat irked; and he felt genuinely sorry for such travelers who were obliged to count their pennies, and who consequently must be finding unexpected hotel bills a severe strain on their resources. But as far as he was personally concerned, he rather enjoyed the renewed consciousness that Spaniards were never too much bound by time; and he did not regret having a week in New York instead of another week at home. Like the news that he had purchased a station wagon, the news that Allan Lambert had received a spurious begging letter from Spain and that, although he recognized its lack of authenticity, had decided to answer it in person, spread like wildfire through the college town which, however dormant, could always be aroused by gossip. Though he had immediately apprised both his cousins and the Dean of his impending departure, he had not thought it necessary to give the main reason for it; it came to their ears through roundabout channels which they could easily have traced back to Charlotte and her mother, if they had taken pains to do so. Charlotte had stubbornly refused to heed her father's sound advice that the less said about the whole thing, the better. Instead, she told everyone who would listen to her that Allan had shown her a letter he had received from an alleged prisoner; and that when Mr. Wendell, through kindness of heart, had gone to warn him, he had laughingly retorted that, of course, he knew the whole thing was a hoax, but that he thought it would be fun to find out what lay behind it! Such a course of conduct was naturally highly reprehensible in a person who had always passed for a serious scholar. It just went to show you could never tell. . . .

Town and gown were both inclined to agree with Charlotte's conclusions. Allan was busy packing and putting his affairs in order generally, preparatory to an absence of indefinite length. Except for taking solitary spins through the countryside in his new station wagon, from which he derived enormous and ever-increasing pleasure, he did not go out unless on business; and when he went to make his arrangements for air conditioning his new treasure, he did not see Mr. Wendell at all, though he asked for him exactly—as the clerk who waited on him said afterward—as if nothing had happened. But he received innumerable callers. Even Marian and Arthur felt that his conduct was scatterbrained and the Dean was still more censorious. He did not hesitate to say that while he himself set down Lambert's course of action to nothing worse than folly, there were some who would inevitably believe that the young professor was going to Spain "intent on larceny." When Allan laughed and asked the Dean why on earth he, Allan, should want to steal, when all he had to do to get more money than he could spend was to cut coupons, the Dean replied that everyone did not realize that—obviously the sender of the letter had not realized that, for all such missives were intended as bait for the unwary. If those who were lacking in caution, experience or sound sense and who could use a little extra money were deceived, that was their misfortune. But when a prudent, intellectual, wealthy man of high standing connived at such wickedness, it was something worse; the kindest thing to say about it might be that it was madness.

"If you feel that by taking a trip to Spain I'm going to bring discredit on the college," Allan remarked quietly, interrupting the Dean at this point, "I'm perfectly willing to hand in my resignation, effective at once. That would give you the summer to find someone to take over my courses permanently, instead of just to look for a temporary substitute."

The Dean instantly realized that he had gone too far. Not only was the possibility of an ideal recreational center slipping away from him, but many other potential benefits to the college. As far as that went, Allan was one of the best teachers on the faculty. Even when he had been without a cent except his salary, he was very valuable. Now his value was immeasurably increased.

"My dear Lambert, I never intended to intimate anything of the sort," the Dean said hastily. "Of course we don't feel that by taking a trip to Spain you're bringing discredit on the college. It's a very logical thing for you to do. In fact, I'm rather surprised, considering your field, that you didn't think of it earlier. It offers endless opportunities for research and study that will be most helpful to your pupils, as well as desirable for yourself. But, as I understand it, you don't propose to spend your time in research and study."

"Excuse me. It looks as if I might be doing quite a little research. And you've been good enough, several times, to call me a natural student. I'm planning to approach the present problem in a very thorough way. . . . Are you sure I couldn't persuade you to take a little light refreshment? It's been a very warm day and I'm sure . . . Oh, excuse me! Casper is rather deaf; he doesn't always hear the telephone and it seems to be ringing quite insistently."

At that moment, Allan welcomed the telephone as an avenue of escape; but more and more he was permitting it to ring insistently without bothering to answer it. It seemed to him that everyone who did not come to see him or write to him was bent on telephoning him. Apparently, he was almost the only person within the radius of his entire acquaintance who had hitherto never heard of the Spanish Prisoner swindle. Articles had been written about it by eminent authors and published in quality magazines with immense circulations. It seemed incredible to him, as it did to all these well-meaning persons who were now hounding him, that he had never read any of these previously. Dog-eared copies of various periodicals, some of them hoary with age, were constantly being sent to him, many of them with marked passages. "A Washington packer, a New York jeweler, a Georgia ice dealer, a Michigan contractor, a California grocer and a Pennsylvania lawyer all admit unhappily that they have followed the train

of the Spanish Prisoner. The United States has been filing names of
victims for over sixty years." So read one of these marked passages and
underneath, in the sender's hand, was written, "Are we now to add 'a New
England professor' to this deplorable list?"

Allan had invited his assistant, poor old Perdido, to come and stay at
his house while he was gone; and in answer to the aged Mexican's objection that he could not be of sufficient use to justify his acceptance, Allan
had suggested that Perdido might screen his mail and forward only such
letters as would give enjoyment in the reading. Thus reassured, Perdido
thankfully took up his residence in the huge historic house and Allan was
relieved of all troublesome correspondence. He drove to New York in high
spirits, put up at a luxurious hotel, and visited the shops by day and the
theater by night. Far from finding that time hung heavy on his hands, he
was really sorry when the morning finally came to take the station wagon
to the pier.

He lacked directions for finding this, having been told only that it was
in Hoboken, at the foot of Eighth Street; and, after making endless turns
to both right and left, sometimes in the wrong order, and roaring through
the Lincoln Tunnel, he discovered that Eighth Street came to a dead end
on a large sandstone bluff. There was not a policeman in sight, but after
several futile attempts to reach his destination, Allan finally caught sight
of a pier and headed toward it, only to discover, through the signs on it,
that it was not the one he sought. While he was trying to turn the station
wagon around, he realized that a dockhand was striving to direct his movements and, thankful for some sign of helpfulness, called out to him.

"Can you tell me where the Eighth Street pier is?"

"What line you look for?" the dockhand inquired in broken English.

"The Spanish Line."

"*Tarragona?*"

"That's right."

"I show you."

Without further ado, he climbed into the station wagon and motioned
toward a steep and bumpy hill. Allan drove slowly down it and, when they
reached its foot, his guide motioned again, indicating that they must follow some railroad tracks. When, after considerable more bumping, they
eventually reached another pier, Allan was interested to note that it was
Number 10; but a policeman was on duty and in comparatively short order,
the station wagon was turned over to the proper authorities, while its owner
was still wondering whether he should have tried to find his way with a
divining rod.

Since nothing more remained to be done on the pier at the moment,
however, he walked back to the guard and inquired whether a taxi might

be available. The reply was affirmative, the policeman obligingly telephoned for one and, as Allan awaited its arrival, entered into conversation with him.

"Not going to take a taxi all the way back to New York, are you?"

"I thought I would. I don't know my way around too well."

"Why, it's easy! Have the taxi take you up to the first bus station, catch onto an 84 bus, and that'll take you right into the Port Authority Station. Which way you headed, uptown or down?"

"Up."

"Well, you can get the subway right there."

"That all sounds rather complicated to me. I think perhaps I'd better stick to the taxi."

"Just as you say, mister. But it'll be a lot more expensive. They'll charge you at least seven-fifty. If you're in a hurry though—"

"I am rather. I've used up a good deal of time trying to find this pier. Do you know why its location's such a secret?"

The policeman laughed. "No. But things'll be better next year. These ships will be leaving from Brooklyn then. Well, here's your taxi. Good luck to you!"

It was completely untrue that Allan was in a hurry, but he had done enough wandering about Hoboken to last him for quite a while and, moreover, he was luxuriating in his escape from penury. He devoted another twenty-four hours to shopping and the theater and himself guided another taxi driver back to Pier Number 10 the following day. Embarkation, according to the latest information received from the company, was to take place between one and four. But as the two morning papers which Allan read did not agree as to sailing time, he decided to take no chances, and was on the pier well before two o'clock. A group of porters, bearing an uncomfortable resemblance to a band of brigands, was lying in wait to relieve him of his baggage, and it was not without some uneasiness that he saw it disappear. After they had exerted themselves to the extent of lifting it from a taxi to a conveyor, they extended eager, unwashed hands to receive their just reward and he could tell by their faces that they were prepared to protest that his tip was too small. He gave them an agreeable surprise and escaped to the elevator.

Early as it was, he found a sizable crowd ahead of him when he reached the embarkation level. No arrangements had been made to separate tourist and first-class passengers, and the number of company officials on hand to check passports and tickets was so limited that the line moved with aggravating slowness. Mothers with small children were vainly trying to keep them from dashing out of reach, alert-looking businessmen were fuming in loud voices and elderly persons of both sexes were showing signs of strain. Allan did not mind the wait; it interested him to size up these various individuals, with whom he would be thrown for the next eight or nine days, and to speculate on which ones he would find the best companions. He did not expect to find any of them boring. He was through with boredom; the fun was beginning.

He finally reached the gangplank, produced his ticket and passport, which had both been thoroughly inspected five minutes earlier, for further scrutiny, and went on toward the deck. A group of swarthy, sleek-haired stewards, wearing immaculate white jackets finished with blue collars so long and narrow that they gave the effect of important ribbons lacking only orders and decorations, was waiting to receive and direct the passengers. One of these stewards, after bowing with grave courtesy worthy of a grandee, stepped forward and solicitously asked Allan the number of his cabin.

"This way, *señor*. If you'll have the goodness to follow me."

He led the way down a narrow passage crowded with passengers and their visitors, threading his way among them with dignity and grace. Then he threw open the door of a cabin marked with a single capital letter.

"If it should not please you, *señor*, the *comisario* will try to change it. It is of course the desire of everyone that you should be perfectly satisfied."

Allan looked about him with amazement. It was years since he had been on an ocean liner, and his parents had always been obliged to travel at minimum rates; he had not been prepared for the changes that time and wealth could make. The cabin was small, but it was furnished and decorated with an elegance that would have done credit to the expensive hotel where he had been staying. The dark woodwork was carved and polished, the bed was flanked by a commodious chest of drawers, and at the windows were frilled white curtains dotted in rose color. A door beside the one by which he had entered revealed a gleaming bathroom; a third door, opposite the entrance, opened into a balcony which had green latticed walls and was furnished in wicker and chintz. The afternoon sun poured in generously and the towers of Manhattan rose against a cloudless sky. Allan drew a long breath and turned toward the waiting steward.

"I couldn't possibly be better pleased. I don't see how anyone could be."

"Thank you, *señor*. If there is anything you should wish, you have only to ring. Your baggage will be sent to you presently."

Allan sat down in one of the wicker chairs and gazed with enthrallment at the scene before him. Ferries, laden with freight cars, were plying back and forth. Excursion boats of the Circle Line went endlessly to and fro. Tugs moved fussily about and barges slipped silently past. The pilot came alongside, departed with a goup of waving well wishers, and returned to await the moment of casting off. Giant airplanes swept overhead on their way out to sea and a helicopter whirled to rest on top of a high flat roof. The dark spire of the Empire State Building clove its way into the bright blue heavens and all the lesser pinnacles which surrounded it seemed to share in its supremacy. . . .

It was not until the sinking sun brought Allan the realization of how much time had passed that he also realized, not only that the announced hour for departure had long since passed, but also that the courteous steward's interpretation of "presently" was different from his. For a moment he thought with uneasiness about his missing possessions, but the concern was fleeting. True, the porters had looked and acted something like brigands; but once the baggage was on the conveyor, it must inevitably reach its destination sooner or later. However, he had his own ideas as to how he wanted it placed and, therefore, he decided to put off inspection of the ship until after his suitcases were safely stowed away. Meanwhile, in spite of his pleasure in his surroundings, time was beginning to drag a little; he wished he had brought along something to read. He should have remembered that he was never contented for long unless he had a book in his hand.

For lack of anything else he took his ticket from his wallet and began to run through the small print, to which, in common with most travelers, he had paid no attention. As he read this text, obviously prepared by someone who believed in literal rather than idiomatic translations, his mouth began to twitch and presently he laughed aloud.

"Passengers are responsible for all infraction of the laws of whatever country the steamer happens to be.

"The passengers are responsible for all injuries or prejudices caused during their stay on board.

"Passengers afflicted with contagious diseases or in a state of dementia will not be admitted on board. Those who during the voyage are attacked by such diseases may be landed at the first port of call with all due precautions. . . ."

"So no passenger will be allowed on board who is in a state of dementia!" Allan said to himself, folding the ticket and restoring it to his wallet. "Lucky for me the company didn't consult anyone in my home town."

Part Two ❦ ETHEL

5.

ALLAN WAS MILDLY SURPRISED to find no passenger list, enclosed in a brochure featuring the *Tarragona's* many attractions, lying on his napkin as he sat down at the table on the second night out. The surprise increased when, the next night, in answer to his question as to its continued absence, his steward informed him that the brochure would make its appearance at the Captain's dinner.

"You mean the evening before we arrive at La Coruña?"

"*Si, señor.*"

The steward's astonishment that it should have been expected any sooner than this was obviously greater than Allan's puzzled amusement over the delay. If such a brochure were designed largely to facilitate identification of fellow passengers, and thus pave the way to the discovery of mutual backgrounds, acquaintances and interests, it certainly would not be of much use if it reached the travelers' hands when they were already packing to disembark; but apparently this aspect of the brochure's usefulness had either escaped the notice of those who directed the ship's destinies or had been considered inconsequential. When he had traveled as a boy with his parents, Allan had always enjoyed finding out that boys from places he had never heard of were traveling with their parents too, and that youthful pursuits and pleasures differed surprisingly little on opposite sides of the globe. This time, he had expected to experience a similar satisfaction in discovering that some of his fellow passengers came from Málaga, and perhaps getting immediate news of long-lost friends. His first impulse was to question the purser, but he decided to suppress this; if he started asking questions, which could be interpreted as revealing undue curiosity, he might arouse undue curiosity about himself. He had no desire to reveal prematurely the object of his visit to Spain. Indeed, his better judgment told him that even if he had wished to do so, such a course would have been injudicious. Quietly, almost cautiously, he began to feel his way about.

At first his progress was slow. The sea was unseasonably rough and many persons were confined to their cabins. Allan had no companions at the swimming pool except a few riotous children. Three of these were Americans, whose exhausted mother was on her way to join her husband—an engineer helping to supervise a bridge building project. The only other Americans on board were a couple whose daughter was expecting a baby;

they were distrustful of their son-in-law, a "foreigner" whom she had unfortunately met during a summer course at the University of Madrid, and of all "foreign" hospitals; and their anxiety was unassuaged by the puzzled barkeeper from whom they persistently sought dry martinis. Allan was able to be of some help in this direction, and the distrustful couple was grateful to him; but he did not find them especially distracting companions.

He fared no better in the dining room. He had been placed at table with three other men, all Mexicans, who were apparently acquainted with each other, but who talked very little, even among themselves, because their devotion to the menu was so intensive as to preclude much conversation. They ate their way steadily through every course, from hors d'oeuvres to fruit and cheese, their gaze concentrated on their laden plates. At the table on the right were two sad-looking aged women, one of them so lame that she had to be helped across the floor, and two others who were slightly younger but already tinged with the drabness born of encroaching years after futile lives. All four were clad in the deepest mourning, as if for some near relative, recently lost. At the table on the left was a family group, consisting of a father, mother, and two pretty young daughters, who wore different dresses at every meal and seemed bright and vivacious. The father, however, was in a morose mood. At intervals he remarked, in a tone loud enough to be overheard, that he might better have remained in Havana and done his business by cable than to spend the rest of his life on the ocean or in ports waiting to sail; by the time they finally reached Bilbao, his correspondents would have despaired of ever seeing him. His wife attempted to soothe him, but her roving glance betrayed disappointment that the daughters' extensive wardrobes were more or less wasted, for there were no sleek young Latins aboard who might serve as acceptable swains, and the ship's officers—all middle-aged or older—sat in a group at a table by themselves and seemed completely unaware of the two lively sisters' charms.

Allan could not see the further tables' occupants when they were seated, and his observations of them as they went back and forth were discouraging. It was not until he went in to dinner the third night out that he noticed a lady, alone at a table hitherto empty, near the extreme end of the room. Even at such a distance, her appearance was sufficiently striking to arrest his attention. She was blond, and in defiance of all prevailing fashion, her abundant hair was fluffed out around her face and then piled high on her head in a mass of burnished gold. She had on an emerald green lace dress with long sleeves, which ended in points over her white wrists and drew immediate attention to the shapeliness of her arms. The molded bodice revealed a dazzlingly white neck and a rounded bosom, modestly veiled. The table concealed the rest of her figure, but Allan could easily visualize it. As she looked up at the steward to give her order and helped herself from the basket of bread beside her plate, the way she made even such slight movements indicated that when she stood and walked, she would do so with distinction.

When Allan was seated himself, this pleasing spectacle was entirely lost to view and, not without a twinge of self-consciousness, he dawdled over his meal until the lace-clad lady rose and passed close to his table before mounting the small staircase which opened into the dining room. It was precisely as he had expected. She moved with consummate grace, and the long sheath skirt of the lace dress accentuated the beautiful lines of hips and legs, just as the sleeves and bodice had accentuated the loveliness of the wearer's arms and breasts. This time he obeyed his first impulse. He excused himself to his tablemates, who were still happily gourmandizing, and followed the lady up the stairs.

He had no trouble in finding her. Coffee and drinks were both served in the tiled and latticed "Alhambra Garden" which was also used later in the evening for moving pictures and dancing or both. He was even saved the slight hazard of venturing unbidden on the initial approach to acquaintance by a smile so charming that it could only be interpreted as one of welcome; and while he was still wondering whether he should address the stranger in Spanish or in English, she spoke to him in English.

"Won't you sit down? I haven't spoken to a soul in three days, and I've been hoping someone would come and talk to me."

"I wish I'd known that sooner."

She laughed pleasantly. "You wouldn't if you knew how disgracefully seasick I've been. Usually I'm a pretty good sailor, but for some reason this time . . . And I'm not going to pretend I had a cold, either, or that I'd been on such a round of farewell parties that my digestion was upset before I got on shipboard. I was just plain seasick, that's all."

Her pleasant laugh was contagious and Allan joined in it. "I might at least have asked your permission to send you champagne, if I'd known about your plight—or your existence," he said. "But I didn't see you on the dock or on shipboard before we got out of the harbor. Surely you weren't seasick that soon!"

"No. But I caught the ship by the skin of my teeth. I'm afraid I shouldn't have made it if we hadn't been so late in casting off. And I really was exhausted that first evening—not from parties, but from traveling. I'd flown up to New York from Tennessee, missing connections everywhere, and running into bad weather everywhere. I went to bed as soon as I was shown to my cabin. And then to have a rough sea at this time of year, after all those thunderstorms and cloudbursts!"

She laughed again, and again Allan joined in her laugh. There was certainly nothing about her now which suggested either exhaustion or sea-sickness, and he would have liked to say so, but refrained for fear the compliment would seem rather brash. Nevertheless, the fact remained that she fairly radiated vitality and closer inspection of the charms which he had first seen only at a distance intensified rather than diminished his admiration of them. She was wearing very little make-up, just a touch of lipstick, perhaps a light dusting of powder; but she had the fresh rosy skin of a very young girl, though he guessed from her complete self-possession that she must be nearer twenty-seven than seventeen; and if the gorgeous color of her hair owed anything to art, the tinting had been so skillfully done that only an expert would have known it. When she laughed she showed beautiful white teeth, and a small dimple just at the left of the lips came into play. Almost immediately Allan found himself watching for it. Then his attention was diverted by a great green stone, suspended from the golden chain around her neck. It could hardly be an emerald, he thought, briefly trying to pretend that it was the stone itself and not its position which had diverted him from the dimple—an emerald of that size would be worth a fortune, and moreover the lady in green was wearing long earrings and an immense ring that matched the pendant. But if it were synthetic, the imitation of the real thing, like the tinting of the hair, was so skillful that it would defy detection by anyone but an expert. And the gold chain was not really too long. It was only the fact that the stone swung back and forth on it, ever so slightly, which made it seem provocative.

Allan told himself all this very firmly. Then, rather belatedly, he asked his new acquaintance if she would not like a liqueur. Coffee had been brought to them automatically, while they were exchanging the first banal-ities, in the course of which he had told her his name and learned that hers was Ethel Crewe. Soon thereafter the cups had been refilled. Now these were empty a second time, and he still had not contributed anything, even conversation, to show his appreciation of this meeting which seemed doubly delightful because he had begun to despair of finding any con-genial company. It was high time he stopped watching a dimple and a green stone swinging from a golden chain, and made some appropriate remark.

The suggestion of a liqueur was favorably received, and while they were sipping it, the American whose children had interfered so effectively with Allan's enjoyment of the swimming pool appeared at the entrance of the "Alhambra Garden," and after hesitating for a moment on the threshold, came and sat down beside them, heaving a deep sigh. She had finally packed those young hellions of hers off to bed, she said. Now, maybe, she would have a little peace. She hoped they didn't mind having her join them. She was feeling sort of lonely. Of course they didn't mind, Allan and Ethel said simultaneously, and Ethel added that she had been a little lonely herself, until Mr. Lambert had finally taken pity on her. She knew exactly how Mrs.—? Oh, yes, Mrs. Graham, felt.

While gratefully gulping down the additional liqueur which Allan hastened to order, the visitor went on talking volubly. She did wish there were more Americans on board, and that more amusements were provided. She had seen last night's movie twice already in Galena, and no one had asked her to dance since they left New York. She supposed the few men on board thought she was too old, but as a matter of fact she loved to dance. She would be thankful when she got to Spain. She understood there were plenty of servants there, dirt cheap, too. She could turn the children over to them—that is, if she could make them understand what she was after. The only trouble was she didn't speak Word One of Spanish . . .

"Have you ever been to Spain before?" she suddenly inquired, addressing Ethel Crewe directly for the first time.

"Yes, twice."

"How did you make out?"

"Fine, thanks."

"I suppose that means you speak Spanish like a native?"

"Not quite that well, I'm afraid. But well enough to get along."

"What do mean by getting along? Have you tried to keep house and manage servants in Spanish?"

"Yes. We have a house in Madrid that we like a lot. Of course, there are a number of good hotels and restaurants and sometimes we take our company to those. But we like having a place of our own too."

"What do you mean by 'we'? Are you married?"

"Yes."

"Then you're on your way to join your husband, just as I am?"

"Well, I gather it's not quite the same. As I said, I've been to Spain twice before, so it's a case of rejoining him on familiar territory, rather than rejoining him in a strange country, so I have a slight advantage over you there. On the other hand, unfortunately, I shan't be able to stay with him very long, and you sound as if you were getting ready to settle down."

"I am. That's where my husband's work is now, worse luck."

"It's where my husband's work is too, and we think that's very good luck. But we have a rather complicated set of family obligations, so I commute between the United States and Spain. And I haven't any children. That makes rather a difference too, doesn't it?"

"I'll say it does."

Mrs. Graham's usual expression of harrassment, which had lightened somewhat while she was questioning Ethel Crewe, now deepened into one of positive gloom. Allan, who at first had regarded her presence as extremely intrusive, had grown less resentful of it as it speedily satisfied his own curiosity on several points, which he would have hesitated to raise himself, while serving only to whet it on several others. He thought that Mrs. Graham was gathering her scattered forces to seek further information of which he would be equally glad, when the record player which supplied the music for dancing suddenly burst into a sound loud enough to drown their voices. At the same instant, the Captain, who had been sitting silently with the same officers with whom he had eaten lunch and dinner every day, rose hurriedly, crossed the floor with the speed and directness of a well-aimed arrow, and bowed before Ethel Crewe. She looked up at him with an expression of pleased surprise, then rose in her turn and nodded smilingly over her shoulder to Allan and Mrs. Graham as she glided away. When the noisy tune subsided into a passage slightly less raucous than that with which it had begun, Mrs. Graham drew her chair closer to Allan's.

"I've heard that the captains on small ships generally have a pet passenger," she hissed in his ear. "I don't believe I need to give you three guesses who it's going to be on this trip. A married woman, too! I think it's simply disgraceful, don't you?"

6.

ALLAN COULD NOT AGREE with Mrs. Graham that it was disgraceful for the Captain to ask Mrs. Crewe for a dance; such an attention seemed to him both courteous and natural, and it was not hard for him to understand why Mrs. Graham herself had lacked partners. However, as the voyage wore on, and the Captain repeated his invitations, Allan began to change his mind. The more Ethel Crewe danced with the Captain the less she had time to dance with him. And, married or not, she was a beautiful dancer.

Fleetingly, he reminded himself that his own attitude was not above reproach. His attentions might be less conspicuous than the other's, because he was only a passenger. Even so, he realized they would not long escape notice and comment, and that it was not the part of a gentleman to subject a lady to anything of the sort. But he found it very easy to disregard the still small voice of conscience; he had set out to have fun and he was having it, much sooner and to a much greater degree than he had expected.

Mrs. Crewe had neglected to reserve a deck chair before succumbing to fatigue and indisposition, so it was a simple matter to arrange that one for her should be placed in the sheltered and secluded section that Allan had already selected for his. The inclement weather was of brief duration, and very shortly they were spending long hours on deck together. In the course of one of their cozy conversations, they became involved in a discussion which proved so absorbing that they did not hear the luncheon bell, and tardily decided that they would have trays sent up; after that it became logical to have all their meals except breakfast together, either on deck or in the dining room. Ethel confessed that her isolation at table had proved little to her liking, though she could not blame it on the chief steward. She had told him she preferred not to be put with strangers. Of course, when she said that, she had not dreamed she would meet one who was so congenial. As a matter of fact, she did not think of Allan as a stranger any longer; she already thought of him as quite an old friend. . . .

There was nothing the Captain could do about the deck chairs or the table plan; but during the evening hours he had his innings. He managed to leave the bridge early enough for a leisurely *apéritif* and to remain absent from his quarters until after the last dance. If Allan and Ethel reached the "Alhambra Garden" before he did, he asked their permission to join them, instead of remaining with the other officers who all filed in together and, except for occasional sallies to the dance floor, remained together. If he were among the first to leave the dining room, he chose a place large enough to accommodate a group, and invited several passengers to join him for coffee. Except for Ethel, these passengers were chosen in rotation, and he scrupulously asked each of the ladies to dance with him once. But Ethel was always asked to join the group. Even the two pretty little Cubans were powerless to divert him, though Allan felt it was a shame they should be so neglected, when they were obviously so ready and eager to please. But he himself did nothing to remedy this neglect, and he was encountering more and more interference all the time. Other male passengers who at first had hesitated to intrude on the Captain's hospitality were becoming bolder and bolder; they lurked in the vicinity of his chosen corner, ready to pounce the minute he rose to perform one of his duty dances. Since Allan's conscience was not so altogether dormant that he did not go through with a few dances too, he did not always get back to the corner in time to prevent Ethel's triumphant capture by one of the waiting interlopers. The evenings became periods of increasing frustration.

Allan was not sure whether it made matters better or worse because all this time Ethel did or said nothing—at least within his presence and his hearing—that could be interpreted as coquettish or even arch. She was pleasant and cordial to everyone and she was quite candid in saying and showing that she greatly enjoyed Allan's society; but there had been nothing to indicate that she would have permitted what, in the college town where he taught, were called "liberties." Much less did she invite these, either openly or by inference; and though she consistently wore beautiful and becoming clothes, they were elegant rather than extreme in style, and none of them, by any stretch of the imagination, could have been considered daring. In one respect and one only she resembled Charlotte: she never appeared in either slacks or shorts; and her bathing suits were actually conservative, if gauged by what they covered rather than by what they outlined. The same was true of her evening dresses. It was not her fault, Allan told himself, as vehemently as if he had been called upon to defend her, that her manner was so irresistibly charming, and that she had the kind of figure which no normal man could look upon entirely unmoved. History was punctuated, though not as frequently as their male contemporaries might have wished, with women like that; there was a quality to their femininity which most women did not possess, that was all.

He dwelt on this persistently. Nevertheless, as the voyage drew toward its end, he found that while all he was telling himself might very well be true—was of course true—he wished very much that it was not. He was having less fun than he had at first, not only because his conscience really had begun to trouble him, but because he saw no course, honorable or otherwise, open to him. Everything that had been lacking in his feeling for Charlotte was all too predominant in his feeling for Ethel; and now, in just a day or two, they would be landing in La Coruña where, as she had told him, spontaneously and happily, her husband would be coming to meet her. Then she would pass out of his life. Meanwhile, unless he had misread everything about her character and conduct, even a swift embrace would meet not with an ardent response but with an indignant rebuff. . . . Or would it?

The question was still unanswered the night of the Captain's dinner. Ethel had declined an invitation for an *apéritif* in the "Alhambra Garden" beforehand, on the ground of a slight migraine and the necessity for some preliminary packing. But when she appeared in the dining room, after everyone else had already begun to drink complimentary Spanish champagne, she did not look as if she had ever had an ache or pain in her life, and certainly she still had some very important packing to do. She was wearing a white tulle dress, sprinkled with tiny gold sequins exactly the color of her hair; and for the first time since she had been aboard ship her bodice was not only sleeveless but strapless, and was cut in a deep V both in front and behind. The chain which hung around her neck was much longer than the one from which the great green stone had been suspended, and this time the jewel was a heart-shaped topaz, not swinging back and forth, but nestling in the hollow between her breasts.

Between courses, Allan leaned forward and took her hands in his. It had been hard to wait until she clasped them lightly in her lap while the plates were being changed.

"I want to talk to you," he said in a tense whisper. "I won't have a chance as long as the dancing goes on. Where will you meet me afterwards?"

"Why, Allan! We've been talking together nearly all day," she said, attempting to draw away her hands.

"I know. But that's not enough. That's not nearly enough."

"Well, we still have all day tomorrow. I think it's such a good idea, don't you, that the Captain's dinner isn't the very last night any more? It used to be so inconvenient, leaving out a party dress and—"

"What I want to say to you won't wait until tomorrow."

"We-e-ell," she said again, more pensively this time, "if it's really so very urgent—and *private*—"

"It's both."

The capable steward was approaching with Baked Alaska. Ethel succeeded in freeing her hands and looked up with her usual charming smile—the smile she gave everyone—as she began to toy with her fork. Then, with apparent appetite, she went on eating.

"I'm trying to think," she said at last. "But, on a small ship like this, there really isn't any place—except maybe the room they call the library, on the boat deck, which seems such a strange place for a library. There aren't any books in it, and I've never seen anyone reading there except the chaplain, who always goes to bed early."

"I suppose this library shows on the boat plan, but I'd forgotten about it and I've never been there. How did you happen to find it?"

"Why, just like that—I happened to."

She looked at him guilelessly. "The Captain didn't help you find it, I suppose?" he shot at her before he could stop himself.

"Of course not! What's the matter with you, Allan? You're not acting a bit like yourself."

"I'm not feeling a bit like myself," he said savagely. "All right, we meet in the library. Right after the dance?"

"We-e-ell, perhaps not *right* after the dance. I'll have to go to my cabin and freshen up a little."

"All right. Say it takes you a quarter of an hour to freshen up. I'll wait for you that long. But if you're not in the library by then, I'll come and get you. I think your cabin is number sixteen, but you'd better tell me—just in case. It might be awkward if I made a mistake or had to ask anybody."

"Why, it is sixteen," she said. "But, Allan, I don't understand. . . ."

"You will," he said quietly.

He had not dreamed it would be so easy. He located the library and, as Ethel had foreseen, no one was there. He looked at his watch, and waited twenty minutes for good measure. Then he walked slowly down the stair-

ways and through the silent corridors. They were in almost complete darkness now, but he had no difficulty in locating Cabin Number Sixteen. He
was already well aware of its position.

He knocked and waited a reasonable length of time, which seemed to
him wholly unreasonable, for an answer. When he received none, he tried
the door. It was not locked. He opened it and went in. The cabin was empty.

Part Three ❧ ANTHONY

7.

ALLAN'S FIRST SENSATION was of rage rather than frustration. He knew comparatively little about the game upon which he had so tardily and impulsively embarked, but he was sure Ethel's conduct was contrary to all the rules: either she should not have made the appointment or she should have kept it. She was neither a good woman nor a good sport.

Though Ethel was not in the cabin now, it was evident that she had been there. The gold-spangled tulle dress had been tossed over the back of the one chair, its full skirt fanning out, in glittering froth, to the floor. Allan picked it up by the unbelievably small bodice and threw it on the bed. Then he seated himself on the chair he had cleared, grimly determined to await the return of the truant. His anger did not abate; it increased. She had actually disrobed before going to another assignation. She must be lost to all shame. . . .

The chair was small and straight and, after an hour or so, Allan began to find it very hard. He also became aware, to his disillusionment, that it was easier to keep his emotions at high pitch when he was not handicapped by discomfort. It further occurred to him that Ethel might be in the habit of taking something to eat or drink at bedtime and that, in this case, her steward would be well informed of her tastes and wants, after a week at sea, and would automatically provide fruit, biscuits or a favorite beverage, without being summoned. He might come bursting in with a small neat tray, well laden, at any moment; and if he found an alien passenger installed in the cabin of the beautiful *señora*, whom he felt honored to serve, it would certainly be a shock to him—and very probably a shock which he would not feel impelled to keep secret. Other practical considerations gradually began to insinuate themselves into Allan's chaotic thoughts. One of these focused itself on Ethel's probable frame of mind when she returned: she might be as angry at finding him still in her cabin as he had been at not finding her there somewhat earlier; in that case, a vulgar quarrel would ensue, rather than tender passages. She might be half asleep, in which case she would be either too pleasantly drowsy for any kind of responsiveness or sulkily resentful at being roused from her blissful torpor. She might be in an ecstatic state, wholly unrelated to him, and, therefore, so indifferent to his presence as to give the impression that it did not matter one way or another. None of these prospects was in the least alluring.

At the end of an hour and a half, Allan rose somewhat stiffly from his hard chair and went out into the corridor, carefully closing the door behind him. He was not a moment too soon. A steward was approaching with just such a small neat tray as Allan had visualized and, though the pitcher on it was covered, he caught a pleasant whiff of cinnamon-scented chocolate. The steward, whose pace, though not exactly rapid, had been purposeful, immediately slackened it.

"The *señor* was searching for someone?" he inquired respectfully.

"No—that is, yes. But it doesn't matter."

"Could I be of service to the *señor*? Possibly his bell is out of order."

"Possibly. Something seems to be."

"If the *señor* would do me the favor to tell me what he would like . . ."

Allan could not suppress a short and entirely mirthless laugh. "It doesn't matter," he said again. "Good night."

"Good night, *señor*. May the angels be with you."

The steward went on down the corridor, in which the aroma of chocolate and cinnamon still lingered. Allan, who had not previously considered the presence of angels desirable, and still did not feel they would be a welcome substitute for the one he had desired, had almost reached the door of his own cabin when he came face to face with Ethel, directly under one of the few overhead lights which had not been extinguished. She had on a simple white sports dress, and she looked neither angry, sleepy nor ecstatic. She stopped short and opened her beautiful blue eyes very wide.

"Why, *Allan!* What on earth are you doing up at this hour?"

"I might ask you the same question," he said sarcastically.

"Don't tell me you didn't get my note!"

"Your note!"

"Yes, of course. I sent you a note to the library, to tell you that a poor friend of mine, who's traveling tourist, had suddenly been taken very ill and asked to have me go to her. I'm thankful to say she's resting more quietly now, but I think I ought to stay with her again tomorrow. She didn't know I was aboard until she read my name in the passenger list this evening and, of course, I didn't know about her, either. But I went as quickly as I could—that is, I changed my dress first, because my white tulle seemed so unsuitable for a sickroom, and I dashed off just a line to you, explaining why I couldn't come to the library. Naturally, I knew you were just joking when you said that if I wasn't there in fifteen minutes you'd go to my cabin."

"As it happens, I wasn't. I've been sitting there, waiting for you, nearly two hours."

"Oh, Allan, how *dreadful!* Suppose the steward had come with my chocolate!"

Up to this point, her voice had sounded exactly as it usually did—pleasant, easy and cordial. Now there was a note of distress, tinged with amazement, in it. Allan, who did not believe a word, either about the sick friend or the note, answered unsympathetically.

"I missed him there by about two minutes. But I met him in the corridor. You'd better get along and drink your chocolate while it's still hot."

"Allan, you sound so *queer!* As if you were annoyed, or something."

"Not really? Well, perhaps this isn't the best time and place to discuss how I feel. Someone else might come along."

"But it wouldn't matter if they did, would it? Because there's no reason why we shouldn't stop and speak to each other for a minute in a public corridor, is there, even if it is late? And I'm really terribly sorry I couldn't have that nice quiet chat with you in the library and I do want to explain. I mightn't sleep if I thought you were really annoyed. I like you such a *lot.*"

Suddenly she put both hands lightly on his shoulders and, with corresponding lightness, kissed him on the cheek. Then she turned and went quickly down the corridor. As the darkness swallowed her up, Allan stood staring after her, rubbing the place her lips had touched. Then, cursing himself for a fool, he went on to his own cabin. To his great surprise, while still calling himself a fool, he did so with less and less rancor; and, before long, he was able to tell himself, quite convincingly, that it was much better things had turned out as they did and not otherwise. Soon thereafter, he found that he was neither pleasantly nor unpleasantly excited any more, but comfortably drowsy; and, eventually, he drifted off to sleep and dreamed, not about Ethel, but about his beautiful new station wagon.

The next morning, his steward, Clemente, with abject apologies, brought him a note. The *Señora* Crewe had charged Clemente to deliver this the evening before, he confessed, and he had forgotten to do so. Allan opened it and found that it contained exactly what Ethel had said it did—a message to the effect that she had been suddenly called to the tourist class for ministry to a poor sick friend. Allan suffered a twinge of conscience for having doubted her, and still more severe twinges when he reached the dining salon and was told by his table steward, Anastasio, that the *Señora* Crewe would not be there for lunch as she was remaining all day with a friend who was ill. The news of the friend's illness and the solicitude of the *Señora* Crewe, which spread rapidly throughout the ship, were received with mingled sympathy and admiration. By the time Allan had finished his packing, eaten two lonely meals and listened, in the "Alhambra Garden," as well as in his cabin and the dining salon, to this touching tale, he had begun to feel like a criminal for having doubted the good faith of a noble woman. He would have liked to tell her how sorry he was, but it was not until they were both engulfed in the maelstrom of disembarkation that he saw her again.

No quarantine formalities took place aboard ship, nor were either passports or baggage examined there. The passengers of both classes streamed ashore in a state of indescribable confusion. Some were holding cages containing fluttering and frightened birds; others had retrieved pet animals which, hitherto, had been confined in kennels, and these creatures were barking, howling and mewing, according to their species. Many persons who had traveled tourist were carrying parcels and packages of every conceivable kind, jostling against each other as they went down the gangplank and shouting to the friends and relatives who had gathered in large numbers to meet them. Once on shore, the laden travelers were squeezed and smothered in fond embraces, relieved of their birds and bundles, and led away for a more general welcome by other friends and relatives who were waiting around the customhouse.

Allan had done his best to keep close to Ethel from the moment he caught sight of her, just ahead of him in the crowd; she had turned and smiled, in her usual untroubled cordial way, and he had not failed to notice that she looked as smart when she was wearing a trim tailored suit and small winged hat as she had in her impeccable sports clothes, with the bright sun shining on her uncovered golden hair. It was also obvious from her easy carriage that she was not burdened with anything heavier than a suitable handbag, though the throng closed in around her so tightly that soon only her head and shoulders were visible to him. Then a woman, carrying on her shoulder a battered and bulging suitcase, tied with rope, came between them and he lost sight of her altogether.

When he saw her again, she had already managed to disentangle herself from the others who had come down the gangplank and was standing apart from them beside a tall, swarthy man, as noticeably well dressed as she was, who would also have been as noticeably good-looking except for a rather ill-formed nose and an expression of impatience, bordering on irritation. The shape of the man's nose was not his fault, Allan told himself quickly, but the expression was something else again. Surely, this must be Ethel's husband, and he should have been grinning from ear to ear with joy over their reunion, instead of betraying such unmistakable annoyance. Allan was still marveling at this phenomenon when he heard Ethel call to him.

"Wedge your way out of that line, can't you, Allan? My husband's so eager to meet you."

Allan did not feel that anything about the man's face and manner indicated special eagerness, but he made the suggested effort and, in time, succeeded in reaching the newly reunited couple. Crewe held out his hand and, though he spoke rather abruptly, as if he were harassed or hurried, on the whole his greeting was agreeable rather than otherwise.

"Ethel's been telling me how pleasant you've made the voyage for her,"

he said. "Perhaps I could best show my appreciation by offering my help
with the customs. I know the ropes pretty well, and there's apt to be considerable delay unless you do—no discourtesy or ill-feeling, you understand,
just Latin lack of organization. And I believe you've got a car with you.
That means a lot more red tape to be untied."

"Why—it's very kind of you, Mr. Crewe. Of course, I'd be grateful for
your help. But possibly you're in a hurry to get off. I wouldn't want to delay
you."

Crewe shrugged his shoulders. "I'd be delayed in any case," he said. "I
expected Ethel would be traveling light—unfortunately, she's only going to
be with me a few weeks. But she's just been telling me that she's got a
wardrobe trunk, one large and one small suitcase, a hatbox, a coatbag, an
overnight bag, a zipper bag and a Scotch cooler with her. They'll be strewn
from one end of the customs shed to the other. The examination won't
amount to anything, once I've got them all together. But, meanwhile, there'll
be plenty of time for the dockhands to get your car unloaded—every car the
Tarragona was bringing, for that matter."

Allan began to understand the other man's unconcealed annoyance. He
thought he would have been annoyed himself if his wife—provided he had
a wife—had arrived to join him for a brief visit bringing with her no less
than seven pieces of baggage, several of them heavy and unwieldy. Of
course, the wardrobe revealed on shipboard would have required some space
to transport—that white tulle dress alone would have filled a good-sized suitcase, and Ethel had worn a different dress every day and every night that
he had seen her. Still . . .

"Well, if you're sure I won't inconvenience you," he said hesitantly.

Crewe shrugged again. "I'm inconvenienced so much already that a little
more or less won't make any difference," he said. "It happens that my car's
out of commission, so I flew over from Madrid to Santiago de Compostela,
about sixty kilometers from here—there isn't any airport in La Coruña. Then
I borrowed a friend's car so that I could come over here and meet Ethel. It's
a small car, like most of those in general use on the Continent—gasoline
so devilish expensive. Now I don't know how we're going to get all this
junk of Ethel's into it, much less how we're going to get it to Madrid. It
would cost a small fortune in excess baggage to take it by air and she vows
she needs most of it right away—that she can't wait to have it come by
truck. There's a very well-organized system of truck transportation in Spain,
one of the best, and she knows it. She'd have everything in a couple of
days, or three at the outside. But that doesn't make any difference to her.
She says all her baggage is brand-new and she doesn't want it banged
around; also, that she didn't have time to pack systematically, that a certain
dress is in one suitcase and the shoes and handbag to go with it in another

and a suitable wrap for it in another and so on and so on. I take it you're not married. You don't know how unreasonable women are about such things."

While Crew had been talking, they had been walking slowly across the wide cobblestoned expanse between the wharf and the customhouse and had now almost reached the latter. Allan had been thinking hard, as well as listening attentively, and, before Crewe finished voicing his difficulties and grievances, had decided how he would reply. To be sure, Ethel had told him she had flown from Tennessee to New York, so her traveling gear must have been assembled before she reached the latter point, since she had also said she caught the ship by the skin of her teeth; therefore, she had already paid a small fortune in excess baggage. But she had never intimated that such an item of expense was troubling her and, indeed, it was logical to assume, from both her clothes and her conversation, that she was never much straitened for funds. He doubted whether her husband was so straitened, either; obviously, Crewe's own car was not of the small economical type that could not have accommodated Ethel's baggage, and clothes, like those her husband was wearing, were produced only by very expensive tailors. Indubitably, it was distaste for feminine foibles, rather than modest circumstances, which caused the man's annoyance and Allan did not feel at all sure he should cater to this. Moreover, though he had inevitably ended by accepting both the story about the delayed note and the one about the sick friend—who somehow seemed to have disappeared from the picture—there were one or two other items which he had not been able to dismiss from his mind: even if Ethel really had thought, as she said, that he was joking about going to her cabin if she did not turn up in the library, he had not been joking about it; he had been in deadly earnest. And though his emotional flare-up had now subsided, he did not feel too certain that this quiescent state was permanent. Certainly, as an honorable man, he should do nothing which would risk disturbing its temporary tranquility. Nevertheless. . . .

"My station wagon has room for any amount of baggage," he said. "And I'm going to Madrid myself—at least, that's my eventual destination. But I'm in no hurry. I'd be glad to go to Santiago de Compostela first, so you could return your friend's car—I'd been thinking of going there anyway, it's so near. It seems a pity not to see anything of Galicia, except the port, if you've never been here before, which I haven't. And I thought I might stop overnight in León, too. I haven't been there, either, and I've always wanted to see the cathedral. The drive from La Coruña to Madrid seemed to me rather long to attempt in one day, though of course I know it can be done. However, we could work out those details later. The point is I'd be very pleased if you'd both join me for the trip."

8.

THE TRIP TO MADRID was a success from almost every viewpoint.

Despite the good offices of Crewe—and they *were* good—it took nearly three hours before the station wagon was released from bondage and ready to roll, and—as he had predicted—it took nearly as long to assemble Ethel's widely distributed baggage, though this was not quite as monumental as Allan had been led to believe. The wardrobe trunk was of relatively modest dimensions, and she had apparently miscounted the other pieces, for there were three less of these than she had previously said, though she now assured her husband that none was missing—it was just that she had forgotten, in the haste of departure, that she had managed to get everything she originally intended to put into the coatbag into the trunk, because she did not need many wraps in the summer, and everything she had intended to put into the smaller suitcase into the hatbox, because hats were worn so little in Spain that she had brought only two or three, which left plenty of room for shoes and lingerie in the side pockets. The zipper bag had also been left behind, because the overnight case had unexpectedly provided room for those last-minute bits and pieces which usually had to be zippered up. Crewe now admitted that she could hardly have been expected to travel with any less than she had brought and Ethel said it was too bad she had annoyed him and perhaps given Mr. Lambert the false impression that her nice husband was naturally short-tempered; and, by the way, she and Mr. Lambert were already calling each other by their first names, it seemed so stilted to do anything else on shipboard, so hadn't the two men better start right in by being Anthony and Allan to each other?

Anthony, whose annoyance had vanished into thin air, agreed that, of course, this was what they should do and Allan echoed the sentiment and overtipped the porters who had stowed Ethel's baggage into the station wagon—which still had all kinds of room for Allan's suitcases, too—and were waiting to protest that they had not received enough. It was now long past lunch time, even by Spanish standards, so they all agreed it was much too late for them to think of pushing on until they had been suitably nourished, and Anthony said they had better go to Lhardy's, which was famous for its seafood. They drove down a long street where the houses appeared to be made almost wholly of glittering glass, because their façades were composed entirely of bay windows on which the sun was shining brightly, and soon reached a restaurant abundantly supplied with *caldeirada* and other delicacies of the region.

An hour and a half later, as he was picking up the check, Allan said he would like very much to see the garden where Sir John Moore was entombed and read the verses about the burial which he had learned in school and which he understood were carved on a tablet there. Anthony and Ethel looked a little vague for a moment, but they said, why certainly, that was a good idea, there would be plenty of time for sight-seeing in Santiago the next day. The garden was found without difficulty, and proved to be a quiet, pleasant place, largely given over to nursemaids and their charges; and it did not take Allan long to find the monument and the inscription in which he was interested and in which the others expressed great interest, too. Then, after they had all paused to admire the view, Anthony said he must go back to the wharf and pick up the car his friend had loaned him; he was sure Allan would understand if Ethel went with him when he switched into this, along with the light baggage she would need immediately; it was so long since they had seen each other, they had a great deal to talk over. But of course, if Allan would rather not drive on to Santiago alone . . .

Allan said that he did not in the least mind driving alone and he meant it. He had enjoyed his luncheon very much, but he would have lingered longer in the garden if he had not sensed that it did not mean as much to the others as it did to him, and he felt the same would be true of the scenery. He told Anthony he was sure he could find the way all right alone, as soon as they were clear of the city, and that they had better not try to keep together, as no doubt his new-found friends liked to drive faster than he did. He was quite right about this, too, for they had not reached the outskirts when Anthony began to swing around corners to the sound of screeching tires and weave his way through traffic in a manner that seemed to Allan a direct invitation to suicide. Then the small car darted out of sight with one of Anthony's hands resting lightly on the wheel while he gaily waved farewell with the other, though two motorcyclists were trying to pass him and a truck was bearing down on him from the top of a hill.

Allan went along at a less dramatic and more leisurely pace, admiring the verdant countryside and puzzling over the tomb-shaped wooden cribs which complemented the other outbuildings of the farmhouses. It occurred to him that it might be very pleasant to linger a few days in Galicia, so that he might see more of such countryside and visit not only the cathedral, but other noteworthy churches in Santiago; he might even make an excursion to the famous fiords in the vicinity. Momentarily, he toyed with the idea of doing all this; then he dismissed it. He had invited the Crewes to go to Madrid with him and doubtless they were more or less in a hurry to reach there. As a matter of fact, he should have been more in a hurry himself; after all, he had not come to Spain to see architectural and scenic wonders, but to solve the intriguing mystery of the Spanish Prisoner letter.

It was still broad daylight when he reached Santiago and, though he made one or two false turns before he reached the great square of the cathedral where an erstwhile palace, now converted into a hotel, was located, he did not regret this, as each mistake enabled him to see more of a city with which he was immediately charmed; and again he toyed with the idea of lingering in the region. Perhaps he would talk this over with the Crewes after all. . . .

They were not in the luxurious lounge when he entered it, but inquiry at the desk revealed that Anthony had made a reservation for him and he was led by a bellboy through a seemingly endless succession of cloisters and patios to a small room dominated by an enormous canopied bed and otherwise adorned with dark religious pictures of sanguinary character. The coffers, *bargueños* and other furnishings with which it was equipped were suggestive of medieval elegance rather than modern convenience, but the adjacent bathroom more than made up for this lack: it had two showers, one encased in gleaming glass, the other connected with shining pipes to the tub, two large basins besides a small one for dental use, and the inevitable *bidet*, which Allan now remembered as an adjunct to all complete Continental bathrooms and many very much less complete. Confronted by so many different sanitary appliances, he could not help wondering whether the guests of the hostel were not expected to spend their time among these, rather than in the rest of the space allotted to them, as it was possible to move around the great bed only by walking sideways, and a single chair, handsomely carved but unconducive to lounging, was the only supplement to the huge chests that lined the walls.

He unpacked the necessities for an overnight stay, indulged in as many forms of bathing as appealed to him and, when these had begun to pall a little, dressed by the feeble light cast from the high-placed electric fixtures designed to suggest candles in more ways than one. Then he sought out the bar, discovering several more patios and cloisters along the way. Anthony and Ethel were already there, drinking *manzanilla*, and, though the barkeeper hastened forward with the suggestion of a martini *con Gordon*, Allan, who had been disillusioned after trying a similar experiment on shipboard, decided on sherry, too. The Crewes were sorry not to have been on hand to welcome him, they told him; they had gone to return their friend's car and he had persuaded them to stay on for a chat; they hoped he was comfortable. Well, he was impressed, Allan said with a grin; he had never seen so much plumbing all in the same bathroom as was provided for him here; he would have been overpowered if all of it had worked, but only a portion of it was practical; he assumed the rest was intended for ornamental purposes. Anthony immediately leaped up, prepared to complain to the management and demand a change of apartment, but Allan dissuaded him; he really had everything he needed; besides, he was sure if he had to try to find his way through any more patios, he would get lost. . . . Then, seeing that his mild attempts at humor were not meeting with exactly the sort of response he had expected, he added that, after all, this was for only one night—at least, he supposed so.

There was a question in his voice and a tinge of regret, but Anthony apparently missed them both. Why yes, he said briskly, that was all, of course. If they got an early start, they could easily make Madrid in a day—incidentally, had Allan made a hotel reservation?

"Not definitely. I ordered my mail sent to the Ritz and wrote the manager that I'd wire him when I knew the exact date of my arrival."

"My dear fellow, the Ritz is not your type at all. At least, I shouldn't think so. You want something less Hollywoodish than that. It'll be a simple matter to have your mail forwarded and, after all, you're not committed to staying there. Now the Wellington's also listed in the luxury category and it has a *gobernanta*—a sort of super-housekeeper—who's the envy of every *hôtelier* in Madrid. She's what I suppose you'd call a lady in reduced circumstances and you wouldn't go far wrong, either—she *is* a lady and, unfortunately, her circumstances are reduced. She's a great friend of ours; she'll see that you have every attention."

"I don't know that I need any special attention," Allan said. "However—"

"However, Leonor de Silva is really worth meeting whether you do or not and she's got a niece in the hotel with her who's a cute little piece. She's in charge of the newsstand, so you'll be running into her, anyway. Be sure to mention my name when you do. I was more or less responsible for getting her the job and, naturally, she can't do enough to please my friends, as a result. . . . Well, as I was saying, the Wellington's quieter than the Ritz; it has a more cultured clientele. You're a professor, you go in for tombstones and cathedrals and museums and all that sort of thing, rather than night clubs and bullfights and racing."

"Well, yes, I do," Allan admitted, without embarrassment. "So, if you think the Wellington's the best place for me, I'll get off a wire right away, asking for a reservation. Not for tomorrow night though, unless you mind very much taking things a little more slowly. It would be a shame, wouldn't it, not to see the silversmiths' shops, now we're here, as well as the cathedral? I understand they're clustered all around it. And, as I said before, I always wanted to go to León. I hope you'll be my guests there. I realize I'm delaying you."

The rather vague expression with which the Crewes had looked at him when he spoke of Sir John Moore returned to their faces at the mention of the Santiago silversmiths and it hardened slightly at this second reference to a stop in León. But he realized he was making a better impression when he asked them to be his guests.

"There's some place on the way, I can't think of its name just now, that's very famous for its chocolate," he went on. "I think we ought to make inquiries and stop there, too, long enough to sample it, since Ethel's so fond of chocolate. . . . By the way," he broke off, conscious that his next remark sounded like a *non sequitur*, "you haven't mentioned your sick friend all day, Ethel. I gather she made a rapid recovery?"

"Not rapid exactly. But I left her feeling much better and I've made every arrangement I could think of for her comfort and well-being—an ambulance to meet the ship at Bilbao and all that. Fortunately, she wasn't planning to disembark at La Coruña and she has lots of relatives; she'll be in good hands. Of course, they were probably planning to meet her anyway, because Spaniards are great on that sort of thing, as you know; but I've wired her brother, to make sure. And speaking of wires, don't you think—"

"Yes, I do," Allan said, rising with alacrity. "I'll get one off to the Wellington right away. And thank you for telling me about your friends. As I said, I'm sure everything will be quite satisfactory as far as my room is concerned and I don't think I need any help about buying a paper. But if you'd like me to make a point of saying I've met you—"

"We would, rather. Then you can report to us later whether or not you think Leonor and Milagrita are really giving super service."

"All right. I'll take notes and tell you as soon as you come around—which, of course, I hope will be very soon."

Again, his mild jest seemed to have miscarried. However, Anthony assured him that they would soon be around.

Despite this assurance, several days passed, after their arrival in Madrid, during the course of which Allan neither saw nor heard anything of the Crewes. They had insisted it would be much simpler if they all went straight to the Wellington, where they would have the doorman call them a taxi, than for Allan to take them home and then try to find his way back to the hotel alone; they lived quite a distance out, on a side street, in one of the new developments, and there were a good many twists and turns along the way which he might find troublesome, especially just at the time of day when traffic was heaviest. Allan felt quite capable of coping with these difficulties alone, but he decided that the point was not worth arguing. He had lingered longer than he intended in the archives of the León cathedral, tempted by a sixth-century palimpset, and, consequently, they had made a late start; then, for some reason, he had not enjoyed his lunch at Palencia as much as he had the one at Lugo the day before—perhaps because his fellow travelers made it plain they hoped he would not do any further learned sight-seeing, and he had been secretly hoping to visit at least the Church of San Miguel, where the marriage of the Cid and Ximena had allegedly taken place. In fact, though they, on the whole, had both been good companions, cheerful and chatty, and Anthony had shown himself very adept at smoothing out minor details of travel which might have been mildly annoying without his expert guidance, they were obviously not the scholarly type and there was no escaping the fact that Allan was. He did not want to escape it. True, this was a pleasure trip, spiced with a possibility of adventure; but that did not mean he must forego the experiences which gave *him* pleasure, whether or not they appealed to anyone else. In fact, he thought the attitude of the Crewes at Palencia had been slightly ungracious, considering the fact that he was paying all the bills. . . .

So he had bid them a temporary good-by, without regrets, at the entrance of the Wellington, where a capable doorman in gray livery secured them a taxi and sent the station wagon to a garage, after overseeing the division of the baggage. Allan registered, surrendered his passport and filled out a form which, like the identical one he had filled out at León the night before, was designed to lay bare his entire life history; then he was shown to a room less oppressively medieval than the one he had occupied at the hostel and connected with a bathroom which was not supplied with quite so much duplication. Again, however, he made the discovery that the light was hardly strong enough for practical purposes and that part of the plumbing was merely ornamental. He was on the point of ringing to see if the *camarero* could do something to remedy this defect when there was a knock at the door, and he opened it to find himself face to face with a lady who, he was sure, must be the Leonor de Silva about whom the Crewes had spoken.

"Good evening, *señor*. I am the *gobernanta* of the hotel," she said quietly. "I have come to make sure everything is satisfactory."

"That's very kind of you. I *should* like stronger bulbs in the electric light fixtures, if that isn't an unreasonable request."

"Certainly not. I will send the electrician to you immediately. Is there anything else?"

"Well, perhaps you might send the plumber, too. But I don't want to be a nuisance."

It did not seem fitting to discuss such matters with the woman before him. She was very tall, as tall as he was, and seemed even taller because she was thin almost to the point of emaciation and because her abundant iron-gray hair was braided in a high coronet around her head. Except for remarkably fine eyes, she was not in any respect beautiful; but neither the nature of her errand nor the nondescript character of her black dress detracted from her essential dignity and distinction. She might, through some strange mischance, have been obliged to become a *gobernanta* in a hotel, but to her dying day she would remain the aristocrat she had been born.

Quite without embarrassment, she walked into the bathroom, quickly located the defective fixture and was about to depart, with a slight inclination of the head and a courteous word of leave-taking, when Allan spoke to her again. "I think you must be *Señora* de Silva," he said. "Some mutual friends spoke to me about you—Mr. and Mrs. Anthony Crewe."

He thought her expression stiffened slightly, though in the dim light he could not be sure. She paused, with her hand on the doorknob.

"Yes," she said noncommittally. It was a question rather than a statement. "The Crewes are old friends of yours?"

"No. Mrs. Crewe and I crossed on the same liner, the *Tarragona*, and we struck up an acquaintance there—you know how it is on shipboard. Then her husband met her at La Coruña and, as his car was out of commission and she had so much baggage with her that she couldn't conveniently travel by air, I invited them to make the trip to Madrid in my station wagon. They recommended this hotel and also suggested that I should look you up—you and your niece."

"I see," said Leonor de Silva. "I thought, when you first spoke, that perhaps you and Mr. Crewe might be associated in business."

"Oh no, nothing like that! I teach Spanish in a small New England college and this is my sabbatical year. I've come to Europe principally for enjoyment, though I may do a little studying and research later on. I don't even know what Crewe's business is. He didn't tell me and I didn't like to ask."

It occurred to Allan that perhaps Leonor de Silva might enlighten him, and that she might say something which showed she valued the friendship of the Crewes and that she was glad to meet someone else who knew them. Instead, she merely remarked that she would send an electrician and a plumber to the room immediately and took a dignified departure. The stronger light bulbs for which Allan had asked arrived within ten minutes; and, before he went down to dinner, he dispatched his second letter to the Prisoner who had appealed to him for help, using the initials and the post office number he had been given and saying he would be available for a conference at any time.

9.

ALLAN DID NOT WISH to commit himself to any definite future engagements until he had received an answer to his letter to the Prisoner, so he made no immediate attempt to get in touch with the American Embassy or with his old friends in Málaga. During the daytime, he was quite content to pass long hours in the Prado Museum looking at the pictures, at the *Rastro* poking through the trash and treasures of this famous "Thieves' Market," or merely wandering about the *Retiro* and the streets, stopping to rest in the shade of the trees clustered around the fountains in the beautiful park, making an occasional purchase on the *Gran' Via,* or sipping a *refresco* at any sidewalk café which happened to be near at hand when he felt thirsty or tired. But the evening hours dragged a little and, eventually, he began to wonder whether he could possibly persuade Milagrita de Silva to go dancing with him.

Within an hour after reaching the hotel, he had bought a paper from her, ostensibly so that he would have something to read while he sat alone at dinner, but actually so that he could decide for himself whether she was "a cute little piece." He would not have described her exactly that way himself, though she was, undeniably, very attractive; and subsequent glimpses of her confirmed his first impression that she might be conservative, as well as selective, when it came to making new acquaintances. She was solicitous about meeting the requirements of her customers, tactful about making suggestions for reading material and souvenirs which they had not asked for, and uniformly patient and pleasant under conditions when she might well have been otherwise. Some of the tourists who came to her little stall dallied endlessly over the possible purchase of knickknacks, tried to bargain with her about prices over which she had no control and finally went away without buying anything. When this happened, she calmly restored the objects which had been handled and rehandled to their proper places and turned her smiling attention to the next group or individual who claimed it. Once or twice, as he passed through the lobby, though not close enough to hear the words, Allan gathered that a man was saying something offensive to her; Milagrita appeared very adept at giving the impression she did not hear them, either. The third time that Allan observed something of the sort happening, he came up to the stall himself.

"Have you succeeded in securing any of the Boston papers for me yet, *señorita?*" he inquired.

He had not previously asked for the Boston papers; he knew they were unavailable and, as a matter of fact, he was perfectly satisfied with the *New York Times* and *Tribune* which were now being sent regularly to his room. Milagrita turned away from the cad who was importuning her and, while the expression of her face and the tone of her voice were both demure, something about the sparkle in her eyes and the wording of her answer led Allan to believe she had not failed to grasp the fact that his seemingly simple question was actually strategic.

"No, *señor*. I am so very sorry. But I shall keep on trying."

"You have perhaps located something from Chicago or San Francisco?"

"I have, as yet, had no success in those directions, either."

"Well, could you suggest anything else?"

"An English paper? We have several of those, as you see. Or, since you have a command of Spanish, why not *ABC* or one of the other local dailies?"

It pleased him that she did not use superlatives, that she said "a command of Spanish" and not "you speak such perfect Spanish." It was a little thing and still it seemed to him significant; she would always be courteous, he believed, but never obsequious. And he was sure now that she recognized a purpose behind his questions; they were playing a little game together and both were enjoying it. The other man was beginning to fidget.

"Well, that might be a good idea. Could I look over a few here before making a decision as to how many I should like to purchase regularly?"

"Certainly, *señor*."

She handed him the London *Times, Mail* and *Express, ABC* and *El Diario*. He laid all except *ABC* down on the counter and slowly turned the pages of the Spanish daily, making an occasional casual comment on one of its many illustrations. The other man gave an exclamation of impatience which he did not even attempt to smother and, after looking daggers first at Allan and then at Milagrita, neither of whom appeared to notice him, swaggered away. When he was out of both sight and hearing, they glanced at each other and Milagrita returned Allan's smile.

"Thank you very much, *señor*," she said and began to gather up the London papers which were still lying on the little counter. Allan went off with *ABC* under his arm.

This trifling episode was a source of both encouragement and discouragement to Allan: encouragement, because it had been so easy to establish understanding between himself and this charming, intelligent girl and discouragement, because he did not wish to risk saying or doing anything that would jeopardize the budding rapprochement. Happily, a solution for his problem presented itself to him in the form of Milagrita's aunt, who came to his room the next afternoon with the maid who brought back his laundry, to help her explain that there had been a little difficulty about one of the suits he had sent to be dry cleaned: it appeared the cleaners did not wish to take the responsibility for the chance either that the material would shrink or that the colors would fade. Should they proceed or not?

"That's quite all right, tell them to go ahead," he said. "It's an old suit. I've got to get some new ones anyway and I understand there are excellent tailors in Madrid." So far, he had not given the subject of clothes much thought; quite probably the suit in question, which antedated the days of his prosperity, was neither preshrunk nor color fast. It was high time he was jolted into getting something better. The maid set down the shallow oval basket containing his beautifully laundered shirts, socks, underwear and handkerchiefs, curtsied slightly and moved toward the door. Leonor de Silva was moving in the same direction when Allan detained her.

"Could I speak to you just a minute about something else?" he asked.

"Certainly, señor. Is the plumbing out of order again?"

"No, it's working quite well—considering. This is different. I want to ask a favor of you. Won't you sit down?"

She hesitated, and then seated herself, not stiffly, but very erectly on a straight-backed chair. It was obvious she had no intention of lingering. Allan decided to go right to the point.

"I'm waiting for a rather important message and, until I get it, I can't make engagements far ahead. But, meanwhile, I naturally want to see all I can of Madrid and I'm getting tired of doing so without anyone to share my enjoyment of it. I don't mean to be presumptuous, to suggest anything you wouldn't consider suitable. But it occurred to me that possibly—just possibly—I could persuade you and your niece to go out with me some evening."

Leonor de Silva looked at him searchingly for a moment, without making any immediate reply. Nevertheless, Allan somehow felt that the request had not been a shock to her, perhaps not even a surprise.

"Surely, your friends, the Crewes—" she said finally.

"They told me it would take a few days for Mrs. Crewe to get settled and that then they'd call me up. I can understand she'd have lots to do after being away for some time. I don't like to seem impatient by calling first. In any case, they apparently have an unlisted number. I don't find it in the telephone book."

If Leonor de Silva knew what it was, which he thought quite likely, she did not enlighten him. "My niece has already spoken to me about you," she said rather slowly. "Milagrita was very grateful for the tact and kindness you showed in dealing with a certain situation yesterday. I, also, am very grateful. Unfortunately, such situations do arise—fairly frequently."

"If you will permit me to say so, I think your niece deals very competently with them herself."

"Yes, you are right. Nonetheless, they are unpleasant. I am regretful that she should be subjected to them."

Again she looked at him fixedly and there was sorrow in her fine eyes— more sorrow than seemed wholly natural. It might be a matter of regret to a woman like this that she and her niece were reduced to earning their living in a hotel, but it could hardly be a matter of sorrow. The stock of which they came was too valorous for easy refuge in grief.

"I am also appreciative of the fact," Leonor de Silva went on after another short silence, "that you approached me, rather than my niece, on this subject. It shows a very welcome delicacy on your part and, also, an understanding of our customs which North Americans do not always possess."

"I am glad you put such gaucheries down to lack of understanding, rather than willful disregard of Spanish social usages," Allan replied. "Believe me, I do not think most of my countrymen mean to give offense when they ask a young girl like your niece to go dancing, without including some older relative in the invitation or without consulting such a relative first. There is a difference in national customs, that is all. I was fortunate enough to spend part of my boyhood in Spain. That is how I happen to know better. I can't take any special credit for it. And, in passing, I should like to say that the man who was annoying your niece yesterday was not a North American. Nor was he a Spaniard. Suppose we do not mention his nationality."

For the first time, Leonor de Silva smiled. Then she rose. "I must go," she said, "and I realize that I have neither accepted nor declined your kind invitation. I should like to think it over a little. After I have done that, if I decide there is no reason why it should not be accepted, as far as I am concerned, I will consult Milagrita. There is always the possibility that she might feel differently. In that case—"

"In that case, of course I will withdraw it," Allan said instantly.

An hour later, as he sat idly turning the pages of *ABC,* in which he found nothing special to divert him, a very small *botones* brought him two letters on a silver tray, with the apologies of the concierge: the *señor* had not asked for his mail and these letters, forwarded from the Ritz, had, in consequence, been overlooked. It was quite true that Allan had made no inquiries, though he had given the necessary forwarding directions; he had failed to miss hearing from home. Now he opened the proffered letters without curiosity. The first was from his cousin Arthur, telling him that the expected twins had arrived, a boy and a girl, and that the boy had been named for him; would he please let Arthur and Marian know, by airmail, when he expected to be back so that they could plan for the christening?

The second letter was from Charlotte, telling him that she had decided to take a highly educational European tour, in the course of which she would see six countries, under careful chaperonage and expert guidance, in as many weeks, and five whole days were to be devoted to Spain. She was sailing almost at once on a suitable Cunarder. Would Allan please let her know, by cable, where to reach him after he left Madrid, as of course she realized that, by this time, he must be finding their separation as hard to bear as she was.

Well, so he was to have a godson before he had a son of his own, and Charlotte was finding their separation unbearable and was prepared to undergo a European education in order to track him down. Neither of these prospects filled him with much pleasure. But when the *botones* appeared again, the note which he was carrying on his silver tray had a more exhilarating effect. A card, bearing an address near the hotel and enclosed in a small envelope, informed him that Leonor de Silva y de la Haya and her niece would be pleased to have him meet them at their apartment about ten-thirty and to dine with him afterward at a quiet restaurant. Allan rather gathered that this program did not include dancing and suffered a mild disappointment; somehow he felt sure that Milagrita would be a beautiful dancer. But, after all, this was beyond the point; the point was that his invitation had not been turned down, and that if one were accepted, another might well be and, the second time, dancing would logically follow.

His pleasurable reflections at this prospect were interrupted by the strident sound of the telephone. He sprang up to answer it, fearful that it might be from the Crewes, tardily inviting him to dine with them that very evening. His suspicions lasted for some minutes, during the course of which he was deafened by a series of loud rattling noises, puzzled by the repeated command of *"Dígame"* and *"Oiga,"* and twice completely disconnected. Then a conversation between two loquacious Spaniards, who had cut in on his line, intervened and did not terminate until they stopped shouting at each other, apparently from sheer exhaustion. At last an unfamiliar voice, which sounded as if it came from a great distance, informed Señor Lambert, in broken English, that the note he had sent to the post office box had been received and that a representative "of the person in whom he was interested" would call on him at eight the following evening, if that would be convenient for him.

10.

THE ADDRESS WHICH Leonor de Silva had sent proved to be that of a rather dingy apartment house with a self-operating elevator designed to hold not more than two persons at the same time. Allan pushed the small white button marked *seis* and was momentarily disturbed when the elevator went creaking on and on, until it came to a stop with a jerk at the top story; then he remembered that he had not made allowances for the fact that the first floor and the ground floor are not one and the same in Europe, that the former is above the latter, and that a mezzanine frequently intervenes even before the so-called first floor is reached. At all events, he could now go no higher, so he turned back the folding doors which opened in the middle, unlatched the grilled gate which served to protect them and edged his way precariously into the hall. Then, standing rather gingerly away from them, he closed first the doors and then the gate before ringing the bell at an apartment on the left which was the only one unmarked by a name.

He was admitted by Milagrita herself, with an immediacy which suggested she might have been waiting nearby, and led from a tiny bare entrance hall into a parlor which was not much larger and which was almost as bare. Leonor was sitting on a stiff little sofa, with a round marble-topped table in front of her, hardly ample enough to hold the decanter of sherry and the twin dishes of olives and almonds set out on it. But Allan, who was observant about such things, noticed that, whereas the furnishings of the flat were sparse and ordinary, indicative of inexpensive and temporary lodgings, the glassware, which its occupants might easily have brought there with them, was fine and fragile; it gave him an immediate clue to the character of their real home and more or less established the fact that this was very different from the place where they were now living. Milagrita, who was always simply but smartly clad, as befitted her type of work, had on much the same sort of dress as she wore at her stall in the hotel. This one was cool green in color, full skirted, tightly belted, with elbow sleeves and a close-fitting bodice fastened with bright buttons almost to the neckline. But Leonor had changed from the nondescript garments of a *gobernanta* into clothing of a very different sort. To be sure, she was still in black, and the style of her dress was somewhat outmoded; but the material was a beautiful brocade, skillfully cut, and with it she was wearing long amethyst earrings and an amethyst cross set in heavy gold. As Allan approached, her shoddy surroundings seemed to fade into insignificance compared to so elegant and distinguished a figure.

"I hope you like sherry," she said cordially, lifting the decanter, "and please smoke if you would care to."

"I like it very much," he said, accepting the tiny etched glass which she held out to him, "and I will smoke presently, too, since you permit it." Milagrita was now offering the almonds and olives, and these he accepted, too, rather mechanically. She smiled at him and he smiled back, but there seemed to be nothing apt to say at the moment, and he decided that, under the circumstances, it would be just as well to say nothing. He hoped and believed that Leonor would take the lead in conversation and he was not mistaken.

"You told me you were awaiting an important message," she said, filling her own glass and sipping slowly from it, "and that, until you received it, your future plans would be uncertain. That must be rather trying. Naturally, you want to make the most of your holiday, when you've come abroad primarily for pleasure."

"It would have been trying if I'd been kept waiting long. But I had a telephone call this afternoon, setting tomorrow for an appointment. After that, I think I'll be able to map out a schedule. And, actually, I'm in no hurry with two whole summers and a winter at my disposal."

"You told me that part of your boyhood was spent in Spain. Was that in Madrid, too?"

"No, in Málaga. My father was American Consul there. I've never been to Madrid before—consuls' salaries are not conducive to much traveling, except when they're being sent from one post to another and then, of course, the government pays their expenses. I do plan to see some of my old friends later on. Right now, I'm very happy to be making some new ones."

"But it appears, from what you've said, that your new friends are somewhat neglectful."

"I wasn't speaking of the Crewes," he said, and waited for an answering smile.

It came, and with it the banality of the first small talk gave way to warmer and more personal conversation. Leonor had passed on the information about Allan's profession to her niece, and Milagrita wanted to know more about the college where he taught. In turn, she told him something about the convent school where she had been educated; she supposed it was very different from those American girls attended. As Allan was not particularly well informed about convent schools, in the United States or anywhere else, he could not give her much information, and encouraged her to go on talking instead. She chatted along, readily and pleasantly, about studies and sports and the setting for these, but she did not say anything about what she did or where she lived during her vacations and Allan learned nothing about the source of the etched glass or the beautiful brocade or the amethyst jewelry. Eventually, he realized that he was not likely to receive any information on these points and that, after all, it would be illogical for him to expect it; he had not said anything about his legacy or his historic house and he had suppressed, as unwise, an impulse to say what had really brought him to Spain. So he merely remarked that the station wagon in which he meant to travel about was at the door to take the ladies wherever they would like to go and that, while they were dining, he would appreciate suggestions as to what he would most enjoy seeing in Spain. Meanwhile, he thought the first suggestion should be in regard to a restaurant.

Leonor glanced at an ormolu clock, which, like the etched glass, indicated an original setting very different from its present one. Eleven o'clock was just striking. "If it were not rather late, even by Spanish standards, I should suggest going to the *Hostería del Estudiante*, at Alcalá de Henares," she began.

"You mean Cervantes' birthplace? I'd like that immensely! Is it really too late?"

"I'm afraid so. It would take us almost an hour to reach there." He could see that she was really regretful, that the reference to Cervantes had pleased her; possibly the average American tourist with whom she came in contact did not respond so readily to a reference of this sort. "Milagrita and I would enjoy the drive in your beautiful station wagon, which we have admired as we saw it parked outside the hotel," she continued. "It would be very refreshing after the heat of the day. And the *Hostería* would interest you. It is picturesque in itself, and it is located in the old university, long since abandoned for purposes of learning and partially in ruins, though it is now undergoing intelligent restoration."

"And does the spirit of San Juan de la Cruz and the other great men who lived and taught there still permeate it?"

This time, her pleasure at his response was even more evident. "I like to believe so. Perhaps, when you do go there, as you must some other time, you will tell me what you think."

"On the spot? You and the *señorita* will go there with me some other evening, when we can make an earlier start?"

"*O tia mia, diga que sí!*"

Leonor turned from her niece to Allan. "You have a very enthusiastic advocate," she said. "But, as it happens, I should have said yes in any case. The great difficulty is that our work—both Milagrita's and mine—generally keeps us so late at the hotel that it is hard to make excursions. We probably could not give you an answer until the evening when we are unexpectedly released a little sooner than usual."

"The answer will be very welcome whenever it comes," Allan assured her. "And now we are going—where?"

"I don't know whether this idea will appeal to you," Leonor told him, "but there are several small restaurants on the *Calle* Velasquez which open extensions in the summertime on the promenade which divides the two sides of the avenue. Little tables are set out among the trees in enclosures of vine-wreathed latticework and approached through open arches. Of course, there is nothing elegant about these small establishments. But they are very typical of Madrid; the food, which is brought out from the parent restaurant, is reasonably good, and the service is prompt and pleasant. Moreover, there is nearly always a breeze stirring and, in the absence of time for a long drive, this would be very refreshing. What do you think?"

"I think it's a marvelous idea," Allan answered. "Let's put it right into action—that is, unless you want to get hats and wraps first."

"Why, *Señor* Lambert, you have been in Spain enough to know that we don't wear hats!" Milagrita reminded him. "And surely, you don't think we need wraps on a warm night like this!"

It was evident that they could not get started too soon to suit her; she was already opening the front door. The little elevator was still suspended where Allan had left it, but she walked briskly over to it and pressed the button which sent it down empty. Allan could not conceal his look of amazement.

"Have you forgotten about elevators, too?" Milagrita asked gaily. "I mean that, except in hotels—hotels with rich foreign clienteles—you're supposed only to ride *up* in them! They're really quite precarious for a downward passage. I know of one large North American lady who went to lunch with a Spanish friend and insisted on riding down, though her friend's apartment was a mere three flights up. The large North American lady neglected to sit exactly in the middle and, of course, that threw everything out of balance. She got stuck between floors and she always declared it was two hours before she was rescued, though actually it was less than one!"

Milagrita was already tripping down the first of the seven flights which they were obliged to cover. Leonor descended almost as lightly and rapidly as her niece. Allan had the feeling that he was galloping in order to keep up with them, and was quite breathless by the time he reached the bottom of the staircase, though neither of his companions showed the slightest sign of strain. They were both so enthusiastic about the appearance and spaciousness of the station wagon that it seemed a pity to use it for only a few blocks; in less than five minutes they had reached the restaurant Leonor had indicated and were seated under a cloudless sky in a bower of greenery. The wide stretch of pavement, on which this was located, was bordered by strips of grass, low hedges and tall trees; and here, innumerable *Madrileños* were

strolling back and forth; young lovers walking hand in hand; young couples
with babies in gocarts and small children frisking along beside them; older
women whose arms were thrust through their husbands' with the confident
ease of long habit; older men, solemn and solitary, leaning heavily on their
canes—all finding obvious pleasure in their leisurely progress and release
from whatever cares had oppressed them during the day. The traffic flowed
endlessly past on either side of their promenade, but they seemed wholly
detached from it; and though some paused for refreshment of one kind or
another, the greater number went quietly on and on, without the slightest
sign of boredom or fatigue. This was the *paseo* of immemorial custom, unchanged and unchangeable, as Spanish as the mantilla and the fan, the
cocido and the *paella*, the *corrida* and the *feria*. Suddenly, Allan felt that
his stay in Spain would not be complete until he had so strolled along such
a pavement, with a girl like Milagrita beside him. *Like* Milagrita! No, with
Milagrita herself!

Meanwhile, he was wholly content with things as they were. There were
not more than a dozen tables all told in the latticed enclosure of the
restaurant and less than half of these were occupied; the hovering waiters
gave Allan and his guests immediate attention. Both ladies insisted that he
should not order mineral water, as the *agua natural* of Madrid was above
reproach; but he was equally insistent and won his point. On the other
hand, he gathered that a fish course was taken for granted, and managed
to conceal his distaste for *merluza frita*—the fried hake for which, from
childhood, he had cherished an incurable aversion. The rest of the menu,
unabashedly *corriente*, occasioned no discussion—the cold vegetable soup
known as *gazpacho*, veal cutlets, boiled potatoes, string beans, fruit, cheese
and a bottle of red table wine. As far as food and drink were concerned,
Allan would have greatly preferred the Ritz or Horcher's Restaurant; but
when it came to the setting and the company, he could not conceive anything pleasanter.

He began, in a desultory way, to talk about other cities he might like
to visit later on. He was not without guile in doing this. It occurred to him
that, through the degree of acquaintance his guests revealed with this place
or that, he might get some clue to their normal habitat, which he felt increasingly sure was not Madrid. But he got nowhere by this method. Leonor
appeared to be equally well informed about every part of Spain which he
mentioned and she took the lead in answering his questions; he could not
gather, from the way she talked, whether she had actually lived in most of
these places—which seemed improbable—whether she had merely visited
them or whether she had only heard about them. She seemed to be wholly
candid, but he eventually decided that she was extremely adroit. Given
the enormous family connections of many Spaniards, which took them

hither and yon merely for visiting, their habit of going to certain resorts for sea bathing, mountain climbing and other pastimes, to certain spas for cures and to certain cities and shrines for special festivals, he did not see how it could be possible for one and the same woman to be equally familiar with Cádiz and Bilbao, Salamanca and Tarragona. At last he turned, almost too abruptly for politeness, from Leonor to Milagrita and asked a direct question.

"Are you as much at home everywhere in Spain as your aunt?" he inquired. The answer came without hesitation.

"Oh, no! But then I haven't been out of school as long as she has! When I'm her age I hope I shall be."

"My dear *marquesa!* What on earth are you doing here?"

The salutation and the inquiry came from a dapper little man who had suddenly come up behind their table and was now bowing over Leonor's hand, which she yielded to him without visible reluctance, but also without spontaneity. As he straightened up, he smiled and nodded in the direction of Milagrita and then looked in a puzzled way at Allan. Leonor made no move to present the stranger to her host.

"But this is a very pleasant place to spend an evening after the heat of the day!" she said, as if in mild protest at his surprise.

"If one is not the fortunate possessor of much pleasanter places or the welcome guest at them!"

"It seems best for me to be in Madrid just now; and, as you know, almost everyone else has left the city, because of the heat."

Her manner was not discourteous, but it certainly was lacking in anything which might be interpreted as an invitation to linger. She still made no move to present Allan and Milagrita still did not speak.

"And the rest of your family?" persisted the dapper little man.

"I have my niece with me, as you see. None of the others."

This time, a definite coolness, which it was impossible to interpret otherwise than as a signal for dismissal, had crept into her tone and manner. The dapper little man bowed once more over her hand, smiled and nodded again to Milagrita and regarded Allan with another questioning stare. Then he moved to a table at the further end of the enclosure, sat down and picked up a menu. Leonor turned back to Allan.

"You were asking me about Valladolid," she said, as if there had been no interruption in their conversation. "I think you would find a stay of several days there very pleasant. Besides the National Museum of Sculpture, which of course has no peer in the world for polychrome statuary, there are many other arresting monuments, including the house where Cervantes, in whom you are so interested, presumably wrote a large part of *Don Quixote*. And the hotel is very comfortable. . . . Shall we go back to the apartment for our coffee? I think the breeze is actually becoming a little too cool for comfort and we very unwisely did not listen when you suggested wraps."

If there actually were a breeze, Allan was not conscious of it; and when, on their return to the apartment, Milagrita asked her aunt if they could not have coffee on the *balcón,* instead of in the salon, Leonor made no objection. To be sure, the little balcony was more protected than the restaurant, for it was enclosed on two sides by projecting masonry. Even so, it was otherwise open to the elements, for the striped awning, which evidently slanted over it in the daytime, had been neatly rolled back and securely tied. In every way, it was a much pleasanter place than the stiff little *salita,* for it was furnished in comfortable, though unpretentious, wicker and adorned with numerous flowering plants; and, while he waited for his hostesses, who had retired together to fetch the coffee, Allan leaned over the parapet and looked first at the brilliantly lighted street below him, where traffic was still flowing past and pedestrians still strolling arm in arm, and then at the resplendent sky above him, where the clustering stars spangled an endless expanse of deep sapphire blue. He was so absorbed in the two sights, wholly different and yet somehow so wholly harmonious, that he did not hear footsteps behind him or the placement of a tray on a little table; and it was not until Milagrita touched him lightly on the arm that he turned.

"Oh, I'm sorry!" he said apologetically, as he saw the coffee service and Leonor sitting beside it.

"Why should you be sorry? It makes me very happy to realize that you are not only seeing Madrid, you are feeling it."

"You're right. But how did you know?"

"How could I help knowing? Day after day, I wait on persons who buy souvenirs, and tell me that these cost too much, and go away muttering they are sorry their tour is keeping them three days in a city where one or two would have been plenty, but that there is no help for this now, because everything has been paid for in advance. And then, at last, someone like you comes to Madrid, who appreciates and understands—and loves."

"My dear, you must not detain *Señor* Lambert with your chatter. The coffee is getting cold."

The coffee was delicious and, if it could have been criticized for anything, this would have been because it was scalding hot. Moreover, Allan did not feel that Leonor was really annoyed because he and Milagrita had lingered for a minute beside the balustrade, talking together. Still he realized that she might be very punctilious about observing all the traditional proprieties, and that he would have to make haste slowly, if the *paseo* and the dancing for which he was longing more eagerly every minute were to become accomplished facts. So he sipped his coffee slowly, asking no more leading questions and making no importunate requests. As a matter of fact, he did comparatively little talking because, though he could control his speech, he found it harder to avert his gaze from Milagrita. She had set her cup down after barely tasting its contents and was sitting quietly, with her hands clasped lightly in her lap—beautiful slim hands, with long, un-ringed fingers and oval nails, pink like the finger tips, but only with natural color. Then his eyes traveled slowly from her dark head, which was now slightly bowed, to her feet, which were crossed at the ankle with the same lightness with which her hands were clasped. He had remarked, ever since his arrival in Spain, the exquisite care which most girls and women gave their magnificent hair and the extreme neatness with which they were shod; therefore, the soft waves brushed smoothly away from a central part and gathered into a knot, equally smooth in spite of its size, at the nape of the neck, gave him no surprise now; neither did the high-heeled black slippers, revealing arched insteps above them. But somehow Milagrita's hair and Milagrita's feet seemed to him far lovelier than any he had previously noticed. And surely he had never seen such long lashes, such white eyelids shielding such shining eyes, such winged brows, such a white fore-head. . . .

Suddenly, she raised her head and looked him full in the face. There was no more abashment than boldness in the look; it was serene and sweet. But there was more in it than serenity and sweetness. It was a look of recognition and of response, as if this young, alien girl, whom he had met the first time only a few days earlier, already knew him for everything he was and could meet him on any common ground.

Allan had difficulty in getting to sleep that night. Nothing really exciting had happened and yet his mind was in a turmoil. He tossed and turned while he tried to reconcile the amethysts and the etched glass with the shoddy little apartment. It had not surprised him to hear Leonor addressed as a *marquesa,* but otherwise he was unable to find any explanation for the dapper little man and for his hostess's obvious disinclination to talk with him or even to remain in the same restaurant with him. These things intrigued and baffled Allan out of all proportion to their importance. But they were by no means alone responsible for his state of turmoil. It was ridiculous, it was fantastic, it was foolhardy, it was everything else that anyone, in-cluding himself, might choose to call it; but unless he was very much mis-taken, he was falling head over heels in love with Milagrita de Silva.

The feeling she inspired was as different from the one of tepid camarade-rie he had enjoyed with Charlotte Wendell as it was from the one of brief and violent infatuation which Ethel Crewe had provoked. He need not have worried lest he be tempted to behave dishonorably during the station wagon trip from La Coruña to Madrid; all such temptation had been totally lacking. He had found that there did not seem to be nearly as much to say to Ethel on land as there had been on shipboard; and though she was, undeniably, very good to look upon, she had made him understand, better than he ever had before, the hidden sting in the reference to beauty which is only skin deep. There were a thousand things he wanted to say to Milagrita which he had had no opportunity to voice and he was consumed by impatience for such an opportunity. Moreover, she seemed to him beautiful through and through. It was not only her looks which enthralled him or her laugh or her voice or even her gallantry; it was a quality which he could not yet define, but which he already knew existed, and that he recognized as one in which the spiritual, the mental and the physical were all exquisitely balanced and blended.

This time, when he finally fell asleep, he did not dream about the station wagon—that is, not primarily. He dreamed that he and Milagrita were riding off in it together and, though he could not see where their road was taking them, he did not care, because she was sitting beside him and there was no one else within sight or hearing.

11.

THE FOLLOWING MORNING, Allan found that the hours had begun to drag, though previously they had not done so in the daytime, only in the evening. For fear that he would call attention to the fact that he was frequenting Milagrita's stall too much, he refrained altogether from going there; he had hitherto not been self-conscious about visiting it, but things seemed different now. He asked the concierge to recommend a tailor, walked to and from the shop suggested, and dawdled over his choice of materials, ending up with the purchase of more suits than he wanted or needed, but consoling himself with the thought that he did not have to worry about how he was going to pay for them. He did not care much for midday drinking, but he whiled away another hour at the bar of the Palace Hotel and was ready to take anyone's word that it was the longest in Europe. Just as he was leaving, he heard someone calling his name, and turned to find himself confronted with Douglas Brooks, a pleasant and wealthy young man whom he had known slightly as a younger classman at Harvard.

"Allan Lambert! What on earth are you doing in Madrid?"

"At the moment, patronizing this bar, as you see—and as you are. I might ask you the same question!"

"I've just been assigned to the Embassy here as third secretary, after three years in Iceland. Gosh, it's good to see you! Where are you staying?"

"At the Wellington."

"Fine! I'll call you up tomorrow and we'll get together. Sorry that I've got to run now, but I'm late for a luncheon date at the Ritz."

He nodded, smiled and was gone. Allan decided to lunch where he was, in the vague hope that he might meet some other acquaintance; he knew that, sooner or later, almost everyone gravitated to this hotel. But no one he knew turned up and, the word Palace having given him another idea, he spent a large part of the afternoon going through the seemingly endless series of public apartments, now denuded of much former grandeur, in the enormous structure where the kings and queens of Spain had, for so many centuries, lived in state. And still it was not eight o'clock or anywhere near it. Because he could think of nothing else to do, he decided to return to the *Rastro*.

On one of his previous visits to this "Thieves' Market," in the section dealing with art objects, ancient and modern, where the *galerías* were grouped about an open court, he had thumbed through a stack of huge parchment music sheets, on which the large square notes were carefully and beautifully lettered. Some of the sheets were adorned in one corner with an illuminated capital letter, picked out in gold against a brilliant blue and crimson background. Without any special stirring of interest, he had noticed an A and an L among them; now it occurred to him that these two sheets, together bearing his initials, were just the right shape and size to replace the frayed silk of a two-paneled screen in the music room of his newly inherited house. Despite its handsome walnut frame, this piece of furniture had jarred his esthetic sensibilities whenever he looked at it, because of the dust-colored, gingerish hue into which it had faded. He decided to go back to the *Galería los Santeros* and buy the music sheets in question.

In the little shop heading the flight of steps leading from the *Rastro* court, Allan found his parchments again and made his purchase with the self-satisfied feeling of a shopper who has obtained exactly what he was seeking with minimum expenditure of effort, time and money. The transaction had been so rapid, in fact, that time was now hanging heavily on his hands again, and he decided to kill some of it in browsing. The shopkeeper, a bent, elderly man, dressed in rusty black, smoothed his thinning gray hair still further back from his high forehead and turned away, leaving his visitor to the latter's own devices. Allan had noticed the extreme deftness with which this man had moved aside a fragile porcelain madonna to make room for the display of the music sheets. Now he was again struck by the swiftness and grace with which this humble salesman used his hands, and by the delicacy with which he refrained from urging further purchases.

There was not much space in which to move about between walls closely hung with pictures, lamps and innumerable figures of angels, and among tables crowded with bric-a-brac and fragments of ecclesiastical stone carvings, intermingled with polychrome figures of saints, ranging in height from six inches to as many feet, and in period from the fifteenth through the eighteenth century. A particularly handsome pair of ancient parchment globes, terrestrial and celestial, magnificently patterned and painted with the imaginative scientific detail of the Renaissance, briefly engaged his attention; but he decided that such treasures belonged in a museum rather than in a private house. The piles of prints, engravings and old maps were more tempting and so were a few volumes bound in old sheepskin and tooled morocco; but eventually he turned aside from these, also, to inspect some well-bound, well-preserved standard works which would really be useful and welcome additions either to the college library or to his own. These were displayed on a table by themselves: a few modern novels, a larger number of nineteenth century poets and some excellent philosophical and theological works, somewhat stained by the years, but otherwise in perfect condition. All these books contained an identical bookplate, showing a heraldic shield with two castles and three pomegranates, the whole encircled by a massive linked chain. Whoever had owned these books, Allan reflected —obviously, they were all from the same library—had cherished a tradition of culture and taste. They were well selected, well cared for and, to judge from the occasional neatly penned marginal comments and queries, thoroughly read. He chose a dozen or so volumes with scholarly ease— among them a first edition of the Duque de Rivas for his own shelves—and was about to beckon the shopkeeper when something quite different caught his eye.

It lay among the books, a deeply incised copper rectangle some four inches by six set in a small wooden frame. No great skill in mirror reading was required to identify it as the original die of the bookplate in the volumes which Allan had been examining. He looked at it more closely and with involuntary shock of compassion. Because he so greatly loved and cherished his own books, he had always felt sorry for people whose libraries found their painful way to the auction table or the secondhand bookstore. He had seen countless volumes in such places, autographed by authors to their personal friends, bearing intimate messages of affection on the flyleaf, or demonstrating, by the way they opened readily at certain marked passages, how often they had been read. Whenever he came upon such books, offered for sale and exposed to public gaze, Allan felt sympathetically aware of the wrench with which their owners must have parted from them. But here was something more poignant and more moving: the owner of the volumes before him had given up not only his library, but his very expectation of ever owning books again; he knew all too surely that he would have no further need for his bookplate.

Allan laid the die on top of his other selections and motioned to the shopkeeper. They lost no time in reaching an agreement about prices; these were not high to begin with, and the old man voluntarily lowered the figure he first mentioned, because the purchase included a number of volumes. The process of doing them up took longer. It involved a hunt for wrappings among old periodicals and odd pieces of paper, differing in size, thickness and color and including rustling sheets of something synthetic and modern, but vaguely resembling papyrus. Eventually, the shopkeeper managed to make two tidy parcels of the books without the use of twine, for which he did not even look. Then, as he wrapped the copper die separately and folded in the ends of tissue, he spoke to Allan rather hesitantly.

"You are especially interested in bookplates, *señor?* A collector of them, perhaps?"

"No, I've never even had one of my own, though now I think I'd like to."

"Perhaps the *señor* is a friend of this one's original owner?"

"No, not so much as an acquaintance. I don't mind telling you that I bought the die wholly out of sentiment. I didn't like to see an emblem which had been identified with so many good books discarded and neglected."

The shopkeeper's eyes met Allan's understandingly.

"The *señor* is right," he said. "And his sentiments do him much credit. Such things are always sad and, in this case, they were especially so. The owner of the die was a great lover of books and the breaking up of his library is a tragedy. I have only a few here from that great collection. Many were bought in one lot for the library of a university in your country—that is, if, as I think, the *señor* is a North American?" And, as Allan smiled and nodded, the old man went on, "Also your Legislature, I believe, bought some of the choicest first editions."

"Our Legislature!" Allan exclaimed, somewhat bewildered.

"*Si, señor.* Your Legislature which now, I am told, possesses the world's greatest library."

"Oh, yes, the Library of Congress. What did it acquire?" Allan asked with interest.

"Lópe de Vega especially, some very fine volumes. And several valuable first editions of the mystic poets. I recall particularly those of Teresa de Jesús, Juan de la Cruz and Luis de León. Also, a great treasure, a missal which had belonged to Juana la Loca and had been given by her in recognition for his faithful services to—" The old man checked himself suddenly and continued in a different tone. "But if the *señor* is interested in such things, a few of the better books from the collection are still to be found in certain Madrid bookshops which specialize in rarities and fine editions —the works of Benavente, for example, and Martínez Sierra and the complete works of Ortega y Gasset, which I believe that author himself never possessed in entirety. All these were especially bound, uniformly and very handsomely. For myself, I could afford to acquire only these volumes which you see here. I wish I might have acquired more. The owner was not only a great lover of books, but a very great gentleman. In fact, he was so true a *caballero*," the old man added after a moment, "that he would understand and approve if he knew I were telling you that he was one of my best friends."

Allan and the old shopkeeper took leave of each other with expressions of mutual good will and the hope and expectation of future meetings. Allan hailed a taxi and went back to the hotel. The hours had ceased to hang heavily on his hands. When he had taken a shower and glanced through the papers, it would be time for his appointment.

The knock for which he had been waiting all day came as the clock on the nearest tower was sonorously striking eight. He hurried to the door and threw it open. On the threshold stood Anthony Crewe.

12.

For a moment, Allan stared at his visitor speechlessly, so dumfounded that he could not frame adequate words of greeting. Then he gathered himself together.

"Why, hello!" he said. "I thought you were going to call me up and arrange for a meeting. Or did you try without getting me? The telephone—"

"Yes, it isn't one of Spain's best features," Crewe agreed readily. "But, as a matter of fact, I haven't called you. However—"

"Then would you mind very much if I asked you to excuse me? I'm expecting another visitor and I don't think—"

"Sorry to contradict and all that," Anthony rejoined, grinning. "You're not expecting someone else. Behold the man!"

"You mean *you* represent—"

"Suppose we don't discuss the matter too publicly. Do you mind if I come in? After all, I'm here at your written invitation—which I have with me, if you need proof."

"No, certainly not. I mean, I don't need proof. And by all means, come in."

Crewe stepped across the threshold and, while Allan closed the door, laid hat, cane and gloves on a nearby table. Then he seated himself in the one armchair, leaned back and lighted a cigarette, obviously quite at his ease. Allan, with more sense of constraint and in a state of considerable bewilderment, took the remaining chair, which was, characteristically, straight and hard.

"I'm afraid you'll have to give me time to get used to the idea of you being—well, you," he said hesitantly.

"Of course," Crewe replied gaily. "I've something of an advantage there, because I got my surprise yesterday morning, when I learned, from the contents of your letter, that you were—well, *you*." He looked up as Allan chuckled. "What's so funny?"

"The whole business, of course. Here we've been together for days, each of us carefully hiding our part in this affair from each other and everyone else, and now—here we are."

"It's rather like a second act curtain line, I suppose. But now that—as you put it—here we are, is there any reason why we shouldn't get down to brass tacks?"

"Certainly not. As a matter of fact, if we had known about this before, we could have had the whole thing wound up by this time.

"In the first place, I suppose you can prove that this is all on the up and up?"

"I'm afraid that's in the second place. What proof can you offer that you are Allan Lambert, to whom the person I represent wrote for assistance some weeks ago?"

"Who else could I be?"

Crewe shrugged. "A *polizonte*, perhaps. An *averiguador* of one degree or another. Possibly even someone connected with the postal service back home, if the real Allan Lambert should perhaps have taken my friend's letter to the U.S. authorities, who might decide to see if, by any chance, it were anything other than genuine. Or someone from the Spanish Secret Service. I am sure they would be most eager to find how such communications could be smuggled out of prison. In any case, both on my friend's account and my own, I must be satisfied, completely satisfied, as to your identity, before we go any further."

Without answering, Allan took his passport, neatly encased in maroon leather, from his breast pocket and passed it to his visitor, who accorded it scarcely a glance.

"If you were connected with the authorities on either side of the Atlantic," Crewe said, "a proper and perfectly genuine passport in the name of Allan Lambert would have been the first thing you would have been given."

"For heaven's sake, show a little judgment!" Allan exclaimed. "What *do* you want? A letter from my pastor? Hand and foot prints taken at the hospital where I was born?"

"I'm not trying to be unreasonable, Professor," Crewe said soothingly. "Try to see this from my point of view. At stake is not merely my own standing, but the fate of a friend—and of his beautiful daughter."

"And perhaps a share in the spoil? As I recall it, the stakes are three hundred thousand American dollars plus, of which I was to receive a third if all went well—not a half, though that would have seemed to me a reasonable division, under all the circumstances. My correspondent did not say that his representative would also receive a third, though that would likewise seem reasonable to me—if he had one. But, as a matter of fact, he did not mention a representative who would call on me. He only spoke of a prison guard on whose discretion I could rely completely. And I take it you are not the guard in question—and in disguise?"

"Of course not," Crewe replied, rather impatiently. "As the situation developed, it seemed better for me to call on you than to have you call at the prison where my friend is confined. And I will not deny that, as a businessman, I feel I should be suitably compensated for the amount of time I am giving to clear this matter up. As a businessman, I also feel I must take all proper precautions."

"Very well." Allan reached in his breast pocket again and drew out a letter of credit and a folder of traveler's checks. "If you'll examine these and the name I'll write on a sheet of hotel paper, you'll see that the signature on them is identical with that on the letter I wrote when I was still at home, as well as the one I wrote the evening I reached Madrid."

This time, Crewe subjected the papers to a careful scrutiny, examining each traveler's check separately and reading the letter of credit with care. Then he extended his hand.

"No one ever got into hot water by being careful to test the temperature first," he said, smiling. "Now, that being settled, let's get down to a working basis."

"Just a minute," Allan retorted, gathering up his possessions without appearing to notice the outstretched hand. "It's my turn to ask questions now. Your charming wife not only knew who I was, but introduced me to you by name when we met at La Coruña. If you have been acting for your friend, you must have known he had addressed his plea for help to me. Then why your surprise yesterday morning at finding me to be the writer of the answer to this communication?"

"In the first place, Ethel knows nothing about what we are discussing. Apart from the fact that this is obviously not the sort of thing a man of discretion broadcasts via the members of his family, I did not come into the picture, in as far as my poor friend Pablo is concerned, until after we got back here to Madrid four days ago."

"I'm afraid that's not as clear as it might be."

"It's really very simple. I had nothing to do with the plea which you received at your home address. I didn't even know such an appeal had been sent. As I believe you were told, it was written with the encouragement of a fellow prisoner, an American named John Smith."

"I was told it was written with the encouragement of a fellow prisoner who knew how to reach me. His name wasn't mentioned—are you quite sure it wasn't José Fulano?" Allan asked the question ironically. "I believe that's the Spanish equivalent for So-and-So."

"Naturally, I knew John Smith wasn't his name. But then, if I were imprisoned in some foreign country and wanted that fact to remain unknown, I would most certainly use an assumed name as much as possible—so would you. The point is that this is the only name my poor friend Pablo knew the man by. John Smith—or José Fulano, if you prefer to call him that—has since been released—he was a seaman arrested for engaging in a drunken brawl and is doubtless halfway across some ocean by this time."

"Doubtless," Allan replied drily. "But I can't help being surprised that this John Smith knew how to reach me. I don't happen to have many intemperate and quarrelsome seamen among my acquaintances."

"He may very well have disguised his occupation as well as his name," Anthony said with increasing impatience. "And he may have been arrested on some trumped-up charge—such things do happen in every country. Anyway, he has disappeared. As the answer to Pablo's letter was to be sent to the friendly prison guard in any case—you'll remember that was the stipulation—Pablo only knew that an answer had come—the guard didn't dare risk showing him the letter—and that another communication to the same post office address would apprise him that the recipient of his plea had arrived in Madrid. The guard—who of course also expects to be suitably rewarded—has been going faithfully to the post office, and when your second letter came in, yesterday morning, he immediately got in touch with me."

"I suppose that's all possible," Allan agreed cautiously. "So, on the score of identity, let's accept each other at par. I'm willing, if you are—though I don't see why I haven't just as much reason to doubt that your name is really Anthony Crewe as you had to doubt that mine is really Allan Lambert. I'm also mildly interested in the nature of your business connections in Spain and your financial status. You already know that I'm a professor at a small New England college and you can't have failed to take note of the amount of funds at my disposal while you were verifying my signature. After all, turnabout is fair play. However, we'll let all that pass—at least for the time being. I assume you have the receipt for the suitcase with you?"

"Of course. Now as to the money to pay the fine, reclaim the suitcase and then go after the trunk—"

"Hold on a minute! Let's not get too far ahead of ourselves! We've merely agreed to accept each other temporarily at face value. But I haven't said yet I'd go along with this scheme. What makes you so sure I would be willing to share embezzled funds? In shorter and uglier words, that I would receive stolen goods?"

"Embezzled? Stolen? What on earth are you talking about?"

"The money, of course. The fifteen thousand in the secret compartment of the suitcase, with the claim check for a trunk that holds the other two hundred and eighty-five thousand."

"But where did you get the idea this was embezzled or stolen?"

"From the letter, of course; the letter I received at home. But that's right. You told me you didn't know what was in the letter asking for help."

"And I don't. But I do know that whatever Don Pablo possesses or claims to possess was come by honorably. I'll put my hand on the chopping block for that!"

"But the letter explicitly says that—"

"The hell with what the letter says. I don't know where the three hundred thousand came from, but the one thing I'll swear on a stack of Bibles from here to yonder is that it wasn't stolen . . . and since that seems to mean something to you—incidentally, I'm proud that it does—let's call it a day now. Before we get together again on this proposition, I'll have the straight about the source of that money."

"You mean from your friend Pablo?"

"Yes, of course."

"Is there any reason why I couldn't be present at the interview?"

"All sorts of reasons. It isn't easy to gain admission to the prison where he is—any prison in any country for that matter. You must know that only near relatives and close friends are permitted to visit the prisoners—at clearly defined times, for brief periods, and usually in the presence of a third person. Since Pablo and I have got a guard on our side, I might get to see Pablo alone. I say I *might*. On the other hand, it's possible I'd have to secure the information by letter."

"I'm sorry, but I think I have to make it a condition that I'm to have a talk with this friend of yours myself before I go much further. Not necessarily to hear all the details of how he came to such a sorry pass. But at least to size him up."

"Well, I'll see what can be done. But I can't hold out any hopes. Unless, of course, he were released on parole. He's been a model prisoner, I know that, and he's in extremely poor health—in fact, he should be in a sanatorium, not a prison. So perhaps something could be worked out along those lines."

Allan smiled pleasantly, but he shook his head. "I'm afraid not," he said. "Pablo's sentence could be shortened by a day for every two days that he's worked, if he's behaved well in the meantime and, since he's been a model prisoner, it probably will be—perhaps soon enough to suit our purposes. I'm not in any particular hurry."

"I tell you he's been sick. He couldn't possibly stand up under hard labor."

"I understand that the term 'work' is very tolerantly interpreted—that even if he were in bed, he could have some kind of occupation that would fall under its heading. And, if he's really sick, he'll be cared for in the infirmary of the institution where he is. But he won't be paroled. I'm rather surprised that you thought he might be, in view of your thorough information about the rules for visitors. Apparently, I know more about some of the other rules here than you do. There isn't any parole system, as we understand it, for prisoners in Spain."

13.

IT WAS CREWE'S TURN to stare speechlessly for a moment. But he recovered himself quickly.

"Oh, you must be mistaken! I'm quite sure—"

Allan rose and went over to his bedside table, which was constructed with a deep shelf underneath a shallow drawer. From this shelf, he removed a rather formidable looking collection of paper-bound books, both large and small, and numerous brochures and pamphlets, all of which he offered to his visitor for inspection.

"I spent a few days in Washington before I sailed," he said. "So I went to the office of the Spanish Cultural Attaché and told him I was especially interested in the Spanish prison system. He was most co-operative. He told me he didn't have much literature on the subject at hand himself, but that he'd gladly give me what he did have and see to it that some more was sent me to the *Tarragona* on its arrival at La Coruña. It was duly delivered to me just before we disembarked and I've been using it for bedtime reading ever since. Very informative it is, too. I can even tell you what prisoners in Spain get to eat." Allan retrieved a small red volume from the collection of books and pamphlets that he had handed to Crewe. "This contains the *Reglamento de los Servicios de Prisiones,*" he said, leafing through the pages rapidly, oblivious of Crewe's deep flush of annoyance. "Ah, here we are! Breakfast is a rather monotonous affair, always bread and coffee, though the milk may be either fresh or tinned. But luncheon permits some scope. On Fridays, the prisoners have chick-peas, potatoes, dried codfish and greens; on Sundays, *paella* with rice, fish, mutton and, of course, plenty of olive oil. On all the other days, there is *cocido completo* with meat and vegetables and rice or vermicelli. Then we should, by no means, overlook the matter of supper—"

"I'm not in the least interested in hearing about the menus offered to Spanish prisoners," Crewe interrupted brusquely. "I suppose I should have realized that, as a professor, you'd go in for statistics of that sort. But I'm a businessman. What interests me is not what my unfortunate friend is eating, but whatever concerns this immense amount of money that's being unjustly withheld from him."

"And your share of it. And the friendly guard's."

"Just so. However, I don't see why you keep harping on that. Probably it's another example of the way a professor's mind works—wholly unlike a businessman's. You go on talking about minor matters. Now I want to get into action. We can take up details later."

"Exactly. And I'm just as eager to get into action as you are. So I suggest that, as our next step, we ask for an appointment with the Minister of Justice, since that's the Department of the Government that prisons come under. I have a letter of introduction to him, but I decided not to present it until I'd had a chance to talk with you—I mean, a chance to talk with the prisoner's representative, whom I never suspected as being you. I'll get it off first thing in the morning."

"I'm sure the Minister of Justice is out of town. None of the big shots stay in Madrid after it begins to get warm here. Besides, it's wholly un-necessary. As I've told you—"

Allan interrupted his visitor. "Well, if the Minister himself is out of town, he must have left some sort of assistant here," he said, without commenting on the latter part of Crewe's speech. "Moreover, I really feel it would be very discourteous not to deliver a letter that's been given me by an attaché of the Spanish Embassy in Washington, and I understand that the Minister is a very distinguished and charming man, with whom it would be a pleasure and a privilege to make connections in any case. But I have a letter to the Director of Prisons, too. I understand that the two gentlemen have their offices in the same building and work together very effectively. If the Minister is really out of town and by some strange chance hasn't left a capable assistant in charge, I'm sure the Director—"

"I tell you it's entirely unnecessary to apply to them at all. In fact, it's not only unnecessary, it's unwise. You'll get hopelessly entangled in red tape and you won't accomplish anything. I know these big brass Spaniards better than you do."

"Maybe. But I did grow up in this country and I have a good many personal friends who are Spaniards. I've been waiting to get in touch with them, too, in the interests of first things first—and I thought this affair with the prisoner did come first. However, I'm sure some of my boyhood acquaintances would be in a position to help and that they'd be glad to, if you think the Spanish big brass, as you call it, wouldn't want to bother. As far as that goes, we can go straight to our own Embassy for help. Of course, my father was only a consul. But he had a very good record."

"A long time ago, wasn't it? I doubt if the present American outfit ever even heard of him. And most of those cookie pushers and muffin hounds are in San Sebastian now, too."

"Oh, come now! Some members of the staff may belong in that category, but not all of them by any means. And the whole outfit isn't in San Sebastian, either. I saw Douglas Brooks, the third secretary, at the Palace bar this noon, just by chance. He's going to call me up tomorrow, to make a date. Incidentally, his father, who was in the Service, too, but with a lot more rank, and mine were very good friends."

"Well, he's the exception that proves the rule, on both counts. And he's a newcomer, without much say. What could a third secretary, who's been here only a few weeks and who probably doesn't speak much, if any, Spanish do in a case like this? Just leave matters in my hands, won't you? I understand this situation better than you do."

"Now at last you've said something with which I'm in complete agreement."

The two men looked levelly at each other, Allan with complete calmness, Crewe with heightened color and an irritation which he was at small pains to conceal. However, after a moment, he answered with an attempt at conciliatory speech.

"A while back, I told you that everything was really very simple and it is. I also told you that before we got together again, I'd find out where Pablo's money came from and I will. Just give me twenty-four hours to work things out my own way, will you?"

"Yes. I'm willing to do that."

"Good! Meanwhile, what about dinner tonight? I'm afraid I can't get much of any real news about Pablo's money for you before tomorrow, but we'll make this a social evening. Ethel's pretty well settled now and she's eager to see you again."

Allan hesitated. He had lost all desire to see Ethel again and, as far as that went, he had no desire to see any more of Crewe than was necessary to clear up the mystery which so greatly intrigued him. But even a "social evening" might well provide him with more clues than he had at the time, and his curiosity was now fully aroused. Well aware as he had been from the beginning that the Spanish Prisoner letter was a hoax, he had not expected to find one of his fellow countrymen connected with the hoax. One? He was now increasingly certain that Ethel, no less than her husband, was some way involved in it, despite Crewe's statement that she knew nothing about the matter. Just how she was involved he did not yet understand, but that involvement existed, he did not doubt. An evening with the couple might be very interesting.

"Yes, I'd be glad to come," he said. "Give me the address, will you? I forgot to ask for it before and you must have forgotten to tell me. And I didn't find you in the telephone book."

He had purposely avoided Milagrita's stall all day, but as he passed through the lobby on his way out to dinner, she smiled at him so invitingly that he could not resist the temptation of stopping to speak with her. In fact, he found he could not resist the temptation of voicing the invitation he had not previously dared to extend.

"I know I shouldn't do this," he said. "But I can't help asking you whether I couldn't persuade you to go dancing with me."

"You mean tonight?"

"No, it couldn't be tonight. I've promised the Crewes to dine with them."

"Oh!"

She had sounded happy and eager when she said, "You mean tonight?" When she said, "Oh!" her tone of voice was entirely different. Allan cursed himself for having been such a fool as to tie himself up and for having disappointed her.

"Could you have gone tonight? That is *could* you? I'm sure I could excuse myself very soon after dinner and—"

"I'm sorry, but I couldn't possibly. First, I'd have to ask my aunt, and I won't have a chance to speak with her for several hours yet. You must have misunderstood me when I said 'Oh!' You see, you told us you hadn't heard anything from the Crewes since you arrived in Madrid, and I was a little surprised to learn that you finally had, after all. Of course, there isn't any reason why I should have been, really. I hope you'll have a very pleasant evening."

"It won't be half so pleasant as last night, I know that. . . . Do you think your aunt would let you go dancing with me tomorrow night?"

"No, I'm afraid not."

"Well, won't you ask her anyway? Or let me?"

"I really think it would be better just to remind her about Alcalá de Henares. We get through earlier on Sundays than we do on week days. We might be able to go then."

"All right, I'll remind her about Alcalá de Henares. And perhaps, if she says yes to that, I might bring up the subject of dancing while we're having dinner at the *Hostería del Estudiante*."

"Yes, perhaps."

Two elderly ladies came up, intent on buying large quantities of American magazines. Allan was obliged to leave the stall with no more encouragement than he had already received. But he did so confidently. There had been the same element of recognition and response in Milagrita's face when she said, "Perhaps," that there had been when she looked at him on the balcony the night before. . . .

He had some difficulty in locating the street where the Crewes lived. It was much further from the center of town than he had anticipated, and, before he located it, he had gone around several circles, missing the proper turns. Then he had been forced to detour because the road was torn up and blocked by large signs reading merely "*Teléfonos.*" Eventually, he reached a section where several buildings were in the process of construction, but where the roads were still unpaved, street lights few and far between and pedestrians practically nonexistent; those he did see could give him no directions. He went bumping along, peering into the darkness and wondering when or whether he would reach his destination.

At last, he came to a house standing by itself on a lot enclosed with a low iron fence, and saw by the light of the twin lamps on the gate that he had found the right number. The front door was promptly opened by a bowing servant, who indicated a short flight of steps leading from an attractive entrance hall into a still more attractive drawing room, where Anthony and Ethel were awaiting their guest. Even before the first greetings were over, Allan was aware of the elegance and taste of his surroundings: the room was airy, spacious and so skillfully furnished that the brocaded sofas and chairs, which were comfortably upholstered, did not seem out of harmony with the inlaid *bargueños*, the polychrome statuettes, the dark paintings, the books bound in vellum and tooled leather and the gold-framed mirrors which all belonged to a far earlier era. He voiced his spontaneous admiration.

"Delighted that you like it," Crewe told him heartily. "We've been picking up these things gradually, and we think they do fit in very well here, even though this is such a modern house. Of course, Ethel's the one who's responsible for the selections and the arrangement." He put his arm around his wife's shoulders and gave her a look of affectionate appreciation. "We'd begun to be afraid you'd lost your way," he went on, turning back to Allan.

"This place is rather hard to find, especially after dark. But it suits us. As you must have gathered, it's in one of the new developments, so construction work is still going on all around us. But, in another year or so, it'll be one of the most desirable residential sections in Madrid. We're very pleased to have got in on the ground floor, so to speak, before prices started skyrocketing. There's plenty of room in our lot for a fine garden, and space for those will be at a premium pretty soon. Ah! Here come the cocktails! I think you'll find Sigismundo's martinis rather better than those on the *Tarragona*, from what Ethel tells me."

The cocktails and the canapés which went with them were, indeed, delicious, and so was the dinner which followed after an easy interval, and which was impeccably served in a dining room which, for spaciousness and elegance, was quite as distinctive as the salon. Ethel was wearing one of the exquisite dresses in which she seemed to specialize—a pale blue one this time, which Allan had not seen on shipboard, with a parure of aquamarines which Allan had not seen either. Her golden curls were as elaborately arranged as ever, and he felt almost guilty because he compared them, mentally and unfavorably, with Milagrita's smooth and simple style of hairdressing. Ethel was a lightweight, there was no doubt of that, and he still felt uncomfortably certain that, in some measure, she was connected with her husband's devious practices, whatever these were. But in her own way she was, undeniably, a siren. He could thank his lucky stars that he had not fallen completely under her spell before it was too late for withdrawal.

Conversation was agreeable and casual. No reference to the prisoner was made during dinner or when coffee was brought afterward into the drawing room. While they were drinking it, however, Sigismundo appeared and apologetically informed Señor Crewe that he was urgently wanted on the telephone. He spoke in broken English, and without giving the matter much thought Allan wondered why his speech sounded vaguely familiar; and why, when the Crewes spoke such good Spanish, they did not use that language in their household. Anthony excused himself and, after an interval when Allan confirmed his previous impression that Ethel's chatter was less intriguing on land than on shipboard, he asked for permission to examine some of the beautifully bound books in the arched recesses on either side of the fireplace at the further end of the room.

"It looks to me as if you had some real treasures there," he said, "and I'm afraid I'm something of a bookworm—not that I've ever been able to indulge my weakness to any great extent. But that doesn't prevent me from appreciating other people's fine libraries."

"By all means, look at the old tomes," Ethel said carelessly. "I bought them in a bunch just to fill in those shelves—we had to have something.

I've hardly opened them. While you're browsing, I'll have another cup of coffee."

He would not have expected her to be interested in rare volumes, but he thought there was a hint of resentment as well as indifference in her tone. Quite conceivably, it was a new experience for her to meet a man who would rather look at books than at her and she might well be piqued because he did not cater to her vanity. Nevertheless, he crossed the room and began to survey the well-stocked shelves. At first, this survey was not intensive; he glanced at titles, leafed through three or four volumes and then inspected three or four others with more careful attention. Next he began taking them down two at a time and replacing them after merely opening them. Then he selected one and brought it over to the table where Ethel still sat sipping her coffee and still seeming rather resentful at his negligence and wholly uninterested in what he was doing.

"Would you and Anthony let me borrow this?" he asked. "It isn't one of a set and I don't think it's especially valuable, as your books go. But it happens to be by an author whose work I've always enjoyed and whose books are difficult to come by—I can't imagine why they've gone out of print so fast, but the fact remains that they have. I've never been able to get hold of this one before."

"By all means, take it along. You don't need to ask Anthony. . . . He's an awfully long time at the telephone, isn't he?"

Allan slipped the slim leather-bound volume into his pocket. "It hasn't seemed long to me," he said. "But then, in your charming company—"

Ethel brightened at once and Allan rose to the occasion. They were engaged in lively repartee when Anthony returned to the room, shaking his head gravely.

"I've had some very bad news," he said, without sitting down. "I've just learned that a poor old friend of mine, who's already been overwhelmed by almost every imaginable disaster, is seriously ill and hasn't the money for proper treatment. I'd like to get some to him tonight, if I possibly could, and it so happens that I've very little cash in the house. I wonder—could you lend me some until tomorrow, Allan?"

Allan reached for his wallet. "I don't keep much with me, either," he said. "Would five thousand *pesetas* do you—I mean, your friend—any good?"

"Well, as a stopgap."

His disappointment was obvious. Nevertheless, he promptly accepted the notes which Allan held out to him.

"You want the money to reach him tonight? I'd be glad to take it anywhere you say. Is your friend at a hospital?"

"Yes, not far from here. But I'm afraid it isn't a very good one. My car's back in commission now, so I'll get the money to him myself and see what else I can do for him. Thanks just the same."

"You'll want to be on your way straight off, I'm sure. I mustn't detain you. Thanks for a wonderful evening. I can't tell you how much I've enjoyed it."

"We've enjoyed it, too. Come again soon, won't you?"

"I'd be glad to."

Allan shook hands with Ethel, who had not moved from the coffee table. Anthony, however, went with their guest to the door and then down the walk toward the gate. As soon as they had left the house, he began speaking in rapid whispers.

"I didn't want to say much in front of my wife—as I've told you already, she doesn't know a thing about the situation with which you've so kindly offered to help. But that telephone message was from our friend the prison guard. Pablo is desperately ill. If we don't act quickly, I'm afraid he'll be dead. And it's quite out of the question for him to receive any visitors, except a priest, who'll administer the Sacraments."

"Not even his daughter? I thought a person in danger of death was always allowed—"

"Well, perhaps his daughter, if she were accessible," Crewe said impatiently. "What I meant was that it was now obviously out of the question for *you* to see him and I doubt if I could."

"I've already advanced you the equivalent of over a hundred dollars and you must have some cash on hand for ordinary household expenses—an establishment like yours doesn't run without something to grease the wheels. You said you only needed to be tided over until tomorrow. I never heard of a hospital that wouldn't wait that long for further funds, if a substantial sum had already been paid on account."

"Then your experience has been different from mine. I've known of emergency cases where a patient hasn't even been admitted until someone had forked out the money for a week's expenses. This time, the patient is there all right, but he's in a public ward without a special nurse or any doctor, except a young intern, looking after him. They won't move him into a private room or give him individual attention until they have at least ten thousand *pesetas*. And to tell you the truth, I haven't got enough cash in the house to make up the difference between that and what you've given me. Besides, I'm rather short just now. You see, we've just bought this new house and, after your first letter came, saying you were starting for Spain, I rather let myself go on modern equipment. Then, as soon as Ethel arrived, she enlarged her scheme of decoration and altogether—"

"In other words, you took it for granted that, if I came at all, I wouldn't ask any awkward questions after I got here."

"That's an ugly way of putting it. But no, I didn't think you'd be so overly cautious and so unjustly suspicious. I still don't see how you can be in the face of such an emergency as I've described. I don't mind being short of cash for myself. But I'd hate to have creditors begin hounding poor Ethel and I'd hate still worse to have my unfortunate friend Pablo suffer for my heedless, but trustful extravagance. So, if you could just see your way clear—"

Allan opened his wallet again and from an inner section took out a hundred-dollar bill. "I told you the truth when I said I didn't have any more *pesetas* with me," he said. "But you ought not have any trouble getting this accepted and it will more than make up the difference between what you have already and what you say you need tonight. I'm afraid I can't undertake to shoulder all *your* financial problems and I won't insist on seeing the patient if he's a dangerously sick man. Besides, I can understand that he'd face death with an easier mind if he knew his daughter was provided for. Suppose you arrange to let me talk with her, if that's possible— I don't know how accessible her convent is—that's one of the things you haven't told me yet. If such an interview can't be arranged, I'd be satisfied to talk with the patient's physician and his confessor."

"What do you expect them to know about the situation? They're both comparative strangers to him."

"You told me Pablo had been sick a great deal, so he may have been treated by this same intern before. In any case, that young man should be able to tell me just what Pablo—I don't know what else to call him—needs in the way of medical treatment and I'll undertake to meet the cost of that, whatever it is—within reason. Moreover, if Pablo's got something on his conscience and is in danger of death, he'd certainly tell his confessor about it. Though the priest couldn't break the seal of the confessional without permission, Pablo could give him that and I'd believe what he told me. I've found that doctors and priests are generally pretty reliable."

"You'd rather trust two strange Spaniards than a fellow American?"

"I didn't say that and I didn't mean to infer it. What I am saying is that I'd rather take the word of a doctor and a priest of any nationality than that of a man of any nationality who's been imprisoned for embezzlement and has approached me only indirectly."

"I've told you there's no question of embezzlement!"

"Yes, I remember. But I haven't forgotten, either, that the man who wrote the letter admitted to 'unfortunate speculations,' flight from the authorities and the payment of a 'ruinous fine.' He wouldn't have been fined or imprisoned for bankruptcy unless he'd entered a plea for it under false pretenses—or pretenses that appeared false to the judge who pronounced the sentence. The way of the transgressor is proverbially hard. I'll be glad to make it easier when I'm certain there's a good reason for it. You assured me you could convince me there was, within twenty-four hours. I'm willing to make that thirty-six or even forty-eight if you like, in view of your friend's illness, and the necessary amount of money will be at your disposal as soon as I *am* convinced. But I'm not handing over fifteen thousand dollars blind to anyone."

As they talked, they had been walking slowly down the path from the house to the gate. As Crewe still seemed disposed to linger and argue, Allan lifted the latch himself and took the keys to the station wagon from his pocket.

"Good night," he said. "And thanks again for a good dinner and an evening that began very pleasantly. I'm sorry to bring it to an end in a way that's disappointing to you and distasteful to us both, but I'm afraid I have to. Let's hope that, by this time tomorrow night, everything will be cleared up."

When Allan reached his room at the Wellington, he found it in its usual pleasant order for the night: the curtains drawn, the bed turned down, his pajamas laid neatly across the folded sheet, a lamp gleaming on the bedside table, but restful darkness elsewhere. He went from switch to switch, turning on the lights of the chandelier, the wall brackets and the desk. The resultant illumination was not as brilliant as he would have wished, but would suffice for his purpose.

The books which he had bought at the *Rastro* were already ranged in a row on a marble shelf over the radiator and the framed die for the bookplate lay beside them. He took one of them over to the desk, where there was the best light, and laid it down so this would fall full upon it. Then he drew the little volume which he had extracted from the Crewes' library out of his pocket and opened it at the flyleaf.

He had not been mistaken. The bookplate was the same in both.

14.

ALLAN HAD ALWAYS enjoyed the sound sleep of good health and a clear conscience. It annoyed him to find himself wakeful and restless again, especially since he could hardly hope that, a second time, he would finally drift off to slumber dreaming that he and Milagrita were riding away in the station wagon together, triumphantly carefree and happy.

Of course, it could be mere coincidence, he told himself over and over again, that the books which Ethel had bought so carelessly had come from the same library as the one from which he had made selections at the *Rastro* and of which the most valuable items had gone to an American university and to the Library of Congress. Indeed, the old shopkeeper whom he had found so *simpático* had told him that the works of some modern writers, formerly included in the collection, could now be found in the better bookstores of Madrid, and he intended to seek these out and buy them himself. But, somehow, he did not believe that the Crewes had come into possession of theirs in this way and, as a matter of fact, the volume he had chosen for comparison with those he had already bought was not the work of a modern writer. In was an 1858 edition of Jovellanos and though he had told the truth when he said it was not part of a set, it was certainly a rare acquisition. With nothing more concrete than instinct to guide him, he was more and more inclined to believe that Crewe had come by the books in a way that did him no credit.

From the books, Allan's restless thoughts darted to the other beautiful things he had seen in the Crewes' house: the inlaid *bargueños*, the polychrome statuettes, the dark paintings and bright mirrors, the shining silver and fragile porcelain. Every one of these might logically have belonged to a great lover of books who was also a great gentleman—so real a *caballero* that he numbered among his friends the humblest as well as the most exalted, which no *nouveau riche* and no social climber could afford to do. In fact, these treasures *must* have belonged to such a person or persons. And they were very valuable. If Crewe were short of money, how could he have paid for them or given Ethel the money to pay for them? As a matter of fact, he had not. He had said as much himself: "I'd hate to see my creditors hounding Ethel . . . I'd hate still worse to have poor Pablo suffer from my extravagance." . . . He was counting on his share of the money which he confidently expected Allan to hand over to pay for the beautiful things he had acquired, by means which looked increasingly foul rather than fair. . . .

Well, Allan would try to clear up at least part of the mystery the next day, or rather that same day, for it was now three o'clock in the morning. He had promised that he would make no attempt to see the Minister of Justice or the Director of Prisons, and that he would not take the initiative in approaching the American Embassy. It was not his fault that he had met Douglas Brooks by chance at the Palace bar, and he would keep his word and say nothing to Douglas or anyone else at the Embassy about this affair of the prisoner, at least until forty-eight hours had elapsed. But he had made no promises about the *Rastro*. Crewe did not even know that he had been to the *Rastro* nor would this self-styled businessman have attached any importance to it if he had. Allan would go back there and ask the old shopkeeper to tell him the name of the great gentleman whose library had been so cruelly sacrificed; he thought that, once convinced there was a good reason for doing this, the shopkeeper might be open to persuasion. Then Allan would ask Crewe outright if he had ever known this *caballero* and ask what the transactions between the two had been.

He would do more than this: he would ask Crewe to explain the nature of the de Silvas' obligations to him. He had said he was "responsible for getting them their jobs." This would indicate a certain amount of affluence and prestige. If he were in financial straits himself, he would hardly be in a position to help other persons out of theirs. Admittedly, he was not even in a position to rescue his friend Pablo. It had been distasteful to Allan, from the beginning, to feel that gentlewomen, like Leonor and Milagrita, were obligated to a man like Crewe. It was a relief to begin believing that, perhaps, they were not so indebted, after all. But there must have been some reason why Crewe wanted to give the impression that they were. If he would not tell, perhaps Leonor, like the shopkeeper, would be open to persuasion —not so easily, not so quickly, but eventually. Allan had not previously considered taking a suite, but now he gave the matter thought. He could not properly detain the *gobernanta* any longer than was absolutely necessary, in the bedroom; but if he had a parlor, all the proprieties would be observed. He would speak to the manager, who seemed most eager to please, the first thing after he went downstairs. Then he would ask Leonor to come to his *salita*. She did not like the Crewes, that was perfectly plain. She had stiffened at the mere mention of their name. She had been obviously relieved when Allan said his acquaintance with them was recent and casual, that it sprang from a meeting on shipboard and was in no way related to business. She had spoken with mild sarcasm about their neglect of their new-found friend after his arrival in Madrid. And she was becoming increasingly well disposed toward Allan. As for her niece. . . .

Yes, as for that niece. The chance meeting with Douglas Brooks might be a godsend. He was undoubtedly asked, all the time, to squire American girls who were visiting Madrid. If he and such a girl could help make up a foursome, Leonor would probably not hesitate to let Milagrita go dancing. For that matter, they could and would ask Leonor to go along. She would not put a damper on such a gathering; she would be a real addition to it. . . .

Having planned everything so tidily, Allan at last went to sleep and, this time, he did not dream, about Milagrita or anyone else. But he was awakened by the ringing of the telephone and, after the usual succession of disconnections, rattles and cracklings, discovered that Douglas Brooks was at the other end of the line. This agreeable young man—so he learned —had been called to Avila, where there were no resident American officials, by the inopportune death of an elderly American tourist, and was about to drive up there for the day; that was why he had called so early. It had occurred to him that Allan might like to go along.

"I'm afraid I won't have a chance to do much sight-seeing with you," Douglas went on, "because of course I'll have to make all the usual rather gruesome arrangements to take care of the body, provide for its transportation and so on. But the ride over is a beautiful one and we'd have a chance to catch up with each other's news on the way back and forth. Perhaps you wouldn't mind wandering around by yourself while I'm otherwise occupied. Avila's a rather interesting old city."

"That's putting it mildly and you needn't be so apologetic. I'd be delighted to go."

"Swell! I'll meet you at the entrance to the Wellington in about an hour."

Allan showered, breakfasted and dressed with dispatch, and had time to cash a fresh supply of traveler's checks and speak to the manager about a suite before Douglas arrived in his Thunderbird. He had not exaggerated the attractions of the drive, which was crowded with contrasts: the ultra-modern buildings of University City; the broad smooth highway, flanked by variegated bloom and inviting restaurants, that stretched from Madrid to Las Rozas; the lengthening plain beyond where clumps of wild yellow broom succeeded the carefully cultivated flower beds of the suburbs; the gradual climb of the Guadarrama Range to its triumphant summit; the descent through fragrant pine woods; and then the seemingly endless boulder-strewn fields of the province toward which they were headed. The character of the traffic changed almost as much as the scenery: the broad boulevards leading out of Madrid were thronged with automobiles of every description, but, presently, the pretentious limousines of wealthy Madrileños ceased to crowd out the small travel-worn cars of tourists and provincials, which chugged busily up hill and down dale. Then the number of these lessened, too, and only the ubiquitous and noisy motorcycles wove their headlong way among the lumbering trucks and creaking horse-drawn carts, under the watchful eye of the Guardia Civil, stationed in well-spaced pairs on either side of the highway. As a concession to the heat, havelocks of olive green cloth, which matched their uniforms, were attached to the patent leather hats which normally constituted their headgear, and mitigated the severity of this. Many of these men leaned, with apparent nonchalance, on their long guns, or took their stance where they could escape the direct brightness of the sun. Nevertheless, even the most casual observer could not remain unaware of their all-seeing vigilance.

"Recently, I came across one of the most ridiculous references I have ever read to the maintenance of law and order in Spain," Allan observed, as they passed the tenth pair of these alert guards. "The author of one of those travel books, written by a person who spends all of a week in some foreign country, calls the *Guardia Civil* the 'secret police.' Secret, my word! You can't go more than a few hundred yards without seeing them and their shiny patent leather hats."

"Not to mention the fact that their headquarters are the most conspicuous feature in every village," Douglas added. "About as secret as a bull ring. I wish creeps who write books like that could be forcibly kept at home, but I suppose there's no way of doing that, so let's not think about them any more than we can help when we're out to enjoy a ride."

The enjoyment lasted from beginning to end. They had a flashing glimpse of the Escorial in the distance and a longer view of a cross-crowned mountain where, Douglas told his friend, a hidden monastery was being hewn from solid rock; further on, the precipitous slopes were dotted by sanatoria, the balconies open to the bracing air and brilliant sunshine. Conical stone posts, banded around the base with white, appeared at regular intervals; these white bands, Douglas explained, marked the heights which the abundant snowfalls, that often rendered the road impassable, had reached the previous season; in the glowing warmth of July, it was hard to visualize this as a cold, impenetrable region. The route was intermittently bordered by fields of ripe wheat and, in some of them, harvesting, by primitive methods, was already under way. It passed through no large towns; but here and there the low, red-roofed houses of a village clustered around a central fountain, or a little church with storks' nests on its belfry stood, in strange solitude, upon a small hill. In the villages, white chickens fluttered frequently and perilously across the driver's path and large black pigs lay complacently beside it or waddled away without haste. Few herds of cattle were in evidence; but flocks of newly shorn sheep again and again detached themselves from a landscape with which they blended almost uncannily and skittered by, under the watchful guidance of their shepherds and the care of their dogs; and patient, heavily laden donkeys went ceaselessly to and fro, or stood drooping under the scant shade of cork trees, awaiting the next summons of their lords and masters. . . .

The infinite variety of the scene robbed the ride of all monotony. Moreover, Allan and Douglas had so much to talk about that, even had the countryside been less arresting, time would have passed almost too quickly. After the careful reserve of the last few weeks, Allan found a welcome release in telling Douglas about his unexpected legacy, and the important architectural and historical features of the fine property he had inherited; his ample means and his sabbatical year supplied reason enough for his trip to Spain. Douglas was ready and able to talk at still greater length of his experiences in Iceland. Despite the cold climate, his house had been very comfortable, as hot water was piped direct from a natural spring. He had

had no language difficulties because—as Allan might remember—he had studied Anglo-Saxon for a whim when they were at Harvard together and this had stood him in good stead. He had admired the highly literate people, especially the pride in their representative government, which went back a thousand years—longer than any other legislative body in the world. As to the scenery, this was superb—the lakes, the mountains, the colors; there was no blue in the world like that of Iceland. And did Allan know that, when William Faulkner came to Iceland a few years back, he had said he felt completely at home because it was so much like Mississippi? The comparison might seem farfetched, ludicrous even. But Douglas, who had spent some time in Mississippi himself, saw what the Nobel prize winner meant. . . .

After they passed Villacastin they were obliged to slow down, more than once, where the roads were torn up by the *Obras Públicas*, which were, eventually, to improve them. However, in less than two hours, to their great surprise, the friends saw that the tower of Avila's cathedral was already rising above the rocky landscape; they could not believe they were at their journey's end so soon. Douglas pulled up the Thunderbird in front of the Hotel Reina Isabel.

"I hate to leave you here," he said, "not even inside the walls yet. But this is where the poor old lady was staying and—"

"I said before, please don't apologize. As a matter of fact, I'm pleased to be here on business of my own and I always enjoy strolling around a strange city, anyway. Just let me know what time you want me back. I'll go in and ask the concierge for a few directions and then I'll be off."

"Well, shall we say two-fifteen, *más o menos*, for lunch at *La Torreón* near the cathedral? It's a rather attractive restaurant, just recently opened and we might as well kill some time there. As you know, everything closes between two and four and I suppose that includes even the mortuary establishments."

"No doubt. Who would be better qualified than undertakers to sleep like the dead?"

Under all the circumstances, Allan did not feel that the grimness of the jest was ill timed. After all, Douglas was on a rather grim errand and, as a matter of fact, his own designs had something of the same quality. He did not plan to go sight-seeing. He planned to visit the leading bank and, afterward, if such a course were indicated, other banks, even if that meant going to all there were in Avila; this might be a good many for a city of that size, since banks, like drugstores, seemed to be more numerous than any given place would suggest. He intended to ask for the director, or directors, and after all traditional preliminaries in the way of exchanged courtesies had been observed, to request that a draft might be made on his letter of credit and that he might open a checking account, in order to give the call some semblance of business purpose; then to submit the communication which had brought him to Spain and which contained the statement that the writer had formerly been a respected banker in Avila, but that he had fled from there and had subsequently been imprisoned. Bank officials were proverbially close-mouthed and properly so; but Allan's financial status was obviously one which deserved respectful consideration and he thought they would be swift to deny that anything which reflected upon the honor of reputable institutions had ever occurred in their city, and that he would be able to tell, without much difficulty, whether such denials were based merely on a desire to shield a good name, or whether they were based on sober and solid fact.

The return drive to Madrid, in the late afternoon, was less jovial than the one in the early morning had been. There was a greater sense of spaciousness and peace, conducive to quiet rather than conversation. There were very few cars and carts on the road now and, though it was the hour of the *paseo*, most of the strollers were as staid and taciturn as the village priests who paced along alone, missal in hand, or mingled unobtrusively with their flocks. The sound of bells, tinkling on the sheep and pealing for the Angelus, were all that broke the companionable silence of the countryside for miles at a stretch. Neither of the two young Americans was disposed to break it, either. Douglas had, naturally, found his day's work distasteful and distressing; Allan had rather enjoyed most of the visits which made up his rounds, but at the end of the day he was unaccountably tired. None of the directors he sought out had declined to see him and all had received him courteously and listened with patient attention to his questions; but at that point, a change had taken place in their attitude. One had expressed himself as deeply shocked that such a statement as the prisoner's letter contained should ever have been made about a respectable banker in Avila, even by a criminal of the deepest dye. Another, equally shocked, seemed to feel chagrin chiefly because Allan had attached enough importance to such derogatory allegations to give them even a passing thought. Two others politely veiled their amusement that he had done so. All had unhesitatingly and categorically denied that any such person as the writer of the letter had ever lived in Avila, much less been connected with the irreproachable institutions handling the public's funds.

Allan could not explain why this oft-repeated assertion should have left him with the feeling of being so let down. After all, it was what he had expected; in fact, it was what he had been perfectly sure would be said to him. He had really had no good reason for using up the time of the busy and worthy men with whom he had talked, only the puerile sensation that he would take satisfaction in telling Crewe he had been to Avila—he had never promised not to do that—had visited every bank in the city, and had discovered that not a single one of them had ever numbered on its staff a defaulter who had been forced to flee. It would give him even more satisfaction to do this than it had to announce that there was no parole system for prisoners in Spain, similar to that in the United States. But that was really no excuse. He might much better have spent the day viewing the incomparable turreted walls from every available angle, visiting the austere cathedral which had done double duty as a fortress, and the shrines associated with the Great Teresa.

When they reached the Wellington, Allan invited Douglas to come in for a drink, but the young diplomat asked for a rain check; it was pretty late already, and he must attend two official cocktail parties before dinner. Allan broached the subject of double-dated dancing and it was well received; perhaps the group could have dinner at Douglas' place beforehand. The friends parted with cordiality but without regret, and Allan went to the reception desk, to see if the matter of a suite had been given attention.

Indeed, yes, he was assured; in fact, under the direction of the *gobernanta*, *Señor* Lambert's belongings had already been carefully transferred by the chambermaid and the *valet de chambre* to the best quarters available in the hotel. The manager hoped and believed everything would be satisfactory. Allan hoped and believed so, too. Unless there were some word from Crewe, which he was very far from expecting, he would dine alone in his own sitting room and go to bed early. . . .

The unexpected message came just as he was beginning his soup. Crewe was on the telephone and even the irritating quality of the connection, which Allan was beginning to regard as inevitable, could not disguise the exultation in his voice. Both the young intern who had been caring for poor Pablo—who was still lingering on, hoping against hope for succor—and the priest who had already administered the Last Rites, would be only too glad to meet Lambert and try to convince him of the unfortunate man's need and condition. There was an implication in the triumphant tone that such a service on their part should have been unnecessary, since Crewe had already informed Lambert fully of all the circumstances. However, these two kindly men had agreed to render it and would be at Crewe's house within half an hour. The friendly guard would accompany them, to give still further weight to their words. He had secured a brief leave from his duties, but he could not be gone from his post long, and neither could the intern, so Crewe hoped very much that Lambert would not keep them waiting, and took it for granted that he would come prepared to keep his part of the bargain. After making this statement, Crewe paused for reassurance.

"If you mean you take it for granted I'll have fifteen thousand dollars in cash on me, I'm afraid I'll have to disappoint you. I've been in Avila all day."

"*Avila!*"

"Yes. Pablo's home town, don't you remember? Well, never mind. I cashed some traveler's checks this morning, so that I could keep my promise about meeting hospital expenses, and now I've opened several accounts, so I could easily give you a negotiable draft, if I'm satisfied circumstances warrant it. At least, I'll have it all prepared."

"Good! I couldn't ask for anything fairer than that. So long!"

"So long and congratulations on your speedy work!"

He spoke civilly, but without warmth and, when he had replaced the receiver, he stood thoughtfully beside the telephone table for some moments. He was sure there was a catch somewhere, explicit as Crewe had been in everything he said. The man's unfamiliarity with prison regulations and his reluctance to confer with the logical authorities pointed unmistakably to double dealing. To a lesser degree, so did his straitened circumstances and his connection with the de Silvas; and Allan had not been able to dismiss from his mind the doubts which the bookplate had aroused, though, admittedly, they might be entirely unfounded. However, the testimony of the Avila bankers was something else again. There could be no question that the letters from the alleged prisoner contained one downright falsehood, with which several other statements were so closely linked that they must be falsehoods, too; and the confident tone of Crewe's voice had changed to one of surprise when Allan mentioned Avila. Indeed, if he were not mistaken, it was tinged with resentment.

In the last analysis, why should he quarrel with all this? He had come to Spain knowing the letter was fraudulent, to a greater or lesser degree, and feeling it would be a lark to track it to its source. Since Crewe had been disclosed as an intermediary, Allan had realized that this "businessman" was in some way connected with the fraud, and yet he had played along with the tricky customer and, until now, had enjoyed the game immensely. It was probably his weariness, after the strenuous day he had put in, which made him feel it was no longer worth the candle. At all events, this was no time to give it up, at the very moment when it promised to become more exciting than ever.

Allan had put down his soup spoon regretfully when the call came in. Now, still more regretfully, he rang again for the waiter, said he had unexpectedly been called out, and that he would order some kind of a light meal and sign the check on his return. Crewe had said nothing about dinner, but this did not strike Allan as strange; after all, their *entente cordiale,* such as it was, had suffered a considerable setback at the gate and, moreover, the Crewes could not be expected to invite a heterogeneous group to dine, or single out one of its members for special hospitality. It seemed to Allan somewhat stranger that the meeting should be taking place at Crewe's house, but the man could not very well give the reasons for this over the telephone, considering all the factors involved. The hospital in question must be the one at the prison, where there could hardly be adequate facilities for conferences; and Crewe had said, the night before, that this was not far from his house. That would make the meeting place still more logical; and if the "hospital" was as hard to locate as the Crewes' residence, Allan felt it was all to the good that he did not have to search for it.

By keeping his mind on his route, rather than by dwelling on the surprise Crewe had sprung, Allan managed to find his way to the new development without any false turns, and was congratulating himself on not having lost his way again when he reached the region of unfinished construction, blocked streets, scanty lighting, and almost deserted sidewalks. He was rounding next to the last corner, as he recalled it, before reaching his destination, when an isolated pedestrian, who had been strolling quietly along, suddenly swung about and darted in front of the station wagon. With a terrible sense of shock, Allan shouted a warning, which he feared would come too late, and slammed on the brakes. As the station wagon jerked to a stop, he flung open the door and jumped out.

The jaywalker had leaped swiftly to safety and was now voicing his threatening rage. Too late, Allan realized that the man whom he had thought was his victim was now his assailant. Then came quick horrible pain and the merciful release of unconsciousness.

Part Four ❧ LEONOR

15.

ALLAN TRIED TO shift his position and found that it hurt to do so. He could
not imagine why. Although he had habitually been such a sound sleeper,
on the exceptional nights when he had been restless, he had thrashed about
in his bed without the least physical discomfort. Now even the effort to
turn slightly gave him acute pain. This puzzled and annoyed him, but he
did not feel it was worth while to analyze the reason for the change. He
drifted off to sleep again.

When he next made a similar attempt, with similar results, he was even
more puzzled and annoyed and, this time, he tried to shake off his drowsiness, only to wonder if he were asleep after all and experiencing some kind
of a very peculiar dream. The bed on which he was lying seemed very high,
very hard and very narrow, not in the least like his low, soft, wide bed at
the Wellington. No wonder he could not turn over easily; in the first place
there was no room to do so and in the second place, the mattress on which
he was lying had no resiliency. It was like the mattress on a hospital bed,
and he had always regarded hospital beds—with which his acquaintance
was fortunately limited—as having been designed wholly for the convenience of doctors and nurses and as representing minor instruments of torture
for patients.

He decided to try turning his head; this, at least, he should be able to do
without discomfort. But he was disappointed; it did not hurt as much as it
did to turn his body—or rather, to attempt the latter—but, even so, it gave
him a very unpleasant sensation. Increasingly baffled and displeased, he
dragged his eyes partly open; they rested on an object as typical of hospitals
as the bed: a small metal table, gleaming with white paint, covered with a
spotless cloth and charged with medicinal supplies. He could not be dreaming; tables like that existed only in such institutions as hospitals. For some
inexplicable reason, he must be in one. He still felt too sleepy to figure out
why. But he sniffed, and the unmistakable odor of disinfectants and anes-
thetics assailed his nostrils. Surer than ever that he had not guessed wrong,
he went back to sleep.

He had no idea how many hours elapsed before he made his third attempt at definite movement and rational wakefulness, but this time he was
more successful. Meanwhile, he had been vaguely conscious, every now
and then, of white-clad forms, subdued voices, and certain ministrations

which seemed to be connected with both; but none of these had interested him to the point of paying them real attention. Now, instead of trying to turn either his body or his head, he hitched himself up slightly on his meager pillow and opened his eyes wide. His impressions, previously so confused, were at last completely clear: the clean gray walls, the clean bare floor, the complete absence of anything that might give the small, almost cell-like room any semblance of character or cheer were characteristic of hospitals all over the world. But where was this one? How and why had he landed in it? As suddenly as he asked himself these questions, he remembered the angry man whom he thought he had run down when he was on his way to the Crewes' and who had leaped out at him; then he remembered the horrible pain which had followed the swift and violent attack. At almost the same moment, he realized that someone was sitting beside his bed; and with even greater surprise, if this were possible, than his condition and his surroundings had aroused, he recognized Mrs. Harvey Wendell.

It could not possibly be anyone else. Her rather battered headgear, her flowered print dress, dark enough not to show the dirt, her "sensible" shoes, designed to ease aching feet through endless days of sight-seeing, her voluminous satchel, far too large to be designated as a handbag—all those might have belonged to any grimly determined tourist. But her face was stamped with a grimness and determination that were unique. No one else whom he had ever seen looked exactly like that and, with a terrible flash of intuition, he realized this was the way Charlotte would also look twenty years hence. Then he realized that Mrs. Wendell must have been watching him very closely, for he had hardly succeeded in shifting his position and opening his eyes when he heard her speaking to him.

"Well, so you've come to at last," she said. "And high time, too. It's just like I told my husband: if he didn't have the gumption to stop you from falling into the clutches of a gang of crooks, there'd be no telling what might happen to you."

"Could you try to tell me?" Allan inquired weakly.

"Sure I can. You were beaten to a pulp by some thieving thugs, who robbed you and left you for dead out yonder in the cornfield, if you get what I mean."

"Yes, I think I get what you mean," Allan replied, hitching himself up a little further in bed and finding, to his immense relief, that it did not hurt very much this time. He was beginning to find his voice, too. "Would you mind going on? I'm very much interested."

"Well, it seems that in this neck of the woods, whoever finds a man that's been beat up and left for dead, same as you were, telephones some sort of a first aid station. I couldn't tell you what it's called any more than I could tell you how this man does the telephoning—I mean the one that finds the man that's been beat up, not him. Where we come from, murder's been done for less than what you've got to put up with if you try to telephone."

With increasing relief, Allan found that it did not hurt to smile. "I think I understand what you mean, Mrs. Wendell," he said. "That is, about the telephone. Now I'd like to know what happened after this particular call did get through."

"Well, after they've got such a call through, heaven help them, they try to find out who the man is—I mean the one that's been beat up—and if they can't, they take him to some other place and try again."

"I see. That is, I think I do. And I gather that, sooner or later, somebody must have found out who I was, because otherwise—"

"Otherwise, I wouldn't be here. Of course not. They finally found out who you were and it was in all the papers. So Charlotte gave up that fine educational trip she was going to take, seeing those six different countries and having a grand time. Instead, she took the first plane she could get that came direct to Madrid."

"Charlotte's in Madrid!"

"That's what I said, isn't it? And Harvey, he got it in his head it would be a good plan if I came along with her. Not that I ever hankered after seeing Spain or any other place out of God's own country."

The door of the cell-like room opened noiselessly and a nun, dressed in a white habit, entered and, after looking reproachfully at Mrs. Wendell, turned anxiously to Allan and felt his pulse. "You are not well enough to have visitors, *Señor* Lambert," she said quietly but with unmistakable firmness. "It is entirely contrary to your physician's orders. The Chief of Police, the Foreign Minister, the American Ambassador, all have been turned away. I have told this lady so. But as it appears she is the mother of your *novia*—"

"Of my what?"

"Of your *novia*," the nun repeated. "She has naturally shared the latter's anxiety for your welfare. So she was finally permitted to come to your room after having promised your friend, *Señor* Brooks, who has been good enough to act as interpreter, that she would let us know as soon as you showed signs of consciousness. I regret that she did not do this, that I knew you had roused only because I heard voices. She must leave at once."

"I really don't think she's done me any harm, Sister. But I'm afraid she's given you a false impression which, perhaps, we'd better correct immediately. I'm not engaged to be married. I haven't any *novia*."

"In that case, she has deceived us. I repeat, she must leave at once."

"But I'm very interested in what she's trying to tell me," protested Allan, who felt his strength returning by leaps and bounds. "You see, I haven't the faintest idea—"

"You will be told, by the proper authorities, everything that it is necessary or advisable for you to know at present. Not by this *señora*."

Mrs. Wendell could not understand a word the nun was saying, but there was no mistaking the implacability of the latter's attitude. She was slender, but the visitor guessed, and rightly, that she was quite capable of forcibly ejecting an intruder if she thought such a course was indicated for the good of her patient. With obvious resentment, Mrs. Wendell rose.

"I guess I'd better be going. I can tell when I'm not wanted around, just as easy as the next person," she said acidly. "Charlotte will be coming, too. She's sorry you didn't show more horse sense. She intends to give you a piece of her mind."

"Perhaps that can wait. Give her my regards and tell her I'm in good hands and that I'm beginning to feel fine. But it seems I'm not expected to have company."

"We'll see about that."

The same grim determination that was stamped on Mrs. Wendell's face sounded in her voice. But the nun, though less grim, was equally determined. She conducted the visitor out of the room and down the corridor and saw her into the elevator. Then she returned, closed the door and placed a thermometer in Allan's mouth.

"Since this North American lady is not the mother of your *novia*, since, indeed, you do not have a *novia*, I think it is better that your next visitor should be Se*ñor* Brooks," she said, after having rendered her patient temporarily incapable of speech. "And if you have not gone back to sleep when your doctor makes his evening rounds, you may ask him how soon you may receive this young gentleman, who has made a very favorable impression on all of us and who will doubtless give you details about everything you wish to know." She did not add that the impression made by Mrs. Wendell was considerably less favorable, but Allan had no difficulty in realizing that this was what she meant to imply. "Meanwhile, I may tell you that you have been in a state of prolonged unconsciousness following an accident and that you had no documents of any kind on your person which would give a clue to your identity. However, through the mercy of God, you *were* eventually identified and brought here to us." She removed the thermometer from his mouth and surveyed it with apparent satisfaction, though, true to the precepts of professional reticence, she made no comment on her reading. "I am happy to tell you that everything now points to your gradual recovery," she said. "Though, at first, we were greatly concerned about you, and with reason. Nor is it advisable for you to talk any more today. You should rest quietly until I bring you some nourishment, which I believe you should now be able to take quite easily by mouth."

"Won't you answer just one question before you go, Sister? Then I promise I won't ask any more."

"Very well. What is the question?"

"I think if it had been *Señor* Brooks who identified me, or the friends I was about to visit when the accident occurred, and who have evidently not been among the persons who wished to see me here, I would have been taken to the British-American Hospital. And this is obviously a Spanish hospital. Would you mind telling me the name of the person who did identify me?"

The nun smoothed the sheet, already quite unrumpled, which was folded neatly over the bedspread, and poured a little water in a glass from the carafe on the bedside table. Then she handed Allan a small capsule and waited until he had obediently swallowed it before she answered. "I thought that would be the question," she said at last. "And I am not sure that I have the lady's name correctly. But, if I am not mistaken, she gave it as Leonor de Silva."

16.

THOUGH HE DID GO to sleep again almost as soon as the nun had fed him, Allan waked before she or anyone else came back to his room and gave considerable thought to the complex situation in which he seemed to be involved. Eventually, she returned, accompanied by a tall spare man, who did not need the stethoscope which hung from his neck to label him as a physician. After saying briefly and gravely that he had been relieved to learn that *Señor* Lambert had, at last, regained consciousness, he proceeded to make a thorough examination, in the course of which he asked no questions of Allan and only two or three of the nun. Then, still very gravely, he addressed himself to his patient.

"I must tell you that you have had a severe concussion of the brain," he said. "Therefore, you should not try to force yourself to think."

"You can't blame me for wanting to unravel the mystery that's responsible for my being here, in this condition."

"No. I can well understand the temptation, under the circumstances. But I will repeat my word of warning. You need complete quiet for some time to come. I'm not speaking of your bruised body. By some miracle you have no broken bones and you are young and strong. It will do you no harm to begin moving about in your bed—in fact, your muscles will be the better for such use as you can give them without pain and, later on, we will also see what mild massage can do for you. But the condition of your head—that is what indicates caution."

"My head really feels fine, Señor Doctor, and I'd have a much quieter mind if I weren't trying to puzzle so many things out."

"Is there some one person who might help you to do this?"

"Yes, my friend, Douglas Brooks—the man that Sister says has made such a good impression here."

"Very well. You may see this friend, Douglas Brooks, for a short time tomorrow afternoon. No one else. Above all, not the lady that Sister Dorotea found ensconced here. And I will see to it that you do not spend the night in puzzlement."

He took a hypodermic needle, which she was already holding in readiness, from the nun and pricked Allan's arm with it, so skillfully that the latter hardly felt the puncture. The doctor was quite right; his patient did not spend the night in puzzlement, but in profound slumber. The next morning, he was still in a state of untroubled lassitude, which permitted him to doze peacefully off and on. During his periods of wakefulness, he experimented with the twisting and turning which, only the day before, had proved so painful and found that he could move with increasing ease; also, that he was quite inordinately hungry. By the time Douglas Brooks was admitted, he had managed to secure a second pillow and, propped up with this, had just made away with a large bowl of soup and a mold of *flan*.

"Hi there!" he said cheerfully, holding out a hand, which, now that he noticed it, looked preternaturally white and thin. "Sit down and tell me the news as fast as you can. I want to hear it before you get thrown out on your ear."

"I'll do my best, but there's quite a long tale to unfold, you know. Do you want me to begin at the beginning and go on as far as I can, or do you want me just to hit a few high spots?"

Allan considered for a minute. "I think it'll probably be more intelligible if you begin at the beginning," he said. "I'll be annoyed if you can't finish, but at least I'll have something to mull over until you get back, unless my doctor sees to it that I don't, as he did last night. I hope he won't. After all, I've apparently been unconscious quite a long time. I don't want to remain in that state forever and I can't see why he's so set on having me do no thinking."

"I can," Douglas retorted. "And so can plenty of other people. What's more, so could you, if you really had your wits about you. The fact that you can't shows that you haven't."

"All right, all right. Let's get going."

"Well, last Friday—"

"How's that again?"

"Last Friday, your solitary supper at the suite into which you'd just moved, at the Wellington, was interrupted by a telephone call. Correct?"

"Correct."

"You rang for the waiter and told him you'd been unexpectedly called out, but that you'd order another snack when you returned. He hadn't heard from you when it was time for him to go off duty. What's more, you hadn't signed the check for the supper you ordered in the first place, so he asked the maître d'hôtel what he ought to do. The maître d'hôtel told him not to worry about the check, but the next morning, when you hadn't ordered any breakfast, either, and your bed hadn't been slept in, the waiter and the chambermaid put their heads together and decided it was time to inform the *gobernanta* about your unexplained absence."

"I see."

"I'm not sure I can follow the sequence of events exactly. But I gather the *gobernanta* seemed to think she knew where you might have gone—or rather, where you might have started to go. So she tried to reach your prospective host of the previous evening by telephone and couldn't get any answer. Then she went to his house and it was empty—the only person on the place was a deaf gardener, who was acting as caretaker. The other servants had been given the week end off. Shall I digress here and say a little more about the prospective host?"

"No, go on about the *gobernanta*."

"Well, she started scouring the first aid stations. There are about ten, all told, in the city limits, and several more in the suburbs. It's a normal part of their routine to receive unconscious persons, drunks and epileptics mostly, but sometimes victims of assault, too—after all, there's no place in the world free from occasional criminal attacks. As a matter of fact, Spanish cities are freer from them than those of most other countries, because the *sereños* supplement police supervision. It was a *sereño* who found you and telephoned for an ambulance. He was terribly upset—still is—over the assault. He says it's the first one that's ever occurred in his district and I believe him."

"Oh, yes. A *sereño* would, of course, enter the picture. I'd forgotten about them. But now I remember how I used to admire them in Málaga when I was a boy—their blue cloaks, and huge staves, and jangling keys. . . ."

For a few moments Allan seemed absorbed in his recollection of the picturesque night watchmen who, during the Middle Ages, patrolled the unlit city streets of Spain and whose successors still perform a similar task. Douglas did not break in on the nostalgic reverie; he felt, and rightly, that Allan, eager as he was for news, was still too weak to absorb it quickly. But presently, the invalid spoke again.

"I assume you have rewarded my *sereño* suitably, but when I'm up and about, I'd like to have a talk with him and give him something myself. I know those trusty fellows don't get very large salaries from the government, or very big tips, either, from the householders who've forgotten or neglected to take their keys with them when they go out and depend on the *sereños* to unlock doors for them. I probably *would* have died if this one hadn't come along."

"Probably. And you're quite right in believing he's been suitably rewarded. Also, in believing that he'd be very pleased if you thanked him personally and that he could use a little extra money."

"Good! Now, as you were about to say when I began to reminisce—"

"As I was about to say, usually the people taken to these *Casas de Socorro*, as they're called, come to fairly quickly, or have something on their persons which identifies them, so that relatives or friends can be notified and come to get them. There'd been no means of identifying you, as I believe you already know, so the *gobernanta* had to try several *Casas de Socorro* before she got a description of anyone who sounded in the least like you. Then she learned that a well-dressed man, apparently in his early thirties, who didn't have a cent of money or a single document in his pockets and who didn't look like a Spaniard, had been found badly beaten in a remote suburb. Evidently, he'd been left there for dead. However, when the ambulance got him to the *Casa de Socorro*, he was still breathing, though unconscious, and, later that same day, he'd been removed to the Provincial Hospital, which is better equipped for the treatment of such cases. She went there at once and identified you, but she thought you needed more individual care than you were getting and that you needed it pretty damn quick. That's why she took the responsibility of having you moved to one of the best private clinics in Madrid, without stopping to get in touch with the American Embassy first. A mighty good thing she did, too, since that's closed over the week end. I can tell you it was touch and go with you for two or three days. And you'd been so damned standoffish that nobody except me—"

"I know, I know. But I had my own reasons."

"Like hell you did. I'll say in passing, I never heard of any worse ones. When the *gobernanta* telephoned the Embassy on Monday, she got more or less of a brushoff—they'd look into the matter, they'd see what could be done, etcetera etcetera. But, since this unconscious man she was running on about didn't have any money on him, how was he going to pay his hospital bills? Since he didn't even have a passport, how could she be sure he was an American citizen? You know there's a little book of rules that tells just exactly what a consul is and isn't supposed to do, right down to the number of cocktails he's allowed to quaff at an official party, and she got hold of one of those characters who creep into our Foreign Service every once in a while and who regard this book as their Bible. She told him you had a suite at the Wellington, that you'd cashed traveler's checks there and that the cashier had taken the number of your passport, which, of course, the management had, too; but she still wasn't getting anywhere fast enough to suit her when the doorman at the Wellington came to the rescue. He'd seen you getting into a Thunderbird with diplomatic license plates and heard you and the friend who came to get you say something about going to Avila for the day. This character at the Embassy knew I had a Thunderbird and that I'd been to Avila, to look after the details when a poor old American tourist died there, so he figured I might be the friend in question; also, that I'd be just the one, with my past experience, to look after a beat-up derelict who was in danger of dying. And that's where I entered this lurid picture. He turned the troublesome *gobernanta* over to me and presto! *todo se ha arreglado!*"

Douglas glanced at his watch. "I'm likely to get thrown out at any moment," he warned, "so you'd better tell me what you want to know next."

"I want to know when and how Mrs. Wendell and her daughter entered this lurid picture."

Douglas laughed. "Well, naturally, there's no keeping such a windfall for the press as this one out of the public prints. All the Spanish papers gave it full play and, of course, the American papers did, too, so the next thing I knew, here were the Wendells hot on my trail. By the way, congratulations! You hadn't told me you were engaged to be married."

"I'm not. Like the reports of Mark Twain's death, the reports of my engagement have been greatly exaggerated. I don't quite know who's responsible for this exaggeration and I understand Mrs. Wendell isn't exactly *persona grata* at the hospital, so I'm afraid I won't have a chance to ask her. I'd prefer to discuss this rather delicate question with Charlotte anyhow, as soon as I'm allowed to see her."

"I'll try to do some missionary work in the meantime. Remember telling me some American girl would be sure to turn up that I'd feel I ought to take dancing? Well, here she is, made to order, in Charlotte! I'll grant you the mother is rather on the grim side, but the daughter wouldn't be bad at all, if she could get over stressing the fact that life is real, life is earnest, and relax a little bit. Now I think of it, I ought to have realized you weren't engaged, that is, not too irrevocably, because this imaginary American girl of yours was needed to make up a foursome in which a Spanish girl was involved. Correct again?"

"Correct again. Now let's go back to the people I was on my way to see when I had my accident."

"I hoped we'd have time for those. Anthony Crewe is the boss con man, the brains behind this swindle you fell for."

"Incorrect this time. I didn't fall for it. I knew it was a swindle. But I was bored and I thought it might be fun to look into it."

"It must have been great fun getting slugged the way you did. Well anyway, as I was saying when you so rudely interrupted me, Anthony Crewe is a crook who did time in the United States for mail fraud. He was sentenced to a year and a day at the correctional institution at Texarkana, but this was commuted to four months of actual service and eight months as a parolee. For the next few years, he wandered around Europe, living chiefly on his wits—living high, wide and handsome most of the time. Finally, he decided to settle in Spain, as providing the most likely source of revenue. Wealthy but inexperienced American tourists from the hinterland have been his principal source of income, and with the tremendous increase in the number of these coming to Spain, it's been a happy hunting ground for him. The authorities—Spanish and American both—have been watching him for some time, but they couldn't actually pin anything on him up to now. There's no criminal action connected with helping innocents abroad, who have no knowledge of foreign languages and want to have a good time. As a matter of fact, I think lots of the people he's fleeced have been very grateful to him—as grateful as he's been to them."

"I take it all this was before he decided to try sending out letters that purported to come from a Spanish prisoner."

"Exactly. That was new. I mean, new for him. Of course, actually the gag is as old as the hills."

"And how did you find out that was what he'd done? I never mentioned it the day we went to Avila."

"I found out from our friend the *gobernanta,* who seems to be very well informed about the Crewes. And I'll hand it to Anthony. He must be about as smart as they come. But I think we have to give Ethel credit for figuring out how neatly the Spanish prisoner would—or at least might—fit into their pattern."

"Ethel!"

"Yes, of course. Undoubtedly, she's Anthony's finger man. In that case, she's kept a close watch out for prospective suckers for a long while. Then, after she thought she'd discovered some—or one—she'd take the same ship or plane with them—him, her. It's surprising how few mistakes she seems to have made. But she made one when she suggested that her husband should send you that Spanish Prisoner letter. You see, she couldn't have heard about your Uncle Nathan's legacy—she must have thought you were a struggling college professor. For once, she wasn't fishing after someone who was already filthy rich—that source of supply might have been temporarily depleted. So she would have been following the time-honored pattern of having letters sent to men of moderate means, living in the smaller cities;

men with some sort of sound business or professional connection, but without much of a backlog. The prospect of a substantial sum of easy money looks pretty good to quite a few men of that sort. You'd be surprised how many have fallen for that Spanish Prisoner gag. Why, I could tell you—"

"I'd like to hear—another day. But I know we're talking against time now."

"Well, when you answered the Prisoner letter and Anthony wrote Ethel airmail, telling her that you had, she thought everything was in the bag. You couldn't have made things easier for her, to begin with. You had obligingly stated what ship you were taking and where you were disembarking and she took immediate steps to do the same and to make herself agreeable to you. I bet you were on pretty good terms with her by the time you reached La Coruña. Well, you needn't look so sheepish. We won't go into that. But then you got on good terms with her husband by inviting this precious pair to come to Madrid in your station wagon."

"Hold everything for a minute! You haven't told me what's become of the station wagon!"

"It's disappeared completely. Of course, the police are looking for it. But, right now, let's go on with the Crewes before Sister Dorotea comes back. You must have begun unsteadying their apple cart when Anthony came to see you—as I believe he may have told you himself later, he didn't think you'd make any difficulties, provided you came to Spain at all. But, evidently, you went on making more and more, until the apple cart was really upset. If you'd forked over fifteen thousand—I believe that's the initial sum usually featured in these Prisoner letters—I think you might have got off easy. Since you didn't, and Crewe was at the point where he really had to have some money, because his high, wide and handsome way of living had got out of bounds, he had to put the heat on somehow. You know better than I do what he did next."

Allan broke in. "That's when I told him I had to meet someone—if not the Prisoner, then his doctor or priest—who could vouch for his story."

"Well then, I suppose he had only one card to play: that is, to tell you all the people you'd asked to have corroborate his story were at his house and next see that you never got there."

The door opened and Sister Dorotea came into the room, as usual, moving noiselessly. She glanced at her patient and smiled. Then she smiled at his visitor. But both men knew that these smiles were signals of dismissal.

"Just ten minutes more! Please, Sister!"

"I am very sorry."

"Well, just five!"

"Well, five. But in five minutes I shall return and see that you are quiet for the night."

"This time, I've two questions to ask before I can be quiet."

"Then ask them quickly."

She left the room, closing the door after her as silently as she had opened it. In his excitement, Allan sat almost bolt upright, but a bad twinge warned him that however promising his prospects of recovery, he must not take chances with it yet.

"Where are the Crewes now?"

"I think they're safely out of Spain and lying low wherever they are. They must have crossed the border in someone else's car, otherwise the customs officials would have a record of it, or else they could have taken a train— they wouldn't have had to give their names when they bought train tickets, as they would have if they had taken a plane. The police are making every effort to track them down, but what's to prove they had anything to do with the robbery and the slugging? As I said before, the station wagon has disappeared. You were found, completely unconscious, presumably dead, on the outskirts of a suburb, north of Madrid, nowhere near the Crewes' house. They made their getaway, well supplied with funds."

"But you said they were practically down and out and Crewe admitted the same thing to me himself. What could he get out of the robbery? I didn't have fifteen thousand dollars or anything like that on me in cash."

"You must have had a lot more than it's healthy to carry around loose. And what about traveler's checks?"

"Yes, I did have a folder of those, but they weren't countersigned. And a personal checkbook and a draft on my bank, made out to Crewe."

"The draft on your bank would be duck soup for Crewe. He could get that honored at any bank he chose, in the first Spanish city where he stopped for gas. That would mean crossing the frontier with more *pesetas* in his possession than he could legally take out of Spain, but it would be a calculated risk. He wouldn't be running nearly as great a chance of getting caught as he would have a few years ago when regulations were stricter."

"All right, that disposes of the draft. What about the checks?"

"Among his other talents, it seems Crewe's an expert forger. If you had one folder of traveler's checks on you, he wouldn't have had any trouble copying your signature, with those to go by. He'd have made them payable to himself, endorsed them and cashed them by showing his passport. With your nonchalance about funds, I don't suppose you kept a separate list of their numbers?"

"That's where you're wrong. The list is in my strongbox at the Wellington, but of course the key to that was among those which were stolen. However, if you'll write out a statement, authorizing the cashier to have the box broken open, and to let you take charge of its contents while he's substituting a new lock and key, I'll sign the authorization. I'm afraid we'd get into trouble with Sister Dorotea if I tried to write the whole thing."

"All right, I'll take the list of numbers to the manager of the American Express office here and you'll get five hundred dollars right away. Also right away, the manager will wire the company's Chief Special Agent in Paris, where there's a guy they call the Head of the Protective Department for all Europe. Once convinced of your good faith and mine, the Paris office will then probably authorize Madrid to supply the rest of the missing funds. This process would normally take only a few days—the trouble is we've lost so much time already. As to the personal checkbook, Crewe may have got away with using that, too, though this is less likely. We can start trying to stop payment on checks right now. However, I think you might as well make up your mind to the fact that you have kissed quite a sizable sum, as well as your station wagon, good-by."

"I'm almost childishly sorry about the station wagon. It's the first good automobile I ever owned and I'd formed a sort of personal attachment for it—I believe that lots of people get to feeling that way about their cars, almost the way they used to feel about their horses when these were their means of transportation. Fortunately, the actual loss of the money doesn't matter too much—there's plenty more where that came from. But the fact that the money was *stolen* and that the robbery was coupled with attempted murder matters a good deal. I wouldn't be human if I didn't want the Crewes brought to justice for that. And something else is bothering me: you seem to have been mighty well informed about my dealing with the Crewes by the *gobernanta*. Have you found out what the actual connection is between them and her?"

"No, I haven't. How much do you think that matters?"

The door had opened again and Sister Dorotea stood on the threshold, unsmiling this time. As he asked his question, Douglas rose and pushed back his chair.

"I think," Allan said, stretching out his hand, "that it probably matters more than anything else in the world."

17.

WHEN THE TALL SPARE physician asked Allan if his "puzzlement" had now been assuaged, the convalescent said impatiently that a few financial details had been satisfactorily discussed, but that the major points still remained obscure—especially one which only *Señora* de Silva could clarify. He demanded permission to see her immediately.

"The Chief of Police is eager for an interview with you. So far, I have been as firm with him as he has tried to be with me; but, possibly, he is the next person you should attempt to see."

"I tell you it is *Señora* de Silva I want."

"Yes, *Señor* Lambert, I heard you. I will undertake the delivery of your message. But I cannot encourage you to talk any more at present."

As before, the doctor took a quick and painless way of bringing an interview to an end; and, when several days passed without any sign of Leonor, Allan began to badger Sister Dorotea. Had she been insistent when she telephoned? Had she made it very clear the doctor felt it essential the patient should have peace of mind and that, to insure it, he must see this lady? Even a nun's resistance can be broken down sometimes, with sufficient provocation. The moment came when Sister Dorotea could suffer his importunities in silence no longer.

"*Señora* de Silva understands that you want to see her and that the doctor has given you permission to do so. Is it not possible that she is delaying her visit for reasons of her own?"

"For reasons of her own! What reasons?"

"How should I know, *Señor* Lambert?"

There seemed to be nothing more that could be accomplished vicariously and, as soon as Allan was allowed pen and paper, he wrote Leonor de Silva a little note, telling her he realized she had saved his life and begging her to let him express his gratitude to her in person. The note remained unanswered and Allan feared he had expressed himself inadequately or clumsily—after all, the Anglo-Saxon was no match for the Latin when it came to voicing his emotions, however sincere or even fervent these might be. He had practically given up hope of getting in direct touch with Leonor, much less with Milagrita, until he went back to the Wellington, when Sister Dorotea came to tell him that *Señora* de Silva was in the reception room, waiting to learn whether he would care to see her.

"Whether I'd care to see her! Tell her if she isn't here within two minutes I'll come and fetch her myself."

Fortunately, no such drastic action was necessary. Leonor followed close behind Sister Dorotea, accepted in a friendly clasp the hand which Allan stretched out to greet her and which had already begun to assume normal color and texture, and seated herself beside him with composure and grace. Then, before he could burst into a flood of comments and questions, she forestalled him by speaking with purposeful calmness.

"I know you must think it very strange that I have not been to see you before, or even written to you. But it has been very hard for me to decide what I ought to do."

"Surely you couldn't think it would do me any harm to come and see me, especially after you had the doctor's permission, and give me a chance to—"

"I am sorry to interrupt you, *Señor* Lambert, but—"

"Couldn't you call me Allan? After all, considering all the circumstances—"

"Very well, I will call you Allan. But it was exactly because you wanted a chance—because indeed you had a right to a chance—to question me, that I did not know just what I ought to do. I could not decide on how far it was right for me to answer you. Not on my own account, but on account of other persons involved."

"Certainly you don't need to consider the Crewes!"

"Not in the way you probably mean when you say 'consider.' Nevertheless, there were obligations."

"To Milagrita?"

Leonor smiled and, though the smile lacked radiance, there was something very appealing about it. "Yes, in a way to Milagrita, who asked to be remembered to you," she said. "But I was not thinking of her when I spoke. I really believe, Allan, that we shall get on better, or at any rate faster, if you do not interrupt me, either. The person most vitally involved in the sordid business which has had many sad aspects, and which came very close to having a tragic end, is my brother, Pablo."

"*Pablo!*"

"Yes, that really is his name. He has several others, but suppose we call him that for the present. It will be simpler. There were a few grains of truth in the Crewes' story, I am sorry to say."

"But surely—" Allan broke in impetuously and checked himself.

"Surely he is not in prison? No, he is in a sanitarium—one of those on the slopes of the Guadarrama that you passed when you went to Avila. He is a very sick man. And it has seemed as though he might be lying in the shadow of a prison, which, of course, has tended to make his condition still more serious."

"But how could he be lying in the shadow of a prison if—"

"My dear Allan, I shall have to repeat what I said before. We shall get on much better if you do not interrupt me—in fact, if we do not interrupt each other. As you have probably found out, a man can't be imprisoned in Spain for bankruptcy, unless his claim is fraudulent, and every effort is made to see if his relatives can't help him out. But Crewe threatened to say my brother's claim was fraudulent and none of his relatives could—or would—help him out. I felt I must see my brother and confer with him, before you and I could talk together with any real satisfaction. And it was not easy for me to arrange this visit. As you know, I have very little free time. I could make the trip to the Guadarrama only on a Sunday and in a private car, since the hours when the public buses run do not fit into my schedule. Of course, I do not have a car of my own, and I was reluctant, for many reasons, to ask the favor of one from a friend—in fact, there is only one friend from whom I was willing to do so and she was in France until very recently. Then the visiting hours at the sanitarium are also strictly limited. In fact, it was only yesterday that I was able to talk with my brother and secure his permission to let you see our family skeleton—or at least one of them. We've had several, I'm sorry to say."

"Doesn't every family? There, I shouldn't have interrupted!"

"That was not an interruption; it was a logical question, prompted by kindness. Yes, I suppose many families do—though I hope not all. The skeleton in our family—at least the one under consideration—does not rattle bones. He rattles dice."

"Yes?"

"Yes. Very disastrously! From generation to generation."

"I think I'm beginning to see a glimmer of light. Your brother—and perhaps your father and grandfather before him—spent more time than was wholesome at the card table."

"Exactly. And with less and less discrimination as to their gambling companions."

"And that is where Crewe entered the picture?"

"You are good at guessing. Ordinarily, as I think you know, he does not gamble with cards, but engages in other games of chance. However, when cards best suit his purpose, he uses those and he plays them extremely well."

"Would you mind telling me just what you mean by 'well'?"

"Adroitly. If he cheats, this hasn't been discovered."

"Adroit is a good word to describe him. He was adroit enough to get away with more than fifteen thousand dollars, and we haven't yet found any way of proving that he broke at least one commandment and tried to break another in the process. To put it more bluntly, robbery and murder, or attempted murder, are still regarded as major crimes and are punishable as such—if you can catch the perpetrator. I take it you believe he probably does cheat at cards."

"I didn't, for a long time. Cheating at cards—"

She stopped and looked at Allan. He realized that, this time, she would not mind if he finished her sentence for her.

"Yes, I know. Cheating at cards is just one of those things that isn't done, even by men who are habitual drunkards and habitual philanderers, or worse. So you didn't think—perhaps you still don't think—that he cheated your brother—only that he ruined him."

"I haven't any proof."

"Any more than I have!"

"Yes. Yes, that's just it. Since I've found out what happened to you, of course I haven't been able to keep from thinking that he cheated when he played cards with my brother. But that's still just supposition. What isn't supposition is what you've just said: he ruined Pablo financially. Pablo couldn't meet his debts of honor. Not even when he'd sold everything he owned."

"Including his library?"

"Yes, including his library. Of course, I saw the books and the bookplate you bought when we moved your things from your bedroom to your suite. The volume of Jovellanos wasn't among the rest that went out of the country and into the bookstores and the *Rastro*. That was a special favorite of Pablo's—he kept it until the very end. Then Crewe wrested that and some other old favorites away from him by saying he'd credit Pablo with a few thousand *pesetas* in exchange for them. By that time, my brother was desperate."

"I figured something of the sort had happened. At least, of course, I didn't know it had happened to your brother, but I felt sure it had happened to some unfortunate victim of foul play. Look, we must start getting that library together again—what hasn't gone out of this country. I'll have Douglas Brooks scour the bookstores. And there must be some way of getting things out of Crewe's house. It wasn't just the books there that had belonged to your brother, either, was it?"

"No, many other belongings of his had gone to the same place. Some of them very recently."

She sat silent for a minute, visualizing the lost treasures. Allan leaned over and took her hand. "We'll get them all back," he said. "I don't know anything about Spanish law, but I'll find out. It didn't take me long to find out about the Spanish prison system," he added with a grin.

"You are very, very kind. But we can't accept such favors."

"Not even from a man who owes his life to you?"

"I wish you wouldn't keep referring to that. I did only what anyone in my position would have done. Indeed, I have been reproaching myself bitterly, because I didn't warn you against Crewe the first time you mentioned his name to me. I certainly should have told you later on. I knew that whether or not he cheated at cards, he was still an evil man. And when he went to see you at the Wellington and you didn't hand over the money—"

"Yes?"

"Well, he came to see me directly afterwards. He told me that very same night about the Spanish Prisoner letter and said I must help him 'put the screws on.' I knew then that I ought to warn you. But I didn't."

"Well, after all, it wasn't your responsibility to warn me. I was nothing to you."

" 'Am I my brother's keeper?' " she quoted bitterly. "We are all our brother's keepers, Allan, in the biblical sense. And I should have remembered that, instead of thinking only of my own brother, in the physical sense. But we were so in debt to Crewe, I was frightened of what might happen if I told you about him. Not on account of myself. On account of Milagrita."

"Of course, I understand. And it's on account of Milagrita, as well as your brother, that we must get all these things back."

"Yes, if we can, legally, but not as a personal gift from you."

"All right, we'll do it legally."

Again Leonor sat silent for a moment and, this time, Allan made no effort to break in on her reverie. She had not withdrawn her hand from his, and he recognized this as a sign of increasing confidence and liking. Presently, she went on speaking with her fine eyes fixed steadily on him.

"My grandmother and my mother were both very rich," she said. "They were able to laugh off—and pay off—their husband's debts, when these gentlemen could not do so themselves; and there was no sense of shame or obligation involved because there was so much actual devotion. That makes a great difference, you know. Besides, there was plenty of money left for other things. You questioned me about different parts of Spain, that evening we went to dine at the little restaurant on the promenade of the *Calle* Velasquez. I know you thought I was trying to evade giving direct answers, and perhaps I was, though, on the other hand, it would really be hard for me to say to which part of Spain I primarily belong, except that, as you guessed, it is not Madrid. The great house on the Castellano was one of the first to be sold and that happened before I was born. But our family connections and our family estates are—or rather, were—almost everywhere else. I married rather late, for a Spanish girl. I had an idea, at one time, that I should like to be a nun. Of course, there is nothing unusual about that; many girls go through such a phase. My parents opposed the project, partly because they realized I did not have a true vocation, and partly because my only sister, who did have one, had already entered a cloistered order. My father and mother were devout, but they were reluctant to lose another daughter. So, to divert my mind, they sent me on a continual round of delightful visits to my relatives, here, there and everywhere. Now we have lost all those beautiful large estates—there is only one little place left, that belonged to my husband's family, which was not a wealthy one. This place is just a *finca* really, or, as we call it, a *dehesa*, not far from Avila. Pablo's wife did not bring him wealth—only complete devotion. In that respect, she was like my mother and my grandmother. She was willing to go without everything for his sake. And now she is dead. And we Spaniards have been through a civil war. This is not the time or place to talk about that, whose fault it was, how much suffering it caused, what its aftermath has been. But my husband was killed in it and after that happened something died in me, too, for when I did marry it was for love and he and I had been very happy together."

Allan pressed the fingers which still rested so confidently in his and Leonor returned their pressure.

"So, after a time, there were only four of us left, since I did not have any children, and Pablo and Modesta had only Milagrita—they had married late, too. And then, as I said, Modesta died and we were only three, and Pablo was already a sick man by that time. But you must not think of him merely as a spendthrift and a gambler. It is true that he was improvident, or rather, that he was impractical. But it was not until he was past middle age that he began to take chances. Up to then, his inherited vice had been dormant. By preference, he lived a very retired life for many years, almost a secluded one. He was deeply religious and he was a great student, I might almost say a great scholar."

"I should have guessed that from his books."

"And he and Modesta were sufficient unto themselves, as my husband and I had been. We had all four withdrawn too much for our own good, as far as our more distant relatives and our friends were concerned. When our time of need came, we were not as close to them as we should have been. Some did not realize that we were actually in want; others had lost everything themselves in the war. Still others thought we had only ourselves to blame for our misfortunes. Besides, it was natural that Pablo would want to do what he could for Milagrita, his only daughter; but he had never been taught how to earn money and he began to think, as all born gamblers do, that he could get it with cards. At first, he showed some discrimination about the company he started to keep, and he had what I believe is called beginner's luck. He won some very substantial sums and, of course, that encouraged him to believe that he could win still larger ones. So he grew more reckless, both about the stakes for which he played and the persons with whom he gambled. It was then that he met Crewe."

"And became indebted to him?"

"Not at first and not much for a long while. Then more and more. So, little by little, Pablo sold everything there was to sell—first the two big houses which were still left, one in the country and one in the city, and then everything in them—last of all, the library, which we had moved to my *dehesa*, where we lived after all the rest was gone. And still, that did not bring in enough to pay the debts, and he was so ill that he needed more care than I could give him and more expert medical attention than he could get from any country doctor. I could not earn money at the *dehesa*. But I thought there might be a place for me at one of the new hotels springing up so fast in Madrid, to accommodate all the Americans who are discovering Spain. So I came here to inquire and, very easily, I secured positions for us at the Wellington—mine first and later the one for Milagrita. Crewe did not get us the positions; I got them myself. But because we were under such obligations to him financially, he liked to give that impression, to humble us still further. We paid him each week part of what we earned, but of course that amounted to nothing by way of clearing the debt—it was just a drop in the bucket. So he had us watched to make sure we were not getting anything or doing anything about which we had not told him and which might be profitable for him."

"By the dapper little man who came to the restaurant?"

"Yes, of course. Crewe was very annoyed because we went to that simple little place. There are many more pretentious restaurants where he could have had a commission if rich Americans had been encouraged to patronize them. But that was not the worst. He was always saying that Milagrita could easily earn much more. And, of course, she could have."

Suddenly Leonor drew away her hand and covered her face. She made no sound, but Allan knew now that she had finished her story, at least as much of it as she could bring herself to tell; she was silently weeping. He felt choked himself and it would have been hard for him to say anything, even if he had thought that he should do so just then. But when Leonor took down her hands, and he saw that somehow she had managed to dry her tears before she did so, the words he wanted came to him.

"It may be a good idea for me to have a short talk with the dapper little man later on," he said. "You must tell me and my Spanish lawyer how to get in touch with him. He might even be quite useful to us as far as the Crewes are concerned. But let us dismiss him from our minds for the present. You said, a little while ago, that there were a few grains of truth in Crewe's story. I'll say there are more than that. There isn't any prisoner— at least not as far as we're concerned. There may be one later on, but if there is, it won't be your brother. And Pablo isn't without a relative in the world except a beautiful daughter. He's got a very wonderful sister. In fact, he has two sisters, and probably the one who's a nun is also wonderful, though I can't believe she's as wonderful as you are."

"Oh, but she is! Much, much more so! You'll see—"

"I'll be glad to see. I'll get to her convent and Pablo's sanitarium as soon as I can. But now that we've checked over Crewe's fabrications, let's talk about the part of the letter that was true—the part about the lovely girl who stood in need of rescue."

"Yes, that part was true."

"All right. Let's start from there. I'm more than pleased to assume the role of rescuer. But that will be only incidental. What I really want is to become a member of your family. I haven't one of my own and I'm much more alone in the world than you are. Would you consider accepting me as a nephew?"

"I'm not sure I understand."

"All right. I'll spell it out. I fell head over heels in love with Milagrita the first time I ever saw her. Have I your permission to ask her to marry me? And, in that general connection it might be helpful if you'd tell me her real name—and yours."

Part Five   THE LITTLE
MIRACLE

18.

THE GLOW OF EXHILARATION in which Leonor left Allan did not subside until late into the night. He was thankful that his physician no longer seemed to feel it necessary to induce profound slumber by artificial means; his wakefulness was one of such triumphant happiness that he wanted to prolong it. Leonor was willing that he should ask Milagrita to marry him— that is, if Pablo were also willing; and though she suggested that the impatient suitor would probably be more successful if he asked Pablo in person for permission to establish his courtship on an official basis, she did not think it would be long before Allan could hope to motor as far as the sanitarium, from what she had been told at the clinic about his progress. Meanwhile, she would prepare her brother for this visit and she would bring Milagrita to the clinic. Not the next morning. The Chief of Police had been kept waiting a long while, and Allan must see him next. But, after that, if the convalescent were not too tired . . .

When his excitement was at last submerged in delicious drowsiness, it was with the visualization of Pablo, Leonor and Milagrita all reinstated in the ancestral *dehesa*, where the library would be almost completely restocked and other apartments in a state of superb restoration. This joyous mental picture, of course, included Allan as a frequent and welcome visitor; he would motor buoyantly back and forth between Avila and Madrid in the station wagon, triumphantly recovered and again as good as new; there would be family conferences, in which he would share, about the rapidly approaching nuptials. Moreover, there would be blissful intervals when he and Milagrita would wander out into the garden—he took it for granted that a garden existed, though none had been mentioned—and he would make love to her in the moonlight. Surely, even in Spain, this must sometimes happen with full parental approval or, at least, with tacit parental assent. And then his former dream would come true: he and Milagrita would be riding off together, with no one else in sight or hearing, and she would be sitting beside him. What was more—and this he had not previously dreamed—they would then be on their honeymoon. It was really better that he had not dreamed this part before; it was all the easier to recognize it now as a reality.

The Crewes were so completely crowded out of this rosy vision, which was as bright when he waked the next morning as it had been the night

before, that it was actually with a sense of surprise that Allan learned the
Chief of Police was waiting to see him and that, as the doctor had now
lifted the ban on visitors—except for the Wendells!—Sister Dorotea thought
it would be not only civil but wise for *Señor* Lambert to receive this func-
tionary as promptly as possible. He proved to be a portly personage, whose
amplitude of figure, controlled by a superbly fitting uniform, added to the
stateliness of his presence rather than detracting from it. He carried himself with great dignity, and spoke with restrained courtesy, expressing his
deep regret that a welcome and distinguished visitor to Spain should have
met with the outrageous, not to say criminal, treatment to which Allan
had been subjected, instead of the unfailingly helpful and kindly treatment
to which he was entitled; but the *Jefe de Policía* did not pursue the subject
to unnecessary and tedious lengths. As soon as the first exchange of greetings was over and Allan had invited his caller to be seated, the latter extracted a small flat notebook from a hidden pocket and began to make
statements and ask questions.

"We have, of course, already conducted a routine investigation," he announced. "The fact is, as I believe *Señor* Brooks, your valued friend—and
ours—has already informed you, the Crewes had been under surveillance
for some time before this most regrettable incident. But they are uncannily
and diabolically clever. It has been impossible to *prove*, so far, that they
were guilty of the misdemeanors of which they were suspected. As long as
their probable guilt was confined to misdemeanors, though we were naturally disturbed, we were not roused to the same pitch of agitation, nor did
we feel impelled to take such immediate and drastic action as we do now
that their probable guilt points toward felony. Is this clear? Or do you have
difficulty in following me?"

"It's completely clear so far. There aren't any language difficulties and I
understand the simpler legal distinctions."

"Then I will proceed. Unfortunately, as your friend *Señor* Brooks has
also pointed out to you, there is nothing we have discovered, so far, to *prove*
that Crewe had anything to do with the robbery and attempted murder.
But their conduct is certainly very suspicious: he telephoned you, asking
you to come to his house to meet persons who do not exist, under circumstances which are also nonexistent; he and his wife hastily took their departure from this handsome new house, in which they were barely settled,
and, apparently, left Madrid in the dead of night, by car. I say 'apparently'
because the lamentable, though inevitable, delay in locating you and
identifying you makes it impossible for us to determine the exact time of
their departure; they had the advantage of three days' leeway before the
Madrid police could alert the provincial police and the border officials to be
on the lookout for them, or report to the F.B.I., asking for material helpful for

identification—a necessary step, since we were trying to cope with the case of American citizens. We have just now established the fact that the Crewes cashed your draft at the *Banco de Santander* in Gerona and that their car is in a garage there, where it was left, ostensibly, for repairs. As a matter of fact, it was in need of considerable attention, due, no doubt, to the reckless speed at which it had been driven. The garage is a reputable one, and its owner well known in the community. We have no reason to doubt the truth of his statement that, when he told Crewe he would need to put some time into working on it, he was assured that he could take all the time he needed, which, unfortunately, is also quite true."

Allan and the *Jefe* exchanged understanding glances, in which there was complete good will, mingled with a little wry amusement. "Crewe must have said he would keep in touch with the garage and find out when the car would be ready for use again," Allan observed.

"Oh, certainly! But he said it would be more practical for him to take the initiative about keeping in touch, as he would be moving from place to place and could not tell exactly when and where he could be reached. That adds another unfortunate truth to our list. He and his wife obviously moved across the frontier before the border officials had received their word of warning."

"By frontier, do you mean the French frontier?"

"Yes, *señor*. If they had intended to cross over into Portugal, they would have gone in exactly the opposite direction. The car would have been left at Badajoz, instead of Gerona."

"You don't think Andorra is a possibility?"

"Almost anything is a possibility. We are not overlooking that one. But Andorra is very small, and offers few opportunities or attractions for fugitives of the Crewes' type. I should think the French Riviera would suit them much better for many reasons. One is that, as soon as we feel perfectly sure it is the French frontier they have crossed, as a matter of courtesy, we will seek the co-operation of the American Embassy at Madrid, in demanding extradition of the probable criminals through the French Embassy in Madrid. Extradition is a procedure which is extremely involved and takes a long time. Meanwhile, the *Sûreté de Paris* and the International Police, generally known as the Interpol—the channel through which the police of different countries work with each other—will have been notified; but, though our man—and our lady—will undoubtedly be found and watched, they will not be arrested until all proper procedures are observed. And this waiting period may be indefinite."

"And you're not perfectly sure yet?"

"We are reasonably sure, from reliable information we have received, that a couple resembling the Crewes went by train from Gerona to Perpignan, just over the border in France, about a fortnight ago. I ventured to remind you that the time element is against us. From Perpignan the track becomes obscure. No one by the name of Crewe, or resembling them in person, has registered at any of the well-known hotels in any of the larger cities. But, of course, that was not to be expected. They would naturally falsify their passports and adopt some form of disguise. However, I have no doubt that the French police will discover these frauds."

"And, meanwhile, the matter is out of your hands?"

"Not entirely. We are by no means overlooking another possibility—a faint one: that Crewe did not actually commit the crime, that he merely instigated it. He may well have had confederates and these confederates may be Spaniards, but we are finding it especially difficult to track down persons who might have been criminally associated with the Crewes. Have you any suggestions?"

"I've been trying to figure that part out myself. I know who some of their victims have been and, naturally, you do, too. I've also seen a bearded man who spies for them; but whether he does anything worse than that, and whether or not he works independently or with a group, I don't know. So, as to criminal associates—"

"Well, for the moment, let us leave out the word 'criminal' and confine ourselves to the word 'associates'—beyond Marcos Estrada, the bearded man of whom you speak, with whom we have already been in touch and with whom we feel competent to deal. We have also been in touch with some card-playing companions of the Duke."

"The Duke! What Duke?"

"The Duke of San Ricardo—that is the title by which he is generally known, though he has a dozen others. I refer to the brother of the *Marquesa* de las Cinco Torres, the father of the *Condesa* de Campo Alegre."

"Oh, yes!" Allan said, blinking a little. Leonor had, indeed, disclosed the titles which the *Jefe* reeled off so casually before she left him the night before. But he had not accustomed himself to them yet. He was still thinking in terms of *Señora* de Silva, Pablo and Milagrita.

"As I was saying," continued the *Jefe,* "we have been in touch with some of the Duke's card-playing companions, both those with whom he gambled before he met Crewe and those with whom he gambled afterward. None of them seems to be subject to suspicion—in fact, the earlier ones are gentlemen of unimpeachable character. Of course, servants very often act as spies, and we are still hoping to get information from some of the Crewes' former employees who have disappeared and who have, so far, eluded us. The only one left on their place, as I believe you know, is a deaf old gardener—we have had him examined by physicians and he really is deaf; he cannot hear the questions we ask him. He is also illiterate, so it does no good to put these questions in writing. We have him under supervision and, no doubt, we shall get something out of him in time, one way or another; but whether or not he has anything of value to reveal remains to be seen. If he has, he will betray himself sooner or later. Meanwhile, I should be most appreciative if you would tell me if you have actually met any persons who were friends or who might have been friends of the Crewes."

"I've heard of two, but I did not meet either of them."

"And these were—"

"Ethel Crewe said she had a friend on the ship, in the tourist class. She told me she didn't know this friend was aboard until the passenger list was published, which was very tardily. Then she looked her up and found she was sick—at least, this is what Ethel claimed. Later, she went on to say that she had arranged to have an ambulance meet the *Tarragona* at Bilbao—the final port—and had notified the invalid's brother, whom the friend was going to visit there."

"But she never mentioned this friend's name?"

"No, never."

The *Jefe* had begun to make quick jottings in his slim notebook. "It will be a simple matter to find out whether an ambulance did meet the *Tarragona* at Bilbao and, if so, for whom it was intended," he said. "I wish we had known about this friend sooner—that is, if she really exists."

"I think she must. That is, I think there must have been someone in tourist whom Ethel Crewe knew and who was ill, or pretending to be ill, and that Ethel visited this person. The reason I think so is because, the day after I heard about her myself, the officers and stewards were talking about the kindness and solicitude of the *Señora* Crewe."

"And you heard about her yourself just when and how?"

"In the middle of the night, about thirty-six hours before we landed. I met Ethel Crewe, quite by chance, in the corridor, and she told me she had just returned from visiting this sick friend. I don't think she expected to be gone so late."

"No?"

"No. Because, just before that, I'd met her steward going to her room with hot chocolate. He wouldn't have taken it quite so soon if he hadn't thought she'd be ready for it. He served her with it every night. Ethel Crewe is very fond of chocolate—drinks it every chance she gets. The Crewes and I purposely stopped in Astorga, on our way to Madrid, so that she could sample its famous specialty. It was about the only place that she showed any enthusiasm for stopping—she couldn't conceal her impatience because I wanted to look at historic monuments in the other cities we went through, and she wasn't interested in the arcaded plaza and the old town hall of Astorga or even in the great clock whose hours are struck by two mechanical figures, representing a *Maragato* and a *Maragata*. I would have liked to find out something about the origin of these mysterious people—nobody seems to know what it is, though they still exist and I believe there's a theory they are descended from the Berbers. I had time to make a few inquiries, because Ethel didn't just sample the chocolate. She drank several cups. But, when she simply couldn't hold any more, she wanted to be on her way."

"I understand that by vocation you are a professor at a university, *señor*. I see you retain your scholarly tastes, even when you are involved in an adventure, and I shall be glad to help you continue your investigations about the *Maragatos* at some future time," the *Jefe* remarked, courteously but casually, as he looked up from his notebook. "Now, about the second friend?"

"Anthony came to La Coruña from Santiago de Compostela in this man's car. His own car was, allegedly, out of commission—perhaps this is chronic, in the light of what you tell me about the garage in Gerona—so he flew from Madrid to Santiago, and then borrowed a car in order to meet Ethel at the dock. The borrowed car wasn't big enough to hold all her baggage and, even if it could have taken this as far as Santiago, it still would have cost a fortune to transport it by air to Madrid. That's how I happened to invite the Crewes to go in my station wagon."

"You saw this friend's car?"

"Yes."

"You couldn't tell me either the color or the make?"

"It was black. It might have been either a Simca or an Opel."

"Then it *was* small?"

"Yes, according to American standards."

"You didn't notice the license number?"

"I didn't make a written note of it, if that's what you mean. As far as I knew, there wasn't any reason why I should have. We piled the baggage into my station wagon and the Crewes and I went to lunch at Lhardy's. Then we went back to the dock, where Crewe picked up his friend's car, and he and Ethel drove to Santiago in it. I did make a *mental* note of the license as we were weaving our way out of the city, but I don't remember it now. I never saw the car again after we left the outskirts of La Coruña. Crewe drove like a bat out of hell—excuse me, he went a lot faster than I would have, in heavy traffic, but that's not unusual over here. The Crewes checked in at the hotel before I did and made a reservation for me, but they weren't there when I arrived, because they returned the car and stayed for a short visit with their friend before they came back."

"And they didn't tell you anything at all about this friend? What his name was? Whether or not he lived in Santiago or was there just temporarily like themselves and, in either case, where this visit took place?"

"No, nothing at all. I'm afraid he may be harder to trace than the sick friend on the *Tarragona*."

The *Jefe* had resumed his jotting. "Not necessarily," he said eventually, looking up. "I don't need to tell you that a great many persons go to Santiago de Compostela on pilgrimages, or alleged pilgrimages, especially in summertime. It's quite within the range of possibility that this friend may live elsewhere and he may be hard to locate, but it is also possible that the information you have given me about these two unidentified friends might be helpful. Is there anything you feel you could add?"

Allan pondered for a moment. "Crewe seemed to be on very good terms with the customs officials and with the managers of the hotels where we stayed," he said. "But that doesn't mean anything, probably, except that he was well known and had found ways of making himself well liked. I understand he's really been very helpful to many innocents abroad, so he may have been of great service to the tourist trade. Besides, he has a very charming wife and he can be very pleasant himself when he's so disposed, even though he does show an ugly streak when he's put out."

"A very ugly streak, I should say. One that has apparently brought him, directly or indirectly, close to felony and murder." The *Jefe* smiled slightly, showing very white teeth. "I do not want to tire you by staying too long, unnecessarily," he said agreeably. "Shall I put away my notebook and take my leave?"

"I'm enjoying your call. You don't need to hurry away on my account. But if I've given you any sort of a lead, or leads, I suppose *you're* in a hurry to follow them up. There are just one or two other items I might mention—"

"I'm all attention, *señor*."

"There's an old man in the *Rastro* who sold me some books—books which had formerly belonged to the Duke of San Ricardo. He's a great admirer of this unfortunate man and very troubled about his downfall. He may know something about those who caused it—or, if he does not, he might be able to find out." Allan paused for a moment and then looked up, smiling, too. "And the Duke has a sister who's a cloistered nun. I believe there's an old saying to the effect that, if you want to know what's going on in the world, you should inquire at a convent. If all else fails, why not try Santa Ana's at Avila?"

"I thank you for the suggestion, *señor*," the *Jefe* said, rising and bowing. "I shall certainly follow it. And, possibly, before all else fails."

19.

ALLAN HAD SOME difficulty in persuading Sister Dorotea that the visit of the *Jefe*—a delightful man!—had not tired him in the least, and that he was quite equal to seeing more visitors the same day; in fact, he thought it was high time he was allowed to get up, put on a dressing gown and slippers, which had been sent over from the hotel in anticipation of his convalescence, and sit in an easy chair. After some hesitation, and a consultation with the doctor, which took place out of Allan's hearing, Sister Dorotea consented to the chair and the garments suitable to its use, on condition that her patient would not be out of bed for more than half an hour and that, afterward, he would take a long siesta. If he actually slept—and she would carefully note whether or not he did—and awoke refreshed, perhaps, just perhaps, he could sit up for another half hour in the late afternoon and have a visitor then. He wanted to have *two* visitors? Really, he was very unreasonable and precipitate, like most Americans! But the *Condesa* de Campo Alegre could not come alone, could she? Allan inquired. A highborn young girl like that? Certainly not! Well, then it should be obvious to Sister Dorotea that her aunt must come with her, and that meant two visitors.

In the end, he got his way. He was, to be sure, a little shaky when he tried to stand and walk; but he manipulated a wheel chair without difficulty and sat in it without apparent fatigue. Then he ate an enormous lunch and lapsed into profound slumber. Sister Dorotea was obliged to confess that she was very pleased with him and, after that, she permitted herself to be persuaded to telephone the *Marquesa*, on condition that Allan would not make the effort of standing to receive her. Seven o'clock was the time set for the visit and Allan, arrayed in a Sulka robe which had been one of his New York purchases, was installed beside the wide window which "gave" so pleasantly on the landscaped surroundings of the clinic, when Leonor and Milagrita arrived.

He had thought Milagrita beautiful from the first moment he laid eyes on her; and from the time that she had looked at him, on the little balcony above the *Calle* Velasquez, with such a clear and candid gaze of recognition and response, he had known that her beauty had a special meaning for him. Now, as she came toward him, he saw that a change had taken place in this, that the avowal of his love, even though this had been made vicariously, had freed her from the reserve which was instinctive in her case, until he had declared himself. Her love for him was no longer a "fountain sealed," but a wellspring of bounty. Her expression, her bearing, even her dress, bore witness to this happy release. She was not grave, she was smiling; she carried herself with less precision and more easy grace; and her dress, instead of being demure in color and cut, was a flowered muslin with a modest yet pleasing décolletage and short puffed sleeves. Her hair was no longer gathered into a knot at the back of her neck, but fell in soft waves over her shoulders and was bound by a rose-colored ribbon which ended in a small bow near the front of its central part. When she entered, she was carrying a large bouquet of pink carnations, a sheaf of magazines and a carved wooden figurine of Don Quixote, all of which she paused to place on his bedside table. Then she ran gladly to his side. While he had sat waiting for her to arrive at the clinic, it was with a sense of keen disappointment because his weakness would not permit him to rush forward to meet her and, also, because a rigid code of propriety, which was alien to him but natural to her, would prevent him from taking her in his arms then and there. But, as she put her slim white fingers into the hand he had stretched out toward her and raised them to his lips, he knew that no impetuous greeting, no passionate embrace, was necessary to strengthen the bond between them. It had been there from the beginning; it would endure to the end of time.

Leonor had already seated herself, smiling, in one of the stiff little chairs which Sister Dorotea had provided for the visitors, long before Milagrita quietly detached her hand from Allan's and took the other seat. Meanwhile, trustfulness and love streamed in such abundance from her touch, and from the dark eyes, shining down on him beneath their long lashes, that he found himself too much moved for any immediate speech beyond the tremulous voicing of her name. Neither she nor Leonor seemed to feel this was in the least strange; and, as Allan gradually recovered from his first overpowering emotion, Leonor spoke tranquilly, yet warmly.

"We can stay only a few minutes—not just on your account, Allan, for, of course, you must not get overtired, but on our own. I have not felt it wise that either Milagrita or I should give up our positions abruptly—indeed, I think it would be most unfair to the management of the Wellington, which has always treated us both with the greatest consideration. It is only the guests who have sometimes proved importunate."

"I know. Complaining about the plumbing and so on." He had regained his composure and found he could speak lightly, almost jestingly, because he was so happy. "I promise not to do that any more, no matter what fails to function, but confess that I'm not the only American to voice annoyance. What about the Wendells, for instance?"

"Oh, the Wendells have left the Wellington for the Ritz," Milagrita interposed archly. "They said this was because it was so much nearer the Prado, but I think there may have been other considerations. The garden, you know, is delightful for either lunching or dancing and, apparently, *Señorita* Carlota does not lack invitations for both. She has become quite a favorite at the American Embassy. And really, you'll hardly know her when you next see her, while the change in her mother is even greater. They have been visiting the best dressmakers—Eisa, Pertegaz, Rodríguez—with quite startling results."

"I can hardly wait to behold the transformation and my gratitude to my friend Douglas keeps increasing by leaps and bounds," Allan answered with even greater lightness than in speaking before. "But I can see that whatever the Wendells have done, you two shouldn't both leave the Wellington hastily. As a matter of fact, it doesn't bother me too much that the *Marquesa* should act the *gobernanta* for a little longer. No doubt, I'll be more comfortable myself with her in charge and have more opportunities for diversion." He met Milagrita's shining eyes and they both laughed a little. "Just the same," he went on more gravely, "you can't blame me for not being very happy about Milagrita's position, after what I've seen occur around that little stall of hers."

"Perhaps not. But you told me yourself that you thought she was very competent in dealing with unpleasant situations."

"I still feel so. But you'll admit that, since then, my viewpoint has become influenced by considerations more personal than they were at first." Again, there was an exchange of smiles before he went on. "No matter how competent she is, I don't relish the idea of having her competence put to the test."

"I understand that. But we have been spared supervision by Marcos Estrada lately."

"That's understandable, if he were spying for the Crewes. With their departure, that would cease to be a source of revenue to him. How much do you know about the man?"

"Only that he's connected with a private detective agency—not one of the best known, but presumably respectable, as such organizations go."

"The Chief of Police told me he knew Estrada and could 'deal' with him, so perhaps we can forget about him for a while, since he's ceased to bother you."

"I agree with you. But I've told the manager of the Wellington that, for family reasons, it may be necessary for Milagrita to resign her position, as soon as we can find a satisfactory substitute for her. I have indicated that it now looks as if my brother's health, over which we have felt so much concern, might permit him, after all, to return to my *dehesa*. That is what you wished me to say, isn't it?"

"Exactly."

"And, in that case, of course he would wish to have his daughter with him."

"Of course. I hope the manager understands how logical this all is."

"I believe he does. I believe there will be no complications there. Naturally, we should not take too much for granted. But, fortunately, Milagrita thought of a schoolmate whose family, like so many in Spain, has undergone financial reverses—a girl a little older than she is, who married very young and whose husband has died, leaving her childless. Milagrita went to see this young lady, and found she would be receptive to the idea of taking over the newspaper and gift stall at the hotel. She is there now, for the period of our visit with you, and she is to return for a few hours every day this next week. Part of this time Milagrita must remain with her, helping her to get adjusted. But part of the time Milagrita will also be free for other diversions. It is agreed that Milagrita may resign in her friend's favor if, at the end of a fortnight, the latter has given satisfaction and is satisfied herself."

"A fortnight! That seems an awfully long time."

"Not really, Allan. We can see that you are getting well fast. But it will still be several days before you can leave the clinic, and then several more before you can stand the trip to the sanitarium on the Guadarrama where my brother is now. Let us say that will use up a week altogether. Meanwhile, I will prepare my brother for your visit."

"And, meanwhile, Milagrita and I can't be formally engaged!"

"No. You cannot give her a bracelet yet. But, after all, you could not select that until you are out of the hospital in any case." Leonor noticed Allan's slightly bewildered expression and added, "Have you forgotten that, in Spain, a girl receives a bracelet instead of a ring as her first gift from her fiancé?"

"I had, if I ever knew it. But that doesn't prevent him from giving her a ring, too, does it, if he happens to be a benighted American and would like to do it?"

"Certainly not—later on. And, unless I'm completely deceived, you and Milagrita have reached a very thorough mutual understanding without any formal engagement or the presents usually associated with it, whether in Spain or in the United States."

"That's so, isn't it, *querida*?" Allan asked, turning toward Milagrita. This much of an endearment he thought he could venture, without risking a reproof. The immediate answer he received more than confirmed this impression.

"Indeed yes, *querido*."

Leonor rose. "Very well. We will say that you two have arrived at an understanding, which might even be called an *in*formal engagement. I shall try to see that neither of you finds conditions this next week irksome. . . . Now, I will go and tell Sister Dorotea that we are leaving, so she can see that you get safely back to bed and that you do not delay doing so. You have had quite enough company for one day. You should rest."

She could, of course, have rung for Sister Dorotea, as they were all quite well aware; and it would not be more than a minute or so before the two came back together, in any case. But this minute or two belonged to Allan and Milagrita. She rose and leaned over his chair, putting her arm around his shoulders and laying her cheek against his. He reached for both her hands and turned his head until their lips met.

20.

Two MORNINGS LATER, Allan was already installed in his chair by the window when the *Jefe* was again announced. The convalescent had been told that, this time, he might sit up an hour in the morning and another hour in the evening. He welcomed his guest cordially.

"I was just thinking of ringing for coffee. Won't you have a cup with me? And perhaps a cigarette?"

"Thank you. I should enjoy both. But I warn you I have some rather discouraging news for you and a few leading questions to ask."

"I'm in a pretty good mood. I think I can take the discouraging news. And I'll do my best to answer the leading questions."

"We have been in touch with Bilbao. It is quite true that an ambulance met the *Tarragona* there, in response to a radio request for one, signed by Ethel Crewe and addressed to a man by the name of Diego Rodríguez. It was needed for his sister, Marta Rodríguez, who had been a passenger in tourist class."

"I don't call that bad news."

"You may when I have finished. Marta Rodríguez is dead."

"Dead!"

"Yes. According to her brother, she had been for some months in the United States, ostensibly as a student. In fact, she was enrolled as such in a college in the southwestern part of your country. Ethel Crewe arranged for this enrollment and paid Marta's passage to and from Spain. Therefore, this plausible lady certainly knew that the Rodríguez girl was on the *Tarragona* long before your meeting in the corridor, which, if I understood you correctly, was only thirty-six hours prior to the time the ship docked. According to Diego, his sister had been ailing for some time and unable to pursue her studies satisfactorily. It seems she had a rather delicate digestion. But it was, apparently, only on the *Tarragona* that her condition became radically worse."

"My God, you're not suggesting that the poor girl was poisoned, are you?"

"I'm not suggesting—not yet, anyway, that she was *purposely* poisoned. But she certainly died because something she had eaten or drunk disagreed with her violently, though it may have been merely a bad case of ptomaine. The ship's surgeon, at first, laid her persistent nausea to severe seasickness. Then he became alarmed and sent for Mrs. Crewe—at night, as you said. But she had been to see Marta before that, on her own initiative, several times. I believe you were told that they were friends and I am sure that is what the ship's officers thought—I mean, that there were no strings attached to this friendship. But I am very much inclined to think they were associated in some way, that Marta Rodríguez was actually in Ethel Crewe's employ. On account of your immigration laws which, if you will permit me to say so, seem to me most unreasonable, of course Marta could not enter the United States as Mrs. Crewe's employee. Only two hundred and fifty Spaniards can legally emigrate there per annum, in comparison to five thousand Italians and heaven knows how many other Europeans who do not use up their quotas. We are at a loss to understand this discrimination. Even those few shepherds who get in because their services are badly needed, cannot take their wives, their minor children nor their aged parents with them or send for these dependents after they themselves have obtained good jobs; and in cases less urgent—as far as the United States is concerned—we have a saying that it is much easier for the wickedest man to get into heaven than for the most upright Spaniard to enter the land of the free and the home of the brave."

For a moment, the *Jefe's* indignation, which Allan, though no politician, could not deny seemed logical, diverted him from his main theme. The *Jefe* took a sip of coffee and lighted a fresh cigarette. Then he went on again.

"With our quota used up fifteen years in advance, it is inevitable that some 'students' should have an ulterior purpose in going to American institutions of learning and manage to have what I believe you would call some 'bootleg' occupations on the side. Of course, they are careful to accept no pay for this—at least, until their return to Spain. But Diego Rodríguez seems to feel very keenly that the Crewes are his sister's debtors, and that since he and his family are in very moderate circumstances, the delay in getting this money and the possibility that they will never get it all are heavy blows to them, in addition to her death."

"I will see that Rodríguez gets whatever money he feels was due his sister when and if we find out what she did to earn it. I take it he didn't mention the nature of her services."

"Only in a very vague and hesitant way. And that brings me to the first of my questions: When you met Ethel Crewe in the corridor that night was she carrying anything? A handbag large enough to contain documents, for instance?"

"Now that you speak of it, I believe she was. She had changed from her evening dress, which was very elaborate, into a simple white sports dress." As he spoke, the vision of the beautiful gold-spangled tulle, tossed over a chair in Ethel's cabin, was vividly re-created, and a feeling of mingled shame and relief swept over Allan. Ethel *had* meant to meet him. It was only because she had been unexpectedly summoned to the tourist class that she had not done so. She had not deliberately been either fickle or virtuous. And, if the assignation had actually taken place, how would he ever have been able to accept Milagrita's trustful and unsullied love almost immediately thereafter? His Puritan conscience told him that it would have been nearly, if not quite, impossible. "I think," he went on slowly, realizing that the *Jefe* was somewhat surprised at being kept waiting so long for a direct answer, "that she had also changed her handbag. She was carrying a small gold one, suitable to go with an evening dress, at dinnertime. And it seems to me, though I can't swear to it, that when I met her in the corridor she was carrying a bag of the so-called envelope type, made of white leather, and capacious enough to hold a few papers, though not large enough to look like a brief case."

"Then, if your memory is not playing you false, doesn't it seem probable to you that, when she so kindly visited her sick friend, she may have removed such papers which, had they been found in the friend's cabin, after her death, might have proved quite incriminating to them both?"

"In what way?"

"To Marta Rodríguez because they might have shown she wasn't spending all her time on the studies for which she allegedly went to the United States; and even more so to Ethel Crewe, because these papers might have proved that she was violating immigration laws, by having Marta work for her; and, worse yet, that this work was connected with fraudulent use of the mails?"

"Yes, now that you point all this out, of course, it makes sense to me. I don't know that it would have otherwise. I haven't had much experience with either adventure or crime heretofore."

"Permit me to say, *señor*, that I think you are making the acquaintance of both with considerable rapidity. Ethel Crewe probably realized, when she saw Marta that night, that the girl's condition was critical—indeed, she must have foreseen this when she was summoned. So she went equipped with a capacious handbag, in which she could remove all incriminating evidence of their association, without inviting suspicion. And, of course, she probably destroyed this evidence as soon as she reached her cabin."

"But, if she was expecting Marta to die—to put it baldly, if she had poisoned her or caused her to be poisoned—why didn't she take away the papers long before that?"

"Because she thought they still might be useful to her and her husband. She wouldn't want to destroy them except as a last resort. And she preferred to have Marta take them ashore, rather than to do so herself. If anyone got caught with them, she didn't intend to be that person. The customs officials would pay very little attention to a sick Spaniard returning with a meager amount of luggage, and no one was likely to search the Rodríguez' humble home. But it was quite possible that a hotel room, occupied by the Crewes, might be searched, or even that they might be detained at the customs, though they were, apparently, on such good terms there. As a matter of fact, I think your presence and evident friendliness may have been a great help to them, for, as you know, they have been under surveillance by the police for some time."

"Following that line of reasoning, Ethel must have expected that Marta would live to reach Bilbao—until that midnight summons was received."

"I think she did. I think that, if poison had been purposely administered, it would have been one of the kinds that work very slowly. Or else, Marta's digestion really was delicate, she really was only seasick at first, and was not poisoned until the voyage was about half over—then, presumably with something that takes a week, more or less, to do its deadly work, but which, for some reason unknown to me, took less time than that. I'm in the midst of conferring with physicians on the subject. It is quite likely we may still find that her illness and death were natural. But this would not alter the possibility that Ethel Crewe may have become alarmed over Marta's condition, and removed documents which might be valuable to us."

"Yes, that's true."

"And you grant it would be unfortunate, if such papers existed, that they should now be at the bottom of the Atlantic, since possession of them would help us to prove that the Crewes were operating illegally?"

"I'll grant that only too willingly."

"Let us cling to the hope that they are not destroyed and that we may still find them, while temporarily considering the friend who was so obliging with the loan of his Simca. We have found a well-regarded resident of Santiago de Compostela who is the owner of a Simca and also an acquaintance of the Crewes. The manager of the hotel was able to identify him as such. He has occasionally been seen at the bar in their company. As you guessed, the manager of that hotel, like other hotel managers with whom we have talked, thinks very highly of the Crewes, who have been instrumental in supplying a great many profitable clients. But this acquaintance seldom leaves his home town. He has hardly done so, except for brief excursions to the fiords, in several years. He is an ardent fisherman, as it appears Crewe is also, and keeps his car largely to facilitate his enjoyment of that sport. However, for the last few weeks, he has not been indulging in it and was, therefore, perfectly willing, upon request, to lend his car to Crewe. He broke his leg a short time ago and is housebound. His wife, a very pious woman; his doctor, one of the most prominent physicians in Santiago; and the friends who live nearby in a respectable neighborhood, all tell the same story."

"Then you didn't get very far in following that clue, either!"

"We did not get very far in Santiago. But, as I told you before, I thought it was possible that a helpful friend might live elsewhere. And I believe we have found him."

"Good God, where?"

"In Aranjuez."

"And how on earth did you happen to look for him in Aranjuez?"

The *Jefe* took another sip of coffee and lighted another cigarette. This time, Allan had the impression that his visitor was not pausing because of indignation, but for better dramatic effect. He was not mistaken.

"I have a pleasant surprise for you," the *Jefe* said, with an emphasis that revealed his own satisfaction at the news. "Your station wagon has been discovered near there, at the bottom of the River Tagus, by some small boys who were in swimming. They had the good sense to notify the local police. The car has been fished out and is now in an excellent garage, where it is undergoing repairs. These may take some time, but I am assured that, eventually, the car will be as good as new; and, meanwhile, of course, we have been active in a direction which, heretofore, as far as we knew, we had no special reason to investigate, just as you had no special reason to make a written note of a license number. But Aranjuez is a comparatively small place and it didn't take us long to comb it thoroughly. A pleasant little city— you have been there, I hope, to see the palace and to feast on asparagus and strawberries?"

21.

Quite forgetful that he was still supposed to be an invalid, Allan bounded from his chair.

"No!" he shouted. "I have not been there to sight-see or to feast! But I shall certainly go there now for a different reason!"

"Suppose you leave the matter in our hands for the present. Your physician encourages me to believe that you will be up and about before long. But, meanwhile, I think we have everything well in hand. And I beg of you, *Señor* Lambert, to calm yourself and be seated again. If Sister Dorotea came in at this moment, she would certainly send me away immediately and forbid my return. Then the natural curiosity I have been fortunate enough to arouse would remain unsatisfied."

Realizing that this was all too true, Allan sank back into his chair. "All right, all right!" he said grudgingly when he had recovered his breath. "But you might at least go on and satisfy some of that natural curiosity now, instead of talking to me about strawberries and asparagus!"

"That was my intention, *señor*, when you startled me by rising so suddenly."

"When *I* startled *you!* Don't you suppose you startled me?"

"As I said, I thought I had a pleasant surprise for you," the *Jefe* said calmly. "And I will now proceed to tell you all I can at the moment. This man whom we have run down was formerly a guide at the royal palace, and was discharged for a minor infraction of the rules—it appears that he was importuned by Crewe to show some of the latter's tourist protégés certain apartments not usually open to the public, and yielded against his better judgment. Crewe professed great concern over his dismissal, and has shown an interest in his welfare ever since to the extent of providing him with odd jobs now and then. The ex-guide also admits to occasional presents which, coupled with some luck in the national lottery, have enabled him to live in reasonable comfort, and even to own a dilapidated old car, though he now has no regular employment. I do not doubt that he has made himself useful to Crewe in ways which we have not yet discovered—they are not as easy to guess as in the case of the unfortunate Marta. This man is unmarried and lives with a crippled brother, also unmarried. The cripple is almost entirely incapacitated; and the ex-guide claims that, instead of being in town the night your station wagon was driven into the Tagus, he was in Linares."

"Linares?"

"Yes, the small city in Jaén, where Manolete, one of our greatest bull-fighters, met his death. . . . I take it you are not an *aficionado?*"

"No, I can't say that I am. Are you suspicious that the Crewes had something to do with the death of Manolete?"

"You are pleased to jest, *señor,* but this is not a jesting matter. On that score, I am afraid we shall have to hold them blameless. But Inocencio Valdez—"

"Inocencio!"

"That is the ex-guide's Christian name—by no means an unusual one. He was present at the fatal event to which I have just referred and he still goes to Linares to attend bullfights, because of a sentimental attachment to Manolete's memory. I must tell you that this bullfighter was regarded as a national hero, and that more persons visit his tomb, in Córdoba, than go to see the world-famous *mezquita* there. Well, a bullfight did take place in Linares the evening of your accident and he went to attend it. Or so he says."

"And you believe him?"

"He was apparently not at home that night. His crippled brother corroborates the statement that Inocencio left Aranjuez early in the morning before your accident, in order to attend the bullfight in Linares. He went alone, expecting to ask friends in Manzanares or Valdepeñas to join him; but he had car trouble—"

"You don't mean to tell me that more car trouble is entering the picture!"

"I can understand your feeling that this seems to be chronic in Spain; but you must remember, *señor,* that most of the cars in general use here are by no means new. At all events, he says that he had car trouble, which delayed him and that, therefore, he decided to drive straight through to Linares, in order to assure himself of a good seat in the ring. As soon as the bullfight was over, he started home again, because he does not like to leave his crippled brother alone too long. And—forgive me—he was again delayed by car trouble. He did not stop at a roadside inn, except for an occasional cup of coffee or glass of beer, so he did not register anywhere; and he did not go to a garage, because he is a fair mechanic himself, and could do the necessary tinkering on the car."

"And you believe all this."

"It is a perfectly plausible story. The only trouble with it is that it lacks corroboration and, since Inocencio is under heavy obligation to Crewe, we are naturally suspicious that he may have co-operated, to a greater or lesser degree, in this crime, though he has no criminal record."

"And you are letting the matter rest there?"

"We have no choice for the moment. So far, we are lacking in witnesses
to the same degree that Inocencio is lacking in alibis; but we by no means
despair of finding some. I will let you know if we do. Also the results of
the autopsy which is to take place in Bilbao, not only in accordance with
our orders, but in conformity with her brother Diego's demands, on the body
of Marta Rodríguez."

22.

THE *Jefe* HAD TOLD the truth when he said the station wagon would be as
good as new. In fact, to Allan, released at last from bondage, it seemed
better than when it was new. As he went zooming along toward the Guadarrama Range, through the pleasant suburbs of Madrid and across the
mighty plain beyond, which, a few weeks earlier, he had crossed in a
Thunderbird with Douglas Brooks, his heart was even lighter than it had
been then. What if a major mystery was still unsolved? What if he had lost
a few thousand dollars? He was on his way to ask for Milagrita's hand in
marriage, and he had reason to hope that the answer would be a favorable
one.

Leonor had kept her word. The period of waiting had not been irksome
to him. When he returned to the Wellington, he found that his suite had
lost the look of stereotyped bareness characteristic of hotels. It was bright
with flowers, and the books which he had bought before his accident had,
in accordance with his instructions, been supplemented by others for which
Douglas Brooks had instigated a search through the shops. These volumes
were all tastefully arranged, between wrought iron book ends and on the
shelves of a small carved cabinet which had not been there before. The two
sheets of illuminated parchment, bought at the *Rastro*, had been framed,
and several small oil paintings and polychrome figurines had also been
added to the décor. *Señor* Brooks was responsible for most of this, Leonor
insisted; but Allan finally wrung from her the admission that some of the
knickknacks were her own; she was just lending them to him, until she
had a better place than her drab little apartment in which to install them.

He had felt immediately at home in these pleasant surroundings, and he
had also enjoyed the visitors, whom he was now allowed to see as frequently
as he chose. The Foreign Office plied him with attention; the American
Embassy, as if to make up for the tardiness of its efforts in his behalf, was
equally cordial. Allan was assured it was giving all possible co-operation to

the Embassy of France in the matter of extradition, and agreeable French-men, as well as agreeable Spaniards and agreeable Americans, frequented his suite and urged him to mention future dates when his strength would permit him to dine with them. Moreover, several of his boyhood friends had come over from Málaga to welcome him back to Spain and say their houses were his and that they were at his disposition. He found himself ordering drinks and hors d'oeuvres throughout the normal calling hours and at other odd times as well. He had dreaded the first encounter with the Wendells, which he realized could not be delayed, once he was out of the hospital; but he had a pleasant surprise: both were beaming with good will. If Mrs. Wendell wore her beautiful new clothes somewhat self-consciously, it was, nevertheless, obvious that she did so with great satisfaction, and Charlotte reflected considerable credit on Spanish *haute couture*. Her man-ner was no longer acquisitive and aggressive; it was nonchalant and sophis-ticated. She could not imagine why her mother had said she and Allan were engaged. Of course, she looked upon him as one of her best friends and, as such, she had naturally been disturbed when she heard about his accident. She hoped their relationship would always remain on this amicable basis, but she had never, for a moment, felt it would develop into a sentimental attachment; it was just too quaint and absurd, the ideas the older generation sometimes got into its head. Allan listened to her with mingled relief, amuse-ment and curiosity. He knew she was talking tongue in cheek, and his suspicions that Douglas had been active along lines other than the haunting of bookshops and the collection of bibelots were duly confirmed. He glanced at Mrs. Wendell, while Charlotte, who had obviously abandoned her plan for an educational tour, rattled on and on about the wonderful time she was having in Madrid; her mother's usually grim expression had changed to one of complacency. Whereas marriage with Allan had once represented the pinnacle of her ambition for her daughter, he was, after all, only a college professor, while Douglas Brooks, who was even richer, was ambassadorial timber. The Wendells were concentrating on him, with pleas-ing results.

True, Allan was not seeing as much of Milagrita as he would have liked; her visits to his suite were discreetly brief and discreetly supervised. But she reported that her friend, Amalia de Chavez, had proved very quick at learning how to manage the gift and newspaper stall and very interested in the work there. What was equally important, the management was entirely content with her grasp of the situation, so Milagrita would be free to resign very shortly now. Having been reassured on this point, Allan began to enjoy himself more and more; and when at last he was pronounced able to dine out, he and Leonor and Milagrita took their long delayed excursion to Alcalá de Henares and feasted, off picturesquely mottoed pottery, on *sopa de ajo* and *paella* and *sangria* in a huge raftered room, flanked with wine-skins, at the *Hostería del Estudiante*. And, in the course of this trip, they discussed at great length what Allan would say to Don Pablo. He was now on his way to say it.

As the station wagon began to climb the Guadarrama, triumphing over the steep ascent and hairpin curves with ease and speed, Allan's pride in his car doubled and redoubled. He had not exaggerated when he told Douglas he had an affection for it, not unlike that which a horseman feels in his mount; and he compared it mentally with the Thunderbird, to the disadvantage of the latter, after the traditional fashion of automobile owners —theirs were always the best. Indeed, his attachment to it had become so personal that he wanted to give it a name of its own, quite apart from its trade name. He turned to Leonor, who was seated beside him, and told her this.

"Have you any suggestions?" he asked.

"I'm afraid not. Surely, you're the person who's best qualified to name it."

"I'd thought of Victoria, but that would be more appropriate after it— she!—has helped to clear everything up. Though she's shown the capacity for triumph already. You'd never believe she's spent nearly two weeks at the bottom of a river, would you?"

"Never. But must you lay that entirely to the superiority of an American car? Doesn't some of the credit belong to Spanish mechanics?"

"Touché! But the good old bus does go like a streak, doesn't it?"

"It does indeed. And here we are."

They had already passed the first two or three of the sanatoria scattered over the eastern slope of the range and seeming to cling, almost precariously, to its rugged incline. The institution whose driveway they now abruptly entered had a somewhat fantastic resemblance to an overgrown Swiss chalet; though it was smaller than most of its fellows, its overhanging eaves, de-signed to give shelter to its upper stories, and the multiple repetition of its small ornate balconies, made it seem at one and the same time alien to its neighbors and more individualistic. The *portero* who appeared promptly at their approach bowed a respectful greeting, indicated a parking place for the station wagon and ushered the visitors into a small stiff reception room.

"The Duke of San Ricardo is expecting you and awaiting you on his balcony," the *portero* said. "But Dr. Benjumea would like to have a word with you first."

Allan could not suppress the feeling that the director of the sanitarium, a compact, self-assured looking man, who appeared promptly in the *portero's* wake, regarded the American stranger with wariness, if not actually with suspicion, despite the correct courtesy of his reception; and, even in address-ing himself to Leonor, there was no warmth in Dr. Benjumea's welcome.

He reminded them both that this was the first time, since the Duke had been admitted to the sanitarium, that he had been allowed to see a visitor other than his sister and his daughter; the director felt it was his duty to tell *Señor* Lambert that it would be very bad for his patient to become overtired, upset or even mildly excited.

"That's what I've been recently hearing about myself, for days on end," Allan retorted, somewhat disrespectfully. "And the most exciting visits were the ones that did me the most good."

"You are young," the doctor said severely, "and, at the time of your unfortunate accident, which has been duly reported to me, you were in excellent health. It is understandable that you should have regained it swiftly. But the Duke of San Ricardo is an old man."

"How old?"

"Actually, he is just over fifty," the director admitted with obvious reluctance. It was evident to Allan that he and this doctor were not going to be congenial spirits and that this was lamentable. "But he has had a long and wasting illness. And, if the *Marquesa* will permit me to say so, great misfortunes."

"I am hoping that his fortunes are going to mend and that I may have some share in their improvement. That's what I've come to talk over with him. I can't help believing that, when he's in better spirits, he'll also be in better health. The *Marquesa* agrees with me. That's why she's been good enough to arrange for this visit—with your permission, of course."

"What *Señor* Lambert says is quite true, *Herr Doktor,*" Leonor said pleasantly. "At all events, the experiment is worth trying, isn't it? May we go up to my brother's room now? I had rather hoped that, after we had seen him, *Señor* Lambert and I might have time to go on to my *dehesa,* to which I am thinking of returning, and still get back to Madrid before dark."

Allan did not fail to note the form of address. Was the director of this sanitarium a German? Or, if not, a German-Swiss or an Austrian? The *portero* had spoken of Dr. Benjumea—was the man's name really Benjamin? He did not see why any of this should make any difference, if it were so, and he grudgingly admitted to himself that the doctor made no further attempt to argue or to detain them, once Leonor had so tactfully made it clear that she had her own reasons for preferring that the visit should take place promptly and that it should be brief. On the other hand, Allan would have preferred that the director should not accompany them, as he seemed determined to do, to Don Pablo's quarters, but should permit him to make the acquaintance of the man he hoped would be his future father-in-law without onlookers to the presentation. In this, Allan was disappointed. Dr. Benjumea—if that were his name!—himself took the visitors up in the small lift and led the way down a long spotless corridor, meanwhile addressing all his remarks to Leonor. At last, he threw open the door of a room not unlike the one which Allan had recently quitted with such thankfulness or, indeed, at first glance, not unlike most hospital rooms; but this proved to have its outer side made almost entirely of glass, thereby admitting an unusual amount of light, and to lead directly on to a small balcony. At the front of this balcony, wrapped in rugs, despite the warmth of the day, sat a small shriveled figure, looking out toward the plain. At the sound of footsteps, the shrouded man turned, and Allan found himself face to face with the Duke of San Ricardo.

His first sensation was one of profound shock. He understood now why the director had spoken of an old man. Don Pablo's hollowed cheeks and thin hands were almost as white as his head of hair, his small pointed beard and his bushy eyebrows. From beneath these brows, his black eyes gleamed with feverish brilliance. He glanced quickly and unsmilingly at the director and Leonor and then gazed steadily at Allan, as if appraising him; it was a gaze so penetrating and so deliberate that Allan found it difficult to meet without flinching. But he succeeded in doing so and, after what was actually only a matter of moments, but which seemed an eternity, the Duke spoke.

From his appearance, Allan had expected that Don Pablo would do so in a feeble or quavering voice. On the contrary, it was with a cool precision which immediately placed each of his visitors in a different category.

"I am glad to see you, Leonor. *Señor* Lambert, I appreciate the kindness which has prompted your visit. *Herr Doktor*, do not let us detain you. I realize there are many urgent matters which require your attention." Then, as the director took his reluctant departure and Leonor leaned over to kiss her brother's forehead, he went on, in an impersonal way which did not seem to the eager suitor to provide much of an opening, "It is a pleasant day. I hope the drive from Madrid was an agreeable one."

"It was delightful," Leonor said quickly. "And it is delightful on this balcony, too, Pablo. I am sure Allan will agree that we Spaniards know how to make good use of balconies."

"I will indeed." As he spoke, the memory, never long absent from his thoughts, of the evening when he and Milagrita had first recognized their mutual love, became so fresh and poignant that it gave him heart to forge forward, even with so discouraging a beginning. "Perhaps your sister has told you, sir, that she was kind enough to invite me to take coffee on the balcony of her apartment in Madrid, and that our acquaintance warmed rapidly into friendship, in those propitious surroundings."

"She has mentioned it. But she has dwelt on your kindness to her and my daughter, rather than on theirs to you."

"Then, with your permission, I should like to tell my side of the story."

"By all means."

Now that he had suddenly been given the hoped-for signal, Allan found himself paralyzed with fear lest he should say the wrong thing. Nothing that he and Milagrita had discussed, when they went to the *Hostería del Estudiante*, seemed fitting or forceful now. How on earth was he to tell a man, as proud as he was poor, and desperately ill into the bargain, that he, Allan Lambert, a complete stranger, an alien American, wanted to assume responsibility for a derelict's physical and financial rehabilitation, without giving mortal offense by seeming to condescend and, worse yet, to proffer charity? How did a small-town New England professor ask for the hand of a grandee's daughter? Allan had not the vaguest idea. The more desperately he sought for a solution, the farther from it he seemed to become. He knew —or at least, he believed—that he had a powerful ally in Leonor; but if she pled his cause for him, it might well weaken this; San Ricardo would look with contempt, and rightly so, upon a man who could not do it for himself. Milagrita loved him, of that he felt certain; but she was young and in-experienced; how could her father be expected to believe that she was wise enough to know her own mind or to follow the dictates of her own heart? It was not reasonable to suppose that he could, even if there were not all the other drawbacks to such a marriage as this presumptuous suitor wanted to urge: difference not only of background and nationality, but of religion, which might be the biggest stumbling block of all. Besides, though Allan was prepared to spend the rest of this summer and all of the next one, not to mention the intervening autumn, winter and spring, in Spain, and to visit it frequently thereafter, he could not become an expatriate; but that was the fate he was on the verge of asking a nobleman, with tremendous national consciousness, to sanction in the case of his only child. The one chance of reaching the desired goal was, apparently, by blind flying.

"I hope you won't think I'm presumptuous, sir, when I say that you and I have several bonds of common interest."

"Such as . . . ?"

"Well, to begin with, we've both been victims of the same scoundrel. Not in the same way, of course, or with the same results. But perhaps we were equally to blame in the beginning. We both put ourselves in a position where he could take advantage of us. If we hadn't been so foolhardy as to do that, he couldn't have got anywhere. Your sister's told me, with your permission, as I understand it, how you became involved with Crewe. I think she's told you how I did. If you hadn't played cards with him, he couldn't have wrecked your fortune and your health. If I hadn't answered an anonymous letter that I knew was a swindle, I wouldn't have been beaten up and left for dead. So you let yourself in for something and so did I—with equally disastrous results. Am I right so far?"

"It pains me to admit it, *señor*, but truth compels me to do so."

"Good! Let's go on from there. We were both foolhardy, but neither of us meant to do anything disgraceful. Card playing's a harmless enough diversion in the eyes of most civilized persons—certainly in yours and mine —unless it leads to reckless gambling and/or cheating. Taking a vacation abroad is what a language teacher is supposed to do when he gets a sabbatical year. But he's also supposed to use some sense in the way he approaches it and improves it. Is that right, too?"

"Yes, indubitably."

"Very well. Then we've both misused our privileges and we've both paid for it. But it isn't too late to mend our ways and get along with something constructive again."

"And your idea of something constructive is . . . ?"

"A sort of partnership. We'd make different contributions to it, just as we fell from grace differently. But these contributions would have equal value. I came, unexpectedly, into money, which, obviously, I didn't know how to use to good advantage at first. But now, with your help, I think I could do something I've dreamed for years of doing: to live for a time, in a quiet, well-ordered Spanish house and, while there, to study Spanish literature with the idea of writing about it. Of course, to have the project amount to anything, the right family would have to own the house and be in residence there. Your sister tells me she has just the sort I've been hoping to find, not far from here. She's going to take me to see it today, after we leave you. If it suits me, as I'm sure it will, she's willing to go back there and run it. But, of course, we'd need you there, too. You're the head of the family."

"You said, when you began your very persuasive argument, that neither of us *meant* to do anything disgraceful. You chose your words well, *Señor* Lambert. I did not mean to bring disgrace on my family, but I have done so. I am no longer fit to be the head of it."

"Isn't that for your sister to decide? Or, perhaps, I should say your sisters, because I believe you have two."

"No, it's something I must decide for myself—or, rather, I must do so if the decision is left to me and not taken from me by God. You must realize that I am a very sick man."

"I do realize it. But I'd like to see you have a consultation of doctors and not depend on one physician's opinion of what's best for you."

"Dr. Benjumea is a graduate of the best medical school in Vienna."

"Oh, so that's why they call him 'Herr Doktor'! I was afraid he wasn't a Spaniard. But, even if he is, he has apparently absorbed so much *Kultur* somewhere along the line that he's rather inflexible. Now there's a doctor in Madrid who's very highly regarded at our Embassy. He's half Spanish and half Scotch—it's a good combination. He says most patients are better off at home, that hospitals are meant only for very sick people."

"But you have agreed that I *am* very sick. You must realize that, merely by looking at me."

"I have, I do. But not many diseases are incurable any longer, after correct diagnosis and with proper care. When you came here, your sister couldn't provide the proper care for you at home. Now, very soon, she can. And, as I've said before, I hope very much that you'll consent to a consultation of physicians, so that we may be sure there's been no mistake in the diagnosis. Of course, I'm speaking only as a layman. But I still feel you'd improve rapidly if you got away from a depressing atmosphere and if you had a renewed reason for recovery. We're agreed that we're both victims of the same scoundrel. That's our first bond of common interest. The second is that we're equally determined to see him brought to justice. Aren't we?"

"It hadn't occurred to me that he could be. I still don't see how he can, much less what I could do to help."

"I don't, either—yet. But this doesn't mean I think it's impossible—only that ways and means have, so far, escaped us. I don't believe they will much longer."

"Would you feel like giving me the reasons for your confidence?"

"I'd rather not, today, because most of it is still conjecture. But I will say this much: we're not the only two men with a grievance."

"No?"

"No, there's a man in Bilbao by the name of Diego Rodríguez who's clamoring for vengeance. His sister was associated with Ethel Crewe in some way, and returned to Spain on the *Tarragona,* the same ship Ethel took and that I took myself. This girl died almost immediately after she reached home and she was already so ill, when she got there, that she couldn't tell a lucid story. But there's reason to believe Ethel may have been under special obligations to Marta and even some suspicions of foul play. Rodríguez is only too ready to see us get even with the Crewes and he might be very useful to us—and you might, too. At least, the Chief of Police seems to feel so and I've come to have great confidence in him."

"It is not misplaced. He is a fine man. I would have been wise to go to him myself. . . . Very well, I will take your word for it that I may be of some slight service beyond that of merely acting as your host—that in itself would not have seemed to justify me in accepting so much from you. And I will wait until your next visit for more details." For a few moments, Don Pablo seemed deep in thought. Then he again turned his penetrating gaze on Allan. "You, also, inspire confidence," he said slowly, "and, as I said before, you are very persuasive. As a result of our talk, I will consent to the consultation which you so strongly advise, and which I hope will include this semi-Spanish, semi-Scotch doctor of whom you speak so highly. If the physicians are agreed that I can safely and properly return to the *dehesa* of my sister Leonor, and if she and my other sister, Pilar, wish me to resume my forfeited place as the head of the family, I will do so. I cannot be so ungracious as to decline the help from you which will make this possible—after all, if Crewe is indeed brought to justice, it perhaps need be only temporary. And I assure you that you will be a most welcome guest at our house whenever you choose to come there. It should, indeed, be a suitable place for the studies you wish to pursue." Don Pablo paused again and, this time, when he began to speak, he did so smilingly. "I somehow gather that these studies will be intermittent," he said. "If I am not mistaken, you wish to do some traveling, not only to satisfy your grievance against the Crewes, but to visit your old friends in Málaga and for the mere enjoyment of your station wagon and the company you might have while using it. Am I not right in believing there was something else you wished to ask me before we parted?"

23.

IT WAS WITH DIFFICULTY that Allan refrained from blurting out, as he and Leonor left the sanitarium, that he would much prefer returning directly to Madrid, rather than continuing almost to Avila, in order to visit the *dehesa*. To be sure, he had been cautioned that he must still not consider his betrothal to Milagrita "official"; but he had also been told, in a way that was not only courteous but friendly, that Don Pablo would give this status "careful consideration"; and that, meanwhile, since it was obvious to him that his daughter and Allan were genuinely attached to each other, and that, as far as he could see, there were no insuperable barriers to an alliance between them, there was no reason why they should not meet in such a way as to suggest that this betrothal was in the offing.

"After all," Don Pablo went on, rather whimsically, "among the people, in my generation, a young man was still obliged to woo his *novia* with an iron grille between them—any other course of conduct would have seemed to them both highly improper. Now the sons and daughters of these same restricted sweethearts are all out strolling, arm in arm, through the public gardens, or sitting close together on park benches, quite unsupervised. The proletariat should not have all the advantages of progress!"

Allan could not possibly have agreed with Don Pablo more wholeheartedly, and his one desire, now that everything seemed under control at the sanitarium, was to get back to Milagrita without delay. Leonor easily read his thoughts and laid her hand lightly on his arm.

"I know in which direction you would like to turn the station wagon," she said pleasantly, "and I am in entire sympathy with your impulse to go speeding down the mountainside and not chugging farther up it. But I am still the *gobernanta* at the Wellington and I do not know when I can have another day off. The sooner I get to the *dehesa,* the sooner I can arrange for my brother's return there; and that likewise means the sooner we can all be there together, a happy and united family."

"You're right, of course—as always. Just let me know when to turn off the main road."

"Soon after we pass Villacastin. The house doesn't show from the highway. There's a long narrow drive leading up to it, bordered by poplars, with great rock-strewn pastures on either side. There's a wooden sign that reads, *Reservada—Dehesa Pinos de la Fidelidad.* But the signboard is rather battered and the lettering's very faded. You could easily miss it. Don't worry. I'll tell you when we're nearly there."

She leaned back, folding her gloved hands and closing her eyes. Allan guessed that she was very tired and that she preferred not to talk; but nothing in her expression indicated that she was unhappy or even troubled; indeed, she looked tranquil and content and, before long, she sat up straighter and opened her eyes.

"I must tell you that you have given my brother not only new hope, but new life," she said. "He told me so himself, after you left us to talk to the *Herr Doktor* about a consultation; and I could see that though, physically, our visit had naturally been something of a strain, mentally and spiritually, it had done wonders for him. I must congratulate you, Allan, on the tact and kindness with which you handled a very difficult situation. If you had said or done the wrong thing, the results would have been very different, not only for Pablo, but for you."

"I'm afraid the outcome's due to good luck rather than good management. I hadn't the dimmest idea how to talk to a grandee. So I just plunged right in."

"I should say that you dived, rather than plunged—a swan dive of exceptional skill and grace, which enabled you to come swiftly and easily to the surface. And you must stop thinking of Pablo as a grandee, though, as a matter of fact, grandees can be approached in the same way that you would approach anyone else—there is a common denominator of conduct and speech among gentlefolk all over the world. But it would be better if you began to think of Pablo as a man who has been terribly humiliated and outdone and knows, as you had the courage to say, that he himself is largely to blame for it; a man whose recovery of self-confidence and pride is almost certainly bound to be slow, especially as he is also grieving because he has lost his beloved and is in frail health besides."

"I know he lost his wife, to whom he was greatly attached, and that he became more and more a recluse. But I don't think you ever told me the exact nature of his illness."

"Well—of course, there was a nervous breakdown. And there were tubercular symptoms, which I believe have largely disappeared—we must give the sanitarium that much credit. And a heart murmur."

"Never angina or a thrombosis or anything like that?"

"No, I don't think so."

"No signs of cancer, either?"

"Not as far as I know."

"Then I'd like to make a wager with you, even though you disapprove of gambling. I think Don Pablo's been the victim of overcautious or pessimistic doctors, as well as evil companions. I think, in a year or so, you'll see him as well as ever."

"I'm not going to bet with you, Allan. I am only going to pray that you are right." She spoke so simply and unaffectedly that her words were not tinged by sanctimony. Allan decided that perhaps it would be better to change the subject.

"About how long do you think it will take to reopen the *dehesa*? I suppose you'll have to hunt up servants and so on."

Leonor sat up still straighter and opened her eyes still wider. "Why, Allan, the *dehesa* has never been completely closed!" she said with surprise. "I told you it had been stripped of its most valuable books and furnishings, which, alas! is true. And some of the younger members of the household staff, at our insistence, sought employment elsewhere. But the servants who have been with us a long time are still there, of course. They would not dream of leaving us in our misfortune, even if they did not get a *peseta* for weeks on end; and, fortunately, I have been able to save a little for them right along, from my salary."

"Is it indiscreet to ask what you mean by a little?"

"It isn't indiscreet, but I hesitate to tell you, because you wouldn't believe me. When times are good, the cook gets about the equivalent of six or seven dollars a month and the *mayordomo* the same—the others less."

"Those are good wages!"

"Yes, indeed. One foreign lady who came here made the great mistake of offering her cook ten dollars a month. The outsider was at once boycotted by the local aristocracy, because she had upset the current wage scale."

"I think it's outrageous," Allan said indignantly. "How can they live on such pay—or less?"

"They subsist largely on a soup made of beans and potatoes and, in cold weather, huddle around a single brazier; but they stay on. They have a sort of loyalty that is indomitable—almost fierce. And, as far as it is within their power, they keep up a pretense that we may be back any day and that they should be ready for us. The bedrooms which are not in use may well have been dismantled. But I think you will find that the drawing room has an air of welcome, even though its tapestries and velvets are gone. Small, silver-framed family photographs will be scattered about, and also larger ones, of various royal personages, all autographed with a flourish. And since it is summertime, and there are still the remnants of a garden, not to mention wild flowers, pathetically cheap or chipped little vases will be filled and put in appropriate places: beside Modesta's picture, for instance, and of course before all the representations of the Blessed Mother and Our Holy Savior."

This time, she spoke not only with her usual unaffected simplicity, but with such assurance that Allan sincerely hoped she would not be mistaken in her expectations, though himself convinced it was almost inevitable that she should be. He had never heard of such servants. Again, Leonor read his thoughts without difficulty.

"If I were willing to wager about anything, I would do so about what I have just told you," she said. "I would even be willing to wager that some servant of the Crewes might be helping to protect them at this very moment; I do not think it is entirely accidental that all their employees have disappeared. Ah—here we are already in sight of the church at Villacastin. It will not be long now before we reach our destination, and you will be able to judge for yourself whether or not I was right, at least as far as our own people are concerned."

She was also correct in believing that he would have missed the entrance to the *dehesa*, if she had not swiftly pointed it out to him, as he was about to go speeding past it. Innumerable rocks, fantastic in shape and gigantic in size, were indeed "strewn" over the surrounding countryside; and though two of these served as crude gateposts to the driveway, this was so narrow and the boulders so similar in character to those on either side, as far as the eye could see, that they did little to identify it. Once off the well-paved highway, the roadbed proved very rough, and the station wagon jolted slowly along, past more rocky pastures and some cleared fields, which showed that harvesting was already completed; beyond these, two or three were planted with vegetables which, no doubt, would later serve as the basis for the soup of which Leonor had spoken. Then came a huge bare courtyard with high walls and a great grilled gate, surmounted by a sculptured coat of arms. The emptiness of this courtyard made it seem doubly big and barren. On its further side, a smaller gate led to another enclosure where unkempt grass was growing, and which permitted the first glimpse of a massive structure beyond. The second gate was padlocked, and there was still no sign of human life; but Leonor had hardly called out the name, "Felipe!" when there came the sound of hurrying footsteps, joyous shouts and barking dogs. So swiftly that Allan did not even hear the creaking of a key, the padlock was swinging on its rusty chain, the gate flung open, and a tall unshaven man, whose dilapidated garments hung loosely on his spare frame and whose wide smile of welcome disclosed a sparse supply of strong yellow teeth, was bowing to the *Marquesa* and, at the same time, futilely trying to suppress the commotion around him. Half a dozen shabbily clad but hearty and happy looking children were cavorting among as many leaping dogs; and suddenly an unseen bell clanged loudly, and the wide, iron-studded door of a great stone house in the background swung slowly open. Out of this came rushing men and women of various ages, vociferous in their greeting. Leonor had barely time to step from the station wagon before they surrounded her, kissing her hand, thanking the saints for her return and plying her with questions.

Allan shut off the engine and sat silently watching the scene before him, while he waited for the first tumult to subside and the propitious moment for his presentation to arrive. He saw that Leonor had indeed not been mistaken. These were really her "people," bound to her by no ties of blood, but by that fierce and indomitable loyalty of which she had spoken with such confidence and such pride. The surging group held his first attention; but looking beyond it, he saw the square twin towers, separated by an upper and a lower gallery, of a building which might well have served, at need, no less as a fortress than as a dwelling place. Most of the windows were grilled and some had heavy shutters as well. Behind the long gallery, whose columns supported a tiled roof, the central part of the house stretched out in solid and spacious amplitude; and beyond the towers, on either side, were great stone wings, apparently as indestructible as the rest of the edifice. It must have been from *castillos* such as this that Old Castile had got its name and Avila the motto on its coat of arms—*Antes Quebrar Que Doblar*.

Allan's scrutiny and meditation did not last long. After responding warmly to their welcome, Leonor disengaged herself from her clamorous retainers and motioned to her guest. As he stepped from the car and came to stand beside her, the group quickly became less noisy and stood respectfully at attention, while she explained that this North American gentleman, *Señor* Lambert, would be their benefactor, as he was already that of their *patrones*. Funds would be left with them that very day to lay in foodstuffs and all other necessities for the reception of Don Pablo, who was to leave the sanitarium and come home, accompanied by a reliable infirmarian. They must hasten and put everything in order. The young *Condesa* would presently join her father, with some suitable companion, and she, the *Marquesa,* would follow as soon as possible. Shortly thereafter, *Señor* Lambert would come to visit them; he would doubtless wish to select at once the apartments which would be most pleasing to him for a bedroom and a study; the family would, of course, occupy the same ones as heretofore.

"And the Chaplain?" one of the older women inquired eagerly. "Will he be coming back, too? It is such a long time since our own chapel has been used and so far to the village church!"

Leonor turned to Allan. "We have always had a chaplain here," she explained in English. "Not a permanent one, in residence, as is customary in many of the more important establishments. However, the Prior of Santo Tomás has been kind enough to supply us with different Dominican Fathers, in rotation. I don't know how you will feel—"

"But of course. You should follow your usual custom in that way—in every way."

"The Chaplain will also return, Josefa," Leonor assured the eager questioner. "The necessary arrangements will be made immediately and the chapel will be open again. I will take *Señor* Lambert to see it before we leave. Unfortunately, we must get back to Madrid tonight, but—"

A chorus of disappointment interrupted her, and one voice was raised in protest above the rest.

"That will not give us time to tell the good news to the shepherds! They are all so far afield that we cannot call them in quickly."

Leonor lifted her hand for silence. "We will be absent only a little while and, meantime, you can prepare the shepherds for our return. Believe me, everything will soon be as it was before. Except that you will probably be getting higher wages. *Señor* Lambert feels very strongly that yours have been inadequate."

Again she was interrupted. "We know that we have always been paid as much as the *Señora Marquesa* was able." The shabby, unshaven man who had opened the gate spoke with dignity.

"Yes, yes, that is so," his companions hastened to agree. But several male members of the group came forward and reached for Allan's hand. He found the clasp warm and firm. One of the older women had begun to cry, and furtively wiped her eyes on a corner of her dingy apron. But the one they called Josefa spoke up stoutly.

"The extra money will mean much to us, *señor*," she said. "But to have Christ with us again—that will mean even more. . . . Your presence, also, will be most welcome," she added, quite innocent of sacrilegious comparison. "It is to be hoped that you will come soon and often throughout a long life."

"That is *Señor* Lambert's hope, too," Leonor said. "So now, let us show him where he will be lodged. We have kept him outside far too long already. *Está es su casa.*"

She took his arm and walked with him along the gallery and through the open door. Some of the group which had surrounded them followed briefly. The others remained in the courtyard, talking among themselves. The vast brick-paved hall which Allan entered with Leonor was unfurnished, except for some benches along the walls, which were paneled in bright tiles. "The service quarters are on this floor," she said. "I suggest that you look at those later, but that now we go directly to the ones we shall be occupying. The staircase is rather long and steep, I am afraid, but you will get used to it."

"It's a beautiful staircase," Allan said quickly. "I can't believe its steps would ever seem steep to me. I'll always be too busy admiring the carved stonework. You didn't prepare me for anything like this."

"Well, never mind. Come and see something for which I did prepare you."

They were in another vast hall, where several figures in armor made a gleaming foreground to the blue and yellow tiles against which they were placed. At one end of this hall, a double doorway stood invitingly open. Leonor stepped across the threshold and turned to Allan with a smile.

It was exactly as she had said. The walls had been denuded of tapestries, and their former important positions were easy to recognize because great rectangles of plaster were paler in tint than the intervening spaces which had been exposed to the light. A blank square in the paneling above the chimney piece betrayed the fact that the painting which had originally been set into the woodwork had also been ruthlessly removed. But some wicker chairs, of modern inexpensive manufacture, had been companionably grouped about, as if waiting to accommodate the visitors deprived of furniture upholstered in velvet and Córdoba leather. On a massive wooden table which, either because of its unwieldiness or some other reason, had been left in place, small family photographs in silver frames were scattered about. A larger photograph, of a very beautiful woman, formed the central ornament, surrounded by autographed likenesses of celebrities, on a grand piano of a size and type which proclaimed its loss of commercial value. A little vase of field flowers stood in front of this picture; and, at the rear of the room, in the recess which faced the fireplace, a gaunt crucifix was banked with red roses.

24.

ALLAN HAD MORE OR less taken it for granted that they would be returning to Villacastin for lunch. But they were hardly ensconced in the drawing room when Josefa reappeared, bearing a tray set with a decanter and two tiny glasses, and proudly put it down in front of Leonor.

"The *Señora Marquesa* knows that I find hiding places for this and that, and provide in advance for possible visits," she said. "It is not enough merely to keep the drawing room in order. There must be refreshment available, too. . . . I still have secreted not only two bottles of Don Pablo's best sherry, of which I have the honor to bring you a sample, but also some sound red *Valdepeñas*, which will go well with your lunch, and several small canisters containing coffee, tea and other delicacies. Shall I set the table here or in the dining room?"

"I think it would be pleasant here, don't you, Allan?"

"But if these poor people have so little to eat—"

"As Josefa has just said, they somehow provide for emergencies." Switching from English to Spanish, Leonor asked, "What are you going to give us, Josefa?"

"First melon, of which there is an abundance just now. Then a *tortilla*— we have just enough eggs for one. And ham—not *jamón de York*, which I know the *señor* would prefer, but some of our own."

"You mean the so-called *jamón Serrano*—the kind that is cured in the snow? But I love it! The *Señora Marquesa* has not yet had time to tell you, Josefa, but I grew up in Spain. I would much rather have Spanish ham than *jamón de York!*"

"I might have known," Josefa replied beaming, "that the *señor* was not actually a foreigner. No outsider is so immediately *simpático* as we have all found him. Yes, I assure you, the matter is being discussed already and there is only one opinion."

"Well, with melon and a *tortilla* and *jamón Serrano*, we shall make out very well."

Josefa held up her hands in horror. "Can the *Señora Marquesa* imagine that is all I can provide? Only yesterday, Felipe had the good fortune to find two partridges."

Neither Leonor nor Allan could refrain from smiling at the use of the word "find," as if the partridges had been discovered nestling among the bushes back of the house; and neither had the heart to suggest that August was out of season for game or that poaching was punishable by law. Instead, Leonor murmured, "Well, as our great Saint Teresa herself said, 'There is a time for penitence and a time for partridges.' "

"Of course, she always knew what she was talking about, that one. And with our partridges, so providentially found, just at the right time, I shall give the *señores* cabbage and rice and a salad," Josefa went on calmly. "And, afterward, *flan* and coffee."

Allan had vowed, when he left the hospital, that nothing would ever induce him to take another spoonful of *flan,* Spain's version of baked custard and its most ubiquitous and standardized sweet. But he could not bring himself to protest against this, any more than against partridge, which he would enjoy. Besides, after melon, omelette, home-cured ham, a main course and salad, he would have very little appetite left anyway, though Josefa now began to apologize because the meal would have to be such a light one.

"If the *Señora Marquesa* had only given us a little warning, there would, of course, have been trout and a suckling pig," she said regretfully, "or tender slices of Avila's best veal, browned to a turn and surrounded by all the *legumbres* readily available now in the *Plaza de la Victoria.* But when the *señores* return—"

"When we return, you will prepare all those things for us," Leonor said with a smile. "Now you must hasten to make ready what is available. The *señor* is somewhat impatient to be on the road again. He has important reasons for wishing to reach Madrid as soon as possible."

Josefa bustled away to return, before the visitors had finished their sherry, with napery and cutlery. The napkins were almost as large as the cloth with which she spread the small table that she placed between the two wicker chairs; and all the linen, though worn thin and carefully darned, was encrusted with huge monograms surmounted by crests. The silverware was correspondingly monogrammed and crested and exceedingly heavy. Leonor picked up a spoon and, after examining it carefully, gave Josefa a questioning look.

"I thought all the set of which this is a part had been sold," she said.

"What! And have nothing left, which had belonged to her sainted mother —may she have eternal rest!—for the *Señorita Condesa* when she marries!"

"So you hid other things besides sherry and *Valdepeñas* and a few canisters filled with delicacies!"

"What would the *Señora Marquesa* expect? . . . But if the North American *señor* is really in a hurry to return to Madrid, we cannot go into all that today. I shall now fetch the melon. I hope the *señores* will find it to their liking."

The melon was excellent. So were the omelette and the ham. The delicate meat of the plump little partridges fell away from their bones at the touch of the heavy forks, and the cabbage which formed the dressing was delicious. Allan did full justice to all these items and felt warranted in refusing the *flan* on the ground that he could not swallow another morsel. But he did not succeed in deceiving Leonor.

"You mean you cannot swallow any more *flan*," she said, laughing. "Well, I do not blame you. Of course, we Spaniards can eat it with enjoyment every day, just as we can eat veal every day. But that is not to be expected of a foreigner."

"Josefa has been good enough to say that I am not actually a foreigner. And I really *do* like *jamón Serrano*."

"Suppose we do not argue that point now! Have you finished your coffee? Then come and have a look at the bedrooms. I want you to choose yours before you leave, so that it may be ready for you on your return."

The bedrooms, like the drawing room, were enormous, and unlike that, as Leonor had foretold, they were dismantled, though tidy. Each was equipped with massive furniture; some had not only one, but two huge beds, wardrobes and dressing tables, and on the old-fashioned marble-topped washstands, twin sets of porcelain bowls and pitchers and the customary utensils to complement these were imposingly set forth. Leonor laughed again as she saw Allan looking at these in astonishment.

"You will not have much cause to complain about the plumbing here, because there is so little of it," she told him. "I am sure you will want to begin your improvements by adding more. Still, we do have two bathrooms of sorts. There was only one when I came here, much larger than necessary, and containing a tub as big as a sarcophagus—in fact, it reminded me of one. So I put up a partition and have always used the smaller section myself."

"So the two are side by side? Quite a cosy arrangement, isn't it?"

"Yes, there at the end of the hall." He was pleased to hear her go on laughing, to see the lightness of her mood. "Well, if I can have my choice, this would be my bedroom," he said, turning back to the smallest one through which he had been conducted. "And please don't think of providing a separate study. I shall be quite overpowered as it is, and I see a desk here, which is the one thing all the bedrooms don't contain."

"Yes. It has been used for a combination study and bedroom before."

"You don't mean by Don Pablo? I wouldn't turn him out for anything!"

"No, by my husband, before we married. I told you this was his family place. And it would make me very happy to have you use it. . . . Now that is settled, let us take a quick look at some of the outbuildings. Of course, we have no riding horses here any more. But perhaps you will want them again?"

"I'm one of those men who '. . . cannot get upon a horse,

By pulleys, ladders, threats or force,'"
Allan answered, quoting gaily. "But I suppose you and Milagrita are expert horsewomen? You'd enjoy riding again?"

"Of course. And so would Pablo, as soon as he's strong enough. It's almost as much of an insult to ask a Castilian if he knows how to ride and likes to do so, as it would be to ask the same question of an Andalusian."

"Then we must, by all means, have riding horses here. . . . In which direction are the stables?"

He was becoming more successful in suppressing his impatience to get back to Madrid. He knew that what Leonor had said was true: the sooner the *dehesa* was reorganized, in all its branches, the sooner a harmonious family life would be possible. And he was really enchanted with the room which Leonor told him had formerly been the head groom's—so tiny that the rest of it was dwarfed by its enormous hooded chimney piece, where twigs were laid ready to start a fire. Brushwood was stacked in a corner beside it and a number of low wooden stools were clustered about it.

"Those are what the shepherds customarily use," Leonor told him. "Now that there is no head groom—or indeed, any groom in residence—this is their favorite meeting place."

"Then we mustn't dislodge them. The new head groom can take up his quarters somewhere else. I can just see those shepherds gathered around their fire, when they come in cold and tired from the fields. And I don't quite know why, but there's something extraordinarily homelike about the whole room." His gaze wandered over the whitewashed walls, bare except for the inevitable crucifix, to the one grilled window, set high above a deep embrasure, and he wondered why he should feel so strongly that this was the case. Yet he knew that some essential element of Old Castile, which he had not yet fathomed, and not only the quaint chimney piece and the low rectangular stools made it so. In his boyhood, he had occasionally visited some of the great estates in the vicinity of Málaga—beautiful villas surrounded by luxuriant gardens, ablaze with color. Now he had come to a sterner, stronger land. He hoped that he could meet its standards. . . .

"Shall we go on?" he heard Leonor ask, breaking in on his reverie. "I did want you to see this—I felt it would say something to you, and I see that it has. But, as far as the kitchen and laundry go, I think you can leave those safely to me. And Felipe is quite capable of improving the barns and increasing the herds, which I am afraid are down to three or four cows and a dozen pigs. You have only to tell him what you want. As to the riding horses, I think you had better discuss those with Milagrita and her father, rather than with me. However—"

"Yes, what have you in mind now?"

"I hesitate to suggest it. But if we left the rest of the premises for our next visit, would you be willing to go on into Avila? We are so near—and it is such a long time since I have seen my sister!"

"You shouldn't have hesitated. Of course, we must go to see your sister. I've been wanting to anyway."

He broke off abruptly. He had never said to Leonor what he had to the Chief of Police: that he thought this sister might be helpful to them. As a matter of fact, in the rush of other impressions and activities, he had almost forgotten about his own idea, and he did not know whether the *Jefe* had ever followed through on it or not. It would be a good plan to find out. . . .

"Are they strict about visiting hours at Santa Ana's?" he inquired.

"Theoretically, yes. But convent rules are not as hard and fast as most Protestants suppose, if there is some good reason for elasticity. And, since we will be dealing with the Abbess—"

"Your sister is the Abbess?"

"Yes. Didn't I mention that before?"

"You know very well you did not!" Allan said explosively. "You Spaniards are exactly like the English in one respect: you have such an aversion to 'putting on side,' as they say, that you leave the poor outsider completely in the dark regarding the identity of VIP's."

"I beg your pardon?"

"Short for very important persons. Like abbesses, for instance—or grandees, for that matter. I hear about 'Pablo' and then I find that he is a duke and a count and heaven knows what several times over in Spain, and that he has valid titles in two or three other countries besides. It took me I don't know how long to discover that the 'Jimmy' people kept talking about was the late Duke of Alba and also the Duke of Berwick and what have you! And we had an inoffensive, rather bashful Scottish visitor at the college once who turned out to be the cousin of the Queen of England, or something of the sort!"

"Well, don't get so excited about it. Wouldn't you rather have us that way than—"

"Than like some Americans? The ones who keep telling you their brother is the head of the Chamber of Commerce at Spodunk, or that their ancestors came over in the *Mayflower*, or that they were in the same class at primary school with the President? Yes, I would, but, after all, there's a happy medium!"

As they talked, they had been strolling away from the stables and through the inner courtyard. The same group which had welcomed them there was now waiting to bid them farewell, and Felipe ran ahead to open the great iron gate. It swung slowly on its hinges, to a chorus of *"Vaya con Dios!"* Then they were jolting down the narrow, poplar-lined driveway again.

"'Go with God.' It's a very moving way of saying good-by, isn't it?" Allan asked.

"I am glad you find it so. . . . Now, before you rebuke me again, let me tell you something about the Convent of Santa Ana. You knew, didn't you, that is where Isabel, as a young princess, was staying when she was first offered the crown of Castile? As soon as we arrive, we will go up the same stone stairway, leading to the main parlor, that was taken by the nobles, under the leadership of the great Carrillo, Archbishop of Toledo, when they came to do so. But she remained behind the grille, at the further end of the room, with the Lady Abbess, and declined the honor on the ground that, as long as he lived, her half brother, Enrique, would be the lawful king."

"No, I didn't know all that. I've always associated Isabel with Granada, never with Avila."

"Well, we must change all that, because she was really an *Avilesa,* born at Madrigal de las Altas Torres, reared at Arévalo, and much later choosing for her summer palace a part of what is now the Convent of Santo Tomás, where her only son lies buried."

She went on, making the great queen, whom Allan had hitherto so vaguely visualized, seem more real and vivid with every kilometer over which they sped. It seemed no time at all before Leonor was directing him to a great stone pile, just outside the wall of the "City of Kings." They went through a large battered door into another of those bare courtyards which Allan was just beginning to accept as stately rather than stark, and were met by a rosy-cheeked, stocky little portress, who fell on Leonor with the same unabashed delight that Josefa and the others had revealed at the *dehesa.* Still chattering and laughing, she indicated another door, at the right of the courtyard, which led into a small and rather gloomy anteroom, where she tugged at an iron bell pull. The voice of an unseen nun answered from within, and the portress spoke with pride, forestalling Leonor's own announcement of her visit.

"Quick! Tell the *Abadesa* that her sister, the *Señora Marquesa,* is here!"

Allan heard another exclamation and another warm greeting, this time from the unseen nun. Then, still very proudly, the portress led the way up a short flight of stone steps and flung wide the door of a huge cold parlor, with a worn carpet on the floor and colored lithographs on the walls. There was a curtained grille at one end of this somewhat cheerless apartment; and almost instantly footsteps could be heard on the further side of

it. Then came the soft-spoken salutation, "*Ave Maria Purísima,*" to which
Leonor responded with the words, "*Sin pecado concebida,*" and the curtains
parted to disclose the black and white-clad figures of the Abbess and her
assistant.

Allan's first impression of the Abbess was one of astonishment: there
was a strong resemblance between her and her younger sister; but, whereas
Leonor was slight and pale, and showed unmistakable signs of strain and
sorrow, Pilar's face and figure were pleasantly rounded, her color fresh and
her smooth skin unmarred by wrinkles. Her companion, obviously much
older than she was, leaned heavily forward, her gnarled hands resting on a
stout cane; but despite her decrepitude, her bearing had a certain dignity
of its own, and when she raised her head to look at her visitors, her seamed
face had something the quality of a Rembrandt portrait—a distinction and
nobility which transcended youth and beauty. Both nuns were smiling, and
the Abbess spoke in such a way as to make Allan conscious of a genuine
welcome, despite the setting which seemed doubly cold and austere to him,
because it was so unfamiliar.

"I rejoice to see you, Leonor. It is a long while since you have been here.
And I am glad you have brought with you the North American friend of
whom you have written. Will you not both please sit down?" Seating herself in a way that disposed her robes gracefully about her, the Abbess went
on, "*Señor* Lambert, the news of your sad mishaps and your good deeds
has preceded you. I thank God, both that the former are safely over, and
that the latter seem to go on and on. Apparently, you are never weary of
well doing. Mother María de los Angeles will confirm my statement that
you have been much in our prayers—first, in petition for your recovery and
then in thanksgiving for your generosity."

"Indeed, *señor,* I cannot too heartily second what our Reverend Mother
has said," the older nun assured him, in a surprisingly young and cheerful
voice.

Allan, who was beginning to feel embarrassed at having his praises so
openly sung, murmured something incoherent in reply. Sensing his malaise,
the Abbess quickly sought to relieve it.

"You will be in need of refreshment after your trip. What would you
prefer—some of our own wine, or milk from our own cows, or perhaps a
cup of chocolate? Do you like our Spanish chocolate, *Señor* Lambert?"

"It's very rich, isn't it?" he said hesitantly. With instinctive distaste, he
suddenly recalled the cloying, cinnamon-scented fragrance wafted toward
him in a ship's corridor; and, unbidden, the image of Ethel at Astorga,
guzzling cup after cup of this sweet dark mixture of a so-called beverage
that was so thick that it was better spooned than drunk, rose to repel him.
As if she had read his thoughts, the Abbess said quietly, "It is not always

the same. Here we have a sister who prepares it very well. But perhaps something has happened to make you dislike it. You had better take wine, I think. I will tell the novice who is waiting for instructions." She rose and, going to the rear of the curtained alcove, spoke to someone Allan could not see. Then, as she returned and resumed her place, she added, still quietly, "Did I guess right?"

"You did, indeed. Was it just a guess—or was it divination? I realize that I am at the very fountainhead of mysticism in Avila, what with the traditions of both Teresa and John of the Cross!"

"And of our own María Vela, of whom perhaps you have not heard—well, we will tell you her story some other time. But I must confess that I have no supernatural gifts. I have only listened with great attention to every detail of a story which the Chief of Police has paid me the compliment of telling me."

"Then he *has* been to see you!"

"Yes, two or three days ago. I told him I would think the matter over and give it prayer. At the moment he approached me, I had no suggestions to make."

"And now?" Allan and Leonor asked simultaneously and with equal eagerness.

"They are perhaps inconsequential, as the item about the chocolate may be—the *Jefe* told me that the woman you are seeking was inordinately fond of it, and that he had included, among the orders he sent out, instructions to watch anyone who seemed to take more than an occasional cup. Of course, it is not normally drunk in France, where she is supposed to be now, as much as it is in Spain. Ah—here is your wine."

Again she went to the rear of the alcove and returned, carrying a small tray which she placed in the *torno* beside the grille. This movable cylinder, encased in wood, revolved slowly and Leonor took the tray from one of its shelves as it reached the main section of the parlor. The wine was flanked by plates of small round cookies, and two tiny napkins, neatly folded, lay beside them. Leonor helped herself and motioned Allan to do the same. He was neither hungry nor thirsty after his enormous lunch, and he was much more keen to hear the results of the Abbess' meditation and prayers than he was to eat and drink. However, he recognized that the refreshments which had been offered him were part of an established pattern and accepted them with as little show of reluctance as he could muster. He was rewarded, for both the wine and the cookies were extremely good, and it was not until he had done justice to both that he asked another question.

"Would it be indiscreet to inquire what the further items may be, however inconsequential they seem?"

"No, I am quite willing to tell you, and you may repeat everything I say to the *Jefe,* for what it is worth. In fact, he halfway prepared me for a visit from you, so this is not an altogether unexpected pleasure. He is so very clever himself, and has the assistance of several such able organizations, that I hardly dare to believe I can suggest anything which has not already occurred to many alert minds. The police will, of course, be looking for a brunette, rather than a blonde, probably a woman wearing dark glasses, clad either in shabby, ill-fitting clothes, deep mourning, or even a sort of habit, such as a *beata* would wear in Spain. And she would be alone. But if she is not at one of the better-known gambling resorts herself—and either the deep mourning or the habit would make that improbable—she would be in touch with one. Let us say, for instance, that she might be at Vence, but that she would communicate frequently with someone at Monte Carlo—a bearded man, also wearing dark glasses and rather ill-fitting clothes, who seldom visits the Casino, but frequently manages to make up a fourth at bridge. Of course, I am using all this just as examples of what the police will naturally be looking for."

"Yes, of course," Allan murmured, more and more beside himself with astonishment.

"Well—the only suggestion I have to make is that the police should also watch the shrines with even greater attention than they would anyway."

"The shrines!"

"Yes. This year marks the centennial celebration at Lourdes. Thousands of pilgrims will be pouring in and out every day. Among the truly devout, there are bound to be some with less lofty motives. Of course, the police know that, too. There are not only vendors of every sort; there are also pickpockets and, quite possibly, would-be assassins."

Allan stared at the Abbess and her assistant. The latter did not speak, but nodded her head sagely and then, still leaning forward heavily on her cane, looked him full in the face as the Superior went on.

"Mother María de los Angeles has joined me in prayer and meditation on this subject, though we have not thought it best to share it with the community as a whole," the Abbess continued. "Even convent walls have cracks in them, occasionally. . . . I have mentioned Lourdes—that was just an example, like Vence and Monte Carlo. I cling to the idea of a shrine. But my own guess is this would not be such an obvious choice as Lourdes. There are several other places of pilgrimage, somewhat less renowned."

"Such as—"

For the last few minutes, Allan had been vaguely conscious of a tolling bell. Now, to his disappointment and distress, the Superior and Mother María de los Angeles both rose.

"We shall have to leave you," the Abbess said, "or we shall be late to Compline and that would set a very bad example. But I hope you will

come again, and that, meanwhile, you will think about what I have said
and talk it over with the *Jefe*. Also, that you will greet my beloved brother
and my dear niece in my behalf. And you may be very sure that the presiding
saints of the shrines will occupy an important place in our prayers."

25.

BETWEEN AVILA and the *Cumbre de los Leones*, which marked the highest
point of the Guadarrama Range over which they passed on their way back
to Madrid, Leonor and Allan talked, the former thoughtfully, the latter
excitedly, over what the Abbess had said. Allan, who was not very well
versed on the subject of shrines, plied his companion with questions concerning all the feasible ones. Leonor, who could name half a dozen easily,
added a word of caution: he should not take it for granted that Pilar was
right; the Abbess had only mentioned the possibilities, and even if she had
guessed correctly, this would not necessarily mean that both Ethel and
Anthony could be tracked down at a place of pilgrimage; Pilar had been
careful to point out that they had probably separated. As far as that went,
Leonor had another theory. But she could not be persuaded to say what
it was. It had just occurred to her, and she wanted to think it over in all
its aspects before mentioning it. . . .

Allan found that neither cajolement nor argument would move her.
When they began the descent of the mountainside, he made a sudden suggestion.

"What do you say that we stop again at the sanitarium? I know there
isn't a chance that they'd let us see Don Pablo twice in one day, but we
could inquire for him, and assure ourselves that he wasn't overtired by our
visit."

"A very good idea. I'm sorry I didn't think of it myself."

The *portero* on duty at the oversize Swiss chalet was not the same who
had ushered them in that morning. This one was neither cordial nor co-
operative.

"We weren't expecting to make a visit, only an inquiry of the director."

"The *Herr Doktor* is not here. He has gone to Madrid."

"Gone to Madrid!" Leonor and Allan exclaimed in unison; and Allan
added emphatically, "Then it is imperative that we should speak with his
assistant. I assure you that you would be well advised to let us do so."

The *portero* still hesitated, but something in Allan's tone compelled acquiescence. Grudgingly, the *portero* opened the door and ushered the visitors into the stiff little waiting room. A considerable time passed before a small, plump man, with blond hair worn *en brosse* and a pink but severe countenance obscured by a pair of thick spectacles, appeared in the doorway and spoke to them sternly.

"This is most irregular," he said brusquely, without any form of courteous greeting. "The *portero* should not have admitted you. As he told you, it is long past visiting hours."

"We came only to make an inquiry as to the Duke of San Ricardo's health."

"You could have done that by telephone. However, since you are here, I will tell you that your visit this morning proved very exhausting. The Duke is now sleeping under heavy sedation."

"Then I should like to see him," Leonor said, with rare impulsiveness.

"And I should like to make another inquiry," Allan said before the blond assistant could frame a forbidding answer. "If the Duke of San Ricardo is in such an exhausted condition, how does it happen that the *Herr Doktor* has chosen this moment to absent himself from such a patient?"

"I believe it was you who insisted on a consultation," the assistant said quickly. "The *Herr Doktor* has gone to Madrid to arrange for this."

"I told him I would make the preliminary arrangements myself. As a matter of courtesy, I should then have asked, of course, whether or not these were agreeable to him; but there is one physician especially, whose advice we were eager to secure, and who is very much *persona grata* at the Embassy. It was through the American Ambassador that I meant to make the first approach."

"That will be quite unnecessary. We are completely capable of handling the situation without American interference. And I may add that I am completely capable of supervising the care of patients, even one of the Duke de San Ricardo's importance to his family, without the presence of the Director. Like him, I am a graduate of the best medical schools on the Continent. As to allowing anyone to see the patient tonight, that is entirely out of the question."

"I think not."

Momentarily, the professor and the physician faced each other. It was the professor who succeeded in outfacing the other.

"The *Marquesa* de las Cinco Torres will remain here tonight," he said. "You will put a room at her disposal, as close as possible to her brother's, and you will see that a nurse furnishes her with whatever is needful for her comfort in the way of toilet articles and a dressing gown. It is to be understood that she may remain either in this room or in her brother's, where an easy chair will be provided for her, just as she prefers or thinks best. It is also understood that she will do nothing which could possibly disturb the patient, much less rouse him. But she will stay. I will wait here until I hear from her that all these details have been cared for to her satisfaction, and that she is also satisfied her brother's abnormally deep slumber gives her no reason for concern. Then I will go on to Madrid and immediately get in touch with the *Herr Doktor*. Be so good as to give me the address at which he can be reached. I will likewise get in touch with the Duke's daughter, who happens to be my fiancée and, whether you approve or not, with the American Embassy."

"Of course I cannot prevent you from getting in touch with your fiancée or your Embassy, whatever I think of the propriety of your doing so, under the circumstances. But it is not our custom to provide accommodations for the relatives of our patients or to give addresses. These high-handed demands are out of order."

"Nevertheless, I think that this time you will manage to depart from custom. It cannot be unknown to you that the events leading up to the Duke's confinement here were, to say the least, unusual. This being so, the *Marquesa*, as his sister, and I, as his future son-in-law, feel justified in asking that unusual concessions should be made in his case. Incidentally, I should like very much to know what sedatives he was given and in what quantities, so that I can report them in Madrid."

"They have already been reported."

"Then it will do no harm to report them again."

Leonor, who had been silent during this inimical exchange of remarks and who had become preternaturally pale, now spoke quietly but firmly. "I am in agreement with everything that *Señor* Lambert has said. Except for another sister, who is a cloistered nun, and his young daughter, who is *Señor* Lambert's fiancée, I am the Duke of San Ricardo's only close relative. I feel that I have a right to remain with him until he wakes and I am assured that his exhaustion has done him no permanent harm; also that the sedatives given him to relieve this exhaustion have had no injurious after-effects. As for the course which my prospective nephew wishes to pursue himself, I think the circumstances warrant it."

"Very well. But should the results, of whatever kind, be unfortunate, I decline to accept the responsibility."

"If the results of anything I have demanded out of order, as you put it, are disastrous, I will accept the responsibility. Of course that does not apply to the results of anything that has previously happened here, nor does it apply to any medication, either past or present."

The hostility of the atmosphere had by no means lessened when the blond doctor, bowing with mock deference, escorted Leonor from the reception room and Allan sat down to await their return. He was seething with fury, though this was less because of anything that he felt convinced had happened than because of the insufferable manner of the man who had been at no pains to conceal the fact that he considered himself an antagonist. Time dragged until Leonor came back and, with every passing moment, Allan found himself increasingly angry. However, when she reappeared, still shadowed by the doctor, nothing in her speech and manner indicated undue concern.

"Pablo seems to be sleeping very quietly," she said, "and an armchair has been put in his room for me, as you requested. No private nurse had previously been provided for night duty, as it had not been thought necessary; now there is one. That is entirely proper—the management cannot be expected to have confidence that I would be completely discreet about avoiding any disturbance of my brother; I should have felt the same way if our positions had been reversed. A very nice room has been prepared for me, but naturally I prefer to remain with Pablo, at least for the present. . . . You will make my apologies at the Wellington, won't you, for not returning to my post at the usual hour? The head chambermaid is very efficient, and I am sure she can function acceptably in my absence. And please ask Amalia de Chavez if she will be so kind as to spend the night with Milagrita at my apartment. I am sure she will be glad to do so. I shall expect to hear from you by telephone in the morning."

"Either that, or I'll be back here. You may continue to feel you'd rather not leave Don Pablo's room, even to take a telephone call."

"Really, *Señor* Lambert, your attitude amounts almost to an insult. This is a highly regarded sanitarium."

"I know. But this doesn't alter the fact that the man who is responsible for the Duke of San Ricardo's presence here is a cardsharp, a forger, a thief and a would-be assassin; or that an employee of this man's wife, who accompanied her from the United States to Spain, died almost immediately after their arrival as a result of slow poisoning by a person or persons as yet unknown. I'm willing to grant that you probably didn't know any of this when you admitted the patient at Crewe's insistence. Nevertheless, you can't blame us for feeling somewhat wary about all his former associates. Incidentally, you haven't told me your name."

"It is Volkman. Hans Volkman."

"You are a German?"

"No, a Swiss—that is, by birth. But a Spaniard by adoption."

"Ah!—then I presume the same is true of the head doctor, whose name, by the way, is—?"

Volkman hesitated but finally said, "He is called Dr. Benjumea."

"I know that. But what is his real name? Is Benjumea a Spanish version of Benjamin?"

"I suppose you might call it that."

"And what is the rest of his name?"

"Buchner. The *Marquesa* could have told you that. He was frequently the Duke's guest at her *dehesa.*"

Allan turned quickly.

"But you *didn't* tell me!" he said, almost accusingly, to Leonor.

"There seemed to be no special reason for it—until now. *Herr Doktor* Buchner, who is indeed a distinguished physician, came first to the *dehesa* not as a medical man, but as a friend—one of several whose names I have not mentioned either, whom my brother was glad to see before he became a recluse—and an invalid. It was only afterwards that *Herr Doktor* Buchner came in his professional capacity."

She was looking at Allan imploringly. So Buchner had been one of those cardplaying companions who, even to the Chief of Police, had been "above suspicion!" And Leonor, who had originally shared this opinion, had flinched from saying any more than she deemed absolutely necessary about those final bouts of gambling which had caused her brother's downfall! Well, here was a new angle, which must be thoroughly explored. But Allan knew that this was not the moment for it. Aloud he said merely, "You are right. Of course there was no previous reason for it. But now I am glad to know it. . . . Do you have *Herr Doktor* Buchner's address and the copy of that prescription ready for me now, *Herr Doktor* Volkman?"

"I have. Permit me to hand them to you."

Allan glanced casually at the neatly typed sheet, nodded, and put it in his pocket. Then he took Leonor's hand and kissed it. The gesture, which a few months ago would have seemed so foreign and artificial to him, was now entirely natural; and, for the first time, as he straightened up, he also kissed her cheek.

"Don't forget I'm your new nephew," he said. "And don't worry. I feel sure everything is under control."

He was in a poor position to say that anyone else drove like a bat out of hell, he told himself, as he went tearing toward Madrid; but he felt no compunction over the speed at which he was going, and fumed when he was caught up in the heavy urban traffic of evening. At the entrance to the Wellington, he asked the friendly doorman to garage the station wagon for him, and charged through the revolving door, intent on reaching Milagrita's stall with the least possible delay. But as he stopped at the *conserjería* to pick up his key, Vitor, its highly efficient chief, held him up.

"There are several messages for the *señor,* all marked urgent. He will perhaps wish to glance through them at once, with a view to immediate attention."

Allan accepted the slips of paper with an unwilling sense of obligation.

But before he began to riffle through them, he handed Vitor the folded sheet Volkman had given him.

"Is that far?" he asked, indicating the address. "If it's fairly near, I'd like to go there tonight, after I have done one or two other things I must see to first." He turned back to Vitor's slips: the Chief of Police had been trying to reach *Señor* Lambert all day by telephone; the call could be returned any time before ten; after that the *Jefe* would be unavailable until morning. The American Embassy had called twice; as the next day was Saturday, it would be closed, but *Señor* Brooks could be reached at his residence, either this evening or tomorrow morning: *Señor* Estrada had come to the hotel in person; he wanted very much to see *Señor* Lambert without delay and would try again in the morning, because it was imperative that they should have a talk. Also another man had come, who did not leave his name; he had said it would mean nothing to *Señor* Lambert, who might, however, be interested to know that he was connected with the *Rastro*; he also would try again. *Señor* Wendell would like *Señor* Lambert to get in touch with him immediately at the Ritz. . . .

"*Señor* Wendell! You mean *Señora* Wendell or *Señorita* Wendell, don't you?"

"No, *señor*. It was a gentleman who spoke. And I understood quite clearly, *Señor* Wendell."

Allan glanced at the clock—twenty past ten. Too late then to reach the *Jefe*. It was out of character for a social favorite like Douglas to be at home and available by telephone throughout the evening; if he were not dining elsewhere, he himself was almost invariably entertaining; probably Allan should do something about that message, but he intended to see Milagrita first. As to the horrible little spy, Estrada, Allan had hoped never to lay eyes on him again. The nice old salesman at the *Rastro* was something else; that he would look into as soon as the deck was cleared of still more urgent matters. The call purporting to come from *Señor* Wendell was clearly a mistake of some sort. . . .

He saw that Vitor, who had been turning the pages of the huge city directory and shaking his head, was looking up with a troubled face. "I am very sorry, *señor*," Vitor said apologetically. "But I have looked carefully, and I cannot find the street indicated by the address you gave me. And I myself have never heard of it. I am a *Madrileño* born and bred and I have been a *conserje* for some years now. I thought it was strange, when you gave me the address, that it was unfamiliar."

Allan snatched the paper from him and turned away, so that Vitor should not see the expression on his face or hear him cursing under his breath; he did not want the pleasant, helpful, *conserje* to think that his rage was caused by the latter's inability to locate a nonexistent street and number.

After a moment he turned again and thanked Vitor, with expressions of regret at having put him to unnecessary trouble; someone was evidently trying to play an ill-timed joke. He then crossed the lobby to the reception desk and gave Leonor's message. The manager regretted to hear of the emergency that caused her absence; but she was quite right; the head chambermaid could manage very well until her return; she was not to bother herself. This matter settled, Allan was at last free to make a dash for Milagrita's stall.

She was waiting for him, wreathed in smiles and wearing a dress of candy-striped taffeta, which was unmistakably the sort she would have put on if she had expected to spend a festive evening. Amalia de Chavez was still with her. Milagrita excitedly interrupted Allan's greeting to herself and the demure little widow.

"Allan, what do you think? *Señor* Brooks telephoned and asked if you and I would not meet him and *Señorita* Carlota at the Ritz, around ten, for dinner and dancing afterward. I told him I would be delighted and that I thought you would be too—of course I did not realize you would be quite so late, but you would have been glad to go anyway, wouldn't you? Then he telephoned again, and said the party was off, because *Señorita* Carlota's father had arrived unexpectedly from the United States and didn't want the evening spent that way; he wanted to have a conference with his wife and daughter and you and *Señor* Brooks. But that could wait till tomorrow, couldn't it? He didn't say anything about including me in it, and I do so want to see you myself!"

"That's just what you're going to do. The conference *can* wait until tomorrow . . . that and a good many other things," Allan added to himself. Aloud he went on, "We'll go dancing with Douglas and Charlotte some other time soon. Tonight, I think it would be nice if you and I could just have a quiet dinner together, in the little trellised restaurant. You could carry on alone awhile longer, couldn't you, *Doña* Amalia? And pretty soon it will be time to shut up shop and you could join Milagrita and me for"— to his surprise he found he could actually laugh a little—"for *flan* and coffee. Then we'll all go to *Tía* Leonor's apartment together. She decided not to come back with me. Yes, I'll explain presently—there's nothing to worry about. But she felt quite sure that *Doña* Amalia would stay with you tonight, *querida*. And she said I could have a little visit with you on the balcony. Come, my dear love."

26.

IT WAS WELL PAST one o'clock before Allan succeeded in tearing himself away from Milagrita. As they ate their leisurely dinner, in the little outdoor restaurant which had become so attractive to him, he gave her an account of the day's happenings: enthusiastic and detailed, as far as his visit to the *dehesa* was concerned; still enthusiastic, but less detailed, as far as the call at Santa Ana's was concerned; he felt perhaps it would be just as well to say nothing about shrines, partly because Milagrita, who was young and inexperienced, might innocently refer to them at an inopportune moment; and partly because Leonor's qualified opinion about her sister's theory had somewhat tempered his own eager acceptance of it. He dwelt on his first stop at the sanitarium with satisfaction; about the second, he said as little as possible. But he did ask one or two seemingly casual questions.

"You have met this *Herr Doktor* Buchner, haven't you, *querida?*"

"Of course. He always received us when we went to the sanitarium."

"You never saw him before that?"

"Yes, a few times, for a few minutes each time, at the *dehesa*. But, you see, I wasn't there very much. I was away at school."

"And you liked the little you saw of him?"

She shrugged her pretty shoulders. "He didn't seem at all like a Spaniard. Of course you don't either, but that's different." She reached across the table for his hand, clasped it warmly and without self-consciousness, and smiled so enchantingly that Allan found it hard not to get up and kiss her then and there. "Otherwise I didn't actually either like or dislike him," Milagrita went on. "He was polite in a stiff sort of way and I knew he was very learned. Besides I realized my father enjoyed *Doktor* Buchner's company—that is, as long as he felt well enough to play cards, and that later, when illness entered the picture, professional advice was necessary. . . . What difference does it make whether I liked him or not?"

"Not much of any. I was just curious to know, because I didn't find him particularly *simpático* myself and I was curious to know whether you did. Have you met the assistant at the sanitarium too?"

"No, it was always the director who received us himself. And remember I haven't been to the sanitarium very often either. First it was hard for me to leave school and then it was hard for me to leave my job. Besides, I was told that even short visits tired my father, that they weren't good for him."

Allan changed the subject. "Your father said I couldn't give you a bracelet yet, but he made no objections to a simple ring. Perhaps I had better confess that I took a chance he mightn't and bought one yesterday. I thought no harm would be done if, after all, there had to be a slight delay. But since there needn't, suppose I give it to you tonight?"

Milagrita thought this a splendid idea. After dinner, they went to Leonor's apartment and left *Doña* Amalia—who, according to previous arrangement had met them at the restaurant—in the *salita*, with a copy of *ABC* and the latest novel by Carmen de Icaza. Then Milagrita and Allan went out on the little balcony and he took a small velvet-covered box from an inner pocket and handed it to his sweetheart. She was so enchanted with the box itself that she did not open it immediately, but turned it over and over in her slim fingers. At last Allan asked her, laughingly, if she were never going to press the little spring at the bottom. When she did so, the lid flew open, disclosing a magnificent diamond imbedded in white satin. The stone itself was so large that the rest of the ring hardly showed at all.

"Why Allan! is that what you call a 'simple ring'?"

"Of course. Just one diamond. What could be simpler?"

"But it's *huge!* I never saw such a big one in a ring before."

"Well then, it's time you did. Aren't you going to let me help you put it on?"

The help occupied considerable time and so did the inevitable aftermath. When they finally returned to the *salita*, Amalia had exhausted the supply of literature they had given her and was doing fine needlework, by the light of a wholly inadequate lamp. But when Allan apologized for the hour, she glanced at the clock and smiled.

"Quarter after one? Why, you should know by now that is practically the edge of the evening in Spain!"

"Thanks for the reminder. . . . Listen *Doña* Amalia, how soon do you think you could take over, entirely, from Milagrita at the stall?"

"Why—within the next few days, if that is agreeable to the management at the Wellington."

"I believe it will be. I'll have a word with the director. And you don't know of anyone, do you, who could take the *Marquesa's* place as *gobernanta?* I feel it's important she should be relieved too, as soon as possible."

"I will think very hard, and ask my mother-in-law to do the same. There might be someone in the family of my late husband—may he have eternal rest!—of whom I would not think myself."

"A very sound idea! Well—even if it is only the edge of the evening, I'm afraid I'll have to say good night. I've had a rather full day and, judging from the messages I found waiting for me at the *conserjería,* I'll have an equally full one tomorrow."

He went back to his hotel suite, flung off his clothes and, to his own surprise, found that he was already so drowsy that he realized there would be no tossing and turning for him in what remained of the night. Moreover, his slumber was so profound that it was permeated by no fantastic dreams, either terrifying or ecstatic. He was finally wakened to unwilling torpor by the consciousness that the telephones in both his rooms were ringing simultaneously. Since the one beside his bed required less effort to answer, he reached for it and said, *"Diga!"* yawning as he did so.

"Diga nothing!" a loud male voice replied indignantly. "Is that you, Allan? Harvey Wendell speaking. Get over to the Ritz on the double! I lost a lot of time yesterday, waiting around for you. I don't want to lose any more."

"I'll get there as soon as I can, Mr. Wendell. But I'm not sure just how quickly that will be. Excuse me, but my other phone is ringing. I'm afraid that's an urgent message too. There were several waiting for me when I got in last night."

Without further apology he hung up the receiver and made a dash for the parlor. As he expected, the Chief of Police was on the line.

"Señor Lambert? Would it be convenient for you to come to my headquarters at once? It will not be possible for me to leave them myself this morning and now that you are no longer an invalid perhaps. . . . Good! I have some news items which I think may be of interest to you. I tried all day yesterday—"

"I know, I know! I'll get to your office just as fast as I can."

He would have felt easier if he could have talked with Leonor before leaving the hotel, but he did not need to be told that it would take at least an hour to get the call through, as the sanitarium was some thirty miles distant from Madrid; neither could he presume to tell the operator to put it in and say that he would accept it at Police Headquarters. It would have to wait until he reached the Ritz. He cut himself while shaving, omitted a shower, and flung on his clothes almost as hastily as he had flung them off a few hours earlier. Then he ran downstairs, deciding that this would be quicker than summoning the elevator. Early as it was, Estrada was lying in wait for him at the rear of the lobby.

"I know you do not wish to speak to me, *Señor* Lambert, but what I have to say is to your advantage and it's very urgent."

"You're right, I do not wish to speak with you. What's more, you're not the only person who has something urgent to say to me this morning and who tried to get hold of me all day yesterday. If you attempt to delay me now, I'll call Vitor and tell him you're molesting me. But if you'll behave yourself and let me get out of here quickly, I'll listen to you this afternoon, if I'm free by that time."

It was all too evident to Estrada that any further effort to detain this incredible North American would result only in disaster. Vitor's watchful eye was already on the intruder and had been, for some minutes past. One of the antiquated taxis, which are not the least noticeable of Madrid's museum pieces, was just drawing up at the entrance, discharging a group of chattering tourists who had arrived on the "luxury train" from Algeciras, upon disembarking there after their voyage on the *Constitution*. As soon as the doorman had dislodged the various raincoats, sweaters, paper parcels, cardboard packages, string bags and other impedimenta wedged in among the passengers, and before the *porteros* had succeeded in removing all the suitcases and hat boxes from the rack on top of the car, Allan was inside it, instructing the driver to get to Police Headquarters in record time.

"*Un momentito, señor!* We cannot leave until the baggage of the other *señores* has been unloaded."

"I realize that. But we can leave before some other tourist has the bright idea that he wants to get to the Prado."

The taxi driver sighed. He had kept hoping for a long while that sometime he would have for a fare a North American who was not in a hurry. But, so far, this hope was unfulfilled, and seemed likely to remain so indefinitely. However, he had to earn his living and these hasty foreigners tipped well. He set his car noisily into motion and went chugging downtown to Police Headquarters, somewhat incongruously housed in the building which had once been the Museum of Ancient Art.

Allan's wait in the corridor, leading to the hall formerly devoted to the Romanesque, was of brief duration. He was admitted to the office of the Chief of Police with great courtesy and with a minimum of delay. It was obvious that the way had been cleared for his immediate reception. The *Jefe* was comfortably seated behind a large desk, smoking an excellent cigar. As usual, he gave the agreeable impression of satisfied well-being, composed efficiency and complete urbanity. He rose, shook hands heartily, and motioned his visitor to a nearby chair.

"As I told you, I have several news items for you. In passing, I will say that I have just received a report from the Avila police, to whom the Abbess had been kind enough to submit some suggestions, after her talk with you. They are entirely in accord with certain theories we entertain here, and which we have already been pursuing, though so far without results. As to more definite progress, I will begin by telling you about the phase of our investigations which appears to me the most important at the moment, though I do not need to tell you that appearances are often deceitful. I think you will be interested to know the results of the autopsy on the body of Marta Rodríguez. I am now in a position to give them to you."

"Interested! I'd say that was the understatement of the year!"

"The report has been slow in coming through, because so many factors were involved. But it now appears certain that Marta was poisoned with antimony salts. Do you know anything about them?"

"Not a thing."

"Well it seems they can be expected to have a lethal effect any time from forty-eight hours to four days after they have been consumed, depending upon the amount that have been given. They produce symptoms of nausea, vomiting and dizziness; in other words, very much the same symptoms as a severe case of seasickness. We have ascertained that the ship's surgeon had none of these deadly salts among his supplies of *materia medica* on the *Tarragona*—indeed there is no reason why he should have, but we have checked to make sure. Therefore, we have every reason to believe that Ethel Crewe had provided herself with them before she went on board, to use in case of emergency, whenever this arose. Where and how she got them we shall probably never know; but it is a lamentable fact that poisons are not as completely inaccessible as they are generally supposed to be. In fact, there has recently been a case of suicide in Bilbao, which was traced to antimony salts, and no one can imagine where the man who killed himself got hold of them."

"So you think Marta was only seasick—very seasick—at first? And that Ethel administered the antimony salts the night I met her in the corridor?"

"Exactly. That theory would fit in perfectly with the official report. The girl had a delicate digestion anyway, as had been frankly stated by her brother; and she was in fact so seasick that the ship's surgeon, who had taken into consideration the possibility of appendicitis, or other intestinal disturbance, became alarmed and sent for Ethel Crewe, who, as he knew, was Marta's employer, and, as he had every reason to believe, her benefactress. He left his patient, after giving her a harmless sedative, confident that she would soon be asleep and that meanwhile she was in good hands. Before he did so, Ethel asked whether or not a cup of bouillon might help to induce slumber, if Marta could retain it, and he said it would, that he would recommend it. The Tourist Class steward has testified that he took a cup of bouillon, late that night, to Marta's cabin, which she had to herself, as Ethel had paid the necessary extra fare to assure single occupancy."

"And Ethel put the poison in the bouillon?"

"It certainly looks that way. The steward had neither motive nor opportunity and we hold him completely guiltless. Antimony salts are undetectable as to both taste and odor when placed in such a solution as bouillon. Ethel was convinced by this time that Marta was so ill from natural causes that she might die at any moment, leaving telltale documents where the authorities, who would then investigate her belongings, could get hold of them. So Ethel decided to take no chances. She poisoned the poor girl, under pretense of ministering to her, and removed all traces of incriminating evidence—or so she thought. She evidently knew how to gauge the amount of the dose very accurately. Marta was desperately ill when she reached Bilbao; the ship's surgeon reported an exaggerated case of seasickness, with a possible complication of appendicitis, to the port doctor; he in turn entrusted her care to the family physician, who came with the ambulance to the dock and, shortly thereafter, found her moribund. All these doctors acted not only with complete good faith, but in accordance with the most approved medical standards. It was only after I learned from you that Ethel Crewe was carrying a capacious handbag the night you met her in the corridor, and passed on this information, that suspicions were aroused in all quarters. By that time Marta had already been buried, and the process of exhumation is one surrounded by considerable formality."

In spite of himself, Allan shuddered. "It's damned grim, isn't it?" he said mournfully. "And I can't help feeling I'm somewhat to blame. If I hadn't answered that letter—"

"You should not blame yourself, señor. Ethel Crewe had arranged for Marta's services long before she ever met you or dispatched that letter. Marta would have had to return to Spain sometime this summer in any case, as her student's visa was good for only one year in an American college. And Ethel would have taken all possible precautions to see that no one found out what her protégée was doing besides her classwork. If they had not taken the *Tarragona* together, they would have taken some other ship, or possibly a plane. Marta's naturally delicate digestion made it easy for Ethel to put an end to her, unsuspected, at any time which seemed expedient."

Allan drew a deep breath. "I suppose you're right," he said. "Just the same, I'm pretty cut up about it."

"Try to dismiss it from your mind, now that you know the facts. Perhaps another news item I have for you will help you to do so. Inocencio has confessed."

"Confessed to *what?*"

"That he did not attend the bullfight in Linares the night of your accident."

"You never thought he did, I believe. But you seemed to be having some difficulty in getting him to admit it."

The *Jefe* coughed slightly. "That difficulty has been overcome," he said, flicking ash from his cigar with a shapely hand. "I will tell you the details about it later, if you are interested. I may add that I believe a large part of his hesitation in confessing earlier was founded on the fact that he didn't want to betray Crewe, who had befriended him."

"I am interested." Allan remembered what Leonor had said concerning almost unshakable loyalty to a *patrón,* and felt a swift stab of sympathy for Inocencio. "But I'm also somewhat pressed for time right now, and I have no doubt you are too," he went on addressing the *Jefe.* "What else did he confess?"

"That it was he who drove your station wagon into the Tagus."

"And it was he who slugged me—at Crewe's instigation of course!" Allan exclaimed, his momentary sympathy engulfed in rage.

"No, not according to his story, and I have reason to believe he is telling the truth now. He says he was told to meet Crewe at a certain point, at a certain hour. He was also told not to come in his own decrepit car, but to take a bus as far as he could and then walk. Shortly after he reached this place which, I need hardly say, was inconspicuously located, two automobiles drove up. One was your station wagon, with Ethel Crewe at the wheel, but otherwise empty. The second car had three men in it, one of them apparently asleep, for he was slumped forward on the seat, but Inocencio could not see him very well."

"This passenger who appeared to be sleeping, rather than knocked out, was no doubt myself."

"No doubt. One of the other men, namely Crewe, emerged from the second car and told Inocencio to take the station wagon to Aranjuez and drive it into the Tagus, as its owner had run afoul of the law and was fleeing from justice. Therefore he had no further use for it and it was important that his car should not be discovered. Inocencio remonstrated on the ground that such a beautiful automobile should not be destroyed; that it would be a prized possession of anyone fortunate enough to get it. But Crewe reminded Inocencio, very bluntly, of his numerous obligations, and of the black mark already against his record, which had caused his dismissal as a palace guide; he had better do as he was told, without any more argument, and without asking any questions. In short, as I believe you would express it, Crewe put the screws on much more forcibly than we have done up to this point. Inocencio was terrified. He may possibly also have been bribed, but this we have no means of proving and I don't by any means feel certain of it. Crewe stood over him until he got into the station wagon and drove away. He did not even dare turn around to see what had become of the other car. He went on going until he reached another inconspicuous place, in the outskirts of Aranjuez. Then, without difficulty, he pushed the station wagon over the bank, which has a sheer drop into the river, which is deep. After that he walked home. It was still dark when he reached there. His crippled brother, not to mention everyone in the neighborhood, was still sleeping. He was entirely unobserved. And of course his co-operation enabled the Crewes to make a much quicker getaway."

"And where is he now?"

"Naturally he is in prison. You were interested in meeting a Spanish prisoner, were you not? Well, here is your opportunity at last."

"And what has become of the crippled brother?"

"We have had to place him in a home for the aged. There was no one else to look after him."

"So their poor little house is empty!"

"For the time being, yes. If nothing worse than theft, aiding and abetting a crime and the destruction of property is proved against Inocencio—in other words, if we can fasten the major crimes on Crewe—Inocencio will be released after serving a normal term."

The *Jefe* leaned back in his chair and relighted his cigar, which had gone out. Allan had the impression that he himself was expected to make the next comment. After a few moments' thought he did so.

"Well, after all, the station wagon has been recovered. And it's as good as new. If you're convinced that Crewe is the major criminal—perhaps I should say *when* you are—possibly the sentence could be shortened for good behavior. Isn't that sometimes done?"

"Yes, sometimes."

"I can't help feeling sorry for the crippled brother. And in a way for that poor devil Inocencio. After all, he and I are fellow victims." Allan remembered that only the day before he had said the same thing to the Duke of San Ricardo. Now, though the circumstances were so different, he found he meant it just as sincerely. "I'd like to go and see him if I may— him and his brother both. That is, if it isn't against rules and regulations."

"Certainly not. We are quite willing to have our institutions visited by responsible persons, whenever they have a valid reason for such visits. And you have one."

"Thank you. And I don't need to tell you how grateful I am for all the trouble you've taken about this."

"*De nada, señor, de nada!*"

"It doesn't seem like nothing to me. It seems like a great deal—so much that I hesitate to ask for any more help."

"There is no reason why you should hesitate. I had not quite finished with my news items. But if there is something special that you wished to ask first—"

"Yes, there is, because it seems to me very important. Are any particular formalities required to get a patient released from a sanitarium?"

"You mean a patient who is sane and who is not so ill that his life would be endangered by such a removal?"

"Yes, exactly. I have a very strong feeling that the Duke of San Ricardo should be taken from that oversized Swiss chalet where he's a patient. There's one thing you didn't tell me, Chief: that the director of that sanitarium was one of the Duke's former cardplaying cronies. You said they were all 'above suspicion.'"

"I said we had every reason to suppose they were—with the exception of Crewe, naturally—though some of the later ones were hardly of the class which the Duke would normally have chosen for companions. I am very sorry if we slipped up there. What exactly is it that you suspect and what exactly is it that you want to do?"

"I don't think the Duke's as sick as he's made out to be. I want a consultation of doctors—physicians of his sister's choosing and mine. And I want to get him away from the sanitarium as quickly as possible. I don't merely think he's being detained there to wring money out of his unfortunate sister, in payment for his gambling debts; I think he's being drugged. I don't mean with lethal doses, but I do mean with ones large enough to stupefy." As briefly as possible, Allan gave an account of his two visits to the sanitarium and of the fictitious address with which he'd been supplied. "I wouldn't be at all surprised if the real reason *Herr Doktor* Buchner came to Madrid wasn't to find physicians suitable for a consultation, but to round up some of the other card players to whom the Duke owes money and get them after him, or after his sister, or after me."

"In that case, we will of course recheck that entire situation at once."

"Thank you. And meanwhile I'd like to get the Duke out of that sanitarium today if possible. It wouldn't even be necessary to wait for an ambulance, if one isn't easily available. He could be transported in my station wagon. The seats are adjustable, so that it is possible to recline in one and the drive to Madrid doesn't take much more than an hour. The Duke could be brought straight to that excellent clinic where I was and Sister Dorotea could care for him. The consultation could take place there."

The *Jefe* smiled and flicked off some more cigar ash. "It will doubtless surprise you to learn that there is no scarcity of ambulances in Spain," he said pleasantly. "I know that foreigners rather like to regard us as backward, but, as a matter of fact, we are quite up-to-date in many respects. However, if it would please you to transport the Duke in your station wagon, and it is really so adaptable, I see no reason why you should not do so. I will look into that situation too, and let you know in an hour or so what I've been able to do. Where are you going next?"

"To the Ritz. An American friend of mine arrived there yesterday, and he's also kept telephoning me. I don't know just what kind of trouble he's in, but evidently some."

"Very well. Go along to the Ritz and see this American friend of yours. I will telephone you at his suite. His name is—?"

"Harvey Wendell. He's just joined his wife and daughter."

"His wife is not by chance the North American lady who made so much disturbance at the clinic?"

"By some chance she is. She rather had the idea that her daughter and I were engaged to be married. But she's got over that now. She has quite a different idea—a much better one, both from her point of view and from mine. Not to mention the daughter's, who, by the way, is a very nice girl. The father isn't after me with a shotgun. Something else must be worrying him."

The *Jefe* laughed comfortably. "Very well," he said again. "Go along to the Ritz and see what you can do to assuage the anxiety of this worried gentleman. I should have said you had enough problems of your own on your hands, without attempting to solve anyone else's. But before you go, I might tell you my other news item. It will take only a moment."

"I'd like very much to hear it."

"Diego Rodríguez left some days ago for France. In fact, shortly after my last visit with you."

"You mean the brother of that poor girl who died?"

"Who else? He never met either of the Crewes—it seems that when the arrangements were made, by an aunt, for his sister to study in the United States, he was in Avila doing research himself. Like you, he is something of a scholar, and he is especially interested in Teresiana. But I do not need to remind you that he is now in a very vengeful mood, though normally he is a mild sort of man; he seems convinced that he can be helpful to Interpol and the French Police. He may possibly be right. At all events, our Bilbao branch has gone so far as to suggest that no impediments be put in his way. Naturally he has been cautioned that Justice should be allowed to take its normal course, and that if it does not, he will be liable to punishment for any rash act of his that may forestall it." The *Jefe* paused for a moment and stared at Allan, but his expression was masklike. "If he *is* right we may be at the end of our search very soon. Then the Police can pounce as soon as the proper signal goes through."

27.

ALLAN MADE GOOD TIME in getting to the Ritz, and the concierge, ordinarily inclined to be somewhat haughty, had received instructions to have him shown immediately to the Wendells' suite. A small *botones* was summoned and, beaming with pride over the importance of his responsibility, led his charge across the lobby to the elevator, bowed him into it, in due course bowed him out of it, preceded him down a long, richly carpeted corridor and knocked at the outsize double doors which obviously led into a spacious suite. Allan had barely time to thrust a five-*peseta* note into the willing hand of the small bellboy, when the doors were flung open by Harvey Wendell himself.

"Well, at last!" he boomed. But though his voice portrayed impatience, it did not sound angry, and he held out his hand and grasped Allan's in a crushing grip. "Come on in. We're all waiting for you."

He turned, passing quickly from the small antechamber into a large circular drawing room, the baroque splendor of which had been somewhat obscured while his ample figure blocked its entrance. It was elegantly equipped with Empire furniture, upholstered in mustard-colored brocade, with draperies of the same tint and texture at the long windows, and the Spanish version of an Aubusson rug on the floor. Allan, with vivid memories of the overstuffed suite in the Wendells' living room at home, its bizarre cretonne curtains and its Axminster floor covering, could not help contrasting the two settings with some amusement. Mrs. Wendell, impressively clad in olive green *crêpe Marocain*, was sitting stiffly on one of the larger sofas; on a love seat, no less impressively clad in biege *peau de soie*, was Charlotte with Douglas beside her. Allan noticed that they were holding hands, and that this was apparently quite in order, as far as Charlotte's parents were concerned. He also noticed that she was wearing a diamond ring, and could not suppress a certain smug satisfaction that the stone in the ring he had given Milagrita the night before was much larger.

"Sit down, sit down, Allan," Mr. Wendell admonished him, still in a booming voice. "Well, I've learned that you and Charlotte have both found someone that suits you better than what seemed likely when you left home, and this suits her mother and me too, as long as it does her. It's all we want, so far as our only child's concerned—that she should be suited. The idea of flying over here didn't just come to me. I sort of got the notion, from what the wife wrote me, that you were shilly-shallying around with my sugar cookie, and I didn't intend to stand for that, not for one minute." Allan could not refrain from looking at Charlotte, and observing, again with some amusement, the withering way in which she was glaring at her father. "However, I knew that wasn't the sort of thing you'd be liable to do, so I didn't jump into the first plane," Mr. Wendell went on. "I figured I'd better wait for developments. And I'm glad I did. I see now I didn't have things sized up right at first, and I've taken a liking to Douglas here, straight off. That is, as a man and a future son-in-law. I'm pleased with him, but I'm not so pleased with his job. Not but what I suppose he's doing the best he can, with higher ups hindering him. But there's no question that the Embassy's shilly-shallying and that gets my goat."

"I'm not sure that I quite follow you, sir," Allan said pleasantly, taking the seat that Mr. Wendell indicated, after having shaken hands all around.

"Why, here it is a month or more since you got beaten up and those criminals are still at large! As an honest-to-God American, it makes my blood boil, just to think of it! It boiled so hard that when I got Charlotte's last letter, I decided I *would* jump into a plane; I'd fly over here and take a hand in things myself. Even if you're not going to be my son-in-law, you're an old friend and a good customer. I propose to see justice done. Not next year either. Right now."

Allan and Douglas exchanged glances. "I don't think you should be too hard on the Embassy, Mr. Wendell," Allan said, still pleasantly. "Since you seem to be very thoroughly informed, you know that though I was found very promptly after the accident, I wasn't identified for several days and I was unconscious for several days after that. Even when I came to, I was in such a serious condition that the hospital authorities wouldn't let me see anyone or talk to anyone. As soon as they could, the Embassy and the Police both got busy, but we'd lost a lot of time."

"The Embassy! The Police!" Mr. Wendell exploded. "And what has either one of them proved so far, I'd like to know?"

"The Embassy has taken all the proper steps to provide for the Crewes' extradition, once they are found, but it's a long process. And I've just come from Police Headquarters. They've cornered the man who ran my station wagon into the Tagus river and made it easier for the Crewes to get away."

"All right, all right!" Mr. Wendell continued vehemently, raising his hand to silence the chorus of eager questions which immediately greeted this exciting announcement. "But they haven't found the *Crewes!* That's what wants doing and what I propose to do myself, if nobody else will."

There was a moment's silence, while Allan gathered his forces. "I appreciate your good will and all the trouble you've taken to come over here," he said eventually. "No doubt you'll think of some angle that hasn't occurred to any of the rest of us."

"*Think* of some angle! I'm not going to stop to think! I'm going to do something!"

Again Allan and Douglas involuntarily exchanged glances, and this time neither one could suppress a smile, though they devoutly hoped that in his agitated condition, Mr. Wendell would not notice this.

"As a matter of fact," Allan went on, "the Chief of Police—whom, incidentally, I like immensely—having discovered who made away with the station wagon, is now following through in two or three other directions. One of them he had no sound reason to investigate before. A rather important piece of evidence had been withheld by someone I'm very fond of—someone I hope is going to be a close relative of mine. She didn't do this maliciously. She did it because she was trying to shield another victim of the Crewes, who's suffered at their hands a lot more than I have. But now that this secret's out, we can carry on a lot further. In fact, I'm expecting a telephone message any minute. I took the liberty of telling the Chief he could call me here."

"All right, all right!" Mr. Wendell said again. "You didn't take any liberty. You know you're welcome to have the Chief of Police or anyone else telephone you at my suite. But is this call you're expecting going to tell us where the Crewes are and what steps are being taken to arrest them?"

"I'm afraid not. But I hope and believe it's going to make life a lot happier for this other victim I've been talking about and that's also very important to me—to me and to his sister and daughter."

Mr. Wendell banged with his fist on an onyx-topped table. "That's all very well. But what's most important to *me* is that those crooks be found and put into jail before they can do any more harm that'll give Americans a bad name abroad. If no one else will go after them, I'm going myself!"

By this time he was actually beating the table, quite oblivious of the fact that the drubbing made no impression on its hard, polished surface, but that his clenched fist was getting redder by the minute. His wife and daughter, each in her own way, endeavored to remonstrate with him.

"Harvey, do stop carrying on so, for goodness sake! The next thing we know, someone will be in here asking what the matter is."

"Somebody *has* gone after them, Poppa! Douglas tried to explain that to you already. There's this organization called Interpol—"

"I don't care who hears me and I'm not interested in any organization. I am going to France on my own, without any help from the Embassy or the Police. The only person I want with me is a good private detective who'll take orders from me and not from anyone else!"

The telephone rang. Without stopping to ask permission, Allan sprang to answer it, and instantly recognized the suave voice of the *Jefe*, despite the usual amount of disturbance on the line.

"*Señor* Lambert? I have more good news for you. There will be nothing to prevent the removal of the person in whom you are interested from the place where he is now, but it will be better if this removal takes place tomorrow or the next day, rather than today. Meanwhile, there is no cause for real anxiety on his account. I am writing you a letter of explanation and sending it by special messenger to the Wellington. You should find it there on your return, which I take it will be in the reasonably near future."

"Yes, in just a few minutes. And thank you again, a thousand times."

"*De nada, amigo, de nada!*"

Allan replaced the receiver on its cradle and turned to his host. "As far as I myself am concerned, I should be perfectly willing to forget all about the Crewes at this point," he said. "But I realize the logic of what you're saying, Mr. Wendell. They mustn't do any more damage if that can be prevented, and they mustn't be allowed to go on giving Americans a black eye in Europe. It may be of interest to you to learn that another man has already started for France in pursuit of them, more or less on his own, though with police approval and co-operation. He's got blood in his eye and if he finds them, I think he'll also find a way to deal with them in short order. But if you want to go too, there's no reason why you shouldn't—freedom of movement isn't confined to the United States, except for the same reasons that it's restricted there. And if you really want to hire a private detective, I think I have just the man for you. The Police wouldn't use him—they look with contempt on any such operator who's not a member of their force. And I wouldn't want him as a traveling companion—in fact, I have a suspicion that he's more or less involved in my own mishaps as well as those of my Spanish friends; and I find him personally repulsive. But that doesn't mean he isn't good at his job."

"Well, that's what I want—a man who's good at his job. I can look after myself better than you can, if you don't mind my saying so; and I don't care what this detective's like personally, if he can do the trick. Didn't you ever hear the good old proverb of, 'Set a thief to catch a thief'?"

"Yes, of course I've heard it. And I've no reason to think this man's a thief —just a spy and a companion of thieves. I don't happen to care for spies."

"What else is a good share of a Police Force or Military Intelligence? Listen, Allan, you're a fine fellow, but you're an idealist. I'm a businessman. Your money came to you easy; you inherited it. I've made every cent of mine, the hard way, and I've made plenty; now I'm in the position to get the most out of it."

Mr. Wendell looked around him with pride: at the Empire furniture upholstered in brocade, at his wife and daughter arrayed in the latest creations of Pertina, at the rising young diplomat seated beside Charlotte and the diamond ring glistening on her finger. Allan sighed. He knew this was not the moment to speak of the long years when he had been underpaid, sometimes underfed, when he had not had a comfortable place to live or the means to increase his slender store of knowledge by travel and association with superior minds; and yet he had persevered. Perhaps he *was* an idealist. But after all his ideals had been those of a gentleman and a scholar; and his one bold sortie into adventure had brought him such untold happiness, such promise of rich reward for himself and others dear to him, that he could not regret it. Perhaps Mr. Wendell *was* more practical; at all events, it was not for him, Allan Lambert, to pass judgment on the course which this successful businessman wanted to pursue. Aloud, he said only, "Well, I happen to know that the detective to whom I referred is at the Wellington right now, lying in wait for me. I want to get back there as soon as I can, not to see him but to see what's in a letter that's been sent me. Would you care to come along with me?"

28.

As ALLAN EXPECTED, Vitor handed him an envelope marked *"Urgente,"* bearing the letterhead of Police Headquarters, as the former went by the *conserjería*; also as he expected, Marcos Estrada was still camping in the lobby. The detective was agreeably surprised when, instead of being again put off, as he had feared he would be, *Señor* Lambert and an older North American gentleman, who looked very prosperous and purposeful, stopped beside him.

"This is *Señor* Wendell, an old friend of mine, Estrada," Allan said. "He has a proposition to make you, which I think might be of more interest to you than anything you and I might talk about; so I suggest you let whatever you have on your mind wait. You may come up to my suite and go over this plan of his with him—you speak enough English to do that, don't you?"

"Of course, *Señor* Lambert. I talk very good English. It is necessary in my work. But I also—"

"You'd better take this chance while you've got it. You may never have one half so good again."

Without more ado, Allan hustled Mr. Wendell and Marcos Estrada into the parlor of his suite, offered them cigarettes and rang for coffee. Then he went into his bedroom, closing the door after him, and tore open the envelope marked *Urgente*.

"*Muy amigo mio*," the letter began. Even in his haste to devour its contents, Allan did not fail to notice the form of salutation. The *Jefe* was addressing him as "My dear friend," instead of "Dear sir" as he would have been if the letter had begun, "*Muy señor mio*." This was a further proof that the two were not only on a professional, but a cordial footing, and Allan was pleased to realize that this was so.

"As I told you over the telephone, I have good news for you," the *Jefe* wrote. "If you proceed in such a way as to allow certain persons a reasonable amount of face-saving, you should have no trouble in carrying out the project you outlined to me earlier this morning. The medical man who came to Madrid yesterday did indeed have other matters in mind besides consultations with physicians. But as a Spaniard, I am proud to say that not a single one of the erstwhile companions at games of chance whom he has succeeded in approaching was willing to press claims against the patient. One or two of them are inaccessible, as they do not live in Madrid; but I am confident that their reply will be the same. So our estimate that this particular group was 'above suspicion' was substantially correct, except in the case of the physician; and surely even the Police must slip up occasionally. The person who wants reimbursement is somewhat chagrined at his failure to find the support he expected, though he will not admit this, which does not surprise me, for I have never known a man of his nationality who would confess to being in the wrong about anything. His chagrin takes the form of saying that he will be satisfied if he is paid in full for his professional services as a physician, and of course he now puts these at a very high figure. He freely admits the use of sedatives for his patient, but reminds me that these are almost invariably used in the treatment of nervous disorders, though doctors disagree as to the amount which should be used and sometimes as to the kind. He is returning to his usual headquarters today, and will be quite ready to receive a medical delegation, as well as yourself, tomorrow. If the consensus of opinion is that the patient may be moved, there will be no further delay—after the huge bill is paid. Meanwhile the amount of sedation has been reduced, the patient is doing well and his sister is welcome to remain with him. I suggest that in the interests of the above mentioned face-saving, you permit an ambulance to be used, but if you insist on the use of your station wagon, I do not think you will be stopped. I believe, however, that it is always best to maintain an atmosphere of harmony, whenever this is possible. Since you may be interested in knowing how I have been able to get results so quickly, I have no objection to telling you that I put through a long-distance telephone call as soon as you left my office and was fortunate in getting a prompt connection—less than half an hour—and in convincing the person with whom I spoke that it would be to his advantage to give me the correct address of his colleague who had come to Madrid. This happened to be fairly near here and one of my lieutenants went there at once and easily persuaded the medical man in question that I required the pleasure of his company.

"Yours with expressions of highest consideration and esteem—"

The letter was signed only with initials. Allan laughed, put it back into his pocket and opened the door into his parlor. Mr. Wendell and Marcos Estrada were obviously reaching a swift and satisfactory understanding over their coffee and cigarettes.

"So you *were* ready to turn state's evidence, Estrada?" Allan said in a slightly mocking tone. And, as the detective looked bewildered, he added, "Never mind what I mean. It's what I supposed you wanted to do, and though I wasn't interested myself, I think you're fortunate in finding someone else who is." He turned to Mr. Wendell. "Of course you and Estrada are quite welcome to stay here until you've settled all the details of your little trip," he said. "But I wonder if you'd excuse me? I have now seen three of the four persons who were vainly trying to get in touch with me yesterday and I'd like to see the fourth one. I think I know where to find him."

The bent, elderly shopkeeper in the *Rastro* was moving rather restlessly about among the trash and treasure which constituted his wares when Allan mounted the steps of the *Galería los Santeros*. No other customers were in sight and the old man straightened up and looked at Allan with a pleased smile of recognition.

"Ah, my friend! So you did get my message! I was hoping that you would come and see me today."

Again Allan experienced an unwonted degree of pleasure of a salutation which began, "My friend." . . . "Yes," he said, "as you see, I did get your message and, as you also see, I have lost no time in responding to it. Of course I am very much interested in knowing why you wanted to see me. I mean specifically. I trust you are always glad to see me."

"I am indeed, *señor*. But there is a certain matter . . ." He paused to indicate a high-backed chair which, despite the worn condition of its crimson velvet and a few fragments missing from its carving, retained an air of ancient elegance.

"Will the *señor* not please be seated?" he asked; and when Allan had taken the designated place, he continued, "Does the name of Sigismundo mean anything to the *señor*?"

"Sigismundo? What is the rest of his name?"

"As a matter of fact, it is Lopez. But the surname does not matter. This man was Crewe's butler. If you remember him at all, it would probably be because he made good cocktails or was exceptionally deft at serving, or something of that sort."

"Lord, you're right! Crewe did call his butler Sigismundo and he made the best martinis I've had in Spain. I remember being surprised that he talked in broken English, instead of Spanish, since the Crewes speak that so well. He must have been the same man who telephoned me to say that the note I had sent to the post office had been received and that a representative of the person in whom I was interested would call on me the following evening."

"He was. Later, when he started adding things up, he realized that there was something fishy about that call, which Crewe had told him to make—and in English. Of course, if anyone had been listening in, it wouldn't have been as much of a giveaway as if he had spoken in Spanish."

"Well, well! So Sigismundo's services were not limited to butlering, though, now that you mention it, I recall that he was very good at that. What is he doing now?"

"Nothing. That is his trouble."

The old shopkeeper paused, and slightly shifted the position of the delicate porcelain Madonna which Allan had noticed the first time that he had gone to the *Galería*. Then the antiquarian went on.

"He and his wife, whom the Crewes had engaged as butler and cook, were given the week end off by way of reward for putting in extra time while the newly rented house was getting settled."

"Newly rented! I thought they owned the house."

"No doubt they had their reasons for giving that impression. The police must, of course, know that it was a false one, but doubtless they have had matters of greater importance to discuss with the *señor.* . . . Well, when Sigismundo and Concepción—what is the matter, *señor?"*

"Nothing. It's simply that I still can't seem to take all of the ordinary Spanish names in my stride. So when Sigismundo and his wife, no doubt prophetically named Concepción, returned from their week end off, they found the Crewes were gone, and the deaf old gardener could give them no information as to their employers' whereabouts, because he could not hear their questions."

"Exactly. And, therefore, Sigismundo and Concepción decided that it would be better if they remained—shall we say in retreat for a while? It seems Sigismundo's suspicions had been roused a second time, because the night after you dined there, Crewe telephoned you, asking you to meet certain persons at his house. The butler overheard the conversation, overheard Crewe calling you by name. It was immediately after this conversation that Crewe generously offered his employees the week end off, and no visitors had arrived at the house by the time the couple had finished their work and went home—they did not live in. Then, as you just said, neither did they find the Crewes in residence when they returned, and presently accounts began to appear in the press about a mysterious disappearance and a mysterious crime. Such people are not normally great readers, but it happens that these two *can* read and the episode was rousing a great deal of excitement; besides seeing the newspapers, they heard the radio reports and the conversation in their family circle. They put two and two together, decided that they did not in any way wish to be implicated, and remained in retreat."

"And do you know what finally decided them to come out from under cover?"

"I am getting to that, *señor*. They were naturally out of work and therefore unpaid—in fact their wages were somewhat in arrears. The week end holiday had allegedly been in partial compensation for these. So finally Sigismundo decided to risk going back for a talk with the gardener who, though he cannot hear, can speak well enough on his own initiative when he wants to. He was still at his post, but he was also unpaid; and though he had managed all right for a time, as long as he had shelter and the wherewithal for food, he did not care to stay on as caretaker much longer. He wants to return to his own *pueblo*. And while he was telling Sigismundo all this, who should drive up but the landlord!"

"Who, I suppose, had not been paid either?"

"Just so. And who proposed to put up with no more nonsense. He had also smelled a rat, but had been content to let matters drift for a time—no one likes to get involved with a crime, no matter how indirectly. However, he wanted to see in what condition the place had been left. Now he intends to apply to the proper authorities to secure new tenants and to have the furniture, which was not his, put up at auction."

"And it was after this pregnant visit that Sigismundo came to see you?"

"Yes. He had been to see me several times before the Crewes' hasty departure. He was very good at doing errands, so it was he who selected on approval a number of the bibelots with which the Crewes had adorned their house. I had waited on him in their behalf. And he knew that the bibelots had not been fully paid for either. So he decided that there would be no dishonesty in returning some of them to me, before the angry landlord could have them put up at auction. At least he persuaded himself that there was no dishonesty in such a course. You can hardly blame the poor man. Concepción's name had indeed proved prophetic and the couple was out of work and frightened."

"And the bibelots are here now?"

"Yes, I have them all grouped together, for the *señor's* convenience. Of course he will not reason like poor Sigismundo who, after all, is more to be pitied than blamed. The *señor* will get in touch with the disappointed landlord and with the proper authorities before taking any other action. But since I knew that he was interested in procuring the Duke of San Ricardo's books, I thought he might be interested in finding out what else was available, here and elsewhere—for of course Sigismundo did not make all his purchases here. I also thought that because of his kind heart, the *señor* might consider doing something to help these poor unfortunate people, who are not in the least to blame for anything that has happened."

"How right you are, about everything! Let's begin by having a look at the bibelots that are here!"

When Allan returned to the Wellington he went at once to Milagrita's stall. He had to wait a few minutes before he could speak with her, because business, at that moment, was brisk. But as soon as opportunity offered, he approached her with an air of undisguised gaiety. "When *Doña* Amalia relieves you, please go home and put on that candy-striped dress again," he said. "This is definitely to be an evening when we should go dancing."

29.

ETHEL CREWE SAT ON THE TERRACE of a small country house near Lisieux, awaiting the arrival of her host, whom she had first met in the garden of the *Hôtel du Parc* a few days earlier, and who had invited her to come and have chocolate with him.

If she had not been so profoundly bored, she would have not accepted the invitation; but she was finding life at the *Hotellerie de Sainte Marthe*, which was run by the Benedictine nuns, utterly "weary, stale, flat and unprofitable." She had a small, narrow room, furnished with a bed, a table, two chairs and an armoire; but it had no proper closet, and though the cubicle at its rear contained *confort moderne*, according to the French interpretation of this, that meant a basin and a *bidet*, nothing more. The view, looking over the little city toward the great white basilica which crowned the hill beyond it, was admittedly a lovely one; but no one could sit all day beside a window, looking through glass at a view. Ethel did not even have a balcony, which would have given her a little more space and the satisfaction of being outdoors. Not that this was always a satisfaction in Normandy. It rained a great deal, and it was often as cold as Madrid in November. . . .

When she was not sitting in this bare little room, Ethel had been going to some service, either in the chapel of the Benedictines, attached to the *hotellerie* where she was staying, or at the church of the Carmelites in the center of town, or at the great white basilica on the hill, which she could see from her window. She would never have believed that so many different services could be crowded into a single day, or that a traveler who had presented herself as a pilgrim, a devotee of the "Little" Saint Thérèse would be expected to attend, automatically, practically all of these; several quavering, black-clad old ladies, who were among the other paying guests at the *hotellerie,* and whose activities, past, present and future, seemed to consist of attending such tiresome services, had offered to accompany her, when she came to Lisieux as a stranger; she had felt it wise to accept their good offices. Now they clung to her company like leeches. They not only dragged her to church, they insisted that they knew the best places to buy souvenirs. The only knickknacks that she had in her bare little room were statuettes of the Little Saint Thérèse and small receptacles of china and German silver, ornamented either with her likeness or with some scene connected with her short and simple life. Ethel thought these were all garish, tasteless and superfluous—a terrible comedown from the marvelous tapestries, the somber, splendid paintings, the polychrome images, the inlaid *bargueños* and other treasures, formerly belonging to the Duke of San Ricardo, which she and Anthony had been fortunate enough to acquire in partial payment of the Duke's debts. . . .

Lourdes had not been as bad as Lisieux. There was more excitement in the air at Lourdes, what with torchlight processions, train loads of invalids under the supervision of clergy, physicians and infirmarians, and the coming and going of eminent personages from all parts of the world. Besides, Lourdes was within easy motoring distance of Pau, where Anthony was staying then, and they still had plenty of funds and a new little French car. But Anthony had got it into his head that they were being watched, despite all their precautions, and that they had better separate completely, at least for the time being. Perhaps later he could come to Deauville, where he would enjoy the Casino, and then they would again be near together and she could have some diversion too. But he had not come to Deauville. He had written her, vaguely, that he was going to take a little trip through Southern and Central France; he had heard of several small places where he felt sure he would find congenial companions. However, he did not tell her the names of these places in his letter, which he had not even signed, and she had not heard from him since. She knew that he blamed her because the *affaire* Lambert had not gone forward according to plan. She should have found out that Allan did not need money, before she sent him that Spanish Prisoner letter; and she should have managed to ensnare him completely afterward. It was easy enough for Anthony to talk. He had slipped up himself, when he had left Allan merely robbed and stunned instead of dead. . . .

She could not go on indefinitely like this, living in a *hotellerie,* which might as well be a convent, staring out of the window, and going only to religious services and such places of pilgrimage as *Les Buissonets,* which had been the childhood home of Saint Thérèse. The *Hôtel du Parc* at least had a pleasant garden, and possibly she might meet someone there who would be harmless, but who would take her mind off her troubles. Certainly the quavering old ladies did not, or the shabby priests who were the only male guests accepted by the Benedictines. There must be some persons who came to Lisieux for reasons other than praying. At least it was worth trying to find out. . . .

At first she had no luck. She was courteously shown to a table, a cheerful, rubicund waiter in a soiled white jacket took her order, and in due course chocolate and *madeleines* were brought to her. But though the occupants of nearby tables looked at her with the frank stares which are not considered particularly bad manners on most of the Continent, no one came to speak with her and the chocolate was not at all to her taste. However, she made it last as long as she could, hoping that something would happen. Nothing did. It was only because she had nowhere else to go except to church that she returned the next day and the next.

It was the third day when something at last did happen. She had pushed away her cup with distaste and spoken sharply to the cheerful rubicund *garçon,* saying it was evident that no one in France knew how to make chocolate. He had at first looked hurt and then indignant, and had gone away shrugging his shoulders and whisking his soiled napkin. It was after this that a quiet-looking man, who had been sitting alone at a nearby table, rose and came over to hers, bowing and speaking to her in Spanish.

"I could not help overhearing what you were saying to that insufferable waiter; I agree with you that this so-called chocolate mixture is almost undrinkable—thin and tasteless. Am I right in believing that I have the pleasure in addressing a fellow countrywoman?"

Ethel had been sorry all the time that her Spanish was not sufficiently foolproof, like Anthony's, to alter not only her name, but her nationality on her passport. She was sorrier than ever now, when at last something vaguely promising had occurred. But at least she was able to answer quite adequately in the stranger's native tongue.

"No, I am an American. But I've had the privilege of spending some time in your country—enough to appreciate your cuisine. Now I like my chocolate thick enough to eat with a spoon instead of drinking it, if I prefer to do so, and heavily flavored with cinnamon. I am sure that is your taste too."

"*Cómo no?*" he said smiling, and added, "Would you permit me to sit down and chat with you a few minutes? You are the first person I have met in this benighted place who speaks Spanish; naturally it is music to my ears." Then as Ethel smiled in return, he seated himself and suggested that he be allowed to order something else. Vermouth perhaps? That at least should be safe. . . .

They fell into easy and casual conversation. Ethel knew that she must be careful, that this nondescript and inoffensive man might be dangerous, directly or indirectly. She encouraged him to do most of the talking, and he seemed quite willing to fall in with her wishes. He was a writer of sorts, interested principally in religious subjects. He had long treasured the plan of preparing a brochure in which the virtues of the Great Saint Teresa of Avila and the Little Saint Thérèse of Lisieux could be compared. Yes, he knew that had already been done, superbly, by an eminent English author; but he had in mind a different type of presentation, briefer, less scholarly, something that could be sold at a popular price. It had been a relatively simple matter to get to Avila—he himself was a resident of Valladolid. But he had been obliged to wait and save before he could come to Lisieux, even traveling third class. It was the old story, there had not been enough money. Now at last he was fortunate: he had not only reached the desired destination, he had succeeded in finding lodgings at a little *pays* only a few kilometers from Lisieux, in fact within easy walking distance. His hosts were not even *petits bourgeois*—just plain farming people; his accommodations were somewhat primitive. But what of that? He was progressing with his work in quiet surroundings. He came into Lisieux every day or so, in connection with his research. And occasionally he allowed himself the extravagance of coming to the garden of the *Hôtel du Parc* for a drink. After all, one could not spend all one's time delving into the story of a saint. Did the *señora* not agree?

She could hardly have done so more heartily. Her purpose in coming to Lisieux had not been exactly like his, she told him; alas! She did not have enough talent to be a writer. Nevertheless, there was a certain similarity between their aims, because she too had been drawn there by her interest in the Little Saint Thérèse. She had been going to all the places of pilgrimage and assembling souvenirs. Now she too was beginning to find that she needed some change, some relaxation, though she was not yet ready to leave. And no, it would not be displeasing to her if they should happen to meet again. . . .

When she returned to the *hotellerie,* she looked at herself thoughtfully in the inadequate mirror provided in her quarters. What she saw was not too discouraging. It had cost her a great deal to cut off her beautiful long fair hair; but now its bright dye, almost orange color, seemed less offensive than it had at first, and she had accustomed herself to a short frizz in place of an elaborate coiffure. Another trial had been the darkening of her fine white teeth and the placing of gold caps on some of them; but she had never been given to broad grins, as if she were advertising a certain brand of toothpaste, and she could smile enchantingly with her lips closed, or nearly so. However, she simply could not stand the hideous clothes, which made her look twice her size, another minute. The next time she went to the garden of the *Hôtel du Parc* she would wear something that more or less fitted her, that had short sleeves and a V neckline. Before prudence could cause her to change her mind, she slipped out of her dress, chopped off the sleeves and began to make other alterations.

It was only a few days after this that her outings began to assume the aspect of a rendezvous. The devout Spaniard, who had disclosed his name as Gaspar Mendoza, and who had offered some of his learned religious writings for her inspection, seemed more and more in need of short breaks in the monotony of his work; and after they had been meeting for about a week he made a suggestion that strongly appealed to Ethel.

"Why not come out to the pleasant little place where I am staying and spend the afternoon with me there? I have asked permission of my landlady to invade her kitchen and make some chocolate of the type we will both enjoy. Do say yes! It will not be exciting, but it will make a pleasant excursion for you."

She had hesitated, but in the end she had consented; the outing had indeed proved very pleasant and the chocolate that Mendoza made delicious. He had escorted her to his lodging the first time she went there, and she had found the walk refreshing and invigorating; they had loitered a little along the way, getting on better terms every minute. Convenient bus service made her return to Lisieux easy, and Mendoza had kissed her hand twice when he bade her farewell. She had not neglected to go to Vespers that same evening.

Now she and her new-found friend had reached the point where she made the outbound and the inbound trip alone, so that he might get on faster with his work and the sooner be free to leave this locality and seek a publisher for his work. Nothing had been said to the effect that when he did, Ethel might leave too. But she was beginning to believe that the idea was forming in his consciousness and the thought of it was not displeasing to her. She was tired of waiting to hear from Anthony and she was heartily sick of Lisieux. Besides, that morning she had received a very severe shock.

When she went to the bank to cash a traveler's check, the Manager, hitherto extremely courteous, had temporized. "We happen to be a little short today of francs in the denominations for which *madame* has shown a preference. Could she perhaps come back tomorrow?"

"It doesn't matter about the denominations. I'll take any you can conveniently let me have."

"Oh, a thousand pardons, *madame!* I see that the cashier has left his *guichet.* I knew he was in a hurry to get home, because of illness in his family. As a matter of fact, it is already closing time and I am somewhat in haste myself. *Au revoir, madame.*"

She had been obliged to leave without money and she was getting short of cash, though she still had plenty of jewelry which she could sell or pawn if worse came to worst. But something told her that she would have no better luck at the bank next day, that her falsified passport had aroused suspicion and that her endorsement of a check, made out to her, signed by Allan Lambert, and cleverly countersigned by Anthony with Allan's signature, would not help her much longer in Lisieux. What was more, if the banking authorities had become suspicious, in little or no time the Police would be suspicious too, if they had not already become so. It was a pity that Mendoza himself was not well-to-do. If he had been, no problem would have existed. But perhaps they could work out something together. And as far as that went, she herself had always been resourceful. . . .

It was unlike him to keep her waiting. His landlady had come out on the terrace to greet her and had apologized in *monsieur's* behalf: he had gone to Norolles, where the Benedictines had first taken refuge after their ancient *Abbaye* had been destroyed in the bombardment, because he had heard there might be something of importance to his work there. But he would be back any minute. Having said this, the good-hearted *fermière* retreated to her kitchen.

Because she had absolutely nothing else to do, Ethel opened her handbag and took from it the folded sheets covered with long lists of names which she still kept there. She knew the prudent course would have been to destroy them long since. But she could not convince herself that they might not still be useful to her, that she might never again be in a position to "guide" rich Americans through Europe, or to find a more tractable recipient of the Spanish Prisoner letter than that miserable Lambert had been. Marta Rodríguez had done her work well. She had ingratiated herself with the gilded youth at the Southwestern college she was attending, a college also attended by any number of young men and women whose parents had come into big money through the discovery of oil. These were to be the future tourists. Marta had also visited the smaller towns in the vicinity of the college and discovered the identity of grocers and merchants who were operating in a modest way, but who were prospering. These were the potential recipients of future Spanish Prisoner letters. Of course Marta did not know this. She only knew that she had been given a great opportunity to study at a North American college for a whole year, with nothing to do in return for this favor but make careful note of those students who had the most spending money and where they came from, and to check on the flourishing mercantile establishments in the surrounding countryside. But Ethel had been lucky to get these lists from her, before it was too late. If they had been found among Marta's belongings, they might have provoked awkward questions. . . .

Ethel heard footsteps and turned to see Mendoza coming toward her, smiling and bearing a tray on which were two steaming cups of chocolate. He must have come from Norolles by the small back road that led off the highway, and entered the *manoir* through a rear door. Anyway, here he was now, profuse in his apologies for keeping her waiting.

"I had no idea I should be gone so long. I found more of importance to me than I should have dreamed possible in so small a place, and my discovery has made it possible for me to finish my brochure in a way that is satisfactory to me, so I lingered to write the final paragraphs. Can you imagine? There is living at his chateau in Norolles a very prominent elderly gentleman, an ex-deputy and a close relative of a former President of the Republic, who knew Thérèse Martin, now canonized as Saint Thérèse, when she was a little girl. The seats his family occupied at the Cathedral were directly behind those of the Martins, and he used to sit lost in admiration of the lovely child's beautiful blond hair. He talked to me about it in detail."

Involuntarily, Ethel winced. She had seen those lovely golden locks, which had been shorn from Thérèse Martin's delicately formed head when she became a Carmelite nun, and which had been carefully preserved in the Carmelite museum—one of the places which Ethel had perforce visited, day after day, in the company of the quavering old ladies. Ethel's own hair, sacrificed to the exigencies of her present situation, had been just as long, just as blond and just as beautiful. And now she had nothing left but an orange-colored frizz!

Mendoza set the tray down on the little tin table from which they customarily took their chocolate, handed Ethel her cup and began to sip from his at the same time that she did from hers. She had not had a moment in which to return the typed sheets to her handbag when he came upon her so suddenly, and though she had shoved this over them, it did not wholly conceal them. Mendoza leaned over and casually drew them from under cover.

"Well, I'm glad you found something to read while I kept you waiting," he said. "But it does not seem to be very interesting—apparently just long lists of names. And what is this letterhead?" He read off the words "Southwestern" giving them a halting Spanish pronunciation. "And what is this name typed in the upper left-hand corner, as if to identify the person who had made the lists? That is easy enough to read, for it might be a Spanish name—Marta Rodríguez."

"Yes, but it has nothing to do with you. I will tell you about it some other time, if you are really curious. However, none of those lists are very interesting, as you just said yourself. Let us drink our delicious chocolate quietly and enjoy this pleasant evening. For a wonder it is quite warm and sunny. And how beautiful the dahlias are at this season! I have never seen such large ones as in Normandy!"

"Oh, but I do find these lists interesting after all! So many queer North American names—Smith and Jones and Harrison and Black! Won't you let me show this paper to our *patronne?* I think she would be interested, too, in such a curiosity."

"No, please, Gaspar, give it back to me! That paper isn't interesting at all, to any stranger! But it happens to be of a rather private nature."

She was too late. Gaspar had already sprung up with the typed sheets in his hand and gone into the *manoir,* closing the terrace door after him. Unless she were prepared to make a scene and provoke questioning which might be embarrassing, Ethel could not pursue him. She finished her chocolate and, after a few minutes, he came back and, still standing, finished his own.

"As it happens," he said slowly, repeating her words, "those sheets are of considerable interest to me—or rather they will be of interest to those persons to whom the *patronne* will show them. They did not tell *me* anything I had not guessed already. I never knew exactly what my sister was doing at that North American college. But I knew it was something besides studying —something useful to Ethel Crewe."

Ethel had sprung to her feet.

"Your sister!" she said hoarsely. "How could she have been your sister? Your name is—"

"Diego Rodríguez. You are not the only person, you know, who can assume a false name, any more than you are the only person who enjoys a cup of chocolate in the afternoon. But you have just enjoyed your last one. As far as that goes, so have I. However, that does not matter. All these formalities about extradition and so on are too complicated and tedious to suit me. I do not believe the Police, who will be here in a few minutes, have enjoyed them either. It has been tedious for them too, following you around. I think they will be glad I took things into my own hands. I am sorry to inconvenience the *patronne,* who has been good to me. But together with your lists and my brochure, I have given her a signed statement, saying it has always been I who prepared the chocolate. I can dabble in poison too, Ethel Crewe."

30.

ALTHOUGH IT WAS ALREADY LATE AFTERNOON, the heat was still intense in the pleasant, sleepy little town, situated in the French *département* of Lot et Garonne, which had become a favorite habitat of Spanish expatriots. They had received a warm welcome from the French in the vicinity, whose political views were similar to their own; and though the sign on their headquarters, which announced it as such, was printed in their native language, and membership in their organization allegedly confined to Spaniards, everyone in town knew what the sign meant, and membership in the organization was actually flexible. A surprising number of Frenchmen in the locality claimed to have close relatives in Catalonia and the Basque country, or to have been born in one of these regions when their parents were visiting the relatives in question; an equally large number of Spaniards made the same claims about Perpignan and Biarritz. The *entente cordiale* was firmly established and was easily recognizable, even by transient visitors, not only through the frequency of business meetings, but through the social gatherings at the café which adjoined party headquarters.

These social gatherings took place inside the café when the weather was inclement, but this was comparatively rare; and the little tables, covered with red and white checked cloths and scattered over the sidewalk, were nearly always surrounded by congenial groups, drinking coffee or red wine, and playing cards. These groups, however congenial, were not always harmonious. Heated arguments were frequent and violent quarrels sometimes occurred. There were differences of political opinion, even in the same party, and national feeling occasionally surmounted apparent assimilation. And there was no getting away from the language barrier. The Spaniards spoke French, after a fashion, still pronouncing every syllable in every word and calling a good honest U an "oo"; the French spoke Spanish after a fashion, also pronouncing it in their own way. When two different nationals wanted to understand each other, they had no difficulty; when the inclination was lacking, a good excuse was automatically furnished.

Hot weather also had the effect of working both ways. Sometimes this effect was definitely soporific; then the coffee was allowed to grow cool, the wine was sipped slowly, the cards were dealt with unconcealed languor. At other times, the rising temperature applied not only to the thermometer but to men's moods. It was too hot to drink coffee. Wine was supposed to be cooling, and temporarily it might be. The Spaniards had introduced *sangria* and had done their best to convince their French friends that this delightful admixture of fruit juice, soda water and ice to their *vin ordinaire* improved it greatly for consumption in warm weather; the French remained skeptical. They continued to drink their wine as it came from the bottle, and in late August it came tepid; but they went on drinking it, telling themselves that sooner or later it would have the desired effect of cooling them off. When a meeting was marred by altercations, or when a card game was taking place at the same time as a drinking party, trouble frequently began to brew among the habitués of the café foregathered in the oasis of shade, provided by the nearby linden trees, which gave an elusive promise of coolness to the open square which separated it from the fields where games of *boule* and *pelota* were both in progress—for youngsters of both nationalities seemed impervious to heat and cold alike, when it came to their favorite sports.

It was the heat, this time, which made their elders wonder how the youngsters could keep tearing around instead of taking their ease. Not that the elders in question were themselves completely at ease. It was almost dark now and they had been drinking and playing cards, not only through the long twilight, but ever since the hours devoted to the *siesta,* which was one of the Spaniards' customs which their French friends heartily approved. A good deal of wine had been consumed and comparatively little of it had gone into *sangrias*—most of it had been drunk straight. And one card player had been winning almost too steadily to please the others. It was beginning to seem unnatural, how steadily he won, and not only this evening either. His luck had been nothing short of phenomenal, almost from the first time it had been hospitably suggested that he might like to take a hand in a game, shortly after his arrival in town, a few weeks earlier. In the case of one of the old habitués, especially one who was a general favorite, such good luck would have been tolerated, perhaps even applauded. But this man was still more or less of a stranger. True, he had proved good company. The Spaniards and the French were both inclined to like him from the beginning; he spoke their languages equally well, he shared their general views and sympathized with their minor differences. Moreover, he offered to stand treat for everyone when his winnings were unusually good. It was not often that a *Madrileño* joined them, but the reasons this one gave seemed sound enough. Oh yes, there was still suppression. There were still dark deeds. . . . His hearers nodded their heads sagely. Haven't they all said the same? The landlord of the café, who had a few rooms to rent, was delighted with this new client. It was seldom that he had the same one for more than a night or two at a time, or a customer who did not complain about prices.

This evening, however, there had been two other new arrivals. The convivial card players had not observed them carefully, when they first drove up in a good-looking American car, because just at that moment the lucky *Madrileño* had turned up another ace, which gave him a still greater advantage over the other players; and they had begun to exchange glances with each other. Such luck was no longer merely phenomenal—there was something fishy about it. The new arrivals had gone straight inside the café, while the glances were being exchanged, and later the two outsiders, accompanied by the landlord, had been heard mounting the stairs, so evidently they meant to spend the night. The landlord would be delighted. Two more customers, rich enough to come in a car, a fine car at that, instead of on the local bus. And they had large leather suitcases too, instead of small ones, made of cheap fabric. The one poor little *sommelier* had really looked overladen when he carried them from the car.

After a time, the two newcomers came down and seated themselves at a table on the very edge of the oasis, some distance from the card players. In the gathering dusk, it was impossible to see them clearly, and as far as that went, no one attempted to do so, because of the absorption in the game, except the *Madrileño*. He looked up and his glance became a steady, startled, stare, which lasted long enough to attract attention.

"Someone you think you know?" one of his companions asked casually.

"No. At first I thought I detected a resemblance to a former acquaintance. But obviously I was mistaken. My play?"

"You lost that last trick. You didn't notice; your attention was elsewhere."

"It was only momentarily diverted. The trick was mine!"

"And I say it wasn't! It was mine."

"He's right, *Madrileño*. There's one you can't get away with."

"Are you suggesting that I've been cheating?"

"If the shoe fits, put it on! That trick is Marcel's. Try to take it away from him and there'll be trouble."

"Try to take it away from *me* and there'll be trouble!"

"All right, come on, let's have trouble!"

The players had all sprung to their feet, so quickly that they overturned the table and scattered the cards. The dice fell rattling to the pavement. Threatening words became shouted oaths, menacing gestures were quickly followed by blows. Angry red faces, strong hairy arms and heavy bodies had already become a single snarl of rage, when the landlord and the *sommelier* came running from the kitchen, and the two strangers from the further side of the oasis pushed the intervening tables aside and stood close to the one the combatants had overturned.

"*Messieurs! messieurs! du calme, du calme!* Otherwise I must call the Police," the landlord yelled ineffectively.

"The tooter the sweeter," one of the two strangers said laconically but emphatically. It was an expression he had learned in the First World War and no one understood it—not that anyone would have paid attention in any case. But the man who was with him started talking rapidly and impellingly and made himself heard above the tumult.

"Friends and comrades! Stop fighting among yourselves and hold fast to that cheat, before he escapes you!"

Although the newcomer was heard, he was not instantly heeded. He went on, giving rapid-fire orders.

"You, Marcel, stop pummeling that man before he knifes you! Pin his arms behind him! I tell you he is a traitor!"

This time the words had their effect. The snarl of red faces and hairy arms and strong bodies began to untangle itself, and the man called Marcel clutched at his antagonist and succeeded, with the help of another, in fending off the *Madrileño's* blows and pinning back his arms. His lip was already cut, his face bloody. He spat out curses.

"You fools, that man over there is the one you should hold, not me! A dirty spy, a double-crosser! He will have you all in jail, unless you make short work of him!"

"And I tell you, if you let this cheat go, he will gyp you and gyp you and gyp you! He will get you to do his dirty work for him and then he will leave you in the lurch, as he did me. He is no more a *Madrileño* than this gentleman beside me, this North American who intends to see justice done!"

The pseudo-*Madrileño*, with a violent effort, wrenched himself free. There was the quick flash of a knife, a pistol shot almost as quick. Then two men fell to the ground, their blood staining the pavement.

Marcos Estrada had got his revenge. But he had paid for it with his life.

EPILOGUE

THE STATION WAGON, which now had the word VICTORIA painted in white letters on both sides, was heading south from Avila; and in it Milagrita was seated beside Allan, just as he had so often pictured her in his rosy dreams.

They had been married a few hours earlier in the private chapel, with Douglas as best man and Charlotte as maid of honor; and Milagrita had been a vision of angelic loveliness, in snowy satin, ancestral lace and sparkling diamonds. Afterward there had been a wedding breakfast at the *dehesa*, and the affectionate greetings among long-lost relatives and the drinking of toasts had gone on indefinitely, or so it seemed to Allan. But he had said firmly, beforehand, that in his country it was customary for the bride and groom to slip away, quietly, for an undisclosed destination, before the other guests left; and though in the beginning Leonor and Pablo had demurred, Allan had finally won his point. Milagrita herself had made only one condition: that first they should go to the Convent of Santa Ana, where she would salute her aunt, the Abbess, and give her the bridal bouquet to separate into clusters of flowers for the adornment of the altar. Such a procedure, though wholly strange to Allan, seemed to him, in advance, rather charming. In retrospect, it seemed more than that; it had been deeply moving.

Neither he nor Milagrita talked very much. As they had told the Abbess all about the wedding ceremony, and the bountiful breakfast, and the family and friends, so long estranged, who had come from far and wide, there was nothing more that needed to be added on those subjects now. And words seemed superfluous to their bliss. They were married, they were on their honeymoon, they were starting their new life together. Tonight they would be in Córdoba—Córdoba with its proud imperishable *Mesquita,* its shop windows filled with incomparable leather, its tomb of Manolete and its secret, scented patios. They would not hurry away from these and all its other wonders. And when they did leave, they would go to Sevilla, to Cádiz, to Málaga, to Granada. It would all be new to Milagrita, for she was a Castilian, born, bred and raised; and it would be new to Allan also, except for Málaga, where he would see all his boyhood friends—not only those who had visited him during his convalescence and those who had come to his wedding, but those whom he had not met for years and years. These friends would arrange swimming parties on the beach at Torre Molinas and festive luncheons at the *Hostería de Gibrafaro* in honor of the bride and groom. Then in Sevilla he and Milagrita would wander through the gardens of the Alcázar, during the cool of the evening and watch the flamenco dancers at midnight. In Granada they would go to drink *sangria* and eat *gazpacho* in those hillside gardens called *carmenes,* which, according to tradition, must contain fruit trees and herbs and vegetables as well as flowers; and then they would go to the Alhambra by moonlight. From Cádiz they would run up to Jerez and visit the *bodegas,* where the great casks of sherry lined innumerable shadowy cellars of richness. In short, they would do everything that tourists did, though not so fast nor with as little sentiment as most; and they would do everything that Spaniards did, in their own country, in their own way, because Milagrita had relatives in all these places, who were waiting to welcome them.

From beginning to end it would be a period of ecstasy and enchantment.

Allan's pulse quickened as they raced farther and farther south, bringing Córdoba nearer and nearer, and with it the benignant darkness in which Milagrita would become wholly his. And there would be countless other nights, hardly less rapturous—perhaps even more so, when they were no longer strange to each other, when Milagrita's virgin innocence had been merged in desire to meet his own. He dwelt on these glorious visions with all the untainted virility of a man who has lived cleanly while knowing the emptiness of such living and yearning for fulfillment. Now this was to be his, in a sense more joyous and complete than he had ever dared to hope.

But this physical union, which would be a spiritual union as well, was not all that lay ahead of him. There would be one quiet day after another in the library at the *dehesa,* when he would be doing the work he had longed to accomplish, not with the same hunger that he had longed for a happy marriage, but with hunger just the same, intense and thwarted. He was a scholar as well as a lover. He would read and study, he would record his findings. All through the winter that lay ahead, he would spend his days in this way, undisturbed, unharassed, tranquil in achievement among the giants of Spanish literature: Luis de León, Cervantes de Saavedra, Lope de Vega, Calderón de la Barca, Benevente Martínez, Concha Espina, and many others. And when another winter came, he would be ready to go back to his classes, to give his students something he had never been able to give them before, because it had not been in him to give. He would share, with liberality, everything that he had learned and gained himself; and meanwhile he would live in his own ancestral home and Milagrita would learn to value and love his American heritage, almost as much as he did. He would never give up his teaching or his legacy from the past, for those were part of him, like his nationality. But every summer he would return to Spain, to go on drinking from its inexhaustible fountainhead of that knowledge which represented his life work.

He was too honest not to admit that his impulse to come to Spain, in response to the alleged Prisoner's letter, had been a mad one, that if he had not been bored with new-found riches, if the fetters which bound him to drudgery had not become insufferable, he would never have broken away, in a manner so completely out of character, from everything that represented his normal life. Perhaps he actually had been in a "state of dementia," as he had laughingly told himself when he read the list of rules and regulations on his steamship ticket. And it was a sobering thought that five persons, two of them wholly innocent, had lost their lives because of his rashness. On the other side of the shield could be inscribed the facts that a great gentleman, who had suffered out of all proportion to his misdoings, had been restored to health and happiness; that two humbler men, who had erred or been close to erring, had been given a new start in life; that a noble woman, who had borne adversity with fortitude, was again installed in her home; and that a beautiful and guileless girl had been rescued from the wolves waiting to prey upon her.

It did Allan's heart good to see Don Pablo gaining daily in health and happiness. He spent long hours in his library, lovingly fingering the books that had been restored to the erstwhile empty shelves, and mapping out a plan of study for his son-in-law to pursue with him that winter. On pleasant days, he tried his legs by pacing slowly up and down the long galleries, whence he could look out on his sister's lands; then, with returning strength, he began to visit the stables and the shepherds' quaint headquarters and to wander over the fields, giving directions for their future cultivation. Never again would he be an absentee landlord, or one content to sit at a gaming table, careless as to whether or not his property and his sister's was productive; the righteous pride of possession, the vehement urge for improvement, were once more alive in him.

Inocencio was still in prison, but Allan was satisfied that his lot there was not too hard a one, and an elderly cousin had been found who was glad to come and stay with his crippled brother, who was back in their own little home. When spring came, if all went well, Inocencio would be back there, too, cultivating strawberries and asparagus in the small kitchen garden. There was even a chance that his position as a guide might be restored to him; Allan had managed to have a talk with the palace authorities, and had convinced them that Inocencio's infringement of the rules, as far as private apartments were concerned, had been wholly Crewe's fault. As to the station wagon—well, Allan had that again, as good as new, and if he could let bygones be bygones in that respect, surely others could do likewise. Hopefully he visualized Inocencio shepherding staring tourists through the long succession of stately rooms, opening into each other to form a vista; pausing to show them the portrait of beautiful Mercedes, who had died so tragically a few months after her happy marriage to Alfonso XII; then, with all due respect, pausing again before the portrait of the same king's second wife, Maria Cristina, and explaining that she had been a noble woman, devoting her life to the upbringing of the son born after his father's death, who was to reign, in due time, as Alfonso XIII.

As to Sigismundo and Concepción, they were already settled in the apartment Allan had taken in Madrid, so that the family would have a *peid-à-terre*, whenever anyone wanted to go there. He had made inquiries about the "big house on the Castellano" which, as Leonor had told him, had been the "first to go" in the wreck of the family fortunes. The present owner was not inclined to sell; but the real estate agent, consulted by Allan, thought that, eventually, he might be persuaded to do so. Such transactions took time in Spain. Meanwhile, Leonor was more than contented at the *dehesa*, restoring tapestries and paintings to their proper places, counting silverware and rearranging furniture. As for Milagrita, here she was beside him; he knew, and rejoiced in the knowledge, that she would be happy wherever she was as long as it was with him.

In his radiant mood, he could even look back on his final visit to the sanitarium with amusement, rather than with anger. He had been received with frigid politeness, as were the physicians who came out from Madrid for the consultation; but there had been no arguments, no outward friction of any kind, and no impediment had been put in the way of Don Pablo's departure in an ambulance. Allan had heeded the *Jefe's* advice about face-saving. He had not insisted on using the station wagon for Pablo's transportation; and he had accepted the huge bill which Buchner handed him "for professional services" and paid it, with a countenance as devoid of expression as the doctor's. Then they had bowed stiffly to each other, without shaking hands, and Allan had departed. That was the end of that. . . .

So perhaps, after all, Marta and Diego had not died in vain. With all his heart, Allan hoped so. In any case, sooner or later, they would have been Ethel's victims, for their fate was already settled before he entered the picture; and he had found a publisher for Diego's brochure, who pronounced it a valuable contribution to Teresiana; perhaps it would be the unfortunate man's memorial. Allan knew that Milagrita was praying for the repose of the souls of both brother and sister. As far as that went, he believed that in her infinite goodness and charity, she was praying that Marcos and the Crewes might be delivered from everlasting punishment. He did not understand such prayers or the reason for them. But he thought that Milagrita must be very near to the Throne of Grace. . . .

He could feel her nestling more closely beside him, and glanced down to see that she was looking at him with eyes of love. After their long silence, which had been one of communion, she was again ready for speech.

"It seems like a miracle, doesn't it?" she said. "I mean, that you received the strange letter and answered it and came to Spain and found me and made us all so happy!"

He reduced the speed of the station wagon, so that he might lean over and kiss her. "*You're* the miracle," he murmured with his lips against hers. "Whoever gave you your name, must somehow have guessed that you would be."